R

PREDESTINED

Jewel Imprint: Amethyst
Medallion Press, Inc.
Florida, USA

Published 2005 by Medallion Press, Inc.
225 Seabreeze Ave.
Palm Beach, FL 33480

Printed in the United States of America

Library of Congress Cataloging-in-Publication Data

Albert, Robin.
  Predestined / Robin Albert a/k/a R. Garland Gray.
     p. cm.
  ISBN 1-932815-52-X
  1. Abandoned children--Fiction. 2. Druids and Druidism--Fiction.
3. Women slaves--Fiction. 4. Prisoners--Fiction. I. Title.
  PS3601.L3347P74 2005
  813'.6--dc22

                                     2005004254

HISTORICAL NOTE

Romans in Ireland? Possibly.

At Drumanagh in the County of Dublin, archaeological excavations in 1996 revealed traces of a Roman coastal fort on a protruding cliff into the Irish Sea. The excavation has been delayed due to a legal dispute.

FOREWORD

As a historical fantasy romance, PREDESTINED borrows from ancient Ireland's loremasters and pre-Christian Celtic mythology. There are references to pagan traditions that offer no scholarly conclusions but simply enhance the mythical feel of the story. The fantastical notions are very much my own.

—*R. Garland Gray*

PROLOGUE

EIRE
LONG AGO

THE PEOPLE SPEAK OF IT at night, in hushed whispers, away from the non-believers.

It is an old Irish legend come down from the north.

On the last eve of the full moon when spring and prosperity had reigned, the first generations of the *Tuatha Dé Danann* became the faery folk. The people named them the *Daoine Sidhe*, their tongues pressed to the roof of their mouths in speech. The "Deena Shee," they said, the dwindled gods.

Before enlightened memory, the *Tuatha Dé Danann* had shed their mundane mortality like unwanted cloaks seeking divinity and their own forever.

Others of the tribe struggled to remain mortal, resisting the temptation that would change their destiny evermore.

Still others wavered in twilight, caught between two worlds, both mortal and faery.

Myth says the *Tuatha Dé Danann* are the faeries. It was said that one, separate and apart, would save them all.

CHAPTER 1

DRUMANAGH, EIRE
KINDRED, RUINS OF A FAERY FORTRESS

HE FELT SLUGGISH AND GRAY, locked in a cold oblivion not of his making. Drugged eyelids crusted open, struggling for focus. Shadows lingered beyond the candlelight in the crumbling tomb of the ancient faery fort.

Tynan shifted cramping muscles. Iron manacles dug into the raw flesh of his wrists and ankles. Painfully, he lifted his head and surveyed his surroundings. He lay on his back on a sacrificial altar of stone, naked and chained, an offering to the otherworld gods, he supposed, his mind still foggy. They had extended his arms above his head and spread his legs apart; leaving him vulnerable.

His head fell back with a heavy thud. He wished he could wake up from this dark dream.

"Doona fight so; let the drug release you."

He startled at the soft lilting voice, so out of place here. A small figure came into view and Tynan blinked to bring the hooded shape into focus.

"Where am I?" he asked. His voice sounded rusty

to his own ears.

"They brought you to the lower tombs of Castle Kindred." The figure moved to stand near his hip, an obscure form carefully crafted to hide the identity of the woman within.

"How do you feel?" she asked.

He felt blurred and queer inside. His body ached in places it had never ached before. The last thing he remembered, dusk had fallen while he bathed in the woodland stream. Low ceiling and stone walls surrounded him now. The damp air attested to the nearness of Eire's wind-swept sea. Black candles burned low in stone crevices, oblivious to the moisture that would extinguish their flames forever.

A movement on the floor caught his attention. He lifted his head. *"Aile Niurin,"* he muttered. Hell Fire. Red beady eyes blinked brazenly back at him before scurrying beneath soiled straw.

"They are only rats looking for food. They will not harm you, warrior. If you feel you can, drink this." She held a flask out to him. "There is little time before they return."

Tynan tried to see the face behind the enticing voice, but the hood's drape hid all features.

"Who comes?" he asked.

Small hands held a silver flask out to him.

"What is in it?" he asked, leery of any offering.

"Water and a crushed apple."

He frowned with indecision, not trusting but

needing nonetheless.

"It is safe, warrior," she reassured. "I prepared it myself before coming here." She took a sip from the flask to prove it.

He nodded, too thirsty to argue and opened his mouth.

She supported the back of his head. Fingers buried in his hair, shifting the black length so it spilled down the stone at his shoulder.

"Slowly, warrior."

The flask touched his cracked lips. Tiny beads of apple slid down his raw throat. The unexpected tartness of the fruit quickly revived him, his mind finally clearing. When finished drinking, he pulled away.

The hooded figure just stood there, watching him, a slight tilt to her head. The scent of lavender teased his nostrils. "Let me see you."

She shook her head and took a small step back. " 'Tis safer not to see my face. If my Roman master found out I ventured to the tombs, he'd order me flayed."

"You are a slave, then?" Tynan could not hide his surprise.

"Aye, to the Roman Centurion that holds this ancient place."

"Do Roman centurions allow their slaves free reign?"

"I am trustworthy and given freedom as long as I remain within my master's boundaries."

"Your master's boundaries do not include the tombs."

"Nay."

"Yet, you are here."

"Aye." She nodded slowly, no doubt wondering where these questions were leading.

He had but one focus lately. "Do you know where the Roman Centurion is holding the faeries?"

The hooded figure stiffened and shook her head. "I doona know anything about that."

Tynan wasn't sure if he believed her.

She turned to the back corridor where voices could be heard.

"They come, warrior. I must leave."

She walked around the altar, and Tynan grabbed a piece of coarse gray cloak. "Who comes?" he demanded.

"The Sorcerer and his minions. They search for the Dark Chieftain of Prophecy."

The woman tugged on her cloak. "Please release me, warrior. If you live, I will find a way to help you."

If I live? He had no intention of dying. Tynan released her. "Hide yourself."

Slipping the silver flask within the folds of her robe, she became part of the darkness, silent and gone as the moments from which she had come. He wondered briefly if he would ever see her again, ever gaze upon her features, but then pushed those thoughts quickly aside for the air became foul with the smell of garlic and sweat.

"The dark sovereign has awakened."

Tynan peered into the shadows trying to locate

the owner of the male voice. *One thing felt certain, his captors knew his name.* Tynan meant dark sovereign among his people.

"Are you the Dark Chieftain of Prophecy?" an older man's voice inquired with a touch of excitement.

"Are you the Sorcerer?" Tynan countered instead. A cloaked man came to stand at his head, face hidden by the drape of the hood. *Does everyone wear hooded robes and cloaks here?*

"I have gone by many names in this life: *Yn Drogh Spyrryd*, Evil One, Dark Druid, but Sorcerer is the name I answer to now. Do you answer to the name of Dark Chieftain?"

Lord Tynan, the Dark Chieftain of the *Tuatha Dé Dananns*, calmed, for his captors did not know whom they held. In his mind, images of purple light and elfin faces flashed and swirled. The imprisoned faeries had become aware of his presence from within the sacred walls of the ancient faery fort.

"Silence will only cause you pain, warrior. I have brought many men down to the tombs to be tested. All have died."

Calloused fingers grazed his temple and Tynan turned away, gripping the manacles.

"Your eyes are faery marked with the color of amethyst, warrior. It is a sure sign of the fey heritage in your blood. Mayhap, my search is finally over."

Tynan ignored his captor's ramblings and tried to see the man's face behind the hood. The rough stone of the altar scraped his bare back. He caught sight of a strong chin and long, black hair, streaked with winter's gray.

"Curious of my face, warrior?"

"Evil has many forms," Tynan answered.

"Think me evil, do you?"

Crooked fingers placed a seventeen-inch black sword on his chest, the blood groove encrusted with lime. Dried leaves draped the double-edges of the iron blade. Tynan shifted, only now becoming aware of the two servants who had stood in the back, out of his line of sight.

The air stirred above him. He looked down his chest. The ancient sword quickly took on a threatening quality. A burning sensation spread into his flesh. He yanked at his chains. "What sorcery is this?"

His captor came around and stood by his shoulder looking down at him, trying to see into his very soul.

"Your blood belongs to the faeries, of that I vow."

He was more mortal than faery thanks to his father's betrayal. "Many of my tribe show the faery claiming in their eyes."

"Not like yours. I think you are their chieftain."

Tynan did not reply.

"Tell me, who is the territorial goddess? I have searched widely for her. The fates are spiteful and keep her hidden."

"The great Evil One cannot find the territorial goddess?" he goaded, trying to turn his captor's interest away from the goddess. All knowledge of her had been lost years before, yet he alone must be the one to find her.

"Tell me her name." The Sorcerer made his demand with spittle and venom. "Tell me or I will spell-bind you in darkness and silence."

"Your threats are weak. I will tell you nothing, Evil One."

"So be it. You are no different than the others before you and so shall suffer for it." he Sorcerer raised his hands and began to chant, something murky and unholy and unrecognizable.

A blood-freezing cold washed over Tynan's face. He reared up in surprise, yanking at the manacles binding him.

The world writhed and slithered into dark and silence.

Slowly his sight winked out. Blind.

Sound wasted away and became only silence. Deaf.

"Nay!" He struggled to breathe in the eternal night and cold stillness engulfing him. His heart pounded erratically in his chest, fear and terror overwhelming him. He felt suspended, lost in a vast ocean of freezing quiet and living blackness.

"TYNAN," the imprisoned faeries trilled in his mind. "HURRY AND FREE US FROM THIS DARK PLACE."

Tynan's jaw clenched.

"DARK CHIEFTAIN. THE EVIL ONE CANNA VEIL OUR FEY GIFT TO YOU. YOU BE OF OUR BLOOD. SEE THE SHAPES WITHIN THE DARKNESS. LOOK INTO IT WITH FEY SIGHT

AND KNOW THAT YOU BE NOT ALONE."

He swallowed hard and focused as his fey brethren decreed.

Suddenly within his blindness, gray shapes moved. He could see form and movement, a living grayness etched with a male's red heat. His faery sight allowed him to see beyond the vileness of the spell, but he could not see details and he could not see color. He could not see the face of his tormentor.

✳✳✳

The Sorcerer pulled back his hood and scowled down upon the sweaty warrior. "Willful. This one shows more strength than most."

Laying his hand beside the warrior's right temple, a sickly smile curved his lips. He opened his fist and released the black spider. "Let us see what he thinks of my creature."

The warrior jerked his head away and the Sorcerer grinned in delight. "Feel the spider at your temple? It feeds upon the senses. It is an ancient creature, spellbound in the old way of magic and obscurity."

The Sorcerer knew the warrior could no longer hear him. Still he spoke, relishing in the sound and echo of his words in these olden tombs. "Live in this world of undying night and silence. Let your senses feed the spider's incessant appetite. In time, your fear shall breed and betray you and then you will tell me all that I need to know."

Chains clanked loudly with the warrior's inner battle and a kind of glee gripped him. "So, the terror begins . . ."

The Sorcerer motioned his servants to leave him. Leaning over, he cupped the warrior's chin harshly, holding him fast, his thin lips inches from the warrior's ear.

"Do you want the answer to your freedom?" He asked with cruel intent. "It is the true kiss of a faery."

He released the warrior and cackled in the way of those doomed. Gazing in satisfaction upon his prisoner, the Sorcerer pulled up his hood and walked away, back to the unending corridors below the ancient castle, back to the unending searches for salvation.

✳✳✳

Tynan blew air out of his lungs. The spell stealing his senses both terrified and enraged him.

"FREE US, NOW." The faeries drummed in his mind, endless demands laced with bad-temper and selfishness.

Jerking the chains, he flung back his head in bitter exasperation. First, he must free himself.

CHAPTER 2

THOUGHTS OF THE CHAINED WARRIOR in the tombs rested heavily on her heart and conscience. Before the predawn hours, Bryna walked under the stone arch and out to the partially completed parapets of the for-tress. At nineteen years old, she had learned resilience, having become a slave early in life. Moving to the un-finished edge, she looked downward. Her coarse gray cloak fluttered behind her in a breeze laced with chill and premonition. Below the walls of the fortress, the black sea crashed against isolated cliffs, carrying the sirens' call of the deep. Spray kissed at her face. She pulled back.

Her Roman master had ignored the warnings of the local villagers and settled in the ruins of an ancient faery fort where he proceeded to build and change it into a fortress of his own making.

Bryna looked west. On the landlocked side of the fortress, beyond the meadow, the white clustered huts of the village and the dried brown fields mingled with the early mist. A harbor nearby supported the Roman's meager trade with the Britons. It was said her Roman master came to protect the trade. Yet, in her heart she believed him to have other plans of campaign, of crusade and of war.

Bryna tugged the frayed hood down her forehead and over winged, black brows. A strand of burnished gold hair, a blending of yellow sunlight and red fire, fluttered across her cheek. She was odd looking, disturbing, a blending of light and shade with eyes cast in the color of silvery mist.

Behind her, a soft familiar shuffle drew near.

"Another mischief night is past," the ancient druidess wheezed. "I am thankful the villagers returned home unhurt from their merrymaking."

"Did the children behave?" Bryna glanced down at her blind teacher. Leathery skin pulled tautly over Derina's gaunt cheekbones. Coarse white hair fell in thick braids to stooped shoulders covered in brown robes.

"Some behaved, others did not." The ancient's one hundred and two year old body shivered in protest of the cold morning. "I dislike being old, child. My bones ache, my stomach grumbles, and my feet hurt."

"I am sorry."

"Age creates a great hindrance to my plans."

Bryna often wondered at those plans. Most villagers believed Derina to be a daughter of Nuada, the Faery King, but some terrible thing had happened to Derina in her youth, something that left her sightless and serving a Roman invader. Out of respect, Bryna never asked her and Derina never offered to share in the telling.

She looked outward upon the surging waves once more. "Is the warrior dead, my Teacher?"

"He lives, child. The Dark Chieftain lives and the time of the prophecy has come this day."

Bryna glanced back into the druidess's empty eye-sockets. "Prophecy?"

"Often, you have heard me speak of the Dark Chieftain Prophecy to the villagers."

"Aye, when they are despondent, when their crops wither in the fields, when there is no food on the table and their children die. You remind them of their legend and give them hope."

"A terrible plague has settled upon our land these past few years. I serve the invader, adding to the suffering and blight. Do you not wonder why?"

"I have wondered."

"I am the guardian of the Lost One. Keeper of the prophecy until he becomes born of flesh and blood."

Bryna did not understand Derina's reference to the lost one, but she understood the other. "You believe that warrior chained in the tombs is the Dark Chieftain." It was a statement.

"It is him, child. Mark me well."

"How do you know?"

"My blood knows. Listen to me now for what I say, I say only once. During faeirin time, I found you on the sacred shores of Loch Gur."

"I know."

"You are the Lost One, destined to be the mate of

the ancient lord."

Bryna scoffed in disbelief. "Prophecy says the ancient lord's mate will be a territorial goddess."

"True."

"I am not a goddess, Teacher. I am a slave as you are well aware."

"Child, you possess the ethereal soul of the faery, though it is hidden by the layers of hardship you have had to endure."

"My destiny is fortitude and endurance, a slave's fate, not a goddess of prophecy. I am not even sure that I believe in the stories you tell."

"You must believe."

"Why, because I was born cursed?"

"Not cursed, blessed."

"Teacher, who else but one cursed can sense changes in the air like those of a coming gale? Who else but one cursed can sense the acid breath of a lie leaving a man's lips?"

"Those so gifted and of faery birth."

Bryna struggled to maintain her patience. "With respect, Teacher, I am not the territorial goddess. I know this because . . . because I dream of one of golden light and purity."

Derina tilted her head, a sudden pausing. "What do you dream, child?"

Bryna scanned the countryside. "In my dreams I see a nighttime glade and a pool of dark rain. At the edge kneels a golden goddess with wings of white lace.

She crushes a pink flower in her hand, a sign of her displeasure. All around her are shadows. I sense danger."

"She is the untrue goddess."

Bryna smiled gently. "I am not a goddess."

"Your time has come, child."

She turned her face away. Her teacher believed her to be of the faeries and there would be no changing her mind.

"The wind blows across the dry fields, yet the mist does not move," she observed quietly, hoping to change the subject. "The air feels thick in my lungs this morning."

"The land prepares for what shall come." The druidess gestured toward the dungeons. "They veil the chieftain with magic and a spider spell."

Bryna turned back to the ancient. "What do you speak of? A spider's spell?"

"It is the Sorcerer's name for it, not mine. It looks like a black spider to me. It feeds off the chieftain, stealing his sight and hearing."

Bryna covered her mouth in alarm, never hearing of such a thing. "Teacher." Her gaze dropped to a glistening spider web in the crevice near her hip; the spider waited in the corner for its next meal. She pulled her hand away from the stone.

"I hid in the dank tombs after you left, child, and watched the black rite," the druidess murmured.

Bryna felt ill to the depths of her soul. To do such a thing to a living being was worse than death. She remembered the tall, skeletal Sorcerer coming to the fortress on a rain-soaked night, many years ago. Some believed him to be the banished Dark High Druid of Leinster. Others whispered that he was the Dark Chieftain of Prophecy, fallen from the favor of the Faery Queen. Whatever his past, twisted evil reigned in him now. With his black candles and foul-smelling breath, he ruled the weak-willed Roman Centurion invader who favored his council.

"What did you see?" she heard herself ask.

"When you bring the chieftain to the waterfall cave I will tell you."

"Teacher, I doona understand you this morning. I canna bring the chieftain. He is a prisoner."

"Listen to me. The Sorcerer belongs to the other-world. He infuses a spider with black magic and the creature has attached itself to the chieftain's temple. You must bring the chieftain to the waterfall cave and remove it there."

Bryna shuddered in revulsion. Normal spiders drank the blood of their paralyzed prey. This one drank a man's senses.

"Witcheyes!" A Roman soldier called abruptly from the courtyard below. That was her Roman master's name for her.

Schooling her expression into cool disinterest, Bryna turned to the soldier in the courtyard below.

"Aye?"

"You are wanted in the great hall."

"I come." A summons from her master boded ill.

"I must go now, Teacher."

The ancient touched her arm.

"Remember what I told you, child. Come to me later and I will tell you what you must do. For now, go and meet your destiny."

Gazing at the druidess with uncertainty, Bryna turned and lifted her gray skirts. She hurried down the unfinished wooden steps to the courtyard below. She did not know what to make of her teacher this morning. The druidess had been acting strangely of late, walking the fields at night and whispering to the moon.

Bryna ran to the massive keep at the south end of the courtyard, the morning dew staining the hem of her gown. Climbing the stone steps, she shoved open the wooden doors and stepped through the arched entrance.

An arcane cold pressed down upon her.

She stopped, sensing the . . .

Daoine Sidhe. The Faeries.

The air in the main hall grew silvery.

In her mind, a whistling sound became butterfly wings, wrapping threads of copper and gold around her. *FREE US. FREE US.*

Her heart pounded in her chest.

She tried to remain calm.

Daoine Sidhe. They call to me yet again. What do you want?

Her hands fisted at her sides, but only silence answered her. "What do you want?" She whispered.

The cold dissipated.

Silver left the air.

The soft sounds of the morning returned with the occasional bark of a hound, the whinny of a horse, the grumbling of men.

Bryna blinked the hall back into focus.

Before her, torches lit crumbling walls. A central gray stone staircase wound its way to the upper levels of the unfinished fortress.

To the left of the staircase, servants scurried from large kitchens with meals on dishes of painted and glazed clay, unaware of the touch of the faeries just moments before.

Gathering her courage, Bryna turned right and walked down the corridor to the great hall, pushing the thought of faeries out of her mind. Since the Roman invaders had come, a vast darkness had spread, shadowing the land with decay. No crops grew in the fields. No rain fell from the sky. Babes had been born dead.

She paused at the entrance of the great hall and peered in.

Red drapes hung in sections, in between the triple narrow windows. A roaring fire hissed and crackled in the stone hearth to the left, chasing away the dampness of the morning.

"Witcheyes!"

Clutching her gray skirts, Bryna hastened to where her Centurion master sat. She knew he was not a typical Roman soldier, but a senior non-commissioned officer, given governorship of the coastal fortress and surrounding land and villages.

"Where have you been?" he demanded. Men wearing tunics of red and black parted, opening a path to the raised dais upon which he sat on his throne of embedded jewels.

"On the parapets, my lord," she replied.

The Centurion's swarthy cheeks flushed in anger. Dressed in his favorite knee-length red tunic, he reminded Bryna of a mean-tempered elf with sunken black eyes hinting at depravity.

She knelt before him. Today would be a day for inner strength and submissiveness. "I am here," she said.

"Lower those damn silver eyes, witch."

Bryna did as he commanded.

"Do not make me wait again. Now, stand beside me."

Bryna rose on silent feet.

"Stand there." His bejeweled fingers gestured to his right, about two arm lengths away from his chair.

She stepped up on the dais and pulled her hood back. Though the Centurion bathed daily in his private bath, he still smelled of sour sweat and unkempt habits and she was glad that he had not ordered her to stand close beside him this day.

"Bring that warrior from the north to me. What do the Britons call them?" The Centurion turned to her for an answer.

"I have heard the Britons call them the Caledonians, but they have other names."

"What do you and the druidess call them?"

"We call them the noble people."

"I have heard another name for them, Witcheyes, something tuatha."

"*Tuatha Dé Danann,*" Bryna replied reluctantly.

"That was it, the magical people." He snickered and then gestured impatiently to the guards at the back door. "Well, get him for me."

The two guards at the back door nodded and hurried to do their master's bidding. While they waited, the men in the room huddled in groups, murmuring amongst themselves of painted men who dyed their bodies blue.

Suddenly the sound of chains could be heard, drawing nearer.

Clanggg . . .

Rr-rattttttle . . .

C-clank . . .

Bryna stared at the doorway.

The guards emerged, dragging the chieftain across the stone floor, a chained animal with no rights but to serve. They brought him before her master, a rebellious prisoner of obvious strength and endurance. Hair, long and black as a wild stallion's mane, fell in plaits and tangled lengths down his back.

The fat Roman guard forced the chieftain to his

knees, pushing down hard on his shoulders.

"He has hair like a woman," the Centurion sneered loudly.

Bryna's heart ached for the chieftain. His large frame trembled with the coiled tension of a captured animal.

"Show me the Sorcerer's spider." Her master sat forward on the edge of his chair with childlike eagerness.

One of the guards grabbed the chieftain's chin and jerked his head sideways.

Bryna's gaze locked on his bruised temple. The spider peeked from beneath a few shiny, black strands of the chieftain's hair. It looked like a wood spider, brown and hairy with eyes that glittered red.

The guard suddenly yelped and jerked his hand back. Blood dripped from teeth marks in his thumb.

"The animal nips." The Centurion chuckled loudly at his guard's injury.

Bryna did not understand this public display, this offense of life. As she stood there locked in dread, the chieftain wiped the blood from his mouth with an unhurried movement of the back of his hand and she knew, knew he was not afraid.

"Where is the Sorcerer?" Her master looked around, yet no one answered. "How do I question my prisoner if he cannot hear me?"

A blond priest in purple robes pushed past Bryna.

"My lord," the priest said in hushed tones. "The Sorcerer said he would come this afternoon to deal with this one. He is in the castle's tomb and not to be disturbed."

"I do not wish to wait." The Centurion motioned the priest back impatiently. "I want to know why the Sorcerer thinks this tuatha prisoner special. He does not look special to me." Several of the Romans nodded in agreement, which only fueled her master's awful thoughts even more.

Bryna knew the Centurion hated this place of magic. She had heard he made a slight misjudgment with a senator's young son and had been banished here to supervise trade. The coastal fort housed only one legion of about four thousand men. He needed more legions if his plans for a glorious military invasion were to be met. She suspected that victory meant liberation to him. He would return to Rome a hero, his villa and slaves restored, the Senate heralding his praise. Bryna would rather die than be brought to Rome.

"Witcheyes, can you tell me what he is thinking?"

She startled out of her musings. "Nay, my lord."

"Try."

She stepped down from the dais on shaky legs. Taking two steps forward, she slammed into an unseen wall of rage from the chieftain. It took her a moment to recover.

"What do you sense, Witcheyes?"

"He is angry."

"Too bad. What else?"

The chieftain tilted his head. Tangles of black hair hid his face. Bryna stared openly at him, unable to help herself.

"Witch, tell me what you sense."

A terrible sadness gripped her heart at the imprisonment of such a beautiful creature. The chieftain shifted again, sending waves of primitive fury crashing into her body. Bryna bit back a sob, shaking her head, and stepped back.

"I want to see his face," the Centurion ordered.

The fat guard immediately complied. Grabbing a handful of black hair, he yanked the chieftain's head back.

Bryna's breath caught.

The face before her was sculpted in hard angles, but what captured her attention were his large eyes. Thick sooty lashes framed violet irises beneath a milky white veil of sightlessness.

The chieftain's jaw clenched in rebellion. The veins in his corded neck bulged. A snarl curled his lips.

Jerking his head out of the guard's grasp, he elbowed his captor in the stomach.

Bryna jumped back, startled at the suddenness of the violence.

The fat guard let out a thick "oof" and fell to one knee. The other, taller guard whipped linked chains around the chieftain's neck and jerked back.

"Restrained, but not broken, I see." The Centurion rubbed his face in disgust. "Well, Witcheyes?"

"I sense nothing," Bryna stated carefully. "I must hear his words to sense if he lies."

"That is not possible, it seems."

" 'Tis not." Bryna agreed.

"Where is the druidess?"

"In the village." She grasped her hands in front of her to keep them from shaking. Servants were lighting the wall torches about the great hall, yet she could not look away from the chains wrapped around the chieftain's neck.

"Ah, Witcheyes," the Centurion sighed mightily. "You disappoint me."

Disappointment often meant death. She quietly repeated her claim. "I sense nothing from the warrior." She dare not call him chieftain, for that would be a sure death sentence.

"So it seems. Stand aside, then." Her master dismissed her with a curt wave.

Relieved, Bryna moved to the stone column on the right and waited.

"Does the animal have a name?" the Centurion demanded.

"They call him Tynan, my lord."

"Release him and step back."

The guard lifted the chains away and the chieftain heaved forward onto his forearms, gasping for air, the muscles in his back and sides flexing with each recovering breath.

"Tynan." The Centurion leaned forward in his

chair, gazing thoughtfully at his coughing prisoner. "I am told that the Sorcerer suspects you are the Dark Chieftain, Tynan. Let me see if I remember this ancient keep's oral tradition." He tilted his head and tapped his chin with an index finger. "If you are Kindred's ancient liege, then you have come to mate with the territorial goddess to restore the land, or," he paused dramatically, "are you just a stupid barbarian?"

Bryna started at her master's understanding of the ancient chieftain prophecy, but he was not finished yet. "Or, should I call you Lord Tynan of the illusive *Tuatha Dé Danann*?" he snarled, leaning forward in his chair. "Which is it? Are you part of the faery tribe that plagues my garrison, or not?"

The castle priest stumbled forward. "My lord, the Sorcerer wishes . . ."

"Shut up, fool! How can you be a priest when you serve a Sorcerer?"

The priest flushed in embarrassment and moved back.

Bryna watched Tynan sit back on his legs. With an arrogant toss, his tangled black mane fell down his back. A thin, red welt marred his neck where the chain had pressed hard into his flesh.

"Who are you?" Her master rose from his chair, tugging at his red tunic. He stepped down from the dais and circled his prisoner.

Tynan's dark head followed her master's movements, to Bryna's growing apprehension. The Centurion huffed in annoyance. "Even spellbound, the animal senses me. Perhaps he needs a little pain to divert those superior senses."

"The Sorcerer, my lord," the priest interrupted. Bryna could hear fear in the man's voice. "He does not want this one harmed."

"Ah, the Sorcerer." Her master returned to his seat, a disgruntled child. "The skeletal one knows I do not like to be kept waiting."

The servants, the men in attendance, all waited for what came next and then suddenly, the chieftain turned to her—a simple act. In that one defining moment, Bryna felt him, a reaching out for her, a touching of warmth and need that stirred her soul.

The Centurion laughed from his seat on the dais. "He senses you, Witcheyes, like a lusty stallion sniffing out a ready mare in heat."

She stood white-faced, unable to move.

"And like any prized stallion he must be taught who is his master. Twenty lashes should make him take to his master's bit. Chain him in the dungeon when finished. I would not want to deprive the Sorcerer of his stallion."

The guards obeyed her master quickly and grabbed the chieftain's upper arms, dragging him backward and out of the hall. Bryna could do nothing. The link between her and the proud chieftain had been severed, leaving her physically weakened.

"Witcheyes, come here." Her master waved for

everyone to leave the hall.

Bryna battled the urge to flee. She walked over to where her master sat in his red finery.

"Lower your eyes."

Some arrogant mischief inside her heart made her disobey.

"Do not test me, Witcheyes. Lower them."

Slowly, she dropped her gaze to the floor.

"Who is this warrior to you?"

"I have not seen him before, my lord." She clasped her hands in front of her.

The Centurion sat back in his chair. "Do you remember when I saved you?"

"Aye." She rubbed the tiny, heart-shaped birthmark on her right hand. It had been seven years since that terrible day.

"Remember when those superstitious villagers tried to burn the evil mark off your hand. It was only my intervention that saved your life."

"I remember."

"And yet you are not grateful."

"I am grateful for your rescue," she said, her tone that of a respectful slave.

"Not grateful enough, it seems." Her master took a sip of wine from his tankard. "Who is this warrior to you?"

"No one."

"Is he this Dark Chieftain that the people speak of?"

"I doona know," she replied, for in truth she did not.

"What do you know?"

She remained silent, not knowing how to answer, and felt his anger shift toward a more dangerous subject.

"Your hair has grown lighter." He reached over and lifted a curl from her breast. "I have never seen a color quite like it. It reminds me of flames." He paused, a secretive smile on his face. "Now, tell me, my lovely witch, what do you know of the castle's ancient lord?"

"He is not ancient, my lord."

He released her hair and sat back. "If you are old enough to notice a man, you are old enough to bed."

Her gaze met his in an act of rebellion, and perhaps idiocy, for with a simple command she knew he could end her life.

"The winter color in your eyes freezes a man's soul, witch. I should blind you for your impertinence."

Always before, he had backed down. Would he again?

"Lower those damn eyes," he snarled. "Something must be done about you."

She waited, staring at the floor, terrified of what he might do.

"Leave me now. I must think."

She turned dutifully, hitching her skirts up and raced out of the hall.

"Sidhe Spawn!" the Centurion growled after her.

"To Hades with the Sorcerer and the castle's oral

tradition. There is no ancient lord to reclaim this foul place." He rose from his chair and reached for his tankard of wine. "Especially not this muscled oaf with woman's hair."

CHAPTER 3

THE OUTSIDE AIR COOLED THE fevered heat ravaging his bruised body. Hands lashed his wrists to posts.

Whoosh . . .

Tynan surged forward with the first slice of the whip. *By the white moon, they whip me!*

Disbelief chilled the blood in his veins. Shrill whistling bombarded his mind. The imprisoned faeries screamed in fear for him.

Whoosh . . .

Stinging pain flicked at his shoulders. *I will show no weakness to these bastards.* He jerked at his bonds.

Crack.

Whoosh . . .

Blades of misery flailed his back.

Whoosh . . . Whoosh . . . Whoosh . . .

He thought of Hawk and the way the boy sought mischief; of Rose speaking to her plants; of the swift vertical swoop of his tribe's falcons; of the piercing kee-kee-kee cry of his mated kestrels; but most of all he thought of castle Kindred and the foul Evil One defiling her tombs.

The whipping continued.

His mind swirled in a haze of pain. Slicing torment

and agony finally cut off thoughts. He prayed to the mother goddess, Dana, to give him strength to die honorably.

His head lowered between bloody shoulders.

He wanted to die a warrior's death.

Not like this . . .

He slipped into unconsciousness, lost to a world of physical pain.

Crack.

Whoosh . . .

❋❋❋

The sun had set by the time Bryna made her way into the dank dungeons below the fortress. The long tunnel before her lay in ragged darkness.

"Please, goddess, give me strength," she murmured. Above her head, torches balanced on the brink of shadows.

From below, the sounds of moaning and weeping faded in and out. She dredged up a prayer of protection from the mother goddess. It seemed impossible that life could survive down here in a tapestry of misplaced souls.

She clutched the heavy basket tighter to her hip.

To her right, a faceted crystal pierced the stone of the wall, breaking into a reflection of cool pink radiance.

Ancient faery magic, Bryna mused. *Remnants of Kindred.*

She continued deeper into the tunnel, her hands becoming clammy and cold.

"You should not be here, Witcheyes." A guard cautiously stood up from his three-legged stool.

Bryna looked down at the dirt floor. "I am to treat the prisoner Tynan's wounds," she replied softly.

"Where is the old druidess?" The guard looked past her for Derina.

"In the village," Bryna said, lying outright, for in truth the ancient waited in the waterfall cave.

She placed the basket at her feet. Flipping back the red cloth, her fingers curved around the clay bowl of seasoned stew. She straightened slowly, holding the bowl so the guard could smell the gamy meat.

"I brought stew to keep you warm," she offered. Laced with valerian root, the stew would hasten the guard's slumber.

From beneath lowered lids, Bryna watched the guard look at the stew, then glance at her, wavering.

He licked his lips. "I suppose it is all right."

Bryna did not move. He took the bowl from her hands and set it carefully down on his stool.

"Follow me and do not touch anything." He turned and walked down a corridor without a backward glance.

Lifting the basket, she settled it against her hip and followed the guard down the narrow path.

"Watch your step here, Witcheyes." The guard pointed to a crumbled step.

Bryna clutched the basket to her and stepped down. Cold, damp air pressed upon her.

The torchlight flickered suddenly as if battling against the murky darkness. Barely discernible blue-white light flickered across her path. She doubted the guard had even noticed.

Her gaze darted over stone walls, searching desperately for the half-moon shaped rock that opened to the castle's secret feypaths. This would be her means of escape.

As a young girl, Derina had taken her from the herb garden one morning and had shown her the secret passages beneath the coastal fortress. She called them feypaths, carved out of rock and dirt a long ago time. The moonbeams, as Derina called the blue-white light, were a feypath's signature.

Bryna's heart leaped into her throat. On her right, the half-moon rock lay wedged in the wall, its once purple brilliance soiled and grubby. The bulging length of it mirrored the size of a small man, but could easily go unnoticed if one did not know what they were looking for.

"Witcheyes," the guard called impatiently ahead of her. She hurried to join him.

The guard removed the key ring from his belt and waited for her in front of a cell.

"Do not stay long," he warned.

"I will not."

He put the key in the cell lock and swung the iron

gate inward.

Bryna stepped through into clinging shadows, her shoes sinking into the damp, mucky straw.

Darkness.

Coldness.

Breathing.

The guard moved one of the wall torches closer and then the gate wheezed shut behind her.

"Please leave it unlocked. I may need to retrieve some healing herbs."

He grunted his displeasure, a moment of hesitation, and then left the gate ajar, anxious to return to his stew.

Bryna waited until he had left. She turned back to the shadows of the large cell. She had come here to free the chieftain and bring him to the waterfall cave as her teacher had instructed.

Torchlight from the tunnel threw slivers of light through the metal bars, showing flashes of silver-furred rats scurrying away in the straw. She held the basket in a death grip and listened to the deep breathing of the chieftain. She did not think him conscious.

He had been chained naked, facing the wall, with manacles at his wrists and ankles, his arms and legs spread wide.

Bryna drew in a steadying breath. Her heart pounded so loudly in her ears she wondered if the guard could hear it.

She moved closer, into the cast of torchlight.

Bloody wounds criss-crossed the chieftain's back. Rivers of blood, now dried, had flowed down his lean waist and firm buttocks to thickly muscled thighs and calves.

She placed the basket at her feet. With trembling fingers, she pushed the red cloth aside and reached for the large flask. It contained a water mixture of onions and honey. The drink would help clear his head and purge lethargy.

Reaching up, she gently pulled his chin to her.

He flinched from her touch.

"Easy," Bryna soothed. While supporting his jaw, she raised the silver flask to his mouth.

He jerked away and Bryna realized that he must think it some sort of poison.

She laid a hand on his shoulder and waited, hoping his need would prompt him to trust her.

His lips were cracked and bleeding, but he was alert now and probably expecting her to force him to drink.

When she did not, he turned to her in wary expectation. Guiding his chin, Bryna allowed several drops of the liquid to spill onto his lips.

A tongue darted out, capturing the precious liquid, testing it.

She waited.

He nodded, opening his mouth.

"Drink slowly," she cautioned, knowing he could not hear. She spoke more for her own comfort than for him.

"Here, now that you made up your mind to trust me." She gave him a small chunk of salty meat. He chewed it slowly as if it required great effort. He took three more from her hand, a wild creature caught and unsure.

Bryna touched his side and his lids cracked open. Beneath black lashes, amethyst colored eyes stared down at her through a white veil of blindness. Despite the spell, it seemed the magic of the past lay in their strange depths.

Tynan waited, painfully alert now. Darkness, silence, and pain receded to bearable levels. His stomach rolled and then settled into manly grumbling. His healer, for that is what he thought of her, squeezed his arm. He felt the trembling of her fingers and waited for what came next. Her touch slid to his back, to his ravaged skin. He recoiled and muttered a curse.

His healer squeezed his arm again, trying to communicate with him. He felt her gently clean his wounds and gripped the chains against the agony of it. Shivering with cold and fevered weakness, he had very little left in him with which to fight. He fixed his mind upon his healer, driving away all else. Was she tall? Was she plump and soft? Did her hair glisten like sunlight, or was it black as pitch like his?

After a time, warm hands spread a numbing paste into the wounds on his back. In relief, he rested his forehead against the cool stone wall and heaved a mighty sigh. He could feel her bandaging his back, up over the left shoulder and then across his chest. A pillowy breast brushed against his bruised ribs where she leaned into him. He focused on that unexpected softness and finally relaxed into her tending.

✳✳✳

"I am done." Bryna stepped back to inspect her work. She could smell the herbs in Derina's poultice, especially the garlic for the infection. The yarrow and toadflax used for the easing of pain and congealing of blood was less pungent.

The chieftain turned his head toward her.

Leaning forward, Bryna squeezed his arm. "I must get the keys. Hopefully, the guard sleeps." She hurried out of the cell, praying the guard had finished the stew laced with the sleeping herb. Silently, she walked back up the tunnel's path. There, slumped against the wall, the man snored gently. She approached him cautiously, removing the key ring from his belt so that it made not a sound.

Hurrying back down the corridor, she heard the clanging noise of chains and became fearful that it might wake the guard.

Once back in Tynan's cell, she quickly returned to his side and grabbed his forearm to prevent another firm yank. His dark head turned to her, the muscles in his arm strained beneath her hands. She knew her only way of communicating with him was by touch. Her fingers slid down his side. His struggles quieted and she remembered her teacher's words. *Let him feel your touch, so he knows you.* Heat rose in her cheeks. She had seen naked men before while helping Derina with the sick and feeble, but nothing prepared her for this, a warrior crafted in form and perfection. She sensed a primitive rage below the surface in him—— that link again, that connection reached out to her. Veiled eyes watched her, oddly seductive and haunting in their intensity.

Bryna felt herself grow bold. Curious, she leaned forward just a wee bit. Within a nest of black curls, she could make out his large, flaccid manhood. She pulled back, embarrassed to her core. *By the white moon, I canna believe I just did that.*

In a fluster, she turned back to her basket. Gathering a large white cloth, she went back to the chieftain and tied the cloth around his hips, making sure his manparts were completely covered.

For a moment, Bryna thought she heard Tynan's soft chuckle. When she looked up, his veiled eyes continued to regard her, but there was a curious tilt to his lips.

He jerked his right arm drawing her attention upward. She would never reach the shackle at his wrist. She looked for something to stand on, a stool, a table, anything, but the barren cell offered only soiled straw and the company of rats.

Bryna's gaze slid back to Tynan's face. He waited, unmoving and expectant.

She would start with the easy task first and free his ankles. Moving her hand from his arm to his waist, she knelt.

He tensed, looking down at her.

"I think you must be wondering why I am kneeling at your feet. Doona worry, my intent is to free you." She struggled to unlock the rusted shackles around his ankles. Once he realized what she was doing, he stilled.

She soon freed both his feet and stood. He yanked impatiently at the chain holding his arms.

"I know, impatient one," she whispered. A ledge jutted out directly in front of him. She ducked under his arm. There wasn't much room between him and the wall so she pushed on a muscled stomach, requesting more space.

He stepped back as far as he could, which was not much given his shackles. A musky male scent pleasantly surrounded her.

She stepped on the ledge and looked up the rock face.

"I shall try to reach your wrists." Reaching up to balance herself, she rested her hand on his right shoulder. He felt hot under her hand and she immediately suspected that in addition to his wounds, he now battled fever.

He stood close behind her, breath warming her

right ear.

Bryna strained upward and choked back a sob of bitter disappointment. "Tynan, I canna reach."

Rising on tiptoe, her fingertips barely brushed the bottom of the shackle. Suddenly a muscular thigh pressed into her leg. She looked down and immediately understood. With one hand on his shoulder, she hiked up her skirts and stepped on his thigh. Within moments, she had both his shackles unlocked.

He made a quick grab for her around the waist and lowered her safely to the ground, but did not let go.

"It is all right." She laid a hand on his bandaged chest, wishing he could hear her. "You are free now."

Tynan struggled to regain his equilibrium. He had no sense of symmetry or evenness in which to steady his world — only touch, only the healer. Swaying a little, he gripped her shoulders. His blood ran cold with the weight of the parasite feeding off his senses. He held the healer in place with one hand while he reached for the thing clinging to his temple. The healer grabbed his wrist with both her hands and tugged. He scowled at her attempt to restrain him. He felt the dark imprint of the evil magic in his mind, thriving off his senses, feeding. He wanted it off! Pulling free from her hands, he touched the thing at his temple. It burned his fingers and he jerked his hand away. *Spellbound!*

Darkness and silence and heat swirled in, stifling his mind. He had to concentrate to remain standing.

Focus on the healer. Focus on the healer. He battled the gray fatigue gripping him and breathed deeply. He was a creature of the senses and they took them away. He hated it.

The healer tugged on his arm.

He hated the blindness.

He hated the silence.

Yet, he felt something, a tingling in the air just within reach. *The faeries.* He wondered if the healer felt it too. She tried to pull free of his hands. His grip tightened on her. She remained the only thing solid and real in his world of eternal silence and night.

He cursed his veiled senses.

He cursed the Evil One.

He cursed the Centurion.

She pinched him.

"Ouch!" he mouthed furiously.

He scowled down at her, letting her know he did not appreciate being pinched.

She pried his left hand from her shoulder and directed his fingers to a mark below her right thumb. It was a small birthmark in the shape of a heart, an easily recognizable mark that he would know her when she touched him.

He sensed that she was talking to him again, though what she was saying only the faeries knew.

His hands slid up graceful arms, shoulders, and up the slim column of her throat to her face, slowly imprinting her youthful features. Soft skin. High cheekbones. Full brows. Lacy eyelashes that feathered the tips of his fingers. It occurred to him that she might possibly be lovely.

He leaned forward and inhaled, taking her lavender scent deep into his lungs. He suspected this to be the same woman who had come to him in the tombs. She squeezed his hand.

He squeezed back and felt her tug.

Tynan followed her lead. She placed his hand on the open cell door and then guided him left.

They walked a short distance upward along a narrowed path and then she stopped abruptly. He nearly toppled over her but caught himself and backed up a step. Reaching out to the wall for balance, he felt a sudden icy draft in the air. A gleaming blue-white light flickered in his black velveteen darkness and then disappeared. The light felt alive in its caress, moonbeams on a winter's night. He tried to see it again by shifting his head, but could not.

She took both his hands in hers and guided them to the wall. Tynan felt the cool smooth shape of a half-moon rock. A queer influence directed his hands. With searching fingers, he found an indentation on the underside and pushed the surface in. The rock slid back from his hands. A burst of cool air hit him along with a sense of dislocation. He pulled back. *An opening? A feypath? By the goddess, my healer knows the secret of the lost feypaths!* Tynan turned to her in astonishment and found his head pulled down by his ear.

She pushed him forward into the opening. He reached out a hand to steady himself and found prickly vines on one side and rough stone on another.

The air tingled with an ancient magic. He inhaled, trying to breathe in the scent of the feypath, a marker or signal so that he could recognize it later. *Nothing.* He suspected the spell had begun to feed on his sense of smell at this point as well. He turned to his healer.

Bryna covered her nose and mouth and gagged. Behind them, the half-moon rock slid close in silence, leaving them in the feypath's odd purple light. She turned into Tynan's bandaged chest for sanctuary.

"The air stinks of rotting crops. I know there are no planted fields, only endless tunnels bathed in purple moonbeams. But it still smells awful in here."

She looked at the tangled canopy of brown vines and silver thorns climbing the walls and ceiling to her right. Derina had explained that the vines were faery cursed and did not need sunlight for growing.

She stepped away from Tynan. "I guess 'tis a blessing that you do not smell this rot."

Bryna looked up into his handsome face. A sense of intense alertness permeated his rugged features.

"Come." She slid her right hand into his. "We must travel far this day." His hand shifted to her wrist, his thumb searching for her birthmark before he once again held her hand. "Aye, 'tis me." She smiled, leading him forward into the strange purple darkness of the ancient feypath.

She had always thought the feypaths an odd setting, a place of blendings, drafts of cold and heat, and of dryness and moisture. The colors of twilight and dusk held sovereignty, reminders of a predator's favorite time. As they traveled westward toward the cliffs, thick vines graced one side of the walls while smooth stones, etched with runic symbols, graced the other.

Bryna decided to travel slowly for the chieftain appeared gravely weakened from what he had suffered. It pained her to see him like this, a being so obviously spirited and strong brought to this low state.

She guided him around a small boulder embedded in the wall. "Here, around this way." Her eyes met his for a brief moment and she felt the magic swirling behind the veil of blindness before he looked away.

In a tiny corner in her heart, Bryna had begun to suspect that this bloody and wounded chieftain might indeed be the one of prophecy.

She continued to guide him forward, careful that he not stumble or bump into anything. "The sounds of the waves grow distant. In this next tunnel we go inward and head to the waterfall cave." She turned away from him to gaze down their intended path and then heard a loud smack.

Bryna jerked her head back and frowned in dismay. "Oh, Tynan."

The poor man had banged his head on a low place in the ceiling and was now rubbing a bruised forehead.

"You are too tall for this place." Reaching up, she pushed his hair away to inspect the new bump. "I am so sorry this has happened to you."

He lifted his head away. His lips thinned and Bryna dropped her hand to her side, attuned to his distress and slightly hurt by his rejection. "I promise to watch you more carefully," she whispered. "Come, we must go this way." Taking his hand, she tried to guide him forward but he would not budge. His chin notched up. Nostrils flared.

Bryna peered over her shoulder into the purple shadows. On either side of the narrow path, silver rock formations glistened with slimy wetness.

"What do you sense that I canna see?" she said urgently.

"Bryna child?"

"Derina?" Bryna called out in surprise

"Aye."

She squeezed Tynan's hand. "My teacher. It is all right." She pulled free and ran into Derina's outstretched arms.

"Child, I feared your delay and came looking."

Bryna hugged her teacher. "We are safe." Resting her cheek on her teacher's shoulder, she inhaled the fragrance of the rosemary herb. The scent belonged to Derina the way the leaves belonged to the trees. The foul stench of the feypath seemed to fade away. She pulled back and smiled brightly through her tears. Her teacher wore a silver brooch and gray cloak this day, blending with the walls of the feypath.

"I have him," she said proudly.

"Aye, though I can sense that he battles weakness."

"He has fever." She moved back to Tynan and wound her arms around his lean waist for support.

"It is all right," she soothed, when he glided his thumb over her birthmark. "My teacher, Derina, is here to help us." She turned back to the ancient. "We must take him to the waterfall cave soon. His skin feels sweaty and hot to the touch."

"Aye, a fever grips him." The ancient moved closer to the wall, her hand outstretched for guidance. "The chieftain is bound by a *geas*. Do you remember what I have taught you?"

Bryna nodded, slightly perplexed by the question. "*Geas* is of magic and obligation."

"And?"

"It is said that faeries imposed a *geas* upon special people like heroes, kings and druids infusing their lives with magic."

"Do you believe this?"

Part of Bryna believed in the magic. The reality part of her, the slave part of her, had trouble believing horses were deities and thorns were sacred to faeries, let alone a binding of obligation through magic. She looked up at the chieftain standing quietly beside her, a regal being mayhap belonging to the faeries. "Even if Tynan has this magical obligation, he will still need to rest and heal."

"True enough. Tynan is his given name then? I dinna know it." She nodded in thought. "It is a good name, a proud name for the prophecy's sovereign. Now, child, you must take the Lord Knight of *Tuatha Dé Dananns* to the waterfall cave."

Bryna searched her teacher's face. "Alone?" she asked. "Do you not come with us?"

"I have left fresh food, healing herbs, and clothes for him there as well."

"Teacher?"

"I canna go with you, child. Now, listen to me carefully. It is a simple thing to free him of this arcane spell."

"I listen."

"You must kiss him."

Bryna's cheeks turned a rosy hue. "Kiss him?"

"Aye, and as you kiss him pull the spider off."

"I can kiss him right here if that is all that he requires."

Her teacher shook her head. "Not here, child. He must be free of the fever first for it encumbers his *geas*, stealing his fire."

"His faery obligation," she nodded in wariness. "Do you know what his *geas* may be?"

The ancient shrugged in a non-committal way.

"Is it something bad?"

"Not bad. Trust me."

"Teacher, you are the only one I have ever trusted."

"I know." Her teacher gestured behind her. "Do

you remember how to get to the waterfall cave from here?"

Bryna looked down the tunnel. "Follow the path right until the square opening of rock."

"Aye, that is the way of it. You must go now."

"Go now," Bryna echoed softly, feeling her life irrevocably changing. Her inclination had always been to leave well enough alone. Yet, since the coming of her woman's moon time, another self had been emerging, another stronger, more formidable self that had the audacity to steal a prisoner from the dungeons.

"Child, doona abandon the land and the prophecy for your own fears."

"Abandon the land? I doona understand what you speak." The chieftain shifted on his feet beside her, a swaying toward the wall.

"You will. Remember, the faery tribe is different in all things."

"I remember." Bryna nodded, keeping her arm locked around the chieftain's waist.

"Especially during their mating time."

"Mating time?"

"Keep that in mind, for the males nip their mates' jaws before mating. It is a normal thing for them to do. Do not fear it."

Bryna frowned at that particular reminder. "I have no inclination to mate with any male."

"I know."

The druidess turned and started walking away.

"You are leaving me now?" Bryna could not believe it.

The ancient looked down, a solemn expression on her face. "For now." She headed toward another tunnel on their left. "Take Kindred's ancient lord to the waterfall cave before the poor man falls down."

CHAPTER 4

A KISS TO FREE HIM was all she needed to do.

She must trust her teacher.

She must trust that his *geas*, whatever it may be, would not harm her.

Kneeling in the soft soil, Bryna looked out upon the waterfall and spray. Sheets of water cascaded down a ten-foot ledge of silver rock into a warm, spring pool. Mist rose above the dark waters. Along the rocky banks of the pool, green moss grew in scattered, uneven clumps.

Her gaze slid to Tynan.

Irritation radiated out of every pore of his body.

He sat on his heels at the far end of the pool, leaning forward. The fever had broken a day ago. Strands of black hair flowed down broad shoulders so that the tips dipped into the swirling pool. He wore a simple pair of faded black breeches and nothing else. Ribbons of pink healing flesh crossed his back. His hands had fast become blistered from repeated attempts to remove the spellbound spider.

It had been five days since they entered the cave. She knew she could wait no longer and reached for the herbal remedy Derina had prepared.

Rolling up her right sleeve, Bryna dipped her hand into the clay pot and coated her arm. It was an herbal protection against possible burns from the spellbound spider. She did not know how it would work, only that Derina instructed her in its use.

Once her arm was coated with the green mixture to the elbow, she stood and walked the length of the cave. Worn black pebbles and tiny shells overlaid the pool's rocky edge. She could see into the deceptively safe shallows where the line would drop off suddenly into swirling black depths.

She came to where Tynan crouched. "I have waited too long to free you from this evil spell." He stared blindly into the water, no awareness of her presence. "It is time to do this thing, Tynan." Leaning forward, she touched his shoulder. He jerked away.

She straightened and sighed deeply. "Aye, you are angry with me and rightly so I suspect." He remained in his crouched position, his patience long since at an end.

Bryna tried again. She touched his shoulder. The muscle beneath her fingertips tensed, but he did not pull away this time.

She knelt beside him.

He exhaled loudly in annoyance and turned to her. A muscle twitched at his jaw.

"My heart is pleased that you trust me still, though your frustration shows." She kept talking to ease her frayed nerves. "Doona be vexed with me," she whispered. "I wanted you strong, for the next battle will be hard."

His lips thinned.

She turned his face so she could view the spell-bound spider and decide how best to grip it. "Let me see the creature that binds your senses."

He pulled out of her hand and stood, scowling down at her, and Bryna knew that the time for gentle coaxing had ended. She stood too, her mind set with stubborn determination.

"We must do this the hard way it seems." She reached for him.

He pushed her hand away and moved around her.

She grabbed a handful of wild mane and yanked him back. Rising on her toes, she planted a kiss full on his mouth.

He froze in surprise. Encouraged, Bryna grabbed hold of his shoulders, balanced on her toes, and kissed him with an urgent purpose born of little knowledge and less experience. She bruised his mouth, mimicking the whores that kissed the soldiers. One whore in particular had taken delight in explaining the art of ravaging a man's mouth. Skimming her tongue over his velvet lips, she tasted only tolerance.

Instinctively she felt the wrongness of it and eased her assault. Her mouth took his with tenderness then, following her own nature. His lips parted slightly. Her tongue delved into the hot cavern between, skimming silk and teasing wetness. Large hands caught at her waist, pulling her into the heat of him.

Tynan kissed her back.

Her lips were swollen from her hell bent urgency to invade his mouth. She must have cut her lip on his teeth, for he tasted blood.

Blood.

A calling stirred in his body.

Faery blood.

A fey longing began to burn, a coercion to possess.

Rich. Dark. Sweet.

Born of magic and obligation.

His *geas* took hold.

A dark urgency pulsed through his veins.

A compulsion to mate.

Now.

Breath beat at his lungs hard and hot. He did not recognize his *geas*, a spell of ancient faery magic, stoking the flames of primordial, spellbound lust. Gray mist swirled seductively in his veiled vision.

Tynan pinned the healer against the wall. He would thrust between her thighs pleasing her for all eternity.

"Fey witch," he murmured hoarsely. His mouth hovered in indecision above hers. "Come ride me." He slanted his mouth over hers, his tongue thrust into her mouth.

She tasted of wild berries and dark mysteries. She squirmed against him, an impotent rebuff that he had no tolerance for.

His body pulsed with the *gá*, the need, instinctively recognizing the woman in his arms as the territorial goddess.

"By the white moon," he rasped against her lips.

Heat scorched his body.

Sharp, primitive hunger surged.

Something wild and untamed roared to life.

The faery compulsion to mate engulfed him in a red haze. Dark, erotic magic streamed through his blood, creating intensely sexual images in his mind.

Of a meadow's caress on his back while small hands locked in his hair.

Of tree bark against his backside while soft lips trailed wetness down his stomach.

Of lying in a streambed while a flame-haired goddess rode him.

Of a goddess' pleasure.

Of his own . . .

Of his *geas*.

A fierce hunger erupted, demanding he mate. He felt the want and madness, the *teastaigh*.

Now.

He must have her now. Tynan held her in a submissive position, giving him better access to her jawline.

"Goddess." Saliva pooled in his mouth. "Take me."

The ancient faery *geas* in his blood compelled him to claim her—his faerymate.

His tongue stroked the right side of her jaw in preparation for his honor-mark.

He whispered an endearment, then his teeth scraped over delicate skin, savoring the salty feminine taste of her.

Bryna choked back a sob. He had nipped her! Somewhere in the back of her mind, she knew this was what Derina had warned her of, the male's mating bite. She pushed against an immovable chest. His hot mouth suckled around the ache in her jaw sending warmth into her quaking limbs. Discomfiture gave way to deep pleasure. Her struggles ceased, her head tilted back giving him better access. She reacted unconsciously, her body crowding up against him. His lips found hers in a passionate kiss. A throaty groan of male pleasure vibrated in her mouth, and then she remembered why she was here.

Freeing her arm, she reached for the spellbound spider at his temple and pushed him hard away. The hairy creature came free in her hand.

Her passionate chieftain roared, grabbing his head and falling to his knees in agony.

Bryna gritted her teeth and held on to the flaying creature while spellbound fire licked up her arm. She ran to the edge of the black pool and threw it in. The spider entered the water with a hissing sound and then disappeared into the depths, forever gone.

She collapsed to her knees at the rocky bank, breathing heavily, weak and shivering in a cold sweat of reprieve. The herbal mixture had shielded her skin, preventing burns, but her arm still tingled hurtfully.

Leaning forward, she dipped her arm in the soothing waters. With gentle strokes, she washed the green
herbal mixture from her very pink flesh. Her bones
ached, a kind of strain as if she had lifted something
too heavy.

She chanced a glance over her shoulder at Tynan.

"*Aile Niurin*," he breathed, holding his head with
both hands.

Rising from the bank, she went to him and knelt.
His black hair seemed to glisten with strands of blue
light. "Tynan, you are free from the spell." Tenderly,
she pushed his hair aside to view his bruised temple
and found herself staring into large eyes no longer
milky and veiled.

More than violet.

More than mortal.

Although his head remained slightly lowered, his
strange gaze held her captive.

"You gave me water in the tombs," Tynan stated
with certainty, gazing curiously at the waif kneeling
before him. She didn't seem older than fifteen summers. Then he caught sight of her lush bosom and
thought better of it.

She frowned, black brows creating a slight furrowing between. "I doona understand," she said in a voice
of alluring softness. "How did you know it was I?"

"You carry the sweet scent of lavender in you
hair, lass."

"Oh." She touched her hair in reflex, hands small

and delicate. Her silvery gaze dropped to her lap. "How do you feel?" she asked.

"I feel addled. Where is this place?"

"The waterfall cave below Kindred, the olden faery fort. Doona worry, we are safe here for a little while more."

Tynan slanted a half-glance around the secluded cave. A fine mist drifted above the pond to the shore. He had never seen a place such as this.

"We are alone?" he inquired.

"Aye." She answered him guardedly as if she thought he might pounce on her. He looked back at his healer. She had a delicate fragility about her that pulled at his masculine core. He studied her downcast eyes; auburn lashes were in abundance, shades darker than her hair. "You are the healer?"

"I am apprenticed to the druidess, Derina. She is the true healer for the villagers."

"The old one?"

She shifted in unease. "How do you know of Derina? You were blinded by the Sorcerer's magic."

"I sensed her." He did not wish to explain about his inner faery sight. "What is your name, gray eyes?"

"Bryna of Loch Gur."

"Bryna of Loch Gur, did you have the knowledge to free me all this time?"

Pink deepened in her cheeks. "Aye."

"Why did you wait so long?"

"I waited for the fever to break."

"My fever broke a day ago," he said slowly.

"I waited the extra day for you to regain your strength."

That made sense to him, considering the condition he had been in when she had first freed him in the dungeon. He touched his tender bottom lip. "Where did you learn to kiss like that?"

"One of the castle whores explained it to me."

"Ah."

His childlike waif looked up at that, her eyes swirling pools of gray mist and light.

"Do you often follow a whore's instruction, Bryna of Loch Gur?"

"Nay." She bit her lip in a sudden pause. "I have never kissed a man before."

"I can believe that." Her auburn eyelashes lowered again, hiding her silvery eyes. He found that gesture odd and took a moment to study her, his mind still foggy on what had gone before. *Faerylike, slender, unspoiled and ethereal.* Those were his first impressions. All gray mist and silver starlight surrounded by hair the color of flames and sun. There was darkness and light in her coloring, as if nature could not decide and crafted her of both. His gaze slid to her jaw, drawn by a slight purpling discoloration. He frowned slightly, his body tightening unexpectedly. "Let me see your jaw."

She tilted her face warily.

His fey senses fell silent at what he saw.

He had honor-marked her.

She looked at him then, with those gray eyes, a child woman of sense and touch, an innocent with the soul-penetrating gaze of his fey brethren.

He had honor-marked her.

Worse, he had honor-marked her without consent.

Tynan came to his feet instantly. Heat pulsed in his blood. His heart pounded in his chest. All senses focused on the faery waif at his feet and then... the world abruptly reeled under him. Bright colors flashed at the corners of his vision so that he felt he might topple over.

"Tynan, may I suggest you sit before you fall?" The voice of reason spoke softly to him.

Tynan dropped down to his knees. His eyes closed. "The earth moves."

"The earth does not move. Allow time for your body to adjust and senses to return. You have been under a spell crafted in evil."

"How long?" He did not like this weakness.

"I doona know. Never have I done this before."

A chuckle rose in his throat. "Neither have I." His eyes cracked open. She watched him in stillness. He looked down at her thumb, searching for the familiar heart-shaped birthmark. "Brown," he muttered and closed his eyes. "I had wondered at the color of the fey mark."

"Do you feel a wee better?"

He took a deep breath. "A little." He opened his eyes and saw that the earth had returned to normal.

"We have been in the waterfall cave too long. You must leave this place, and soon." She climbed to her feet.

He looked up at her. "You are young," he said in observation.

Her head lifted. "I am nineteen summers," she huffed.

"You do not look it."

"How old are you?" she countered in a righteous temper.

He fought back a grin. "I am twenty-seven summers, eight summers older than you." He climbed slowly to his feet and found that he was not as steady as he had thought.

"Here, lean on me."

"I can stand on my own. I doona need your help." He pushed her hands aside.

She stiffened at his rejection and turned away.

Tynan muttered an oath. "Lass, I did not mean my words to sound so harsh. A man needs to stand on his own."

She nodded but kept on walking.

A sensitive waif, he mused, just his luck, and then noticed her right arm. "Are you injured?" She probably did not realize that she held her arm close to her stomach, protectively. She looked to the pond and replied, "Bruised but a little."

He glanced at the pond then back at her retreating back. "From what?"

"The spellbound spider," she offered as a matter-of-fact, and headed toward the basket of food on the other end of the pond.

Unfortunately, he had no idea of what she spoke. Tynan rubbed his throbbing temple. "What is a spell-bound spider?"

"The Sorcerer attached a spellbound spider to your temple," she explained, still not looking at him. "Derina said it fed off your senses. That is why you could not see or hear. When I pulled it off, it tried to burn me."

"Spider? So, that is it. When did you pull it off?"

"When I . . . when we kissed."

"Where is the unholy thing?"

She pointed to the pond. "I threw it in the water."

He stopped to look into the pond. Moss curled about his bare toes, a slimy sensation. "I see only dark-ness in the water depths."

"The waters are deep. It probably settled to the bottom by now." Tynan turned back and saw her kneel near the baskets. He watched her rummage through the obviously meager provisions. Her right arm was pink from the fingers to her elbow.

He came up beside her and knelt. "Let me see your arm." He could see that he unnerved her with his closeness.

"I am fine," she said, shifting away.

"Let me see your arm, Bryna." He pitched his voice low and calm and waited.

She looked at him with indecision and then held out her arm for his inspection.

Gently, he touched her wrist. "Does it hurt?"

"It tingles some." She pulled back, reached for a slice of bread and handed it to him.

"There is not much."

He stared at the dark bread in his hands. "Why did you help me, Bryna? It is a brave thing that you did."

Bryna shrugged. She never thought of herself as brave, only resilient and mayhap naïve, for she had been molded by isolation.

He took a bite of the stale bread. "Tell me, how do you know the name Kindred?"

She put the rest of the bread back in the basket. "Kindred is the ancient name of this place. It is an old faery fort of forgotten magic."

"It is old, but not forgotten." Bryna found herself the focus of an unsettling intensity. "What do you know of the feypaths?" he asked.

She looked down at her lap, detecting an undercurrent in his tone. "Little."

"Your downcast eyes suggest a deceiver."

She was not a deceiver and glared at him. "Never am I a deceiver."

For several long moments, silver mist swirled in displeasure at amethyst fire.

Tynan's breathing quickened. Her faery gaze pulled him back to his past.

Faery eyes.

Faery vow.

Faery betrayal.

His tribe belonged to an ancient and separate sect of the *Tuatha Dé Dananns*, the noble people of the mother goddess Dana. His ancestors, assisted by the Good People, built Kindred. He was the last direct descendent of that ancient bloodline. Kindred belonged to him by birthright; the imprisoned faeries were his tribe's brethren.

Faery eyes.

Faery vow.

Faery betrayal.

Every hundred years, one of the ancient bloodline promised to mate with a *Daoine Sidhe* in order to keep the kingship of the land. His father broke the promise, and with that came the invaders, persecution, and hardships.

Tynan felt his body quicken.

He had vowed to keep the promise no matter the personal cost. He never allowed himself to think about bedding a creature of twilight. He knew his duty.

He stared at Bryna.

Small.

Slender.

Pure.

Translucent skin.

Large, silver-mist eyes.

Black winged brows.

Burnished gold hair.

"Daoine Sidhe," he whispered in sudden recognition and understanding. "I have honor-marked a faery."

Her eyes widened in dismay, white tones of silver that reminded him of moonstone on a winter's night. "Nay, I am not."

"You are faery bred." Tynan stated with a growing conviction.

"You are greatly mistaken."

He did not believe her and stood, not sure how to deal with so wrong a denial.

"Do you sense things, feel things that others do not?"

She refused to answer him.

"You are silent." Tynan held her gaze. "Your fear makes you lie to yourself."

She looked away. "I am a slave to a Roman invader, nothing more."

"Invaders often bring slaves with them from other lands."

"I am of this land."

His *geas* confirmed this for his body already pulsed with awareness of her as faery.

"Where is your birthplace, Bryna?"

"Derina found me on the shores of Loch Gur wrapped in rags."

"Loch Gur is a sacred lake to the faeries."

"I know this," she snapped.

A smile tugged at his lips. "You are faery."

She stood and faced him in a virtuous anger, a

magnificent sight for so slight a being.

"Where are my wings then, oh great warrior?" Small hands waved in the air and he half expected to be brought down to his knees for some punishment.

"Do the storms come at my command?" she demanded. "Why dinna I not just turn you into a toad at the first sign of my displeasure?"

Tynan's lips curved into a grin. He could not help it. "And you are just as fiery and willful as the faery folk."

"I am not faery."

"As you say."

Bryna looked away. The echoes of his words were like rays of light in her gloomy darkness. Her denials were becoming more for herself than for others. What if she were faery? What then? And what of her dreams? What of the golden territorial goddess kneeling in the nighttime glade? What did it mean to be a creature of twilight? She didn't dare think of it and hurriedly pushed those thoughts aside.

She wiped at her skirt. "Tynan."

"Aye."

"You must leave this cave before the Sorcerer and his searching minions find this place."

A large hand wrapped warmth around her left forearm and held her firmly. Bryna stared at his hand on her arm and froze in place. His touch was gentle, a hold not meant to hurt. A quickening began in her blood, in her womb. It frightened her.

"Look at me, Bryna."

She shook her head. "My eyes reflect evil in a man's soul."

He released her and pulled back. "What fool said that?"

"The Centurion." She could feel the heat of his gaze, could smell the clean scent of land and water on his skin.

"Is that why you look to the dirt?" His inflection was one of curiosity and not suspicion.

She gave a curt nod, a hollow feeling welling up inside her.

"Foolish faery," he chuckled softly, catching her off guard.

Bryna looked up at him in surprise.

"Good, for I doona like talking to the top of your lovely head."

"My eyes doona frighten you," she said in amazement.

He shook his head slowly, a kind of confirmation that gladdened her heart. She could not let the Sorcerer find him. She had to protect him.

"Tynan."

"Aye, faery."

"You must leave," she said adamantly. "You have to leave."

He nodded. "We will leave together."

"Are you mad?" she blurted, and then covered her mouth.

His lips turned up in amusement. "Methinks not so much today."

She had to fight back a smile. "I belong to the Centurion," she added in all seriousness. "He will come after me."

His head tilted in thought. "You have been gone for five days, lass, will he not punish you when he finds you?"

"Nay," Bryna locked her hands under her chin. "I doona think so. My teacher will have said that I am helping a sick villager. It has happened before and I only received a minor punishment."

"A minor punishment? You will not be punished this time, for he will not find you."

"He always finds me."

His gaze slid to her bruised jaw and Bryna detected a sudden change in him.

"He will not find you, for you are going with me."

CHAPTER 5

It had already begun.

The fey compulsion.

He wanted to mate; deep down where souls touched and passion lingered. His *geas* saturated his blood now, an unending, primitive desire for her.

Tynan inhaled, taking her feminine scent deep into his lungs. He had never met a virgin faery. They were always mated to the earth, loch, or air. Something about predestinies and blood ties, he mused, secrets forbidden even from the ancients. He dare not touch her until he confirmed her heritage. For now, he must endure the *gá,* the need.

She knelt again before him, rummaging through moldy cheese in a wicker basket. She was different from other women, other faeries, a waiflike combination of fortitude and fragile innocence.

She looked up at him, a sideways observance that slid away and left him heated. Her eyes were faery marked, but then so were his. It was the way of such things.

"What do you see when you look into my eyes, Bryna?"

"Violet and gold," she answered stiffly.

"You doona like my eyes?"

"I am not used to meeting another's gaze."

"You have lovely eyes, Bryna."

She looked up at him as if he had lost his mind. Her gaze dropped to his chest and dipped to the dark line of hair that started at his navel and disappeared beneath the waistband of his breeches. Tynan smiled at the pink coming into her cheeks.

She gestured to the pile of clothes in the corner.

"There are clothes over there that you can use for the journey."

He looked at the pile and nodded. "Although my tribe travel barefoot, I prefer covering on my feet." It was a small concession that he allowed himself.

"There may be shoes over there." He heard her breathe a sigh of relief when he turned away and grinned. Looking at the clothes, he reached for a forest green tunic and shrugged into it.

It was obviously too small, but it appeared to be the largest in the pile. The front laces pulled taut, exposing a large portion of his chest. He tested the seams by moving his arms.

"The tunic is too small," she stated and Tynan smiled to himself. She watched him.

"Mayhap another would fit," she offered in female advice.

"This is the largest in the pile." He gathered his long hair behind him with a piece of rope.

"Tynan, the sleeves tear at the seams . . ."

"It gives me more room to move." He retrieved a pair of brown, calf-high boots and tried them on.

"Do the boots fit?"

"They are snug, but not greatly so. Either way, they will have to do." Tynan straightened and looked over his shoulder. Gray eyes were inspecting his legs. He waited until their eyes met.

"Do you like watching me dress, faery?"

She muttered something about males under her breath and turned away.

Tynan threw back his head and laughed.

He felt strong.

He felt invigorated.

He felt restless with an aching desire that he could not quench. Aye, he may not enjoy her body for now, but he'd enjoy her wit.

"Ah, you do like what you see," he said. "Good." When the time came to woo her to his bed, it would make it much easier. He would not think of the possibility of the faery or tribe rejection of her for his mate.

He moved to the edge of the waterfall and listened to the sounds of vibrating life. The black waters stirred as his lust stirred, deep and constant. The *gá*, the need would get worse, he knew. The need to mate with the flame-haired Bryna would eventually drive him insane if he fought it. The imprisoned faeries would have to wait. They would be safe as long as the Dark Chieftain remained free.

He looked over his shoulder. "How did you come

to know my name?"

"The Centurion called you Tynan."

"How did he know my name?"

"I believe the Sorcerer told his servants who in turn told the guards."

"Ah, I wonder how the Sorcerer knew."

She shrugged and then flexed her jaw; a small grimace delineated her features.

He felt her pain down to his bones and stilled. "My mark brings you discomfort." Blood began to pound in his temples, removing all thoughts but those of his honor-mark. He must ease the ending of it, for she had pulled away before he could finish it.

"Very little," she replied.

"Bryna, my request may seem odd to you but I must ease the bruising of my mark."

"The wound gives me little hurt," she reassured.

" 'Tis not a wound, Bryna."

"I meant to say . . . the mating bite."

" 'Tis not a mating bite either."

She looked at him, her black brows curved in a small frown of confusion. "Derina had instructed me about mating bites and I assumed that this," she pointed to her jaw, "is one. I apologize if I have caused you insult."

"There is no insult and it is my need, faery." Reclaiming Kindred depended on observing his *geas*. To break the *geas* was unthinkable. It would be contrary to his honor and to nature, and the result would be catastrophic for his people. Each *geas* is unique and intimate, and those that where so possessed often kept it secret because an enemy could use it against them.

"Your need?" she echoed.

Tynan turned away before reaching for her. She had to come willingly into his arms. There could be no other way for him to complete the binding of his honor-mark on her.

He walked to the wall behind the pile of clothes. Already the *duil*, the desire, burned in his loins from the fey compulsion. He was the knight of *Tuatha Dé Dananns*, Dark Chieftain to the faery castle Kindred and he would not be driven to mate like a mindless animal.

He glanced over his shoulder. She stood unmoving, hands by her sides, eyes unblinking like a faery, silver and intent.

"What are you doing, Tynan?"

"I need to rest a moment." With his back pressed to the wall, he slid down and sat in the dirt.

Damned spiteful faeries and their spells. The borrowed breeches pulled taut against his erection. He raised one leg higher to hide his discomfort, hoping she did not see his arousal.

"Do you feel ill?" she asked in concern, taking a step toward him.

"Nay," he replied softly.

"How long do you intend to rest?"

"Until you allow me the easing of my mark."

"I doona understand any of this."

"Come to me, then." He let his voice coax her. "Let me relieve any discomfort that I may have caused you."

"Derina said the noble tribe are different from the rest of us. She once told me that a noble male's saliva is soothing for their mating bite."

"Derina is wise," Tynan murmured.

"She is a druidess. She knows of many things."

"That is it, then."

"Methinks, she does not know of this."

His lips curved into a smile. "Mayhap. Come to me," he urged.

She approached cautiously, a butterfly ready to take flight. There was a small silence while she studied him.

"You need to do this easing? It is part of some ritual?"

"Aye, it is unfinished."

"Will you nip me again?"

He shook his head.

She stepped between his legs and Tynan released the breath he had been holding. With a slow gentleness designed not to frighten her, he reached up and took her left hand in his.

"Sit." He guided her down. "Closer to me." He patted his inner right thigh.

She knelt, distrustful, yet curious.

"My mark was not meant to give you discomfort, only pleasure. Do you understand?"

She nodded.

"Your eyes are darkening, Tynan," she whispered.

"What color do you see?"

"They are as night."

Tynan closed his eyes and nodded. It had begun. His *geas* would darken the light in his eyes to pitch until tears of blood formed, but he still had time. It was too early yet for the madness to take hold.

"Tynan?"

He opened his eyes and looked into a sea of swirling silver. She belonged to the contrasts of in-between, of both faery and mortal, and now she belonged to him.

He drank her in, every delectable part of her embedding in his senses. He listened to the increased beat of her heart, the mysterious whisper of her breath, the slight, trembling sigh. Her reaction to him was as ancient and elemental as his faery *geas*.

"Frightened of me?" he asked.

"Aye, a little."

" 'Tis only natural to fear the unknown. I need you to remain calm and concentrate on me." He scrutinized his honor-mark on her jaw. Tiny spots of blood had risen to the surface of her purpling bruise, making him even angrier with himself. "My touch my seem strange at first, but 'tis our way."

She did not move. He took that as affirmation and then proceeded to explain the ancient male to female healing practiced by his tribe.

Bryna's eyes widened in alarm. She made a small,

strangled sound low in her throat. She did not know what to do. Derina had taught her that there were different forms of healing and that she needed to keep an open mind, but she felt exceedingly uncomfortable about him suckling her jaw, even though the saliva was meant to heal.

He touched her chin, his thumb brushing the bruised skin.

She pulled back.

"Hurts?" he asked.

She nodded, going rigid next to him.

"I will not hurt you." His hand entwined in her silken hair, tilting her head back.

"What are you doing?"

"I am tilting your head back so that I may have better access to your jaw." Gently, Tynan kissed her cheek; his lips moved down and slid along her jawline to his mark. He tasted the sweet nectar of her blood and the saltiness of her skin, taking great care to go slow with her. He suckled her jaw and felt her tremble in his arms. He pulled back a little. "I must do this," he said against her cheek. "Doona fear."

His lips returned to his honor-mark. With each feathery stroke of his tongue, his mark healed, binding her closer to him. Her shoulder pressed into his chest. He knew she could feel the increased beat of his heart against her arm.

She shifted her legs, her hip coming to rest intimately on his inner thigh.

Tynan stilled at the unexpected contact.

She shifted again.

"Bryna," he barely managed, his voice throaty with need. "You need to settle down."

He shifted back into the wall to give her more room.

"Did I hurt you?" she asked in mortification.

He shook his head. "Nay."

"Your voice sounds strange."

He nodded, knowing the cause. "Hold still then and let me finish." *Before I dishonor myself.*

She settled closer to him and Tynan felt a cold sweat come on. He resumed stroking saliva into his mark, praying for it to heal quickly.

He shut his eyes in determination. A primitive urge to bind her to him roared in his blood and then she sighed . . .

He froze at the distinctive sound of female surrender. His hands slid down to her shoulders and tightened.

Her eyes fluttered open, a gaze of molten silver burning a path to his soul. Fey need pulsed in him, ripping away his hard fought control.

"By the white moon, faery. I canna..."

Suddenly, jagged shapes slashed through his fey lust and compulsion.

Shapes.

Movement.

Tynan turned toward the feypath entrance.

"Tynan, what is wrong?"

His hands slid to her dainty wrists. "Be still and listen."

"The cave is safe," she whispered.

"The threat comes from the feypaths." In one swift move, he brought them both quickly to their feet.

"We must leave, now faery." Distant shapes filled his inner senses. "Which way?" He pulled her with him toward the pool.

"What?"

"The Evil One searches with many, Bryna. Is there another way out of this cave?"

She pointed to the shimmering waterfall. "Behind the waterfall lies a narrow path that leads to the outside."

"Show me." Gently, he pushed her forward.

"Nay, I canna go with you."

"You have no choice."

✳✳✳

The sunlight blinded them as they emerged from the secret waterfall cave, slightly disoriented.

A rolling landscape faced bright sunrise and Bryna thought they were somewhere near the western border of Laigin. As she had never ventured from the waterfall cave before, she was unsure, yet the land before them shone of sunlit hues in deep blues, greens, and golds. Majestic oaks and sycamores sprinkled over the plains. It was a place of light, of shore, and of a once fertile time. She could see the land struggling to return to its former glory.

Once outside, Tynan assumed the lead, urgency riding his heels. The day felt warm for this time of year and Bryna suspected he wanted to take advantage of it.

She had problems keeping up with his fast pace on the rocky hill, but valiantly struggled on. Tall grass brushed against her gray skirts. They strode around the leafy blackthorn trees with thorny branches and ancient standing stones that were level with her hip. In *Marta*, March, the busy month, Bryna knew these prickly trees offered blue-black fruit and beautiful white flowers, but not now.

Caught up in her musings, she stumbled on a protruding rock and cried out, losing her footing.

The chieftain pivoted and grabbed her upper arm, steadying her against him. Catching hold of his broad shoulders for support, Bryna stared at a muscular chest and a sweat dampened tunic. A powerful pulse beat at the base of his neck. Above her, warm breath teased the hair at her temple. He did not seem to be letting go, so she looked up.

He indeed watched her with a silent regard. Gold flecks glittered in large amethyst orbs framed by sinfully long black lashes. He was past and twilight, an ethereal mystery of long ago magic.

"Are you hurt, faery?"

"What?"

He glanced down at her feet, at her worn slippers cut from one piece of leather and sewn with an ornate seam.

"I am fine." She stepped back out of his arms. "Tynan, I canna go with you. I must go back to the fortress."

His gaze returned to her face and narrowed. "I think not." He pulled her forward firmly. "'Tis not safe for you anymore. The Evil One will know that you helped me, faery."

"How will he know?"

"He will know. You canna go back."

Bryna glanced over her shoulder. She felt a strong urge to return to Kindred that she could not explain. Derina had said she must go with the chieftain, yet she worried for the safety of her teacher. What would the Centurion do to the ancient druidess when his Witcheyes went missing? In the past, she had always believed situations would resolve themselves if left alone. She no longer felt that way and knew she must act. Later, when the chieftain rested, she would escape him and return to the fortress.

Through the morning and long afternoon, she walked beside him in silence. High above, the sun moved across the blue sky. They walked away from the sea cliffs and bramble-covered mounds, over rolling green hills dotted with mature yews, and around an unbroken ring of gray stones.

"Tynan, where do we go?" She shoved her hair

back over her shoulder.

"My home."

They were moving deeper inland, toward the place where the faery woodlands were said to be. Purple shadows crept across the land, turning the living world into the timeless dominion of the faeries.

"Twilight approaches. We can rest here for the night," he said.

To Bryna's vast relief, he stopped before a thicket of silver thorns that masked the entrance to a small cave. It was a good thing; for she was so tired that she swayed on her feet.

"Wait here." He sniffed the air, and then disappeared into the cave's darkness.

She wrapped her arms around herself and looked to the horizon. In the twilight sky, the buttered moon had begun its slow rise. She fervently wished for some toffee apples and mulled wine, cake, and a roaring fire to drive the cold away. She should flee now, but could not muster the strength in her legs.

"Bryna," he called, stepping from the thicket. "The cave is safe. Walk around the thicket."

She stood rooted to the spot. "I need to..."

He nodded in understanding. "Doona go far. The night closes in upon us." He walked back into the cave and gave her privacy.

In the underbrush, Bryna attended to her personal needs.

With the setting of the sun, crispness settled in the

air warning of a cold night. She shivered and glanced apprehensively at the dark cave entrance. She did not want to go in there. Neither did she want to spend her eve out in the open.

✳✳✳

In the cave, Tynan built a small fire with sticks, dried leaves, and moss. He settled himself down on a makeshift bed of dried leaves and waited for Bryna. The ground felt hard and cold beneath his weary body despite his best efforts. He ran a hand through his hair. He should hunt for food, but was too tired to do so. Beyond everything else, his body needed rest. His strength had waned quickly as he had not fully recovered from the Evil One's spell.

He reclined on the bed that he made and shifted to his side, bracing on one arm. Tynan stared at the cave entrance in growing annoyance at her delay. "Bryna?" he called out, breaking a small branch in his hands.

"I come." She entered the cave on silent feet and settled down on the other side of the fire, color high on her cheeks.

It came as something of a jolt to him, that this waif could be his territorial goddess. It would not bother him in the least to mate with a creature this beautiful. He leisurely explored her face.

She returned his regard with an icy blank expression that would set a lesser man in his place.

He patted the bed of leaves before him. "Come here and join me." His voice vibrated deep in the small confines of the cave.

Fear flickered in her eyes for just a moment. "I will not lie with you."

He patted the leaves again. "Come, Bryna."

She shook her head.

"I have no patience for stubbornness this night." In one swift motion, he rose. Coming around the fire, he pulled her to her feet.

She kicked his shin, causing him to hop back.

"Why did you do that?"

"Let go of my wrist!"

He scowled at her and then dragged her around the fire to the makeshift bed.

"Tynan, let go of me."

"Do not make me expend what little strength I have left in fighting with you. The night will be cold."

"I doona care how cold it gets." She kicked out, catching him off balance. They tumbled down in a wave of flailing limbs.

Tynan twisted, taking the brunt of the fall. She landed on top of him, her elbow jabbing his stomach. He grunted, rolling to his side and taking her with him.

"Settle down!"

She turned, her knee barely missing his manparts.

He grunted, twisting her around so that her back pressed into his chest.

"Stop fighting me," he hissed through clenched teeth, locking her arms across her chest and forcing her compliance.

"I will not lie with you!"

Tynan was in no mood to tolerate disobedience. "All I wanted was to share my warmth and sleep with you."

"Sleep?"

"Aye, sleep. I will not dishonor you."

"Do I have your word?"

He chuckled. "Aye, you have my word. Now, can we sleep? My body aches more at this moment than it did before."

"I thought . . ."

"I know what you thought." Tynan released his hold on her and laid down on his back.

She settled in beside him.

"Rest, faery," he said wearily. "You are safe from the bad chieftain this night."

"Safe," she murmured. "I know not what safe is." Soon, her trembling subsided and she slid into a mindless slumber.

After a time, Tynan locked his hands behind his head and listened to her breathing. She would always be safe with him. He stared up at the black ceiling of the cave. The flutter of tiny wings moved the air above him. Two brown bats left the shelter of the cave to forage in the night.

His mind finally calmed, giving his body the rest he

sorely needed. His last thoughts were of the silver-eyed faery mumbling in her sleep about a golden goddess.

CHAPTER 6

BRYNA DREAMED OF THE GOLDEN territorial goddess again, an ill omen, a dream turned menacing. The goddess knelt in a glade beside a pool of black rain-water, an elfin vision of blond beauty and rage. As the dream held her immobile, bars of red fire sprouted from the dirt, locking the goddess in a cage, a cage belonging to castle Kindred. The vision began to fade, nightmare and mist streaming over a fading glade into nothingness.

The warm world under her shifted.

And then again . . .

She snuggled closer to the sloping hardness be-neath her cheek and hand. Strength slowly encircled her upper back, caressing the curve of her shoulder. Throbbing warmth pulsed against her inner thigh. Adjusting her position, she did not recognize the press-ing length of masculine desire.

A hand pushed her knee down.

Bryna's eyes fluttered open.

"You need to move, faery," a black velvet voice urged softly.

Bryna blinked, not yet fully awake.

Hips shifted under her.

She looked down at her body draping his, at her knee, at the large bulge pressing against her inner thigh.

She scampered back in a blind panic, bruising her hip on an outcropping of hard, mineral-laden rocks, and rolled over with a firm thump.

"Oh," she gasped as the world tilted precariously.

The chieftain levered himself up on one arm. His amethyst eyes fixed unblinkingly on her. "Morning, skittish one."

Bryna took a steadying breath to regain her senses and rubbed her bruised hip. "Morning."

"Are you hurt?" He was looking at her, a slight frown arching a dark brow.

"Just a little bump." She looked over at the smooth planes of a male chest that lay exposed beneath the green laces of his tunic.

Tugging down the hem of her rumpled gown, she then adjusted the bodice, which had twisted sideways during the night. Gazing down at the frayed material, she realized the straining seams would soon need a needle and thread.

A masculine groan echoed in the morning silence. She peered up at him from beneath her lashes; he had lain on his back, his arm covering his eyes.

"Tynan, are you feeling ill this morning?" she inquired.

"Not ill," he answered emphatically. He dropped his arm to his side and stared up at the ceiling in a most perplexing way.

"Tynan?"

He grimaced and sat up.

"If you doona feel ill, what is wrong then?"

"I am annoyed." Reaching behind his back, he pulled out an offending rock and tossed it aside.

"By that rock?"

He looked at her with great displeasure, as if she had done something terribly wrong. "Faery, can you not repair that gown?"

Wincing at his tone, she absently touched the frayed bodice. "Not without a needle and thread. Is that why you feel annoyed? By my gown?"

"Partly."

She tilted her head and studied him, but his gaze had slid away. "Derina said some men awake in a temper."

"Aye, they do," he agreed in irritation. "Damn Sidhe spells and honor." In one swift move, he stood.

"What spells do you speak of?"

He stood in front of her, a distinctive male bulge between his legs.

"Does it hurt when it gets like that?"

He glanced down at himself and then gave her a very strange look. "Have you not seen the shape of a man before?"

"I have."

"When?" His tone was exceedingly male and honed with the knowledge and the mystery of experience.

"When helping Derina with the ill. I am not a complete innocent. I have just never seen a bulge so large before."

"We come in varying sizes, faery," he said in a slow throaty voice. "Curious of my shape? Would you like to see?"

Bryna stood abruptly at the offering and shook her head. " 'Tis not decent."

A faint smile graced his lips before his expression slipped subtly into darkness. "Not today, then."

His face grew shadowed.

Sensing danger, she gestured behind her, wishing to go outside.

His eyes drifted to the cave entrance and then back to her. He shook his head.

The cave became strangely quiet. She could not seem to breathe and took a step back without looking. Her right foot slid off a rock. Flinging her arms out for balance, she heard a distinctive ripping of fabric before regaining her balance. She looked down at herself in astonishment. Three vertical seams on the front of the bodice had completely unraveled and now gaped open, exposing her breasts.

She heard his harsh intake of breath before he growled, "Cover yourself."

Bryna tried to shield herself with her hands.

" 'Tis not my fault," she said shakily. She looked up and felt devoured by his gaze. "The gown is old and the repairs no longer hold." She spun away and tripped again over the infernal rock. With a startled gasp, she pitched forward before strong arms locked around her waist, yanking back into a hard body.

"Bryna." His voice came out in an odd rasp near her ear. He leaned over her slowly. His hand grazed the underside of her breast and she could not draw away.

He cupped her, kneading her flesh, his thumb teasing the rose-tipped nipple.

She held on to his wrist, her head pressed back into his shoulder.

"You are more beautiful than I could have ever imagined."

Her breast felt heavy in his hand, and the other ached for his touch.

He turned her around and backed her against the cold wall.

Bryna could only stare in wonder as he dropped down to his knees in front of her. Warm lips slid over her right nipple, taking her into the moist heat of his mouth. Her legs nearly gave out at the stream of hot pleasure. She tangled her hands in his silken hair, holding him to her.

He suckled her, igniting flames in her womb.

She gasped softly, lost in sensations beyond her experience, her body becoming liquid.

"Tynan," she sighed.

He went rigid and released her breast.

Rocking to his feet, he stepped back, a strange tension outlining his features.

Bryna stared up at him in puzzlement.

He reached for the edges of her torn bodice and

slowly pulled them closed, his knuckles sliding over her sensitive skin. Her hands covered his, holding the tattered fabric together.

"Tynan?"

"I canna take you."

She could feel the slow ebbing of pleasure in her body being replaced with the cold hurt of rejection. Pulling back from him, she searched his face.

"Bryna, I canna forswear my oath to mate with the territorial goddess. My faery brethren and tribe must approve of my mate. Do you understand?"

She did. He had mistakenly honor-marked her. She was not this goddess but a slave. Turning away, she stared through her tears at the wall. With trembling fingers, she struggled to repair the bodice, knowing it to be hopeless.

Behind her, heavy breathing warned of his edginess. She possessed no thread and no extra fabric. Glancing down at her skirts, she thought possibly that she could tear a piece from the hem, but then her legs would be exposed.

The sound of fabric ripping startled her. She looked over her shoulder. He had torn off the sleeves from his green tunic.

"Here, use these."

She did not move.

"Hold the bodice closed." He tied the ends of the sleeves together. Leaning forward, he pulled the sleeves under her arms. In several turns, he managed to cover her thoroughly. He then pushed her hair out of the way and knotted the sleeve ends behind her back.

Bryna looked down at herself and nearly laughed out of nervous tension. He stepped in front of her, inspecting his work.

" 'Tis a peculiar bodice," she said softly.

"It will do." He turned and walked away.

She stared after him, a great sadness taking hold of her. Turning, she headed in the opposite direction, toward the cave entrance.

"Bryna?"

She paused beside the opening thicket. Sunlight streamed in upon her legs.

"Where are you going?"

"I need to go outside."

He nodded once. "Let me check first." He walked past her, the scent and heat of him a momentary flash before he was gone. He returned a few moments later, his gaze hooded and withdrawn. "The land is quiet, but stay close to the cave."

She nodded that she would.

***

Tynan watched the gentle sway of her hips as she disappeared into the morning light and then turned back into the cave. Some days provided more challenges than others did, and this day was starting high in his estimation. He stared at the makeshift bed of leaves. Shutting his eyes in bitter frustration, he tilted his head back and exhaled loudly.

Damn the faeries.

Straightening, he stared once more at the bed of leaves. He would fight the spellbound compulsion with all of his willpower and strength. Never would he lose sight of the ultimate goal to redeem his bloodline and return prosperity to the land.

Damn his father's weakness.

He would not succumb. He would endure. His pride and determination would overcome.

From beneath lowered lids, he looked sideways at the cave entrance, at the spilling of sunlight across the black, moist soil. It was best his lovely faery waif remained out of his sight for a while. He needed time to regain his self-control and grace.

Sidhe spells and honor.

The words tumbled in his brain, a muttered oath of downfall and duty. Grimacing, he reached down and loosened the waist of his pants, easing some of the pressure off his arousal. He needed looser pants.

His gaze slid to the cave's shadowed entrance again, drawn to the warmth of the morning light. Yellow and gold streamed through the thicket to the dirt floor. He stared at the blackness of the soil and his thoughts turned inward once again, dim and dark with yearnings long suppressed. *Why did you not keep the faery promise, Father? Why?* It pained him, the memory of it, the memory of his father's dishonor and his own abandonment. He rolled his head, a vain attempt to relieve some of the stress coiling in his body, but there would be no relief for him.

For now, his body was burdened with twice the obligation and twice the desire. He would endure.

✳✳✳

Outside, pleasing sunlight warmed her chilled skin. Bryna tipped her face to the resplendent blue sky, soaking in the wonder of puffy, white clouds and the clearness of the day. Summoning an inner calm, she listened to the whispery movement of the clouds, unaware that no mortal had ever heard such a breath of sound or seen such shades of blue and white.

The small clearing beckoned her admiration. In the previous day's twilight it had remained hidden but now, all its beauty unfolded. Two large oaks stood on the outskirts, dwarfing all beneath their outstretched branches. Silver-capped boulders, positioned by faeries no doubt, gouged the land in a strange circular pattern. It was said that clearings were sacred to the druids and she reasoned that it must be so, for never had she seen such natural splendor. At the base of each boulder, fuchsia bloomed in riotous colors of pink, lavender, and white. Vibrant green bushes splashed the landscape with berry-laden branches causing her mouth to water from the glistening harvest. She walked over to one of the bushes and with care, gathered red berries in her palm. At the end of branches, tiny white flowers fluttered musically in the cool morning breeze, a greeting of sorts from one to another. Drenched with morning dew, the berries tasted ripe with sweetness. She plopped a few more into her mouth and let the juice trickle down her throat.

Inhaling the fragrance of the new day, Bryna walked along the tufts of grass growing in the black soil. She glanced upon a small violet flower and paused, gazing down into the exact shade of Tynan's eyes.

From above, a piercing kee-kee cry rent the air, startling her. Bryna looked up, shielding her eyes from the morning sun. A large, rust-colored kestrel settled on the top branch of the oak. The bird looked down at her with a mythical wisdom not of his kind, and she sensed a shadow come over the clearing.

"She will not eat you," Tynan said, watching his faery waif with a strange possessiveness.

"I know. She seems to want something, Tynan."

He met the bird's black beady eyes and felt the chilly air of her warning.

"She gives us caution," he replied, and nodded to the kestrel which then took flight, disappearing into the blue sky.

"Do you talk to birds?"

"Nay, they talk to me." Tynan scanned the immediate area for this new threat. There were three men, mayhap more, moving quietly along the outskirts of the clearing. He glanced back at Bryna and held out his hand for her to come to him. He wished she would not look at him with such feminine curiosity, and instead went to her and took her arm.

"My berries, Tynan," she protested.

"Listen, faery." He tilted his head, indicating the shrubbery on the west side of the clearing.

"Is something out there?"

Tynan reached out with his fey senses, a slow smile curving his lips. "Men," he answered, the tension leaving his body, "and mayhap food."

"How do you know that?"

"I know. Trust me."

"Trust has little to do with it."

"Does it not? You are safe with me and shall always be safe with me." He looked over her bright head toward the sound of footfalls. Emerging from the dark shrubbery, a young man with red hair approached them.

"Edwin." Tynan smiled warmly at his younger tribesman.

"Sire."

"You scout ahead, Edwin?" He scanned the area for the arrival of the rest of the group. His tribesmen never traveled alone.

"Aye. Once again, our leaders bade us search for the mysterious feypaths."

Tynan looked at his silver-eyed faery. She knew at least one of the feypaths, and he vowed to gently coax the rest of the secrets from her, but that would come later.

✳✳✳

Bryna watched Tynan speak with the broad-shouldered youth. The young man wore forest green breeches and long-sleeved tunic that matched the land. About his neck rested a thick, gold neck ring. She heard the adornment referred to as a torc. On his green tunic, several gold brooches glittered and gold bracelets wrapped each thick wrist.

She looked back to Tynan. The morning light caught at the blue-black length of his long hair. Again, the feeling of ancient faery magic radiated from him. It saturated her, making her feel luminescent, changing the morning gold to shades of purple twilight.

"Bryna, come meet my tribesman, Edwin." He gestured for her to come forward. "This is Bryna of Loch Gur, Edwin."

"Lady," The youth replied, and bowed his head.

Bryna smiled warmly and suddenly five warriors emerged from the berry bushes carrying bows and axes.

"Easy, faery," Tynan said when she backed up into him. "They are my tribesmen. Doona fear."

Leather-wrapped scabbards strapped to their backs held swords with solid wood handles flanked with brass tang guards and tips. All wore the same green and brown clothes, subdued and mixing with the colors of the land. Sheathed at their waists, Bryna saw the glint of six-inch daggers with black, leather-wrapped handles. Some wore gold beads woven in their long braids; others wore their hair unadorned. They were the tallest men she had ever seen, and she felt a trifle overwhelmed by their imposing presence.

The tallest of them came forward. Long, brown hair fell to his shoulders with thin braids on either side of his temple. Sheathing his curved dagger in his belt, he bowed his head in acknowledgement.

"Cousin," the tall man said pointedly.

"Eamon," Tynan responded just as coldly.

To Bryna, this greeting felt more like an encounter between enemies than tribesmen.

"Edwin has told me that you search for the fey-paths, Eamon."

The tall warrior called Eamon snorted. "Aye, again we search for the accursed feypaths! I tell Rose they do not exist, but does she listen to me?" He shook his head in disgust. "She insists, so we search. I grow tired of this endless searching. It is a waste of my time."

Beside her, Tynan said nothing. She felt uneasy with his prolonged silence. So, too, did the other men, it seemed.

"You come from Kindred?" Eamon quickly changed the subject.

With that question, honesty and truth slipped away and Bryna felt the full force of her accursed gift.

Horrible sweetness spilled from the man's mouth, a beginning of lies yet unspoken. She stifled back a cough, her throat closing reflexively.

"Aye, we come from Kindred," Tynan answered in measured tones, almost as if he too sensed Eamon's falsehoods.

"I heard telling of a spider's spell."

Bryna watched as something sly crept across Eamon's features. She felt a hand on her shoulder; Tynan's gaze searched hers for an explanation of her discomfiture, but she could only give him a wane smile, shaking her head. How could she explain it?

Her chieftain turned back to his tribesmen. "How do you know of the Sorcerer's spider spell, cousin?"

So simple a question, indeed, was loaded with meaning.

"We have heard talk," Eamon answered, evasive and unrevealing.

"What talk?"

Bryna saw hatred burning behind Eamon's eyes, hatred and jealousy of Tynan. The red scar across his chin crinkled, giving him a hunted look.

Lies and deceit were being spun here and Bryna felt caught between the two. Suddenly, the youth Edwin stepped in front of her.

"Thirsty?" He held up a water flask in offering. His eyes implored her to take the flask and defuse the volatile situation developing between Tynan and Eamon.

Bryna reached for the silver flask. "My thanks, Edwin.

I am thirsty." She looked up at Tynan for approval.

He nodded curtly to her. "Drink, faery."

Bryna brought the narrow neck of the flask to her lips, very much aware of the men's attention on her. Chilled water streamed into her mouth, hurting her teeth.

"Slowly." Tynan pulled the flask away from her mouth. "Cold water hurts an empty stomach and we have not eaten. Drink it slowly."

She nodded and did so.

The men continued to watch her, their gazes skirting her jawline in knowledge and question before gliding away. They were curious of her place beside their chieftain.

When she had finished drinking, she handed the flask to Tynan.

Raising it to his own lips, he drank what remained of the water.

Beside her, Edwin cleared his throat. "We have food, sire, if you wish to eat before traveling."

Tynan nodded and handed the flask back to Edwin. "My thanks, Edwin." He wiped his mouth with the back of his hand. "Let us eat before journeying home. My stomach feels empty." He gestured toward the cave's hidden entrance. "There is a cave beyond the thicket. Let us eat in there."

Bryna felt his hand centered on her back, guiding her forward.

***

A damp coolness resided in the cave. Along the uneven walls, shadows mimicked the men's movements.

Tynan took Bryna's arm and guided her to sit next to him on his right. His tribesmen formed a circle outward from them and settled down to eat, Eamon to his left, and Edwin to Bryna's right.

His faery waif knelt beside him with her hands folded in her lap, a posture of an obedient slave that irked him for no reason.

"Will you introduce us to the maid, cousin?" Eamon asked.

"Bryna," Tynan began his introductions, "this is Eamon, my cousin."

"Lady." Eamon dipped his head.

"The blond ones that sit across from us are the brothers, Declan and Lachlan. Ian is the one holding the longbow. Adian sits to Edwin's right and is his first cousin on his mother's side. You already know Edwin."

She dipped her head to all of them.

He suspected that Bryna had no idea why they addressed her as "Lady." His tribesmen had already recognized his honor-mark on her and waited for his explanation, an explanation he did not intend to give this day.

"Is the *Yn Drogh Spyrryd* still at Kindred?" Eamon prompted, leaning forward to unpack supplies.

Tynan detected a trace of resentment in the other man's voice.

"Aye, the Evil One lives in the castle's ancient tombs."

Beside him his faery stared at the ground, her cheeks suddenly pale as if battling some sickness.

He touched her leg and she shook her head adamantly. He grew concerned at her odd behavior.

"The maid looks ill, cousin. Mayhap your honor-mark is false."

Tynan turned to his cousin, his face darkened in anger. "Be forewarned, Eamon."

"I am only concerned for her."

"Your concern gives you credit if that is all of it. She is mine, Eamon."

"My apologies, Dark Chieftain. I meant no disrespect."

"Temper you tone and mayhap the apology would be more believable." Tynan glared his displeasure a moment longer. "Let us eat. The day passes and I am anxious to journey home."

He glanced at his faery and then looked away.

Staring at the dirt floor, Bryna froze, coming to an abrupt awareness.

Eamon had called Tynan Dark Chieftain.

Dark Chieftain.

She had never truly believed it.

Never wanted to believe it.

Never wanted to hope for it.

Never, until now.

She had thought Tynan only some powerful chieftain of one of the fey tribes, but if it were true, if Tynan was the one prophesied to drive the invaders from the land, then she could be free.

"Dark Chieftain," she murmured, unaware that she had spoken aloud.

The Dark Chieftain tilted his head to her and waited.

Slowly, Bryna looked up at him, seeing him in a new light, hopes rising in her. "You are the Dark Chieftain of Prophecy?"

"Aye, does that frighten you?"

She shook her head even though it did frighten her, frightened her deep down inside; change always did.

"Why *Dark* Chieftain?" she asked. "Why not just chieftain?"

"There is a faery darkness that comes into the eyes when I am . . ." he did not finish, but took a deeper breath. "You have already seen the change in me, Bryna. Do you understand?"

She did. When passions rode him hard, the color of his eyes slid to pitch.

One large hand covered her hand and squeezed. "We will talk later in my home. You are not at all what I expected. The territorial goddess belongs to the Dark Chieftain, as he does to her. I thought you would know all this. But, it seems I must be the teacher instead of the student."

"I doona know what you mean. I am a slave."

He turned away from her without responding, accepting food from one of his tribesmen.

Bryna frowned in thoughtful silence. What did he mean about being the teacher instead of the student? Was the goddess meant to teach him something? She knew nothing other than a slave's survival.

More dried food and cold water were being passed around.

"Lady?" Edwin called quietly to her right.

A large portion of food was placed in her lap. Bryna looked down at the chunks of spicy dried meat and black bread. She shook her head at Edwin and his generous offering. "Edwin, I canna eat all this." She tried handing some of it back.

The Dark Chieftain leaned closer and whispered in her ear. "Do you not like the food, Bryna?"

She turned to him. "It is not that. Only, I canna accept all this."

"To return it would be an insult to Edwin."

She turned back to Edwin. The youth had bowed his head.

"My thanks, Edwin. I am indeed hungry." She caught sight of a red blush creeping into his cheeks.

"Lady." He returned to his seat.

Bryna turned back to Tynan. "I meant no insult."

"I know. Eat now for we have a long journey to make and I wish you to be strong."

She turned her attention to the food, her mouth already watering.

Tynan wondered how many men she had helped escape the Evil One's clutches. He inhaled her scent, a world of knowledge entering his body. She was not bled, a virgin faery, untouched by the land. Inconceivable, he mused. His fey senses reached out to her. Her woman's courses drew near. He would wait until after her time before making his claim.

Eating a stale cake, he took a mouthful of water to wash it down. His older cousin watched him with resentful eyes. Never would there be kinship there. Eamon's envy consumed him. No, there would never be a kinship, but mayhap an enemy. He hoped not. He hoped that he was wrong. His gaze slid back to his faery waif.

Bryna found a strange peace in the presence of these strong men. They did not scowl at her or call her Witcheyes. They instead called her "Lady," for no reason that she could fathom but felt grateful for their gentle courtesy.

She took another bite of the moist black bread and felt the heat of Eamon's gaze. She shifted back, uncomfortable with his interest. Knowing very little about the ways of the illusive *Tuatha Dé Dananns,* her womanhood warned her to stay away from Eamon and not instigate a challenge between the men. Derina had told her that the men folk of Tynan's tribe were highly competitive in their mating claims. Since she bore Tynan's mark on her jaw, she could only reason that she belonged to him, at least for now.

"We scout ahead." Eamon spoke authoritatively into the silence. "The tribe elders wish to reclaim Kindred soon. They are intent upon it."

"If only the ancient feypaths could be found," the youth Edwin concurred.

Bryna stopped eating at the mention of the feypaths.

"Desperation guides us." Eamon grunted. "I have a distaste for the tribe elders' decision."

"There are better ways to achieve our goals than a direct attack upon our enemy." Tynan spoke to them all in a voice of calm leadership.

"You have a plan, cousin?"

Bryna felt her mouth go dry with Eamon's impertinent tone. She had a distinct urge to slap him.

"I will speak with our tribe elders first." Tynan gestured to Edwin. "The feypaths exist lad and we will use them to regain what is rightfully ours."

Bryna knew that Tynan intended for her to show them the secret feypaths. She felt the eyes of the men move between them, their chieftain and her. In her stomach, the food began to turn to acid. The feypaths were not meant for human kind. She did not know how she knew this, but she did.

"And what of her?" Eamon motioned in her direction, his cold blue eyes hard with desire.

" 'Tis not your concern, Eamon," Ian said in warning. "The maid belongs to our chieftain."

"Are your senses dulled, cousin," Tynan growled, "that you doona recognize my mark?"

Bryna could taste the man's unspoken challenge in the currents of the morning air.

"She is not bled, and is not handfasted."

All the men came to their feet in a single rush.

"Stand back," Tynan commanded. "Eamon challenges for the maid."

"I do!"

Bryna climbed quickly to her feet. "Tynan, stop this."

"Protect her, Edwin." He shoved her into the youth's arms.

Bryna found herself pulled out of harm's way. Her mind raced on how to resolve the situation without violence, but before she could act Tynan's large fist had connected with Eamon's jaw, sending the taller man flying backwards into the dirt. He flipped his cousin to his stomach and jammed his knee into the man's back. Yanking Eamon's arms behind him, Tynan twisted his cousin's wrists up behind his back.

Bryna stood on shaking legs. She had lived around violence all her life, yet each encounter still unnerved her.

Tynan leaned forward on his knee, snarling his warning so all could hear. "Doona question my mark on her again, Eamon. The maid is mine. Do you yield?"

"Aye," Eamon grumbled, "I yield."

"I canna hear you."

"Aye, Dark Chieftain. I yield your claim."

Tynan released Eamon's arm and jumped to his

feet. For a brief moment, Bryna met his gaze and then looked away.

Tynan knew what she saw.

The darkening in his eyes.

The mating fire now raged in his blood from the challenge.

Damn Eamon and his lust! In another place, he would claim Bryna as his prize. But not today; he must keep his focus and maintain control.

"Ian, have the men make ready. We travel to the woodlands this day."

Reaching for Bryna, he guided her around Edwin. His young tribesman did a quick bow before rushing back to gather his belonging.

"Tynan, you hurt me."

He eased his grip, but the need to claim her did not ease inside him. He steered her to the front of the cave. Yellow sunlight streamed through the thicket across the dirt floor onto their feet.

He looked sightlessly into the vine's under-growth, struggling to regain control of the tempest in his blood.

"Tynan?"

He pulled her into his arms, closed his eyes and rested his heated cheek upon the top of her silky head. He breathed in her intoxicating lavender fragrance, the compulsion riding him hard. If only she knew what his faery obligation demanded, what he needed from her.

"Tynan, what is wrong?"

He knew she felt the strangeness in him.

"Doona move away from me." He held her tighter. Her shoulder pressed into his damp chest. "Bryna, I canna explain right now."

"Is it your *geas*?"

His breath touched the top of her ear. "Stay with me."

She nodded under his chin, shifting closer to him rather than away. He needed to calm down or mate with her here and now, and that was not an option for him.

He inhaled the scent of his honor-mark on her, destining her to be his faerymate, his goddess. She was going to be the death of him, if he did not get some relief from this fey coercion soon.

CHAPTER 7

LONG HOURS SLID BY SINCE they left the cave. Behind their lord, the men walked in single file to hide their numbers. Above them, a group of blackbirds flew in silence. Their orange-yellow beaks and eye rings shone in the sun's setting light. Bryna watched them fly away, wistful for her own freedom.

She followed behind young Edwin. They walked around a large stone circle flanked by decayed trees with black twisted trunks. In the center, three upright stones were set with a space between and capped with a horizontal stone. Bryna recognized the ancient structure as a dolmen. Some villagers believed treasure lay beneath these giant tombs and had ventured in search of them, never to return. From Derina's teachings, she knew dolmens were guarded by spriggans. Spriggans were described as nasty elfin folk, if one believed in elfin folk. It was said that if one squinted their eyes just so — and Bryna tried it — one could see the tiny creature with its large head and puny shoulders.

She shielded her eyes from the late sun and squinted harder.

At one of the black twisted trunks, a shriveled old man with a large head shimmered into view. He wore a red velvet tunic with ruby buttons. A sinister smile curved white lips. He bowed his head to her and then hissed, "Goddess."

Bryna's eyes widened in shock.

"As pledged, only you I let see and hear me."

She turned quickly away only to find herself looking back over her shoulder, but the spriggan had disappeared.

Raising her skirts, she hurried across limestone slabs, keeping pace with the line of men and putting distance between herself and the dolmen. Already her mind had rationalized the creature away.

Another hour passed before her nerves had settled down and she felt comfortable enough to look about once again. Across the wild land, shadows of the past lingered in stone blocks and head-high bracken. Ruins and quaking bogs haunted the rocky countryside, places of long ago mysteries that she would have liked to explore, if she had been free.

In the distance, buried in the afternoon's peculiar white mist, the mystical faery woodlands glistened into view, treetops kissing a soft blue sky. Anticipation stirred in her blood. No one had ever seen the fey woodlands and lived to tell of it. It was a place of enchantment where music played in the air and massive white roses grew in impenetrable thorn thickets of silver and gold.

Bryna dashed a wayward curl from her eye and blinked. The fey woodlands were still there, monarchs dwarfing all living creatures that came near.

"My lord suffers the *tuaicthe*." Edwin glanced over his shoulder at her.

It took her a moment to respond. "What is the *tuaicthe*?"

" 'Tis the anguished heart, my Lady."

She looked up ahead to where Tynan led his men. "He doona look anguished."

"The honor-mark burns him, my Lady."

Bryna took an extra step to walk abreast with Edwin and waited for him to continue.

"The honor-mark is an ancient promise our faery brethren cast in the bloodline of our tribe's true lord. We are the noble tribe, a spirit race belonging to the earth and lochs, to the breezes and sky, and to the goddess Dana, or Aine, as I hear the villagers call her."

"Tell me more."

"The honor-mark pledges our tribe's chieftain to a faery mating. It is his *geas*. Every one-hundred years a mating must take place to maintain the pattern of continuity, harmony, trust, and kingship of the land."

"Kingship?" She touched her jaw reflexively.

"What do you wish to know?" Tynan inquired tersely from behind her.

"Sire, I . . ." Edwin stammered in apology. An apple red flush spotted his cheeks.

"Walk on, Edwin," Tynan ordered.

"Lady." Edwin bowed and then hurled himself forward.

Bryna felt terrible and came to the youth's defense. "Edwin did no wrong."

"He did not," Tynan agreed softly. He motioned her forward. "Walk with me, Bryna."

She nodded and fell into step beside him. "Are the faery woodlands far ahead, Tynan?" She looked ahead at the groves of giant trees. Afternoon light shone through the silvery mist ahead of them.

" 'Tis not far." He took her arm and assisted her over a rocky outcropping. "We arrive by twilight."

"Faery time, how appropriate."

"Tired?" he asked.

She shook her head. She would not admit to being tired, even if she were. A slave would never confess to something that could be perceived as weakness.

"I only wonder when you plan to release me."

"Are you anxious to return to your Roman master, then?"

Shadows seemed to come over his features, waiting for her response. She managed a slight smile. "Nay, I only miss Derina's comfort and company."

He looked away, vowing to find some way to bring the ancient to the woodlands. "I can understand that. Bryna, I ask that you might consider my tribe as your new home. It is a good place and we are in need of more simplers."

"Healers?" she said with interest.

"We call our healers simplers."

"I am not a slave, then?"

"Nay, faery."

Mayhap Tynan's people would look upon her differently than the Romans. "I will consider it."

" 'Tis all I ask."

They walked side by side for a short while before Bryna became aware of a growing tension in him. "Do you wish to speak more with me?" She looked up at his face.

He nodded, but did not answer right away. "Edwin spoke of my honor-mark. It is a private concern, and I would prefer you ask your questions of me rather than another."

"I understand."

"If you are not comfortable asking me, Rose will answer."

"Rose?"

"Rose is our lead simpler. She is very wise and will explain about our rituals. I would have you understand about our way of life."

"I honestly doona know what to think, Tynan. Your ways seem so different than my own."

"Then ask me, Bryna."

At once she felt uncomfortable, but decided knowing was better than not. "Is your honor-mark different than the mating bite?"

"Aye," he seemed to answer with difficulty. "The mating bite is a confirmation of life, freely given by a male and freely accepted by a female. It is a binding promise to mate." He paused in his description. "The honor-mark belongs only to the chieftain of prophecy, Bryna. It is an ancient faery spell that flows in his blood, in my blood, from my ancestors."

She slowed their pace, Tynan's tribesmen leaving them alone. "Can it be undone?"

"Do you wish it undone?"

"To be truthful, I doona know what I wish. I doona understand any of this, yet there is a deep reckoning inside me."

"Then let me tell you more of our ways so that you will better understand."

"I would like that."

He looked back to the path ahead. "Once in a great war, my tribe aided the faeries. In return for our help, they built a castle of stone above their faery fort that would always protect us."

"Kindred."

"Aye, Kindred," he agreed softly. "The Faery Queen was a selfish creature and became besotted with my ancestor, a dark-haired chieftain. When he refused her attentions, she imposed a great *geas* upon him and his descendants to mate with a faery." He turned to her. "Do you know what a *geas* is?"

She nodded. "A spell of obligation."

"Aye, it is of obligation and of penance and so much more that I canna describe it. This *geas* bound our tribe to the faeries in trust and loyalty to the land. Every hundred years or so a male descendent of the chieftain must lay with a creature of twilight to conceive a child, thus maintaining the trust."

"You are faery born, then." Bryna's voice lowered in awe.

"My father dinna observe his *geas*. He broke the promise by taking a mate within our tribe. I am more mortal than faery because of this." His gaze took on a faraway look. "My father broke the trust because of his love for my mother. Our enemies then took Kindred and we became the hunted."

"What happened?"

He looked back to the path, his voice roughened with emotion. "My father's mind turned dark. He disappeared into the faery woodlands on a rain-soaked night many years ago. I have not seen him since."

"And your mother? What happened to her?"

"She died when I was very young. I doona remember much of her except that she had dark hair like me. Rose raised me."

Bryna touched his arm, saddened by his loss. "I am sorry, Tynan."

They stopped walking and faced each other.

"Forgive me," she whispered. "Memories such as these best be forgotten."

"Not forgotten." A flood of intensity glinted in his eyes. "I mean to fulfill the promise of my tribe, Bryna."

"I understand."

"Do you?" he whispered, and then leaned forward and inhaled her.

Bryna drew back. "Why do you always do that?"

"It is our way. Your faery blood is well hidden."

"I am not faery." The denial came out reflexively.

"My body and *geas* say differently."

Bryna could not respond to that. She needed time to think of what he had told her. Gathering her skirts higher, she followed the path the men had taken.

The land changed, reflecting the radiant twilight sky. All around her ribbons of gold and silver danced in the wind-scored hills, marking the woodland's border of enchantment. The giant trees slipped in and out of faded colors and gray mist.

She stopped to catch her breath.

The handsome chieftain was right behind her and came round to face her. "You canna run from what you are. Why do you deny the faery blood that flows in your veins?"

"I doona know." She had no answer for him, or an answer for herself. She wanted to drive him away; yet, she wanted to drive him closer.

Silver-mists began to swirl about their ankles.

"Shall I prove it to you, Bryna?" He pulled her close before she could escape.

"Release me," she said, not looking up at him.

"Shall I take you now and make the land shudder with your unearthly passion? Shall I renew the promise between your soft thighs and bury my seed deep in your faery womb?"

She began to tremble, fear and unknown wants taking hold of her.

"Your moon time approaches," he whispered huskily against her temple. "Your body readies itself for a mating."

Her cheeks flushed in mortification. "It readies every month, Tynan. That is the way of life."

"Aye, 'tis life's way." He pulled back and Bryna watched a single bead of sweat run down his cheek to his jawline.

"Let me go, Tynan." She pushed against his chest.

"I will." His voice vibrated deeply with male need. He shackled her wrists. "But not before I taste what is mine."

Bryna looked up into a face chiseled in savage male beauty.

"You would hold me against my will?"

"I hold you so you doona hurt yourself. Your will is your own."

His gaze burned her with a deep, hard possession.

"Fiery faery, I wish to taste that fire." He buried his hand in the sweat-dampened hair at her nape and pulled her closer.

"Doona fear me," he said gently. "I canna let you go. You are mine by ancient promise as I belong to you."

His head lowered. "You are my destiny, Bryna."

Part of her wanted to be that destiny, but then the golden goddess of her dreams flashed in her mind and she could not help but say, "There is another."

"There is no other."

He tilted her chin upward. His eyes fixed on her face.

"See the changing color in my eyes, Bryna. Know the promise of the ancient lord. Know that I will regain Kindred and build a kingdom of dawn as the faeries have foretold."

He framed her face.

"Know that you are mine." He closed the distance between their mouths and brushed her lips with his.

"My faerymate," he murmured, sliding his lips over hers and taking what belonged to him.

Heat and need bloomed within her. Bryna closed her eyes. The legacy of her hidden faery birth shimmered deep within her heart, threatening to wreck the pattern of her ordinary life.

"Taste me," he murmured seductively against her sensitive lips. "Open for me, Bryna. Doona fear the ancient promise." He held her face tenderly and she felt a strange compulsion to mimic what he did to her. She swirled her tongue in his mouth. He tasted of nighttime stars, of clear streams, of fragrant hills, and of all things magic.

She whimpered and wrapped her arms around his corded neck.

In her mouth, Tynan murmured encouragingly. He breathed deeply of his honor-mark calling him to mate now — with this young woman, in this unlikely place.

He should stop this madness.

His hands caressed her back and fitted low over her rounded bottom. Like the rhythm of waves upon her shore, he moved against her, undulating back and forth, seeking relief in her feminine response. His hands slid her gown up her slender thighs to silken hips, a reminder of what was forbidden. He pulled away from her.

"Tynan?"

Seeking respite, he turned from her lovely face and swollen lips and raked a hand through his hair. "Bryna, I canna forswear my oath but, by the gods, you are tempting."

Sidhe spells and honor. The words echoed in his heated body and mind.

Sidhe spells and honor.

He turned around, but his faery had flown from him over the rocky hill where his men had disappeared.

He looked up into the new twilight sky, his body still hot and hard. A hawk soared above, caught in the deepening purple light.

The ancient promise flowed in his blood creating a tide of lust pulsing with magic, a magic that shone in his eyes. He detested it, detested the loss of control.

His life and his tribesmen's lives were interwoven with the faery folk. They were no longer ordinary mortals, but caught in between the worlds of the mortal and faery.

Suddenly the sound of droning bees filled his ears blanking, out his musings. Tynan had to smile in reluctant amusement.

"I hear you," he said.

The invisible piskies, tiny kin to his faery folk, scolded him for his delay and then commented on the beauty of his faery.

"I know."

It was believed that the piskies bore the souls of the virtuous. Although no one had ever seen them, except mayhap in dreams, their helpfulness toward the aged and infirm were often balanced with their prankish ways.

Tynan looked where Bryna had disappeared.

The earlier mist receded. Jagged shapes filled his inner sight. The men of his tribe waited for him just beyond the rise.

"Tell Ian that I come."

A sprinkling of gold mist, and then they were gone. Silence returned to the air.

Tynan let the silence soothe his ravaged spirit and started walking up the hill. He watched a red fox hurriedly cross his path and disappear in a thick hedgerow. The animal searched for its prey, as he had searched for the territorial goddess. Bryna was not at all what he had expected in a fey mate; too mortal, too innocent, and way too lovely for his peace of mind.

They had reached the woodlands.

Bryna inspected the roundhouse where Edwin

had told her to wait. Built of oak timbers, it appeared slightly larger than the rest of the circular homes dotting the woodlands. The other homes were made of poles, stakes, twigs, and tree branches bound with clay and mud. Hazelnuts woven into animal skins hung over the door entrances.

She glanced back into the house. In the center of the dirt floor lay a circle of small gray stones for the fire. Straw and fragrant rushes covered selected areas that were away from the fire pit. In the back, spread out in welcome, lay a large bed of sheepskins and woven blankets. A finely carved trestle table and benches stood to the right. On the table, white candles lit the space.

She turned back to the music of the night, complete with the hum of frogs and crickets and an occasional hooting owl.

To her right, a decayed ruin of fallen stones lay buried beneath a massive thicket of silver thorns.

She watched brown wrens forage through the undergrowth at the edge of the woodlands, envious of their freedom. The active birds often startled decent people with their sudden movements and their constant searches for spiders and bugs, but they never startled her. A part of her always seemed to know when animals were near.

The faery woodlands were a place of ancient oaks, red-berried rowans, and fine-grained yews whose wood was favored by archers. She felt the elemental cycle of nature in her blood. Every bracken, stone, and stream glimmered with enchantment. It was folly to deny her senses, to deny what she felt. She had always thirsted for the sweetness of the land. *Do others feel like this?* She often wondered. *Do others feel the breath of a butterfly; hear the echo of a ripple of water, or the sighs of grasshoppers?*

She continued to look outward, cramming her senses with all that she could, her heart calming, sliding into a new-found peace.

The faery tribe lived on the edge of a large sylvan thicket. Below the giant trees, silver mists lingered among the holly bushes and whispering ferns. Vines of tiny white flowers opened for the moon's kiss. It was a fey place, a belonging place. Fires kindled and the smell of cooking meat made her mouth water.

Smiling with a strange contentment, she went back into the roundhouse and stopped.

"Oh, I dinna know anyone is here."

An ancient noble female stood in the candlelit darkness. Sprigs of holly and gold beads adorned her long, wavy black hair streaked with gray. Bryna had never seen anything like it. The older woman wore a green woolen gown beneath a girdle of silver chains. Around her neck rested a thick bronze torc. She wore arm bands, bracelets, and finger rings. She had heard the faery tribe was fond of personal decoration, but this seemed excessive to her.

"I have brought warm water." The woman gestured

to the back where three candles lit a dark corner. "And clean clothes for you to change into. You may bathe. Then we talk."

Bryna looked past the woman to the back. Candlelight glowed over steaming water lapping in a brown bucket large enough to sit in. A white cloth and soap rested on the trestle table behind the bucket. The flames of three white candles flickered in the corner.

"Do you know the meaning of the candles?" the woman asked.

Bryna knew their meaning from Derina's teachings. "The candles are a triad illuminating knowledge, nature, and truth."

"Go on."

"Some believe the triadic goddess embodies fertility, sexual pleasure, and magical warfare. My beliefs are simpler. They involve the maid, the mother, and the crone."

"So do mine. Bathe. I will await you outside."

Bryna watched the woman leave and then walked to the back of the roundhouse. The flickering shadows gave her a sense of privacy. Undressing, she stepped into the large bucket and lowered herself in. The warm water felt amazingly good. Her knees drew to her breasts, but she did not care. She washed her hair and body with the surprisingly fragrant soap. Finishing quickly, she rose and dried herself.

The older woman had provided a simple dark green gown, which lay on the bed. Bryna slipped it on. The tight bodice fit snugly over her breasts, but the rest of the gown would do well enough. Twisting her hair into a tight rope, she squeezed the remaining water out.

"Daoine Sidhe," the woman called from outside. "Come."

Bryna went outside, feeling the chilling dampness against her skin. She did not correct the woman, but met her blue gaze, a gaze that regarded her from an ageless face shaped round and white.

"Put this on." The woman held out a green cloak edged with fringe, and a lovely bronze brooch.

Murmuring her thanks, Bryna accepted the cloak and wrapped it around her shoulders. She clasped the brooch under her chin.

"Come, let us sit by the west fire. I am Rose."

✱✱✱

Refreshed from his bath in the chilled woodland stream, Tynan waited restlessly in Rose's roundhouse. He donned forest green breeches and a tunic for the unusually cool night. A pair of calf-high boots hugged his legs. Around his neck, he wore his mother's thin gold torc, a personal honor he kept quiet within himself. His hand rested easily on the belt dagger around his waist.

Shelves of healing plants from Rose's garden and wreathes cluttered the home. He stood in front of the table and leaned down to smell one of the dried herbs. *Lavender.* He would always associate that particular scent with Bryna.

"Welcome to my home, Dark Chieftain," the simpler said upon entering.

Tynan glanced over his shoulder at the tribe elder and nodded his greeting, "Rose."

"What brings you here this late in the eve?"

"Is Bryna of our faery brethren?"

The simpler moved to her table of plants, her fingers gently working in the soil.

"Rose, doona make me wait in this."

She glanced up at him with those gold-flecked faery eyes, full of wisdom and calm. "I doona know."

"You doona know?" He could not believe that.

"Bryna feels things deeply, of that I'm certain. She guards her emotions behind a wall of remoteness. Methinks she is faery and mortal, most unusual. Her link to the land is shadowed by turmoil and inattentiveness, but her awareness grows."

"What does that mean?"

The simpler continued to fuss with a remedy of Bilar Trá, for the malady of open sores in the mouth.

"Rose," he said impatiently.

"What does your body say, Lordling? Is she faery? Is she the territorial goddess?"

He looked down. His body hummed with the *gá*, the need, for Bryna. He did not want his male torment known.

"Lordling, leave that plant alone."

Tynan pulled back his hands. In preoccupation, he had bruised the tender leaf of one of her plants.

When he looked up, she watched him intently, her bushy brows drawing down.

"You burn in the *gá*."

"Aye."

She faced him with her hands on her hips and Tynan prepared for the worst.

"Why did you honor-mark her without consent?"

He spoke slowly, calmly. "I was spellbound in magic by the Evil One."

"*Yn Drogh Spyrryd*." Her eyes widened. "Did he touch you?" she asked hurriedly. "Speak to you?"

Tynan frowned at the urgency in her voice.

"The Evil One," she prompted. "Did he touch you, Lordling?"

Tynan blinked. The memory came unbidden.

Be you mine, the Sorcerer had said.

Tynan shook his head.

"I doona remember," he answered. "He had drugged me."

She nodded and turned from him to face the table. Her hands appeared to be shaking.

"Rose?"

She shook her head. "Your body and blood recognizes Bryna for what she is even though her heart is closed to the truth. She is hurt deeply and not open to her own nature."

"She is the territorial goddess?" Anticipation exploded in him.

"I am uncertain. She is *idir*, between." The simpler shrugged. "Mayhap the faeries test you as punishment for your father's sins. Mayhap they hide the goddess so that you must prove your loyalty to them and the land. I doona know."

"The faeries punish us all, then. I ask again, simpler, can I take her to mate and fulfill the promise?"

"I will speak with the elders about handfasting."

"Handfasting is a trial-marriage. It is only temporary."

"Aye, for year and a day unless she fulfills the goddess' promise and conceives an heir. You must still seek our faery approval."

Tynan muttered an oath and stalked past the simpler without a glance.

"Patience, Lordling."

"Patience," he echoed caustically, and stopped just inside the entrance. He looked out to the starry night, the aloneness of his spellbound blood humming inside him. "The faeries are imprisoned in Kindred by the Evil One's magic. To get their approval, I must first free them."

"The Roman invaders want the Dark Chieftain and use our fey brethren for lure."

"Aye, and I want Kindred, but to get Kindred I must mate with the territorial goddess. I canna . . ."

"Wait?"

He turned back to her, struggling with the fey compulsion inside him. "Speak with the elders."

"I will, but you must wait for their decision."

"Rose." His voice lowered. His sense of destiny came from deep within himself and the need to right his father's wrong. He learned early on that he must seize control to succeed and to live. "The forces inside me are strong and ancient."

"Strong and ancient you may be, my virile lordling." She raked him with a disapproving look. "But doona voice your claim on her. Wait for tribe approval of the handfasting."

"I doona want a temporary arrangement. I want a full marriage."

"Go through the handfasting ceremony until we are sure of Bryna's true nature. There are other ways to ease your manly plight."

A sense of doom filled him. Tynan knew he would never forswear the promise. He would never jeopardize his tribe's future. His gaze returned to the unforgiving night.

"Two days you have." He glanced over his shoulder and met her gold-flecked faery cursed eyes. "Two days, Rose." He turned and stepped out into the night.

"Willful," Rose murmured, and then smiled.

Back at Kindred, the Sorcerer's black rage knew no

bounds. He slaughtered innocents in a seething fury, and shredded men of warrior strength until the frenzy inside him lulled to a dull roar.

People scurried from his path. Even the Roman Centurion had ordered his soldiers to keep their distance from him, afraid he'd conjure some terrible plague. *If only it were so*, the Sorcerer mused. If only he could change the past.

He strode through the tombs until he stood at the edge of the stone crater. He studied the small mountain of red jewels. From within the prison's faceted depths, unblinking faery eyes of gold, silver, and bronze watched him warily.

Aye, he mused, they had come when he cried out for help. The small handful of woodland nymphs mistook his spellbound voice for the younger version and fell into his trap.

A wicked smile curved his thin lips.

"Soon, my son will come."

He turned away. His mind filled with the best way to get his blood back.

When only one Dark Chieftain remained, the faeries would have no choice but to forgive him. He licked his lips in eager anticipation.

He'd make them slither in the dirt like worms.

CHAPTER 8

GLOAMING ARRIVED IN TRIUMPHANT SHADES of purple, changing the woodlands into a shimmering place. Shade and dimness vied for the gleaming of the silver tipped ferns, the luminescence of the air, and the dark moist bark of branches.

Bryna felt a little dispirited as the day slipped into a cool evening. She did not notice the faery sparkle of the land, or the acorn-fed pigs that stared up at her curiously before moving on.

Standing outside Lyn Cerrig's home, she waited quietly for Rose. She had been assisting the simpler all day and had learned that the tribe of the *Tuatha De Danann* were a people of knowledge and crafts.

Cerrig, the tribe's blacksmith, was highly prized for his skill in chariot design. He had summoned Rose to treat a festering cut on his left shin and was now receiving a thorough scolding from the angry simpler for waiting so long.

Bryna stared at the black dirt. Three days had passed since she met with the tribe elders and five days since Tynan had left. She spent most of her time with Rose, helping tend the ill as she had once done with Derina.

Her single braid fell down one shoulder. Her hands remained locked in front of her, playing with the folds of her green cloak.

Rose stepped from the circular house and took a moment to compose herself.

"Is Cerrig all right?" Bryna asked.

"That man is amazingly stubborn." The simpler adjusted one of her brooches and then waved her hands, setting her gray streaked braids flying. "As are most men."

A tiny smile curved Bryna's lips. She had learned early on that the lead simpler of Tynan's tribe was a woman of high emotion.

"Bryna." The simpler put a finger under her chin, tilting her head up. "He doona want you to look in the dirt anymore."

"He?"

The simpler's lips curved in a perceptive smile.

"Ah," Bryna nodded. "Lord Tynan." She had also learned that the *Tuatha de Danann* called Tynan "lord." Who else could the all-powerful "he" be?

She dinna want to look at the dirt any more than the "he" wanted her to. Moreover, if the "he" commanded her to look his tribesmen in the eye, well then, that was exactly what she would do.

Bryna nodded. "All right, Rose. No more looking at the ground."

"Good. He will be pleased."

"Do any others need tending?" She reached for Rose's

medicinal basket at her feet and lifted it in her arms.

"There are always others who need tending. We are a people of excellence in crafts and challenge, and therefore injury."

Bryna rested the weight of the basket on her hip. It felt heavy like Derina's baskets often were. She missed her teacher.

"Methinks we will visit Oth next." The simpler strode away, heading toward a brown circular house nestled underneath a canopy of small trees. Her black cloak billowed behind her.

"Oth," Bryna echoed, and followed. From then on, she struggled to meet everyone's gaze whether narrowed in wariness or openly friendly.

She met Oth, the golden bard with the most amazing grin she had ever seen and whose swollen left eye needed tending. Bryna suggested that he duck the next time, to which he heartedly agreed.

Next, she met Rhiannia whose wary eyes spoke openly of her distrust, so Bryna decided to wait outside the hut for Rose.

In the afternoon, young Fionn ate too many nuts and complained of stomach pain. *No wonder*, Bryna thought, and so the day went.

When they finished tending the needs of the tribe for that day, Bryna returned to her hut. Night had come upon them on soft feet and the buttery moon rose in the darkening sky of twilight.

Having completed her bath, Bryna now stood at

the roundhouse's entrance clad only in one of Rose's white shifts and her own warm green cloak. This night the ancient oak trees were wrapped in cool mists and magic.

She wondered about Tynan, feeling slightly abandoned by him. She wondered if he thought of her since bringing her here and then leaving.

Her gaze swept the shadows of the land. Etched in shades, the woodlands were primal and separate from the natural world.

Footfalls came from her right.

"Good eve, Rose," she greeted the simpler

"Good eve. Did you like the goat's milk?"

The simpler had left a bowl of goat's milk and drisheen, black pudding made from the blood of sheep, and a loaf of bread on the trestle table inside.

"I am not hungry, Rose. Mayhap later."

"He will not be pleased."

Bryna nodded. "Lord Tynan," she murmured.

"Comfortable here?" The simpler indicated the roundhouse behind them.

"Aye, 'tis a fine home. Much bigger than my tiny room in the fortress."

"Aye, 'tis a fine home. 'Tis our chieftain's home."

Bryna's black brows drew together in a frown.

"His home," she echoed and looked over her shoulder. The dark brown roundhouse was nestled against two large limestone boulders in the center of a sprawling cluster of circular houses. Moonlight bathed everything in a golden glow.

"Rose, I canna stay here," she voiced her thoughts aloud.

"Shush. 'Tis an honor he gives you, Bryna. No other woman has shared his home. He would not allow you to stay anywhere else."

She shook her head in confusion. "Why does he do this?"

"Look to your heart."

Long ago she had learned her place within this world, and that had little to do with heart's desire. "My heart is silent, Rose."

"Silent?"

Bryna looked away. As an abandoned child, left to die on the shores of a sacred loch, she had been raised by an old druidess with ancient dreams. Outcast and scorned, her fate had been to serve the needs of a Roman Centurion, not follow her heart. So, she had never listened to her own desires, but chose instead to survive.

"Rose, I am not special in any way, not like the Dark Chieftain with magic coursing in his blood. The honor-mark is a mistake. I am not this goddess to meet his prophecy."

"It is not *his* prophecy, but belonging to all of us as the rolling hills, as the glittering lochs, as the blue skies belong to all of us."

Bryna shook her head, looking out upon the many small fires where family groups gathered. Laughter filled the night air. Tynan's tribesmen wore cloaks with long raveled edges that danced in the air. Gold and silver brooches, neck rings, and arm rings reflected the firelight.

"Do you see and feel things differently?"

"Differently than what, Rose?" What felt normal and right to her seemed not to others. When people learned of her abilities, they both feared and cursed her. She did not want that to happen here, not with these people who treated her gently and with respect.

The simpler grew silent.

"I am not special, Rose," Bryna murmured into the long quiet.

"Our chieftain disagrees, Bryna. He petitions the elders for a handfasting."

"Handfasting?" Bryna looked at the simpler.

"Aye, that is our trial-marriage. 'Tis not a true marriage unless he begets an heir off you."

"I know of handfasting. It is a test to see if the man and woman get along with each other. They are bound together in a temporary agreement that expires after a year and a day."

The simpler adjusted her cloak. "It can be made permanent after a time if our faery brethren approve of the match."

"I canna marry him, Rose."

"Did he ask you to handfast?"

Bryna shook her head vehemently, sending damp curls flying, and for the first time saw the simpler blush and look away.

"Then, I've spoken out of turn and will probably suffer for it." She laughed softly with amusement. " 'Tis not the first time."

"Rose, I canna do this." Bryna felt a kind of panic setting in.

The simpler touched her arm with reassurance. "Let the fates decide, Bryna. All will be as it should be."

Bryna did not think so. "Will you ask if there is another place I may stay?"

"I will ask."

But her tone inferred there would be none. "My thanks." Bryna held her cloak closed. A sudden chill had come to the air and seeped into her flesh.

"Doona worry about the handfasting. Both of you must agree before it comes to pass." The simpler squeezed her wrist before letting go. "I bid you good eve. Sleep well, Bryna."

"Good eve, Rose."

Bryna turned back into Tynan's home. He wanted to handfast with her, a short-term marriage, a vow not meant to last. He would lie with her at night; share his body and his seed. But what then, when his true goddess presented herself? What then would become of her?

Bryna's hands pressed to her heated face. Why did she watch for his return? Why did she listen for the sound of his voice?

This growing infatuation must end.

She was not his territorial goddess.

How could she be?

Bryna skimmed the interior. In the back, a thick pallet of straw, heavy blankets and furs made a comfortable bed on the floor.

Tynan's home.

Tynan's bed.

She had always wished for a home.

She had always wished for a bed of her own.

It would not be here.

***

Sunday morning, Bryna awoke to a heavy chill in the air. She sat up slowly, tilted her head back and closed her eyes. The nightmare still lingered in her mind.

"Golden one," she spoke to the empty air, "you exchange the glade for imprisoned fire and night." Her dreams of the golden territorial goddess were of darkness and confinement now. It worried her, these visitations in the unconscious realm. "Tynan petitions tribe elders for a handfasting with me. Do you know of this?" she asked the goddess of her dreams.

No answer.

Bryna opened her eyes.

"Why do you not answer me?" she asked in agonized whispers. "Why do you visit only in my dreams?" Her hands fisted in her lap. "Why do you not speak to me? I doona know what you want."

Silence and the sound of her own breathing were the only answers she would have this morning.

Bryna sighed deeply. "So be it."

She thought about last eve. Rose's assurances about handfasting had rung with some truth. She must agree to be handfasted to Tynan before the trial-marriage ceremony could take place. She just would not agree.

Noises outside spoke of people being out of bed. Bryna rose. A drawing in her womb slowed her movements, a signaling of her approaching moon time.

"Not now." She must remember to speak to Rose about the herbs for her woman's courses. The woman herbs often eased the discomfort and pain during her moon time. Bryna donned the familiar green gown and laced up the snug bodice over her sensitive breasts. She wore no jewelry, unlike the rest of Tynan's tribe. They had gifted her with bracelets and finger rings as payment for tending their ailments.

She thought to refuse the jewelry, but decided against it. She did not want to insult anyone and the pieces could be bartered for food and clothing, if need be. She slid her feet into the brown slippers that Rose had given her.

Deciding to leave her hair unbound, Bryna reached for the floor-length green cloak. She swung it about her shoulders and fastened it with the brooch under her chin.

"Today is the first Sunday of the new month, *Nollaig*, December," Bryna said aloud. "I shall feel good about myself and pay tribute to the holy well in the *nematon* with the rest of the tribe." The *nematon* was a place of divine and earthly union, as anyone knew, Rose had explained. Here, it was located in the circular clearing in the woodlands. The sacred water in the well would link the tribe to the faery world.

"Bryna?" Rose called from outside. "Are you ready? The time grows late."

"Aye, Rose. I am ready" Bryna hurried out of the roundhouse, holding her skirts high. The outside air felt crisp this new morning and smelled sweet. The simpler wore a black cloak about her shoulders and four gold brooches. Her gray-streaked, black hair fell unbound too, with gold beads woven amongst braids that fell behind her ears.

"No adornment?"

Bryna looked down her plain clothes. "Nay, I doona feel right to wear anything."

The simpler clearly disagreed and gestured forward impatiently. "We must hurry. I have risen later than usual because of my husband's frolicking. They will not start the celebration without me."

Bryna wondered who was Rose's husband. She had not met the man in all the time that she had spent with the simpler.

They walked to the meadow where the tribe's noble horses grazed in groups of twos and threes. The beauty of the animals took all other thoughts away. A most odd thing; she paused to look at them. The horses all wore silver ribbons braided in their flowing manes.

"Rose, why are the horses wearing ribbons?"

"Last night the piskies braided ribbons in their manes."

"Why would they do that?" Holding her skirts, she hurried after the simpler.

"Why do piskies do anything? Mischievous sprites, they are. They celebrate too, a new goddess among them, I suppose. Better they braid horses manes with silver ribbons than some other mischief. Hurry, Bryna. I am late for the celebration. No doubt the elders shall scowl at me."

"You may blame me," Bryna offered, "if you like."

" 'Tis my husband's fault, not yours."

Green and gold ferns grew along the worn path to the small clearing. Shafts of yellow sunlight filtered through the canopy of ancient trees. A fine morning, Bryna thought, and prepared to enjoy the new day.

"The faeries are kind enough to share their woodlands with us," the simpler said, slightly out of breath. "We must show our thanks."

Bryna intended to do so. Over these past days, she had begun to believe in the fey, a sprinkling of awareness and possibility and perhaps just a little bit of hope. She followed the simpler to a clearing where women and men knelt in small groups. In the center of the clearing, a square stone well rose before a thicket of silver thorns from a hilly backdrop of granite boulders. Four stone columns grew out of the well at each end, rising high, shaped tips blunted and pointing to the sky.

"Why do brown vines and white roses twist around the base of the well?" Bryna asked, following Rose around a group of kneeling people.

"The needles of the vines protect the well. The tiny roses give sweet fragrance and beauty. Beauty must be in all things faery, and this is a special place of elemental forces and magic."

The simpler gestured to a space free of the green and lavender ferns. "Sit here. The ferns part for us."

Bryna knelt beside Rose and tucked her cloak about her. She placed her palms upon the black dirt of the land and felt a pulsing of warmth and magic.

The simpler gave her a knowing smile. "No matter the weather beyond the woodlands, warmth always seeps from the soil here, a fey gift from our brethren."

Bryna sat back. In front of the well, five maidens gathered, not much younger than her. They wore white robes and neck rings of gold and holly. Gold beads laced into their long, wavy hair. Cheeks flushed a rosy hue and eyes sparkled in excitement.

Seeing the simpler kneel, the maidens had spread out in a single row in front of the stone well, preparing for the communal celebration.

They faced west.

Rose nodded to them.

Their voices rose in song, filling the clearing.

WE GATHER IN PERFECT TRUST.
WE GATHER IN PERFECT LOYALTY.
WE ASK THEE TO BLESS OUR OFFERING.
BLESSED BE.
BY THE ANCIENT.
BY THE MYSTICAL.
BY THE ELEMENT OF WATER . . .

The melody handed down by the faeries of the well, inspired courage and loyalty in all living things.

Bryna had never heard voices so beautiful. So immersed in the moment and song, she did not see Eamon make his way toward her.

"Do you pay tribute to the spirits of the well?" Eamon asked, kneeling beside her.

Bryna pushed burnished gold curls from her cheek and glanced over her shoulder at Eamon. "They sing beautifully," she answered, wary of his intention.

He leaned closer, smelling of mead and something far more threatening. Hot breath puffed against her cheek.

"Our chieftain's scent is not on you." He spoke for her ears only.

Bryna pulled back. "Why do you sit so close to me?"

"Lord Tynan will not claim you, my golden beauty."

"It matters not," she said low, knowing her own words for a lie. For it had begun to matter to her; it had begun to matter greatly.

He raised a dubious brow. A large hand slid over

both of hers in her lap and squeezed.

Bryna looked down at his hand and felt only revulsion.

"I am not bound by a faery *geas*, Bryna. The faeries are wrong in their choice of chieftain. I would have been the better leader. With you by my side, I can sway them."

Bryna didn't know what to say. Something in her face must have encouraged him. He moved closer, his eyes bright and intense.

"Believe me, I will be gentle with you."

. . . be gentle with you. Sweetness spilled from his lips, from his lies, and into the air. She shook her head and pulled her hands out from under his. There was evil in his words, deceit and falsehoods that turned her stomach. In this moment, she stared into his face and thought herself better off dead than in his bed.

"Eamon," Tynan snarled in warning from behind her. She would recognize that voice anywhere. Bryna twisted around and caught her breath at the sight of him.

The maidens' high song stuttered to a stop.

"Touch her again and I will kill you." His threat rang out in the clearing.

The Dark Chieftain stood poised in the morning shadows of the massive trees. Above their heads, thousands of white doves had taken flight in the treetops, wings flapping in soundless fright. He reminded her of a faery king returning from *Tir Na n'Óg,* the land of youth. Surrounded by morning mist, the air glimmered softly, welcoming him back to the world of mortals.

Beside her, she sensed Eamon stiffening in rage, but all her senses focused forward where Tynan stepped out of the shadows into the shafts of sunlight. His brown boots made no sound. His right hand rested easily upon a large silver dagger sheathed at his waist. Tiny lavender jewels, encrusted in the sheath, winked with faery eyes.

Raven black hair glistened with dampness. A gold torc rested at the base of his neck. He wore a sleeveless green tunic that laced down the front, and gold arm bands wrapped powerful upper arms. Snug green breeches rode low on his lean hips.

Bryna started to rise but the simpler's hand stayed her.

"Doona interfere, Bryna."

"Remember what I said, Bryna." Eamon slowly rose and moved away from her, his hands spread wide at his hips in a non-threatening gesture.

"My apologizes, sire." Eamon bowed slightly at the waist. "I come only to give tribute to the well."

"Pay your tribute then on the other side of the clearing," Tynan said in a voice of great displeasure.

"He dinna challenge, Lordling," the simpler spoke up.

Tynan frowned at the simpler's attempt to soothe his rage, but it was Bryna's silvery gaze that snared him, Bryna's gaze that held him in a pool of restraint.

"Leave us, Eamon," he commanded, not looking at his cousin. Out of the corner of his eye, he saw Eamon nod and move to join the other single men at the west end of the clearing.

Tynan knew his cousin wanted Bryna. He had to secure his claim soon without forswearing his *geas*. He hoped to handfast without the fey claim, hold Bryna by pledge until the time became appropriate to mate with her.

The two days he had given the tribe elders to approve a handfasting had turned into a month.

A month.

His control was weakening under the onslaught of the fey compulsion.

He looked away from her. His dark amethyst gaze swept the clearing in thoughtful intensity. Faces stared back at him in silence and uncertainty. His people did not understand his recent intolerances. They knew only that the time to retake Kindred drew near. In truth, he did not understand his recent rages himself.

His heart grew heavy at what he saw reflected in their eyes. *They are afraid of me,* he realized, and that angered him.

He looked back to Bryna once again. He had tried to stay away, tried to fight the pulse in his blood, the burning ache in his loins. He could no more stay away from her than a bee could stay away from a succulent flower.

She smiled up at him in innocent invitation and Tynan felt his body tighten.

"Welcome, Dark Chieftain." She spoke in a voice loud enough so that all could hear and patted the ground next to her. "Come join us."

He raised an eyebrow at that. Did she understand the implications if he acted upon her offering?

"Oh, do sit, Lordling," Rose huffed, "before you frighten the maidens away and the well faeries become vindictive."

Tynan's eyes lifted to the wide-eyed maidens standing near the well. Faces flushed, they turned away from him, having been caught in open stares.

"I doona frighten maidens," he said gruffly.

"Then sit," the simpler ordered.

He lowered himself down beside Bryna and had to admit that the maidens looked about ready to bolt.

"Welcome," his faery waif said.

He grunted in response, battling the siren call of her in his blood.

"May that be a faery greeting, my lord? I doona know it." She tilted her head in devilment and then mimicked his grunt. No way did it sound gruntlike to him, but it served her purpose well; for the simpler snorted and covered her mouth in suppressed laughter. Tribesmen sitting near enough to hear the peculiar sound chuckled loudly in enjoyment.

Tynan fought back a grin. "Well done, but the grunt needs to be deeper, like this." He grunted again to show her.

"I shall practice." She smiled, brightening this new day.

"My lord, are you finished?" the simpler demanded on the other side of Bryna. "The celebration awaits."

Tynan leaned across Bryna's lap, his hair spilling over his shoulder into her lap. "Proceed at your own pleasure, simpler," he replied softly.

"My pleasure?" Rose muttered a foul word under her breath. "As usual, you have disrupted another ceremony."

" 'Twas not my intention, Rose."

" 'Tis never your intention, Lordling, but you always manage to do so."

Tynan grinned. "True enough." He felt a tug at his scalp and glanced down. Bryna's fingers had somehow become intertwined in his hair. He glanced sideways at her before sitting back.

"What are you doing, Bryna?"

A lovely shade of pink stained her cheeks.

"Lordling," the simpler called in high irritation.

He looked back at her.

"May we continue?" she snapped in annoyance.

"Aye, continue." He felt a sharp twinge in his scalp and looked down. His faerymate was trying to disentangle her fingers from his wet hair.

He covered her small hands with his. "Bryna, stop."

Around them, several grins had slowly begun to spread across the faces of his people. It appeared they were the center of attention, not a good thing with the faeries.

Another tug at his scalp ended his patience. "Bryna."

"Oh, let me." She yanked her hands back, taking several strands of hair.

"Ouch!" He bellowed and glared at her, rubbing his abused scalp.

She smiled openly, the mischievous waif.

"Sire," Ian called from where he knelt with his family, barely able to contain his mirth, "Do you need help?"

"Nay, Ian, the faery has released me but has taken several strands of my hair with her."

One of the maidens at the well started giggling and soon other giggles joined hers.

Bryna held up her hands and wiggled her fingers for all to see her new found freedom.

Tynan broke out in a grin. Reaching over, he brought her hands closer and kissed her fingertips.

"My thanks, Bryna." The tension that he had brought with him to the clearing faded away.

Releasing her, he gestured for the maidens to sing.

"Continue with the celebration." He tossed his mane of black hair behind him, removing temptation.

"Men and their hair," the simpler grumbled. Climbing to her feet, she moved away, waving her thin arms in the air.

"Start the song from the beginning," she ordered.

The maidens faced west again, their lilting voices

rose once more in song, promising loyalty to the land in return for the water of the well.

"Why do they face west?" his faerymate inquired.

"West be where the element of water flows," Tynan explained, moving closer to her. "They turn South now for the blessing of fire and East for new beginnings where we ask for the blessing of air. This brings us truth, wisdom, and vision.

"And North?"

"North be where the element of earth resides, deeply grounded in strength and support."

"Your ways are very strange to me, Tynan."

He supposed that they would be. "New ways are always strange, Bryna. You must keep an open heart and see with more than your eyes. See and feel with the center of your spirit."

She nodded and looked back to the well.

He did, too, enjoying this gentle respite, this moment of unaccustomed peace. His compulsion had suspiciously quieted and he welcomed it without question.

Soon, he would need to talk to her about the future, but not now. He just wanted to live in this very precious moment.

"Father?"

He glanced over his shoulder at his son of eight summers. "Hawk."

"I waited to give tribute with you." The boy settled down in the small space between him and Bryna, holding a large pink rock in his hands.

"Hello, my name is Hawk."

Bryna found herself staring into a child's brown eyes that were full of life and childhood curiosity.

"I am gratified to meet you, Hawk." She smiled warmly in greeting. "I am Bryna of Loch Gur."

"I know. My father says you are pretty, like sunlight and mist."

"Am I?" she whispered, fighting the urge to look up at the father. *Tynan has a son?*

"Do you like my father?"

"Verra much, I do."

"I do too." He held up the pink rock for her to see. "I come to give tribute to the well faeries for Elf."

"Who is Elf?" Bryna took the pink rock from his outstretched hands. The rock was surprisingly heavy for a child to carry.

"Elfin Song is my horse."

"Ah." She turned the rock carefully this way and that, all the while feeling the watchful gazes of both father and son.

"It carries the beauty of a pink sky at twilight," she offered.

"Aye, 'tis a fine offering," Tynan said in agreement, ruffling the boy's head.

The child beamed at her compliment.

"Good, for it contains faery magic like me."

She handed the rock back to him, careful that he took it with both his hands.

"Go give your tribute, Hawk," Tynan commanded gently, helping the boy stand. "The spirits of the well await."

The boy tucked the pink rock close to his chest and hurried toward the well. Bryna watched him go, wondering about the mother.

"He is mine in all ways that matter," Tynan said beside her.

She turned back to him and waited.

"I found him in an abandoned hawk's nest on the cliffs."

That surprised her. "His parents?" she asked.

"Gone, I know not where. Faery mischief, Rose thinks."

She nodded, her heart less pinched in her chest.

"Does that make you feel better, faery?"

How well he was beginning to understand her. "I doona know what you mean."

"Ah." He smiled. "Well then, I spoke out of turn."

Bryna clasped her hands in her lap. Hawk was Tynan's son by pledge, not blood. As she watched, the boy moved deftly between the maidens to get to the stone well behind them.

The haunting chant had ended sometime during her conversation with the child. People now rose in small groups to bring their tribute, their own hopes and prayers for the future. Many carried flowers, some offered jewelry, and still others carried makings of their own design.

Had she known, she would have brought an offering

of her own. She glanced at Tynan and frowned slightly; he carried no offering either.

"You doona care for the faeries to make an offering?" she asked thoughtfully.

" 'Tis not that, Bryna. They can be damned unforgiving at times."

"Unforgiving?"

"Aye. They want without regard, almost as if envy eats at them. I canna put it into words."

"They hurt you." She knew, coming to a deeper understanding of him.

"Not I alone. They have hurt many with their ways."

She turned back to the sacred well and Hawk . . .

"Tynan!" she cried out, but he had already bolted for his son.

The child had climbed up the stone well and now teetered on the edge near one of the stone columns, clutching the pink rock high above his head, ready to throw it in.

Tynan grabbed Hawk around the waist and jerked back. The pink rock that had been going forward in the child's hands suddenly came flying back into his temple. Bryna heard the painful smack as both father and son went down, scattering the maidens into a flowing mass of shrieks and robes.

She jumped up and ran to them.

Tynan lay flat on his back, his eyes closed in a painful grimace. "Hawk, you will be the death of me one of these days."

Bryna knelt and touched Tynan's shoulder. "Are you hurt?"

"My pride only." His eyes remained shut as if in pain.

"Liar," she scolded, worried for him.

"True enough."

He squinted his eyes at her.

"Am I still in one piece, faery?"

"Aye."

He looked to his very quiet son.

"Hawk, are you hurt?"

"My rock dinna go in the well."

"I know. It landed on my head." He squeezed his son's waist and dropped his head back upon the ground.

"Let me see your temple." Gently, Bryna pushed aside his hair to see the swiftly purpling bruise.

He stiffened at her touch and pulled away. "I am fine, faery. 'Tis just another bruise from my son." He braced himself up on his elbows.

"Are you mad at me?" The boy sat up between his father's long legs.

"Should I be?" Tynan responded.

"Are you mad at Bryna, then?"

Tynan exhaled loudly. "I am not mad."

"Why do you have the mad face, then?" The boy scowled like his father.

Bryna struggled to keep a straight face.

"Dirt smudged whirlwind," Tynan muttered, "I am not mad. Now, can you toss the rock in the well from here?" His eyebrows rose in challenge.

His son took the bait.

"Aye." The boy reached for the pink rock that had landed near his foot.

"Then do so and let us hope the spirits of the well are quicker than I and step out of the way."

Bryna enjoyed the interaction between father and son. It was obvious that Tynan loved the child very much.

The boy stood, spread his legs, and positioned himself for the throw.

Bryna ducked when Hawk held the rock behind his head. The pink rock sailed through the air and disappeared into the depths of the sacred well.

Hawk let out a loud shout of glee.

"Well done, Hawk." Tynan complimented his son proudly. "Now, let us listen for its fall."

Bryna leaned forward, tilting her head, but no splash marked the end of the rock's journey in the deep well.

She looked at Tynan. "There was no splash. What does that mean?"

He motioned his son to answer.

"The faeries are pleased?" Hawk answered with uncertainty.

"Aye, Hawk. They are well pleased."

"I did it." Hawk jumped up in triumph, a child's joy, his right heel perilously close to grinding down his father's manparts.

Tynan scooted back, but not soon enough. Bryna caught the child's foot, the back of her hand brushing hard against the father's inner thigh.

The boy hugged her and ran off to where the simpler waited.

Bryna held her flushed face and laughed. She rested her hand on Tynan's thigh and turned to him. "He is delightful, Tynan."

Her smile slowly wilted.

Black amber eyes watched her, cast in a feral light.

"Did I hurt you?" she whispered. "I only meant to protect you from Hawk's heel."

"Remove your hand from my leg."

She pulled her hand back, holding it to her.

"Doona touch me again unless you mean it." He climbed to his feet and stalked off into the woodlands.

Bryna looked to the ground, her heart hurting. Within her blurred vision the simpler's small feet appeared.

"What did I do, Rose?" She looked up.

"Not you. It is his *geas*, Bryna. Do you know what that means?"

"His faery obligation."

"You do know, then. It heats his blood with compulsion and pain if he battles it."

Bryna did not want to think of Tynan in pain. "What can I do to help him?"

"The tribe elders have agreed to the handfasting ceremony owing to the chieftain's honor-mark on you. Without our faery brethren's approval, they canna in good conscience consent to a permanent consort for him."

Bryna nodded, biting her lip in silence.

CHAPTER 9

IN THE FLICKERING LIGHT OF candles, Bryna stood in the back of the roundhouse finishing her cloth bath. Night had fallen many hours ago, leaving a fey stillness in the green woodlands, a watchfulness of things yet to be. Leaning over the bronze bucket, she squeezed water from her dripping hair. Shadows caressed her damp skin. In the fire circle of gray stones behind her, orange flames crackled and spat, giving out heat in the roundhouse.

She twisted her hair one last time before shaking it out and then reached for a cloth to dry herself. This day she learned that tending the ill included the tribe's numerous animals. After the morning tribute to the holy well, she had helped Rose and Hawk tend an orphaned wolf cub covered in mud, and a magnificent brown mare with a swollen fetlock.

Combing out her hair, she wove the damp tresses into a single braid down her back and tied it with a cord. She knew most of the *Tuatha Dé Danann* slept without clothes, but Bryna could not bring herself to do that. As a slave, she always kept herself covered for safety. She slipped into a long, white sleeping garment that Rose had thoughtfully provided. It was many sizes too large and the front panel required lacing up. She looked down at herself. The panel exposed a sliver of flesh down to her navel, but she was too weary to deal with the intricate laces. Besides, no one was here to witness her immodesty.

She felt weary inside her body. Tynan's anger at the well this morning drained her to the core. Bryna glanced over her shoulder at the trestle table.

In the center of the wooden table, the flames of three white candles danced. Bunches of wild flowers and fragrant herbs tied with silver ribbons lay beside the candles. They were a gift from the mysterious piskies, Rose had said.

"My thanks for the gifts, little ones," she whispered. Since coming to the woodlands, a new deep-rooted belief in the fey magic had begun to take hold of her. "The flowers are lovely."

Above the table, tiny giggles lit the air with threads of gold and then disappeared.

"I knew you waited for notice." She smiled gently and walked over to the table. There indeed were faeries. Her fingertips caressed the yellow petal of a flower and then moved to the clay bowls filled with goat cheese and bread. She had eaten little this eve, yet felt no hunger.

Turning away solemnly, she wondered where Tynan slept this night. Dropping down to the bed, she snuggled into the soft furs. She ran her fingers through the soft pelts and closed her eyes, imagining

Tynan's strong arms around her. She yearned to be held by him.

To feel his touch . . .

To feel his lips . . .

To feel every part of his large body pressing her down into the furs . . .

Suddenly, a primordial presence made itself felt, heavy and flowing like liquid shade. Bryna opened her eyes and slowly sat up. The darkness shifted near the front of the roundhouse, a parting of shadows and stillness. Cool air from the outside rushed in causing the flames in the fire circle to flicker.

At the entrance, stood a tall dark shape.

"Tynan?" she called hesitantly.

The shape came closer and Bryna found herself staring at a half-naked savage, clad only in green breeches. His amethyst eyes glowed with an unearthly light.

"Tynan, what is wrong?"

Faery magic, as old as the sea-swept shores of Eire, looked down upon her. His chest and shoulders gleamed with sweat. The scent of fallen trees, woodland mist, and fey yearning lay heavily on his skin. He was breathing hard, a struggling against some great inner battle.

Her hands fisted in the pelts at his continuing silence. He frightened her a wee bit. He seemed otherworldly, a creature trapped in darkness and obsession.

Black hair flowed over one powerful shoulder.

Gold bands woven around powerful biceps glimmered in the soft glow of candlelight.

He knelt and bowed his head.

That surprised her and eased her fear of his *geas* somewhat.

"Do you find my home to your liking?" he asked in a voice of darkness and need.

"Aye, 'tis warm and welcoming."

He looked up slowly. Blushing, she hastily pulled the laces of the sleeping gown closed. The air shimmered around him with gold and silver threads that evaporated into shadows.

"Do you come from the woodlands?" she asked.

"Aye."

" 'Tis a fey night." Bryna felt the presence of the faery spell swirling thick within his perspiration and unspoken desire.

He inhaled, and then exhaled, a controlling of the relentless drive inside him.

" 'Tis fey," he answered slowly.

Bryna clutched the panels of the sleeping gown nervously. "Tynan, what is wrong? You act strange."

"You smell of lavender." Dark eyes stared at her with such primitive hunger she could barely breathe, and then he asked, "Do you want me, Bryna of Loch Gur?"

"Want?"

His gaze dropped. Beads of sweat dripped down his temple, down his face, down his chest and arms.

"I canna wait any longer for you. The fever burns me."

"Your *geas*?"

"Aye," he rasped.

"What do you need of me?"

"A promise from you to handfast with me."

"Why? How will that help?"

He looked up. "An easing for me. A shield of protection for you, from my *geas*, from my compulsion should I weaken and dishonor you."

"You would not weaken."

He looked away. "It is also a guard of protection for you should my faery brethren disapprove of my honor-mark and choose another mate for me. In this way, never would you be labeled a fallen woman."

"You would do this for me?"

His gaze slid back to her, a dark and magical watching. "Is there another male that you want?"

She shook her head slowly. "There is no other, Tynan."

He visibly relaxed, a small reprieve, she guessed, from the fever smoldering inside him.

"Handfast with me, Bryna."

"You ask for a promise only?"

"I ask for a full handfasting, but for now the promise will do. I can no longer think clearly, and I must, in order to recapture Kindred and free the imprisoned faeries."

Bryna could not bear him suffering for the mistake of honor-marking her. "I agree to a handfasting. Rose said it would be for a year and a day, a temporary vow between us until the golden territorial goddess claims you."

Tynan heard only two words, "I agree." With trembling fingers, he touched her cheek.

"Tomorrow, Bryna? We handfast tomorrow?" he asked in longing.

"Tomorrow."

With her agreement, Tynan felt a shifting inside his body, a lessening of misery and chaos.

He had her word.

"I must give you pleasure now."

"What?"

For his own relief as well as hers. He stared at the ripeness of her mouth. "Do you want me, Bryna?" He traced the moist outline and pink curve of her lips with one fingertip.

She licked her lips, touching his finger with her tongue. "You taste of hazelnuts."

He waited for her answer to his question.

"Should we not wait until after the handfasting ceremony?"

"Aye, I will wait. But what I speak of tonight is another matter." He leaned forward, his warm lips brushed her sensitive jaw. "If you want me, I will mark you again tonight to ease my honor-mark." His tongue slid wetness along her jaw, savoring her skin.

"You wish to honor-mark me again?" she choked, leaning away, bracing herself in the pelts.

Tynan did not move. The fey lust had worsened since the elders' approval of the handfasting. Nothing had eased the hunger raging in his body.

And he had tried.

Oh, how he had tried.

He hunted in the deep woodlands with his kestrels until his body neared collapse.

He brushed the coats of every damned horse in the clearing until the animals stomped their impatience and Edwin asked him politely to leave.

And still, the ancient promise of his faery brethren burned in his blood. The damned honor-mark called and called until he could no longer deny it. Now that she had agreed to handfast with him . . .

Tynan looked deeply into her eyes and disliked what he saw reflected there.

Beast. Go slower. You terrify her.

He must gain her trust.

. . . and reclaim Kindred, reclaim the land, reclaim his soul.

He would bury himself so deep inside her they would be one for all time.

But not now.

Not this night.

"I doona mean to frighten you. I must honor-mark you again. It is part of the easing for me." He looked away, disgusted with himself.

A soft hand reached out and touched his forearm. He stared down at it, unable to move, his body trembling.

"All things unfamiliar are frightening. You must

go slow with me."

Pain rippled low and deep in his belly. He dropped his head down between his shoulders and muttered, "I have become a beast." He was shamed to the core of his being by this uncontrollable need to possess her, to be brought to this base level.

"Tynan." She cupped his sweaty cheek.

"Tame me, Bryna. Only you can ease this torment."

He pressed his face into the cool softness of her hand, closing his burning eyes, unable to speak.

He savored her.

This moment.

Her touch.

Her scent.

He could stay this way forever.

" 'Tis all right. Tell me what to do."

Sweet relief flooded his body with her offering. Her soothing voice and touch calmed the brute inside him.

"The magic beats at me," he admitted hoarsely. "The ancient spell in my blood demands something in between."

She chewed her bottom lip. "What is in between?"

"I need to honor-mark you again and bring you pleasure, and in doing so, gain respite."

"Will it hurt like before?" Her hand dropped from his face.

"I will not hurt you."

"What is this pleasure, a glass of mead?" she teased

guardedly.

"Nay, lass. 'Tis the kind that leaves your virtue intact."

"Oh," she thought on that a moment. "I suppose," she answered slowly, "then it would be all right. Your eyes are turning all black. Are you in pain now?"

"Nay." He did not want her responding to his discomfort.

"You lie to me, Dark Chieftain."

He pulled back but she grabbed his wrist and held him.

"I accept," she said softly.

Tynan stared at her in stunned surprise. "You accept?"

She released his wrist. "Aye, I accept. How shall we begin?"

He did not move.

"I will not nip you," she added.

Tynan's lips twitched. He could not help it. "You may nip me if you wish it," he replied very seriously. He would welcome the distraction of pain.

A long silence came and went while neither of them moved.

"Tynan." She whispered his name into the shadows, a fusion of yearnings and confusion that matched his own.

"Be sure, faery."

"I am."

Slowly, he crawled around her and settled behind

her back.

"Let go of the laces," he breathed against her bare shoulder. She let go and the oversized gown slipped off one shoulder.

"Why do you kneel behind me?"

"I honor-mark you as my faerymate," he answered huskily.

"From behind? It feels odd this way."

"Like this." Beneath the furs, he slid his hands around her smooth waist, pulling her closer into his heat.

"Wait." She grabbed his forearms.

He stopped.

"Go slow, Tynan."

He nodded, pressing his chest into her silky back, making sure she felt the raging heat in his body.

"The night is cold. I will keep you warm."

"Hot, you mean."

He chuckled low, pressing his face into her cool nape. "You smell so good, Bryna."

"I bathed earlier."

"I speak not of cleanliness, but of the scent of your skin." He gathered her damp, burnished gold braid in his hands and gently slid it over a smooth shoulder to clear his way.

"So soft. I never thought a faery could feel so soft in my hands." He cupped full breasts.

She held onto his thick wrists. "This is not honor-marking."

"It is the beginning of it. Relax into me, Bryna. Feel my hands on your body," he soothed. "I prepare you."

"For what?" she asked in sudden defiance.

He nibbled at the base of her neck. "For what comes after this. Do you like my touch?"

"I doona know."

" 'Tis your innocence that answers."

His hands continued caressing, arousing her.

The hard length of him pressed up against her backside, and she dropped her head back with a whisper of female surrender. "I want to see you, Tynan."

"This eve is for my touch and mark only. After we handfast, you may see me. Trust me, faery. I do this for both of us and will not hurt you."

"I trust you, Tynan."

Tynan slid his mouth over her jaw. The hand at her waist slid down her rounded belly and cupped her womanly softness. He held her in his hand, letting her get accustomed to his touch.

She shifted her hips, seeking that which remained out of her reach.

"I feel your need," he murmured huskily, and gently stroked her there.

Slowly.

Building the fire.

Her hips rocked forward.

"Aye, faery."

She pushed down on his hand. "Tynan?"

He caressed her throat with his tongue. "Feel."

With a single finger, he entered the warmth of her essence. She felt wet and ready for him . . . and tight, so blessed tight. *By the goddess, a virgin faery sheath.*

Small hands clenched on his thighs. Her head rolled back on his shoulder.

Tynan rubbed the tiny nub hidden within the damp petals of her womanhood. Pleasure mounted within him, a mirror image of her own. The air glimmered with magic, pulsing, primitive and unattainable — her pleasure, her need burned through his body.

"Please," she moaned, bucking in front of him.

Breath left her straining lungs in rapid bursts.

"Let it come," he rasped against her ear while she pushed down and rode his hand.

Sweat poured off him. "Let it come." His mouth slid over her jaw to his mark.

Her body quivered.

Innocence faltered.

And then...

She gasped and arched, a shattering of a thousand shards of faery light . . .

. . . taking him with her.

Tynan's hips bucked in unison with hers. And then, just then, when her hips rocked forward and she climaxed in his hand, he honor-marked her.

Relief came instantly, drenching his body like a warm summer rain. Reprieve spread through his blood, loosening tense muscles and easing the compulsion to mate.

He suckled her jaw, spreading saliva with his tongue.

His *geas* calmed.

His body eased into quietness.

A deep fatigue weighted his limbs.

Slowly, he removed his hand from her dampness.

Pulling her back into the pelts with him, he continued to suckle her jaw. Her head rolled back on his shoulder, eyes fluttered, but remained closed. The roughness of his tongue lulled her into a deep, replenishing sleep.

Peace invaded his body, invaded his soul. Exhaustion greeted him like an old friend.

Holding Bryna possessively in his arms, Tynan lay down, closed his eyes, and welcomed the sweet, dark caress of sleep.

***

Bryna awoke alone.

A growing tightness grew into discomfort in her lower womb. It was early morning. Her fickle moon time had finally arrived almost a fortnight late.

"My thanks, goddess," she murmured, ever practical. "Please may it not be too painful this month."

With all that had happened, she had forgotten to speak to Rose about preparing the woman herbs.

Tynan was not in the roundhouse and she thanked

the mother goddess again for that small blessing. Last night she had agreed to handfast with Tynan today, but her body had other plans.

With a wave of cramping, reality crashed in. Bryna stifled a moan and attended to her personal needs with a slowness that spoke of her distress. In the corner of the roundhouse, she slowly prepared her woman's wrappings for her courses. She had begun to feel very ill.

"And this is only the morning," she muttered in loathing. Each month proved difficult for her as if her body fought some invisible battle. Other women did not suffer the cramping pain and weakness that brought her to her knees and made her wish she were dead. She did not understand, only that she must suffer this womanly affliction in silence.

"How can I possibly go through a handfasting ceremony today?" she murmured in pain. Her dreams of the golden territorial goddess were ominous of late, and always ended in a cage of fire and night.

She sat down on the bed, wretched in both body and spirit. Why did the golden goddess of her dreams not come to Tynan? Why did his *geas* recognize her as the territorial goddess? A new wave of cramping washed over her and she could not think beyond that.

Looking over her shoulder, she shuddered. She always had a rough time each month even with Derina's woman herbs. On those days when her courses were particularly painful, she would curl up in a dark bend of the fortress and endure the agony in silence. It was a penance for some wrong, she supposed, but could find no reason for it.

"Please, goddess." A crippling contraction wracked her body. "I am going to be handfasted today."

"Bryna," Hawk called. The boy charged into his father's roundhouse. He gripped a bow and arrow and stopped dead in his tracks. His eyes widened in a child's fear. "Bryna, what is wrong?"

She looked up from where she had been kneeling, crouched over in pain.

"Hawk, doona be afraid." She tried to soothe the boy from her curled position in the dirt, but he ran out of the roundhouse, yelling for his father.

"Aile Niurin." Bryna muttered the boy's favorite oath.

Curling into herself, her body felt tight and constricted. She tensed as another wave of pain drained her. *Please goddess. I canna . . .* She did not want Tynan to see her like this.

A few moments later, she heard Tynan cursing. He charged into the roundhouse and stopped dead just like his son had. His face drained of all color.

"Bryna? What is wrong?" He dove to her side and wrapped his arms around her shoulders.

"Hawk found you."

"Aye, the boy said you were dying." His hand stroked her back.

"I think I frightened him."

"I will deal with him later."

Another contraction hit, low and painful. She squeezed her eyes shut and bit her lip to stifle a moan.

"Bryna!" His tone rose in alarm. "What is wrong? Did I hurt you last night?"

"Nay," she said, low. Embarrassment stained her cheeks with a high color. "Last night was wonderful, Tynan," she tried to reassure him, but her efforts proved pitiful even to her own ears. "Please, go away."

He watched her with a curious expression, his nostrils twitching.

"Go away, Tynan."

"I think not, faery."

A warm hand slid down and rested in the small of her back. The heat from his hand felt good, providing a momentary respite.

" 'Tis your moon time," he stated with sudden male insight that irked her. "I had wondered at the delay."

"Do I have no secrets from you?" Straightening from her squat position on the dirt, she balanced on her hand and looked sideways at him.

He was different.

The composure and serenity that the *geas* had robbed him of had now returned. Gone was the darkness of his compulsion. Gone was the pain that it had wrought. Amethyst light, bright with golden flecks, scrutinized her with concern and nothing else.

"You are better now?" she asked, knowing it for truth.

"Aye. Because of what we shared last night, my body will remain at peace for a short time."

"How long?"

"I doona know. Enough of me. You are in much pain, faery?" He rubbed her lower back with infinite gentleness.

"Little," she replied, looking away.

"Liar. You have trouble with blood flow."

Bryna blinked back at him in mortification, her arm pressed to her painful side. "Men do not discuss such things."

He tilted his head. "My tribesmen do. We care for our women."

"Go away," she choked, and lay down on her side.

"For a moment I will go."

He left her and Bryna did not know if she felt grateful or not. She rested her left cheek on the edge of the bed. The fur tickled her nose, but she did not have the strength or the will to move.

As the next wave of cramping hit, she began to rock back and forth.

"Bryna?"

She stifled a moan and looked up from her torture. Both Rose and Tynan were on their knees beside her, Tynan behind and Rose in front.

The simpler held a large, brown cloth bag.

Bryna wiggled her nose and instantly recognized the scent of woman herbs. "Blue Cohosh roots,

Raspberry leaves, Sarsaparilla, Blessed Thistle?" she rattled off a few that she recognized. They were the same herbs that Derina gave her for her courses. They helped sometimes.

"Aye, let me help you," the simpler soothed. "I have seen this many times with young virgins." She gestured to Tynan. "Help her sit up, Lordling."

Bryna allowed Tynan to take her in his arms, her back pressed against his chest, his chin resting near her right temple as he too gazed at the simpler's cloth bag. He felt so wonderfully warm pressing into her like that, and the scents of the woodlands upon him offered a tiny measure of comfort to her. She suspected he knew much about the ways of women, though it embarrassed her to think so. His people did not seem to have the same reservations as her Roman master. They were much freer and less inhibited with their bodies.

"Has it always been this way, Bryna?" Rose asked.

"Aye." She tried not to sound so pitiful.

"Help her," Tynan said firmly. He seemed to feel her pain as if it were his own.

Bryna clutched her bloated abdomen and shuddered through another round of cramping.

"*Aile Niurin*," he growled, his arms holding her trembling body. She broke out in a cold sweat.

"Patience, Lordling," the simpler said, gesturing toward the entranceway. "Get the milkwater from my home. 'Tis more serious than I thought."

Gently, he pulled away from her and disappeared out of the roundhouse. Bryna missed his support and heat, but he returned within moments.

Handing a brown leather bag to the simpler, he settled down once again behind her.

Rose reached into the first bag. "Watch me, Bryna. Bitter herbs and my milkwater will help your body do what it needs to do. Later I will show you our place of growing woman herbs." As Bryna watched, the older woman crushed the bitter herbs from her first bag into the bag containing the milkwater.

"This is the remedy I used, and my mother before me. You should also not eat a day or two before your moon time. If you must eat, choose only the fruits."

Bryna held her stomach and nodded once.

"Here now, drink slowly."

With trembling hands, she reached for it, but Tynan took the bag from Rose and held it up to her lips.

"Drink, Bryna."

Reaching for the bag's lip, she pulled it to her mouth. She swallowed the slightly bitter liquid, slowly at first and then with more confidence as her trust and hope in Rose's remedy grew.

"Many virgins have difficulty with their moon time."

Bryna concentrated on swallowing the liquid and felt its presence in her pain-racked body almost immediately . . . releasing, soothing, calming.

Tynan brushed a stray curl from her dampened

cheek. "Why does she suffer?"

Rose shrugged. " 'Tis the way of it, sometimes. I doona know. I've never seen it this bad before, a one-sidedness. My herbs will help her."

"Is there something I can do?"

"Get her with child soon."

Bryna coughed at the simpler's statement of the old wives tale. However, images of a mating with Tynan had already skirted her imagination. If she were not suffering so, no doubt the images would have been more vivid.

"How will that help, Rose?" Tynan demanded.

Bryna was not up for this discussion. "I wish to rest," she whispered, touching his forearm. Closing her eyes, her head rolled back into his supporting shoulder. Warm relief began to flood her tortured womb.

"Bryna, it takes time for the body's acceptance." The simpler squeezed her chilled hand.

Bryna cracked her eyes open and looked upon the simpler with such heartfelt thanks that she thought she saw tears forming in the woman's blue eyes.

"I feel better, Rose," she murmured, deeply grateful.

"Relax and let my remedy work. Do you know how to use your chieftain mate's presence?"

Bryna shook her head. It was hard to think of Tynan as her mate, even though she had agreed to handfast with him.

The simpler guided Tynan's large hand over her stomach.

Bryna pulled back.

"Easy, child," Rose reassured. "Feel his warmth. Our males are so very warm."

She watched Tynan's long fingers instinctively settle over the area of pain on her lower left side.

"Relax back into him, Bryna."

This day she did as she was told.

"That is it. Drink more. Let the milkwater work."

Tynan held the bag up to her and Bryna sipped at what was left in it.

"Lordling, Bryna is small inside and will always have trouble during this time."

"He doona need to know," Bryna grumbled.

"Aye, I do," Tynan interrupted her. "You are my faerymate. 'Tis my duty to care for you."

How could she argue with that?

"Bryna, the pain shall become the whisper of the wind instead of a raging storm if you allow it. Acceptance of your faery blood, of your body, of who you are, only this will ease your pain, ease the one-siding."

"One-siding?" Bryna echoed, understanding blooming inside her.

"The balance. Listen to your faery spirit. Listen, Bryna, and heal thyself."

Bryna closed her eyes, her body had calmed, yet she remained apprehensive of what lived inside her, fearful of the knowing and of the change.

"Listen." The simpler's soothing words compelled her. "Doona fear. It is only Bryna, your faery self."

The milkwater eased her body, a slowing and slackening within. She opened her heart and mind to the *meadh*, the balance, between worlds both mortal and faery.

Tears glistened down her cheek.

A young villager had once asked, what does it mean to be faery? Frightened by the question, she had remained stubbornly mute. Now, she acknowledged the living force of the land, a sacred vow of trust that had always echoed inside her.

Illuminating her soul.

A collective wisdom.

A harmonious knowledge.

"Bryna?"

"Hush, Lordling. Let her recognize what is within. Let her understand."

It means to be free, Bryna thought in swift insight, to understand and share the world in its entirety.

To be a sister to the primordial whispers of the land . . .

To be a mother to the sacred lochs . . .

To exchange mortality for the divine energy, and in so doing, merge with the supernatural.

And in that one defining moment, she knew. She knew what it was to be faery.

So simple.

It meant to BELONG.

Perhaps it was the relief from the cramps that allowed her to see and hear and feel what had always been within her, compelling the acceptance in her heart and mind.

Perhaps it was this enchanted place of mist and woods.

Perhaps it was the powerful chieftain that held her so tenderly in his arms.

She did not know.

Did not care.

Enlightenment filled her being.

Visions of small, willowy folk, barely knee high, floated in her mind, forgotten memories pushed aside long ago. They were beautiful, with pale and delicate complexions. Silver bells tinkled on their heads. Some sprouted wings of silver, diamonds, and gold. Some wore lace, velvet, or satin.

But she was not so much like them, as something more than they were. Something still repressed, still entangled in darkness and fear in a small corner of her being. She was afraid to take that final step and look. For now, it was enough that she knew.

"Bryna?" her chieftain mate whispered hoarsely, anxious for her.

She squeezed his arm, turning her face into his corded neck. His chin lowered to her, brushing her temple, his arms holding her close.

"I am here," he said quietly. "You are not alone."

She breathed in the scent of him, knowing she would never be truly alone again. Her journey was about to begin. She looked at the simpler through her lashes. "My thanks. I begin to see."

"It will take time."

"I know." Bryna snuggled deeper into Tynan's arms.

"My work is done here. I will take my leave of you now." The simpler rose to her feet.

"My thanks, Rose," Tynan said with gentle gravity. "Delay the handfasting ceremony until my faerymate feels better."

"I will speak with the elders on you behalf, Lordling. Bryna, let our chieftain's strength hold you while my herbs and milkwater balance your body."

"Rose." She could never thank this wise woman enough.

"I know, rest now."

Bryna watched the simpler leave.

"I am here for as long as you need me," Tynan murmured against her temple.

"I know." She closed her eyes.

The massive cramping ebbed to small whispers as the simpler had promised. The tightness fled her body, leaving a deep exhaustion. She felt the blood flow freely from her womb and she knew the imbalance in her no longer existed.

The simpler's bitter herbs and milkwater soothed her body, but the awakening and recognition of her inner self was her own.

She was faery bred.

The pain would never come again.

Throughout the day, the Dark Chieftain of *Tuatha*

Dé Danann held her and Bryna listened to her body and slept in his warm embrace.

✱✱✱

Shades of a pink twilight filtered into Tynan's home, marking the day's passing into twilight. Coolness kissed the air. She had slept the day away tucked safely in Tynan's arms. She could still feel his warmth about her and smell his scent.

Bryna sat up, feeling rested. She drank the rest of the milkwater and noticed a new milkwater bag lay at the foot of the pelts along with a pink rock. *Hawk*.

She smiled, listening to this new inner peace and harmony of her body. She had not dreamed of the golden territorial goddess, but of light and contentment. Peacefulness settled over her. For the first time in her life, she felt almost whole.

Bryna rose from the bed with a new sense of self. She attended to her personal needs, taking great joy in the washing of her hair and body. Within her, there remained only a faint aching whisper in her womb to remind her of her woman's monthly pain. She thanked the mother goddess for her patience with her.

Donning the green gown once again, she braided her damp hair into a single braid, satisfied that she looked presentable. With a happy heart, Bryna turned and stumbled into a wide male chest. She stared up at a scarred chin.

"Eamon."

Blue eyes stared down at her with an animal's hunger.

"You bleed," he said icily.

"You should not be here." She stepped back but he grabbed her hard, his demanding mouth covering her own.

She gagged at the vile taste of his kiss and bit down on his lip, gaining her release. But it was short lived.

He grabbed her again and dragged her back into the roundhouse.

Bryna pummeled his chest. "Let me go, Eamon."

His hold tightened hurtfully. "Your moon time is unfortunate, Bryna. But it will not stop me. I want what is mine."

Bryna pushed against him. He smelled of stale sweat and lust and she wanted no part of him.

He chuckled at her attempts for escape. Changing tactics, she stomped on his foot.

"Stop this." He shook her. "You are faery bred and still he does not claim you."

She glared up at him through angry tears.

"My cousin is a fool. Were I the ancient liege you would have felt my thrusts between your white thighs immediately."

Dread slowly began to replace the anger.

"He does not care for you." He held her face in a hard grip. "If he cared, he'd voice his claim. Instead, he leaves you open for challenge, Bryna."

Bryna blinked. Tynan cared for her, did he not? He would not have asked her to handfast with him if he did not care for her. He would not have held her with such gentleness yesterday when she was in such pain.

Eamon pulled her around and pressed his palm against her lower stomach.

"Nay, Eamon," Bryna cried, trying to push his hand away.

"It is said taking a woman during her moon time weakens a man. But I dare not wait."

Bryna prayed that Tynan would return before Eamon raped her. He jerked her head back, his nose pressed to her jaw.

"He has marked you again, yet still there is no claim. Does he think that his mark will stop me from taking what is rightfully mine? I should have been the chieftain."

Bryna ceased struggling as a black rage swept over her senses. *Tynan.*

"That is better, my winsome faery," Eamon said, thinking her submissive. "Tonight I will lay my seed in your womb and make my claim."

"I have already claimed her, Eamon."

Eamon jerked around, taking her with him.

"Are you all right?" Tynan asked.

She gave a curt nod. "I am unhurt."

He turned back to her attacker.

"Eamon, you know better than anyone that I will not tolerate another's claim on her. Release her now or

I will be forced to kill you, cousin."

"You did not voice the faery honor-mark claim. I have right of challenge."

Tynan watched Eamon pull Bryna against his chest. The man's thick forearm pressed into her delicate neck.

He burned with fury that his cousin would dare touch what belonged to him.

Suddenly, footfalls filled the silence and Tynan recognized the sounds of the tribe elders. They were coming to his roundhouse. He fingered the dagger at his waist, deciding to end this farce here and now.

Eamon growled out his challenge. "I, Eamon of the *Tuatha Dé Danann*, challenge . . . ugh!"

Tynan launched himself at Eamon. Pinning his blade to his cousin's neck, he jerked him back, forcing Bryna's release.

"LORD TYNAN!" Dafyd bellowed at the entrance, Rose by his side. The leader of the tribe elders pounded the blunt end of his hazelwood walking stick into the ground. "Release Eamon, I say."

"Not yet, Dafyd. We have unfinished matters to discuss."

"Release him and let us settle this dispute once and for all."

Though he thought better of it, Tynan shoved Eamon away from him and returned his dagger to the sheath at his waist. To his right, Bryna stood pale but resilient.

"Much better," the elder huffed. "Faery child, come here, my fey senses are getting old."

Tynan nodded for her to go.

She stepped forward and stood proudly before the gaunt elder.

"I am Dafyd, leader of the tribe elders."

"I am Bryna."

"I know, faery child."

"Honor-marked twice, my husband," the simpler said and Tynan suspected some foul pretense afoot.

"I know, wife." Dafyd straightened, leaning hard on his walking stick. "It is as you said, and I am not that old that I canna tell a twice given honor-mark. Our lord has honor-marked the maid once before the handfasting approval and then once after. Is that not right, Lord Tynan?"

"It is right."

The elder nodded and turned his attention back to Bryna. "Let me see the honor-mark, Bryna." His callused fingers inspected her jaw and out of the corner of his eye, Tynan saw Eamon flash a triumphant smile.

"Did my young warriors hurt you?" the elder inquired. "You look about to faint."

Tynan muttered an oath, knowing the reason for her sudden pallor. He retrieved the milkwater bag.

"Nay, they did not hurt me," she whispered.

Without asking, he put the bag under her nose and ordered her to drink.

With trembling fingers, she took the bag but did

not move to drink.

"Dafyd, give us a moment." Tynan made the request in a low tone and the elder nodded in understanding.

He gently pulled Bryna aside. Taking the brown bag from her hands, he held it to her lips.

"Drink," he whispered, using his body to block out the others. "They will wait."

She drank for him, eyes closed, auburn lashes splayed against white cheeks.

"Are you in pain?" he asked softly.

She wiped her mouth and shook her head. "Nay, Tynan. I am fine."

"Keep the bag with you," he ordered. Moving back, he gestured for the elder to continue.

"Bryna, do you feel well enough to answer my questions?"

"I do."

The elder leaned on his walking stick. "Did Lord Tynan truly honor-mark you the first time or is this mark a result of the Evil One's magic? Doona glance at our chieftain for your answer, faery child. Tell me your feelings."

"The first honor-mark is not true to my way of thinking."

"Why is that?"

"The Dark Chieftain was spellbound."

"Ah," the elder said with a single nod.

"ENOUGH!" Tynan said loudly, startling everyone

He had had enough and stepped forward to make his claim. "I honor-marked Bryna. She is mine by ancient promise. I am bound as she is bound. To twilight. To honor. To land."

"Nay, 'tis too late for the claim! My challenge stands," Eamon bellowed his objection.

"Oh, shut up," the simpler snapped in annoyance.

"Quiet!" Dafyd ordered loudly. "I have no choice. The claim has come after the challenge."

"Dafyd," Tynan said in warning.

"The challenge stands, Lord Tynan. Your request for handfasting must wait until after the challenge. That is, if you accept?"

"I accept Eamon's challenge," Tynan growled, wanting to punch his cousin in the face.

"And what of the promise?"

Tynan could not believe the elder dared to remind him of his vow. "If our faery brethren doona accept Bryna as my faerymate, I will lay with one of their choosing."

"And what of the maid Bryna?"

Tynan locked gazes with the older man. "I will free her to make her own choice," he replied tightly.

The elder nodded, seemingly satisfied with his answer.

"Is this agreeable to you, Bryna?" he asked.

The simpler went and stood by his faerymate's side as he could not.

"I accept," she whispered and with that, Tynan felt

the fire of battle begin to warm his blood.

"Let the challenge begin." Dafyd turned and limped out of the roundhouse. "Wife, bring the maid and let the males prepare."

CHAPTER 10

ON A SMALL HILLTOP AT the crossroads and beyond the shelter of the faery woodlands, a bonfire roared to life in the black, predawn sky. A spiritual force unto itself, it possessed both destructiveness and cleansing. Blue dancing flames spiked high, and then splintered red sparks into the chilled air.

Bryna felt the heat and energy of the fire like a living thing. Properly cleaned and chaperoned, she now sat amidst a group of aging females who wore bright, fringed cloaks that fell to their ankles. Thick pelts had been thrown on the ground where Rose now sat beside her.

She had been told the challenge would begin when her woman's courses ended.

The time had come last eve and the simpler wasted no time in insisting she be prepared for the sacred handfasting ceremony. Rose had explained that in doing this the women showed their preference for the Dark Chieftain.

So, in the middle of the night, beneath a full moon's buttery glow, Bryna had endured a bath in the woodland's icy stream. Black waters murmured of their endless journey, gliding past her thighs and

disappearing around the bend while she shivered uncontrollably. Maidens lined the banks, holding white
candles, while old women washed her hair and rubbed
fragrant soap into her skin until she pleaded with
them to stop.

Shaking with cold, Bryna moved to the hard bank,
only to be scented with lavender oils, wrapped in a red
cloak, and escorted to Rose's home.

An aura of expectation gripped the women and as
they walked from the stream, their voices whispered
of faery magic and a male's hard desire.

The simpler waited at the entrance to her home in
a warm blue cloak with silver fringe that moved in the
night's breeze.

"Come, Bryna." Rose wrapped her arms around
her quivering shoulders. "We must prepare you."

"P-prepppare? Rose, I'm sooo coold, I canna feel
my body."

" 'Tis the cleansing. Come now."

Bryna allowed the simpler to lead her into the
small roundhouse. They allowed her to sit on the hard
bench in front of a trestle table. On the table top lay
bunches of dried herbs and fragrant wreaths so that a
pleasant sweetness filled the air. White candles burned
in clusters of three, illuminating the darkness.

"Mmmaid, Mmmother, Cccrone," Bryna said, her
teeth chattering with cold.

Rose came around the table and smiled.

"Maid, mother, crone. Aye, we are all of them, but

you are faery as well."

"I'm so ccccold."

"Aye, Bryna, I know. But that soon will pass."

Numb with fatigue, she could raise no objection to the women who surrounded her and began to weave rose ribbons and gold beads into her wet hair.

They pulled the red cloak from her shoulders despite her protests, and urged her to stand. A rose red gown was dropped over her head.

Warmth came instantly, a cascade of heat scented with a light fragrance of wild roses. Bryna looked down upon herself in wonderment. Clusters of shiny stones and gold threads decorated the bodice, which hugged her breasts as if made for her. The rest of the otherworldly fabric draped in a clinging silhouette with slits on either side exposing her from ankle to mid-thigh. The fey gown felt petal soft against her skin. Red slippers, infused with heat, were also placed onto her feet.

"The warmth comes from the enchantment," Rose said.

Bryna looked up at the simpler. "I feel it, Rose. 'Tis warm and woven from the wild roses that grow in the meadows."

"Aye, the gown is a gift from the faeries. It is spun from spring roses and tears of joy. It will keep you warm."

And it had.

Now in the predawn darkness, the warriors of the

Tuatha Dé Danann gathered around the bonfire.

Sitting on white pelts with her legs tucked under her, Bryna filled her eyes with the dawn spectacle.

She did not feel the crisp temperatures of the new morning, for the warmth of the fey gown and red cloak bathed her in comfort and calm. She would have preferred a brooch to hold the cloak closed, but for now it was fine. The drape overlapped in front.

The simpler tapped her arm and pointed to the far side of the fire. "Look, our men gather."

Bryna left thoughts of the previous night's activity behind. The men of the *Tuatha Dé Danann* were tall and muscular in their sleeveless tunics and dark breeches. Unlike the Romans, they wore their hair long and adorned with beads. Bronze and silver arm bands glittered on their arms and belted daggers shone at lean waists. They looked wild and formidable, mirroring the land that they protected.

A feeling of expectation pulsed about them, a kind of primitive competitiveness and sexual desire.

Bryna felt glad they had seated her at a small distance away from all that male expectation.

"The men feel our chieftain's turmoil and grow anxious by it," the simpler remarked. "Look, my husband and our leaders come now."

Indeed, Dafyd and the tribe elders had moved to stand in front of the bonfire.

For Tynan this was the beginning, a sensation of hunger and battle pumping through his blood. The icy mask of the hunter slid into place, a predator waiting for the battle yet to come. He glanced sideways and Eamon nodded tensely. Ian stood beyond, a trusted friend and guardian of the chieftain.

Tynan turned his attention back to the elders and ceremony. From the opposite side of the fire, they approached, men and women of age and wisdom, their youth long since past. Clean white robes rested on stooped shoulders. Massive hoods draped lined faces so out of place in this moment of primitiveness.

Dafyd tapped his staff into the dirt. "Ian, step back."

Tynan nodded and his friend backed up, out of his line of sight.

"Step forward, Lord Tynan. Step forward, Eamon. We must begin in the East and ask for the blessings of the element of Air, which brings truth, wisdom, and vision to us. We are *Tuatha Dé Danann*, the proud and spirited people of the goddess Dana. Only she understands our ancient lord's blood *geas* and sacrifice. Only she knows the fire that burns within him." The elder turned to Eamon.

"Eamon, I am disappointed by this challenge, but not surprised by it. Do you still challenge our lord's honor-mark?"

"I do," his cousin responded, and Tynan felt the quickening of battle grow within. They had played together as children and grown together into manhood. Never had he imagined his cousin as an enemy.

"If you should win the day," the elder continued,

"you have first claim to the maid, but only with her approval. Do you agree, Eamon?"

"I agree."

Tynan waited for Dafyd's dark eyes to slide to him, feeling the heavy responsibility of his tribe and what was expected.

"Lord Tynan of *Tuatha Dé Danann*, is your honor-mark on the maid Bryna of Loch Gur true?"

"It is true," he answered, a quick response.

"If you should win the day, we will honor your request for the handfasting. Be that as it may, you must not consummate the vow until our faery brethren give their approval."

Tynan's dark brow rose slightly. "Did you think I would not?"

"Lord Tynan, what I think is of little importance here. You are the ancient lord of prophecy, the chosen one."

"Let us not forget that, tribe leader."

The leader's walking stick pounded into the ground once again. "I will not forget that, you arrogant cub." He stepped back. "Mark him. Eamon, step aside and wait by the fire."

Tynan's eyes narrowed considerably at the two youngsters accompanying Hawk. He did not like this. The children approached him, each with a clay bowl of blue dye made from the woad plant.

"I dislike the dye, Dafyd."

"This dye will not make you itch. It has been

specially prepared for you and you will be marked. As Kindred's ancient liege, we offer tribute, as is our brethren's way. Carry on, young Hawk. Your father awaits this honor."

The two youngsters had stopped at his growl of protest, but Hawk came forward without fear.

Tynan stared down at his son's quick movements. Kindred's runic inscriptions of loch, sky and earth were fast being drawn on his lower stomach and left forearm.

They were symbols of protection, blessing, and success. There was no hope for it, now. He knelt obediently on one knee so his son could reach his shoulders and back.

From across the clearing he felt the gazes of the women. He looked up slowly, awareness of his faerymate burning within him, her name echoing in his head. *Bryna*.

Her silvery eyes captured and held him, locking the world out. Her fear, a concern far deeper then any of the others, warmed his soul. Within this small measure of time, their bond had grown.

His son patted his shoulder. "I am done."

Tynan stood, his gaze never leaving Bryna.

Sudden mirth lighted her face. He looked down his body, at his son's intention. A figure took shape on the area of his breeches that shielded his manhood.

"Hawk, what are you doing?"

The boy stepped back with a big grin. "The hawk

symbol gives you strength." He looked into his son's bright gaze and blue smudged cheeks.

"So it will. My thanks."

"This is foolishness," Eamon complained.

Tynan glanced over his shoulder. His cousin was flushed, his body tight with anticipation of the fight. He gently pushed his son back into the safety of Dafyd's waiting arms. Checking to make sure the other two children were safe, he turned and faced Eamon, his dagger drawn. His cousin's strength was legendary in his tribe; he would have to be swifter. Much depended on his victory this day.

Out of the corner of his eye, he saw the elder lift his walking staff high for all to see.

"Begin the challenge," he called loudly, and stepped back.

Eamon lunged.

Tynan sidestepped his cousin's upward thrust and knew instantly it had been meant as a death-blow. Eamon was not out for first blood, but for death's blood. He tightened his grip on his dagger and moved in.

The orange glow of the fire flickered, shadow and light mingled in the field of battle.

Bryna could not look away from the fight. Dawn approached, pink ribbons entwined with flat gray clouds. The air whispered to her of a new storm, fueling the growing tension inside her. Even the faery gown's gentle influence could no longer contain her dread.

Tynan's strong back was to her now, his thrusts fast and strong. Eamon ducked and dodged.

"First blood," Rose whispered into her ear.

Bryna gave the older woman a quick glance.

"The male to draw first blood wins the claim. You are in dispute, my dear. They fight for the mating rights to you."

"But, I thought Lord Tynan's honor-mark meant I belonged to him."

"It would have, but Lordling did not voice his claim. Eamon had the right of challenge then."

Bryna bit her lip. He did not voice his claim because he needed to wait for the faeries' approval. Now, if he wins, he would be forced to issue it. Would the golden territorial goddess of her dreams be angry? Would the faeries be angry? Would they take their spite out on the land and Tynan's people? She could not let that happen.

"The honor-mark is the faeries' spell of binding and intent," the simpler said. "Tynan's body recognized you as a possible mate to fulfill the promise. The claim is Lordling's final acceptance."

"My faery blood doona matter to Eamon?"

"Only Lordling is bound to mate with a faery. Not Eamon."

"If Lord Tynan should lose . . ." Bryna could not finish.

"The honor-mark will release him to find another faery mate."

"What does that mean?"

"The attraction, the driving lust that binds him to you, is gone."

"Gone," Bryna repeated dimly, looking back to the fight. She thought, *it was Tynan's geas and not his heart that binds him to me.* A kind of sadness came with that and she struggled to push it aside. All that mattered now was that he win.

"You will make a fine faerymate for our prideful lord. My only hope is that our faery brethren agree. They will be cross that Lord Tynan made the claim before seeking their approval. And they will be most annoyed that he has not yet freed those of them imprisoned."

"He will free them," Bryna stated with conviction. She recognized now that the fey voices calling to her at the fortress had been pleas for help. In her innocence and self-condemnation, she had not understood.

"Have you ever met the Evil One?"

"W-what?" Bryna blinked at the change of subject.

"The Sorcerer, have you met him, Bryna?" The simpler's voice was curiously intent.

"Once, on the parapets."

"What is your impression?"

"My impression." She thought back to that windy night on the parapets when she had first seen the Sorcerer. He stood unmoving, lost in the folds of his brown robe, staring outward upon the stars. She watched him for only moments before he had ordered

her away. "He is a tortured soul, full of loss and vengeance, methinks. He seems to grieve for something,
yet I doona know what." She shook her head to rid
herself of the disturbing memory. "There is much bit-
terness in him. I stayed away whenever possible."

"Our faery brethren are unforgiving," the simpler
murmured.

Bryna did not understand the melancholy in the
simpler's voice and focused back on the men fighting
over her.

"If Eamon wins, will I be given to him?" she asked.

"Lord Tynan shall win."

"How can you be sure?"

"I am always right, most of the time."

Bryna did not find that comforting.

"Eamon knows our history and prophesy, Bryna.
Envy eats at him. Neither is he the chosen male, nor
does the ancient bloodline flow in his veins, and my
proud Lordling is stubborn."

Bryna looked at the simpler.

"Doona be upset with us, Bryna. You were destined for Lordling from the time of his birth. I have no
doubt who will be blooded in this fight." With that,
the simpler smiled and Bryna turned back just in time
to see Tynan slash at Eamon's left cheek.

First blood had been drawn.

The fight was over.

Tynan stepped back, his body filmed in sweat and
blue dye.

" 'Tis done, Eamon. Lower your weapon." He clutched the bloodied dagger in his hand. His cousin's warm blood trickled between his fingers. This would be the first time his cousin had been bested in a two-man fight. The quickness of the faeries had been with him this day.

He stared into Eamon's burning eyes and waited.

Eamon could not believe that he had lost. *Yn Drogh Spyrryd*, the Evil One, promised him riches if he delivered the ancient lord to him. And he had. It had been so easy, slipping the potion in Tynan's drink. Then everything went wrong. When he dropped the unconscious Tynan at the Evil One's feet, he felt such hatred from the creature that the air seemed to boil. The promise of riches had been just that, promises only. The Evil One's hard fist hit him across the face, and he'd been dragged out of the dungeon like a dog. He received nothing for his troubles. And then Tynan had escaped. He wanted to bury the dagger in Tynan's chest and be done with it. Eamon dropped the dagger in the dirt and bowed his head in feigned defeat. His vengeance must wait for another day.

Tynan watched Eamon's eyes, a great unease settling within him.

" 'Tis done," his cousin rasped.

A crowd of men gathered around in anticipation of the relinquishing of his claim, and Tynan saw a flash of angry reaction in his cousin's face.

"Do you withdraw your claim, Eamon?"

"Aye, Dark Chieftain. I relinquish my claim to the maid, Bryna of Loch Gur."

"I accept, then," Tynan replied. "You may leave, Eamon."

His cousin cast him a final look of fury before disappearing into the crowd of men. A fathomless rage brewed there that Tynan did not understand, not just over the loss of Bryna, but something far greater. It would come back to haunt him, he did not doubt.

For now though, he had won his rights back.

He walked over to where the elders waited and handed Dafyd the bloody dagger. Hawk plowed through the aged tribe leaders and collided bodily with him, forcing him to take a step back to regain his balance. Small arms hugged his thighs in a death grip.

"Hush, Hawk." His hand soothed the boy's trembling shoulders. Tynan thought he heard a strangled sob against his thigh and shot an angry glance at the elders.

"He should not have been allowed to watch," he growled.

"Your son would not leave and he is old enough to know the ways of our brethren." Dafyd turned and faced the men. "Are there any other challenges for the maid Bryna?"

Tynan searched the faces of his tribesmen. Their eyes were bright, but no challenge did he see.

The elder turned back. "Your claim is free. We begin the handfasting ceremony."

"Now?" Tynan remarked in surprise. "You wish to do it now? Should I not clean up first?"

His son suddenly pushed away from him to stand near the elder's side.

"You must enter the circle marked with Kindred's runes," the boy said in a teary voice, slowly regaining his composure. "We worked on it all night so you could handfast today." His son pointed and the men parted. There, just a few steps east of the bonfire, lay a large circle of stones and crystal rocks. His people fell silent, showing their confidence in him. Never did they think he might lose.

He gave his son a proud smile " 'Tis a fine circle, Hawk."

The boy beamed.

"Now, with your permission, I must make my claim first."

His son's small chin bobbed up and down before he broke out in a grin. "You have my permission, Lordling."

"Lordling?" Tynan echoed in amusement. "You have spent too much time with Rose. We will correct that." Chuckling, he glanced over his shoulder.

The women were standing around his faerymate, an offering of her to him. Waves of burnished gold fell about her shoulders in a vision of loveliness.

Hunger surged through his heated body.

He could no more stop the faeries' lust than a rock could stop the flow of water in a stream. Fever burned in his loins now, a reminder of his *geas*, of his spell-induced obligation to mate with a faery.

He felt the mindless lust reaching to take hold of his mind and fought it. He turned back to the fire and inhaled the heat.

His tribe waited for him to voice his claim.

He filled his lungs, the spirit of the fire touching him, sending a river of sweat down his face and chest. He welcomed it, a feeling of victory and a silent fervent prayer offered to the mother goddess that his mating claim would not offend the faeries, for it was their damned *geas* that had forced him to it.

"I honor-marked Bryna of Loch Gur," his voice rang out. "She is mine by ancient promise. I am bound as she is bound. To twilight. To honor. To land."

With arms raised, the men of the faery tribe roared their approval.

"The claim is made," Rose said beside her.

In relief, Bryna clutched the red cloak about her. She belonged to him now. Joy filled her heart until she looked up. A half-naked, sweaty, blue-stained savage turned from the tribe elders and started walking in her direction.

"Rose?" Bryna felt her mouth go dry.

"Be gentle with him, Bryna." The simpler picked up her cloak and started walking away.

Bryna flashed her a look of disbelief. "Be gentle with him?"

He looked wild to her. His black hair lifted and spread out behind him. The blue runic symbols on his chest and arms were no longer recognizable, for he gleamed with sweat.

Bryna held still when he stopped in front of her. His fierce scowl scattered the remaining women, leaving them alone on this side of the bonfire.

An instinct of self-preservation whispered for her to lower her eyes and step back, a familiar reaction, a slave's response. One she would not do.

Then surprisingly, he did what she would not.

Lids lowering, his gaze dropped to the ground in supplication. He held out his hand, palm open, a male's simple offering.

"Will you handfast with me, faery?" he asked in a low voice laced with need.

Bryna looked down at his hand, calloused and cleaned of Eamon's blood. She became aware of the sudden silence around them. It was as if the land waited, poised for her decision.

Without hesitation, she slid her hand into his much larger one.

"Aye, Tynan," she whispered. "A trial-marriage I consent to."

His gaze lifted, a dark compelling triumph glittered there, and Bryna could only smile.

Strong fingers closed around her hand, a forever vow of belonging.

Three bells clanged on the other side of the fire and then chaos and shouts erupted.

Bryna startled and looked around. "What is happening?"

"It is time to gather around the sacred circle of stones where the handfasting ceremony shall take place."

"Now? I thought we would have more time."

"Walk with me, faery." He guided her forward, around the bonfire. "We must enter the sacred circle from the east, the direction of sunrise and growth."

On the east end, his tribe waited around the large circle of stones and crystal rock. Maidens dressed in robes of white tossed red rose petals along the perimeter of the stone circle. Candles were lit to mark the four cardinal directions.

"Do we begin the handfasting ceremony now?"

He led her once around the circle and then entered it from the east.

"Aye, 'tis the beginning of it."

"What is required of me?" Bryna held the red cloak closed under her chin.

"To stand by my side and answer truthfully." Warm hands on her shoulders guided her to the center of the circle.

In front of them, Hawk placed a wooden altar. Upon the surface rested a silver knife, red cord, a small silver box, and a trowel.

Bryna looked at the trowel. She did not understand any of this, but was willing to learn.

Dafyd rang the bell three more times and Bryna supposed that it was to mark the beginning of the ceremony. Giving the bell to another, the elder entered the circle, faced them and began the hand-fasting blessing.

⋘⋙

"Let us begin in the east. Here we ask for the blessings of the element of Air, which brings truth, wisdom, and vision. May East and Air bless Tynan and Bryna throughout their lives."

⋘⋙

"Now, we turn to the south. Here we ask for the blessings of the element of Fire, home of passion, plea-sure, joy, and happiness. May South and Fire bless Tynan and Bryna throughout their lives."

⋘⋙

"Now, let us turn to the west. Here we ask for the blessings of the element of Water, bringing tranquil-ity, peace, emotion, and serenity. May West and Water bless Tynan and Bryna throughout their lives."

⋘⋙

"Now, we turn to the north, where the element of Earth resides, deeply grounded in strength, comfort, and support. May North and Earth bless Tynan and

Bryna throughout their lives."

≈⊱≈

"And in the Center and all around us, above and below, resides the Spirit who brings blessings of love, magic, friendship, and community. May the Spirit of all things divine join us and bless Tynan and Bryna on this sacred day."

≈⊱≈

Bryna faced Tynan.

"Bryna, let go of the cloak and take my hands," he whispered.

She slipped her hands in his, allowing the cloak to part and hint at the gown.

"Do any here challenge this joining?" the elder leader asked, and made a big show of looking around, so much so that Bryna fought back a giggle.

"Then, let us begin the joining," he said, and faced them once more.

"Tynan, do you come of your own free will?"

"I do."

"Bryna, do you come of your own free will?"

"I do," she replied softly.

"Then state your vows."

Bryna did not know what to say.

Tynan squeezed her hands. "Say these words with me, faerymate."

She nodded, grateful to him.

"We commit ourselves to be with each other in joy and in adversity."

Bryna repeated his words.

"In wholeness and brokenness."

"In wholeness and brokenness," she echoed, feeling her world shift.

"In peace and turmoil."

"In peace and turmoil," she repeated. This all felt frighteningly permanent to her.

"Living together faithfully all our days." Tynan's voice carried through the air. "May the Gods and Goddesses give us the strength to keep these vows. So be it."

She repeated the final phrase.

The elder stepped forward and placed a red cord over and around their right hands.

"Red symbolizes life and a handfasting commitment for one year and a day," the elder said. "If our faery brethren approve, you may return and repeat the vows with the cord tightly knotted to show a permanent joining. If not, the trial-marriage ends and you must go your separate ways."

He bowed over the red cord, said a prayer, and then removed it, returning it to the altar. Picking up the small knife, he handed it to Tynan.

Tynan held the knife in his right hand. She watched him cut one of her curls and place it in the silver box the elder held.

He then held the knife in an open palm for her to take. Bryna took the knife and followed his actions. She cut a thick lock of Tynan's black hair and placed it in the silver box over her own flame-colored curl.

The elder closed the silver box. "For the future." He returned the box to the altar.

Tynan took both her hands in his again.

"Be understanding and patient with each other," the elder murmured, backing away. "Be free in the giving of affection and warmth. Have no fear and let not the ways of the unenlightened give you unease, for the Gods and Goddesses be with you." He stepped out of the circle.

Tynan picked up the silver box and handed it to her.

"Is the ceremony over?" she inquired.

"Not yet. Together we must bury the silver box in the center of the circle to safeguard our future. Place your right hand over mine." He picked up the trowel.

Bryna did as instructed and leaned forward with him.

He did all the work and dug a small hole.

Together they placed the silver box in the hole and covered it beneath a mound of dirt.

From outside the circle, the elder called out, "The circle is open but unbroken. May the peace of the Old Ones go in our hearts. They are handfasted."

The bell rang three times.

"Faerymate, you are mine."

"For a year and a day," Bryna replied.

Tynan smiled at her answer, a grin of devilment. "For a year and a day. Come, Bryna." He led her out of the circle. "We must walk around the circle once before we greet our people."

Our people? It sounded good to her ears.

"It is time to feast and celebrate!" Dafyd raised his stick high. "Our chieftain has found his faerymate."

A loud, joyous roar rose in the morning air.

✳✳✳

Finally able to excuse herself, Bryna headed for Tynan's roundhouse, intent upon finding a brooch from her many gifts to hold the infernal cloak closed. Her fingers were aching.

She only made it to the top of the hill.

"Bryna?"

She stopped, the cloak slipping off one bare shoulder.

"Tynan, I need to get a brooch."

He came to her and reached for the cloak, pulling it aside.

"Let me see what you hide."

He pulled the cloak away and Bryna saw the faery darkness come into his gaze.

"I always knew you were beautiful." He tossed the cloak behind him and touched the material at her waist. "What is this made of?"

Bryna shrugged, watching his slow perusal. "I

doona know. 'Tis a fey gift from your brethren."

"Our brethren," he corrected, taking her hand and pulling her forward. He drew her down the rolling hill and back through the cluster of roundhouses.

Above their heads, thunder rumbled. Lightning sliced through the sky, warming her blood with anticipation and a maiden's trepidation. Stumbling on the gown's hem, she reached down to draw up its length and felt the bodice slip.

"*Aile Niurin*," he choked beside her.

Bryna blinked at his expletive and straightened quickly, holding the gaping bodice to her breast.

She met his darkening gaze.

Tynan felt the very essence of his soul yearning so intensely that he thought the pores of his skin would bleed if she denied him. He wanted to take her now, in this moment. With strength of will that had seen him through many battles, he struggled to fight the compulsion and gently guided her to his roundhouse ahead.

A light rain began to fall on his heated flesh, sipping at his strength. It was as if the faeries sought to weaken his resolve. He stepped into his home behind her, a creature slipping into lust and darkness.

"You are lovely, Bryna."

She stepped back from him, an uncertainty that he quickly took note of.

"Lovely like the storms that you bring, all fey and clean."

Outside, the afternoon had turned dark gray with an unnatural suddenness. He tilted his head toward the howling winds.

"You bring the rain storm to me, faery? To cool my *geas*?"

"I canna control storms, Tynan."

"You control more than storms, Bryna of Loch Gur. You control me."

"Why do you look at me that way?"

"I need to end this fey madness," he said in vehemence, taking a step toward her.

She flinched from him and immediately Tynan stilled, his eyes searching, then dropping to the ground.

"I am not a beast," he muttered, and moved away from her. "I will not be a beast." He looked up slowly, seeing alarm in the silver of her eyes, but he could also see awareness and desire. She waited upon him, a creature of purity and innocence.

"I will not force you, Bryna." Tynan shut his eyes and dropped down heavily to his knees.

"I will not force her," he called to the stormy skies above, compulsion changing to fury. "Do you hear me? I will not force her."

"Tynan, please . . ."

He opened his eyes. Never had he looked upon such beauty, or ever felt such desire. She was ethereal and mortal to him, faery spirit and warm flesh. He looked down at his hands and recoiled. "I canna do this." He had to wait for his faery brethren's approval.

Pain could be endured. The handfasting had been meant to keep her safely in his home and under his care. Never was it meant for mating. *Never!*

He knew he risked his own sanity by denying the compulsion to take her. He no longer cared. A new sea of pain raked his body. Tynan flung back his head and roared his rage, a howling of misery, a wounded animal fallen in capture.

He welcomed the icy shroud of night.

Welcomed the silent darkness engulfing him . . .

Welcomed the oblivion...

She touched him, a bright light staying his darkness. It was enough to stop his journey into madness.

He opened his eyes and met her gaze before looking away.

"Tynan?" Bryna knelt before him, terrified to her very core. Black ribbons of hair clung from the sweat at his temples down his chest and arms and back.

"Look at me," she said, hoping desperately that he would obey her.

His nostrils flared, sucking in the moist air.

Slowly, he met her eyes. Dark sensual magic held her. She felt like she was looking in upon a sea of misery.

"This is your *geas*?"

He nodded slowly, a stranger looking upon her with Tynan's eyes. Reaching up, she tangled her fingers in the hair at his temples. To her horror, a blood red tear gathered and fell down his cheek.

"I am faery, Tynan. Your body recognized what I

am before I did. Mayhap your territorial goddess can forgive me, for I can no longer bear witness to your pain. Claim me, as is your right."

His lips parted in a harsh breath.

"Claim me," she said more softly. "Ease this torment that drives you to madness."

"Be certain." His haunted gaze searched her face. "There is no going back once I touch you."

Bryna prayed the goddess of her dreams would understand and forgive her. "I am," she replied.

"Forgive me," Tynan said, and his mouth clamped over hers in claim, demanding her compliance, forcing her back upon the cold ground.

She clutched at his shoulders.

"*Daoine Sidhe*," he breathed fiercely against her lips. "You are mine."

The last vestiges of control were gone now.

He swept her up in his arms and carried her to the back of his roundhouse. They fell together on the bed. Around them, the air crackled with humidity and the rainstorm's windy fury.

He shifted above her and stripped off his sweat-stained breeches.

"Kiss me, faery." Hunger pulsed through his blood. "Let me taste your magic."

His mouth took hers while the winds bayed outside and rain poured from the dark sky, pummeling the roundhouse.

His hands stroked her body, memorizing every

delicious curve and hollow. At her hip, Tynan grasped the delicate red fabric that seemed spun of faery webs. It pulsed in his hand, a tingling sensation of heat and ice. Blue wisps of light danced behind his eyes and then the air stirred. His hand came away, taking the enchanted gown with it.

Tynan broke the heated kiss and glanced down. The gown floated to her side, leaving her gloriously naked before him.

Bryna felt the cool air against her skin. Suddenly frightened, she pushed against his chest. His lips settled over her swollen mouth in response. His tongue thrust in, demanding her surrender and taking possession.

Callused hands found the weight of her breasts and kneaded the silken flesh. Fingers teased her nipples into hurtful peaks and then he broke the kiss, his lips blazing a moist trail down her throat.

Flicking his tongue out, Tynan stroked the satiny pink nipple and drew it hungrily into his mouth, suckling her.

Her shocked cry rippled through him, fueling his compulsion and lust. He cupped her other breast.

Bryna closed her eyes in unbelievable pleasure. Her hands tangled in a waterfall of black hair, holding him to her, wanting more. Heat licked at her breasts and she writhed under him in chaotic desire.

He pinned her slender hips to the white pelts with his thigh. His left hand released her breast and skimmed down the curve of her stomach to her auburn down. One finger delved into her swollen petals and Bryna gasped at the burning tightness.

He stroked her there, a terrible yearning pouring into her womb. She pushed down against his hand, wanting.

He shifted, pulling his hand away and settling his hips between her thighs.

"Take me," he rasped, and Bryna felt his heavy arousal pressing into that secret place.

With one quick thrust, he buried himself deep in her velvet sheath, breaching her innocence. She cried out in surprise and momentary pain . . .

Tynan did not hear her.

His *geas* had triggered a bestial response in him.

Waves of lust began to beat at his body.

Lost in sensations he could not control, he thrust harder into her sheath, her body yielding to his demands. Urgency flared, unleashing the blaze low in his belly. It consumed him, muscles bunching, wet, tight, deeper and deeper, until . . .

He flung his head back in ecstasy.

His body exploded, pleasure so intense he could not breathe while his seed pumped into her faery womb.

The compulsion released him.

The fey conception had been made.

Awareness flooded him instantaneously.

Against his chest, soft sobs were muffled, piercing his soul.

"Hush, faery," he soothed, kissing her tear-stained face, guilt riding him hard. He caressed her trembling body with calming strokes.

She tried to shift out from under him.

"Bryna, stay with me." He kissed her throat and collarbone.

"Nay, Tynan."

The anguish in her voice tore through him.

Small hands pushed at his chest.

He kissed her ear, tasting the delicate salty shell. "For you, faery." He moved his hips, his body already hardening by design, a promise kept in the aftermath of the compulsion. Slow, sultry, continuous strokes meant for her pleasure alone.

Startled, she looked up at him.

"Your pleasure," he murmured.

Tears streamed down her cheeks and he captured them with his tongue. "Feel me inside you."

She did. Heat began to spread through her, replacing the discomfort that came before. A tender throbbing began in her womb, a different blooming this time.

"Aye," he whispered roughly, his body moving above hers. "For you, Bryna. The compulsion is over."

His hand cradled her head. He kissed her, coaxing her mouth open to accept his gentle invasion. His warm tongue stroked a response from her while his manhood bore longer and deeper into her womb.

She whimpered, rocking under him, struggling to match his steady rhythm.

"Please Tynan, I need..." She spread her legs wider, aching for more. His hips slowed, grinding deeper inside her moist heat, prolonging it, making her . . .

Bryna gasped. Pleasure and brilliance seared through her body, through her blood. He pumped into her, her hands catching at his sweaty shoulders. She writhed in heat and ecstasy unlike any sensation she had ever felt before.

Tynan flung back his head and roared in triumph.

She was his.

Belonging only to him.

Finally.

CHAPTER 11

GRAYNESS EVAPORATED INTO A NIGHT quenched with low hanging stars.

Tynan awoke with a sense of harmony unlike any he had ever known. It settled inside him, a gathering of tranquility and calm, of mornings drenched in dew, of nights caressed with moonbeams, of all things that peace can and should be.

He listened to the echo of the new quiet and silently thanked the mother goddess for his faerymate. Outside, the rain-soaked land slumbered serenely within the cool eve.

They had slept and made love throughout the rainy afternoon.

A myriad of white candles burned low on the trestle table. Yellow flames flickered, creating shadows upon the walls. Wax dripped into tiny, irregular pools, spreading outward.

Tynan closed his eyes in contentment. His beautiful, naked faery lay sprawled on top of him. Her face was nestled in the curve of his neck, full breasts crushed to his side, a silken arm and leg thrown over him in complete abandon.

He caressed her lower back with slow, steady

strokes, marveling at the smooth texture of her skin beneath his fingertips.

Brushing her forehead with his lips, he inhaled her fragrance. The scents of their mating sweat lingered. He took it deep in his lungs and felt himself harden with the memory of her unearthly passion, rapture beyond anything experienced except, perhaps, only in dreams.

She fulfilled him in all ways.

They would do well together.

Tenderly, he brushed a stray curl from her flushed cheek.

Her breathing quickened, a sign of awakening. He felt the delicate flutter of lashes against his neck and slowly she pulled back to look at him.

"Faery," he murmured, seeing how she searched his face.

"The blackness is gone, Tynan. You are at peace?"

"Aye, forevermore." He looked in awe upon the swirling grays and silver threads in her eyes. Her reddened lips were slightly swollen from the force of his kisses. Auburn lashes, tipped with gold, fluttered down, hiding her thoughts.

For a moment, guilt surged in him, raw and painful, a spear wound in the heart. He'd taken her innocence, an animal locked in lust.

She must have seen it in his face, for she touched his cheek.

"Nay, Tynan. 'Tis the way of a virgin mating.

Derina told me of this first time pain. I wanted you, guilt has no place here."

"Bryna, my heart." His fingers stroked her back in a long caress. "If given a choice, know that I would have chosen you for my goddess mate."

Light and warmth ebbed from her eyes. "If given a choice, I would have chosen you too." She looked away. Her lips parted, then closed without a sound. Inhaling shakily, she pulled away and sat up.

Tynan supported himself on his elbow. "Bryna, talk to me. Whatever this is, this dread that leeches color from your skin, I'll make it right."

"You canna make it right. Only I can, Tynan." Bryna knew this all too well. With her growing awareness of her faery spirit, she understood things on a level beyond mortality.

The land whispered and she heard.

A link of profound longing pulsed, of a union forbidden and of a territorial goddess that waited, held captive in a dank tomb.

"I dream, Tynan."

"What do you dream?"

She looked up at him, this naked faery king enticed into a mortal world. Confusion glittered within the gold shards in his amethyst eyes; confusion and suspicion.

"You must listen to what I have to say."

He shifted on his hip. The pelts slipped down his body, revealing the hard planes of a smooth chest, and a rippling stomach. A stream of dark hair flowed down from his navel and disappeared beneath the furs. Bryna knew the dark nest of pleasure at the end, knew the surge and feel of him between her thighs.

"I will listen," he murmured.

"For many months now I have dreamed of a golden territorial goddess with white lace wings. At first, she kneels in a glade beside a black rain pool. In her hand, she crushes a pink flower, a sign of her displeasure with me."

"With you?"

"Aye, with me."

"Go on."

"In the glade, bars of red fire sprout from the land and lock her in a cage of night. I feel her surprise and rage. She is confined against her will, Tynan."

He said not a word and Bryna felt a sense of doom seeping into her soul.

"You are the Dark Chieftain of the *Tuatha Dé Danann*." She paused to gather her courage. "The ancient lord of Kindred destined to restore loyalty and bounty to the land who must . . ."

"I know this. Tell me of what bothers you."

Bryna clutched the pelts to her breasts. "You must mate with the territorial goddess, Tynan. I am not she The golden one in my dreams is your true mate."

She met his gaze and then looked away.

Tynan stilled.

Silence fell in dark waves about him.

He did not answer right away.

His heart and body disagreed with her declaration. She was his territorial goddess.

He could not feel this way for another.

"You are of faery," he stated firmly and with control.

"I am of faery. I see and feel of things you canna imagine. But I am not your territorial goddess, Tynan."

"Why did you agree to handfast with me?"

Tears welled in her eyes. "To stop your suffering. For your need I handfasted with you, and for my own need as well."

Tynan rose slowly from their bed and went to the roundhouse's entrance to stare out. His body vibrated with tension, gone was the peace that saturated his heart only moments before. He looked up. Stars lit the night sky.

"How can you not be my territorial goddess when my body feels sated and whole?"

"I doona know. Mayhap you responded to my faery blood."

Tynan could not imagine a lifetime without her, sharing the joys of living, bearing his sons and daughters. How could something that feels right be wrong?

"How do you know you are not my goddess?" he demanded, glaring back at her. "You cried out your pleasure in my arms and the storm winked out, leaving only the stars. The night approves of our joining." He gestured outside. "The air approves." He pointed to the ground. "The land pulses with joy beneath my feet."

He watched her. Naked beneath his pelts, she looked small and vulnerable, a wee girl, unsure in her lover's bed.

"How can you not be my goddess?" he demanded.

She shook her head.

"Please explain it to me."

"I canna explain it. 'Tis a shimmering that fills the emptiness inside me. Why would the golden goddess come to me in my dreams?"

"What does your faery spirit say? What does the golden goddess say?" he asked very softly. "I must know."

"Tynan," she began shakily, then stopped.

"What does she say to you?"

"She has never spoken to me, only looked upon me with eyes of liquid amber. Her tresses are of pale sunlight and her wings are of delicate lace."

"I care not what she looks like." He took a step back into his roundhouse. "You are uncertain, Bryna."

"I am not. She is your territorial goddess."

He looked away and did not question her further.

She was faery bred, attuned to the land, loch and sky. She knew.

But why did his body and blood recognize Bryna as his territorial goddess?

Why did calm replace the torment of his *geas*?

Somewhere a mistake had been made.

He turned back to the crisp, dark night. Outside the thicket of thorns beside his roundhouse glimmered silver in the moonlight. A humid breeze rustled the entrance flap of animal skin beside his shoulder. In silent fury, he cursed the first Faery Queen that had forced his ancestor to take a faery mate.

"She is confined at Kindred, I think," Bryna spoke from behind him, "with the other faeries."

"Are you sure?" he asked.

"Aye, I am."

He waited for her to say something more, but she did not. He would not forswear the promise, nor would he give Bryna up. If the territorial goddess was among the imprisoned faeries, so be it. She would not be his goddess. He had made his claim.

He glanced back over his shoulder.

His faerymate would not look at him. Her head bowed, burnished gold curls tumbled in disarray about her pale shoulders.

He ached to hold her.

Tynan crushed down the need and focused.

No longer dazed by the fey compulsion, a plan to reclaim his future quickly took form in his mind.

"Bryna, can you tell me about the feypaths? Is there a marker of some kind to show their location?"

She seemed to grow paler, cold with certainty that he would now set her aside. She looked up at him, her eyes dull and bruised.

"There is a marker for them and you touched it in the dungeon, remember?" she prodded gently.

He thought back a moment, feeling the remembered sensation of it in his hands. "A rock smooth to the touch and shaped in a half-moon?"

"Aye, the half-moon rock feels smooth to the hand. It looks like a dark purple crystal when cleaned. Sometimes, if you walk by it at just the right moment, a blue-white light can be seen. My teacher calls the fey light moonbeams."

"Do you know the location of the half-moon rocks?"

"I know only a few but they exist along the storm swept cliffs, in caves hidden by bracken, and in secret places along the deserted moors. All lead to the ancient feypaths beneath the land."

He nodded, turning away from her to stare out into the night. "How did you come to know of the feypaths? The knowledge was lost to my people long ago."

"Derina showed me."

"The old druidess with no eyes? She sees more than most men."

"Aye. She knows of many things, but I doona know how she knows of them."

He nodded. Someday he would talk to this druidess and find out how she knew of things belonging only to his people. For now though, he must turn his mind toward what lay before him. "Bryna, the time has come for me to retake Kindred. There is much preparation to be done. I must leave for a few days and make ready."

"I understand. What has been will never be again."

He looked back at her, his eyes narrowed slightly at her down turned face. "This is not over between us, faery."

Tynan left, welcoming the embrace of the dark night. He headed for the woodland's icy stream.

CHAPTER 12

NIGHT FELL UPON THE LAND and the full moon rose in shades of buttery yellow that called to the nocturnal creatures in silky whispers.

Tynan strode quietly into the woodlands, dressed in black. In his right hand, he carried his best battle weapon. The sword was well oiled, the iron blade reflecting like a still pool of rainwater. The blood groove, down the center, had been made exact and true to catch the enemy's blood. In his left hand, he held his shield. In the metal were the etched runes in the language of his faery brethren, a blessing of protection and strength.

With these in hand, he strode forward, his heart heavy in his chest.

Across his path spilled the glow of the moon and the long shadows of the massive tree trunks of the ancient oaks. Three gray wolves studied him from behind a grouping of fine-grained yew trees. Their amber eyes glittered with enhanced intelligence.

"Be at rest, I come to speak to our brethren and do not breach your territory." It was a strange thing that he did not fear the predators of the woodlands. They were faery bred, like him, like the other creatures that made this place their home.

The sweet, seductive call of the night filled his senses with longing — for her, still.

Two days had passed since leaving her bed.

Two days since he had felt the rapid beat of her pulse against his own.

Two days since her hips had met his thrusts. He could not free his mind of her, which only confirmed his belief.

She was his goddess.

Somewhere, a mistake had been made.

A mistake that he would rectify.

He walked into the silent beauty of the fey clearing and stopped. A light mist swirled in greeting around his ankles, rising to his calves in a tender caress. Before him, the enchanted well waited. Gray stones, more ancient than time, were slashed with silver shards of light.

The thicket of thorns glimmered at the well's base. Thorns were the faery mark of possession like the golden shards in his eyes.

He looked up. Silence surrounded him. It seemed the animals of the woodlands waited too for a sign of the magic that pulsed so richly in the fey land.

"I come to ask thee for help." Tynan dropped down to his knees. Warmth immediately seeped up his thighs. Beneath his black tunic, his chest bore the runes of Kindred in blue dye. He wore a gold torc about his neck and gold and silver arm bands. At the waist of his breeches rested his jeweled dagger.

He laid the heavy shield on the ground by his side. With two hands, he gripped the hilt of his sword and pointed the blade to the sky. Closing his eyes, he prayed silently to the mother goddess Dana for her blessing.

"Make me strong and quick, for I go to Kindred this night. Make my warriors fearless, for I go to reclaim all that has been wrongfully taken."

Heat shot into his hands.

Tynan opened his eyes.

Silvery mist swirled up his forearms, his hands, and into the sword, covering the blood groove and infusing the blade with magic and strength.

It felt like a woman's passionate caress on his skin, the sword's brass tang guard and tip glowing yellow.

"THE GODDESS DANA HEARS YOUR REQUEST AND HAS SENT ME. RECEIVE MY GIFT OF STRENGTH, DARK CHIEFTAIN." the voice of the clearing breathed in a resonance of many whispers. He could not tell if it was female or male. "FOR, YOU SHALL FIND TRUTH AND SORROW AT KINDRED, A PASSAGE OF TIME ILL SPENT, AND ALL THAT HAS COME BEFORE SHALL BE AGAIN."

Tynan bowed his head in reverence. "I accept thy gift."

The strange white mist retreated, dissipating upon the land and leaving him chilled.

"Doona leave."

At the edge of his sight, small shapes moved in the darkness. Dana's messenger may have gone, but the piskies remained.

"Little friends, I go to Kindred to free the imprisoned faeries." His hands clenched around the sword's hilt, fingers gripping the familiar hold. The blade shimmered, reflecting the amethyst and gold in his gaze, but Tynan saw only beautiful eyes of silvery mist.

"I care for her." He spoke into the nightshade and pressed his forehead to the smoothness of the cool blade. He would not give voice to his heart. He would not give the faeries a weapon with which to control him. If they took Bryna away, he could not endure it. It would be an eternal bleeding of his soul. Yet, this yearning and desire within him could be denied no longer. He hoped the piskies would understand and give in to his request.

"Help me to convince our brethren that Bryna is my true faerymate."

He listened for their answer, but only silence met his plea; they waited for him to declare his love — only then would they help. When he did not, they left, winking out into the night.

The glimmering in the clearing faded and Tynan bowed his head.

He nodded once and climbed to his feet.

It was the first day of *Eanair,* January, known as the "cold air" month, known too as the dead month, and Bryna felt the chill of apprehension.

The woodlands, a place of eternal magic and mist, could only be seen by those favored by the faeries. So, it was often said that the *Tuatha Dé Danann*, the faery tribe, lived in the bark of trees, underneath boulders and in the clear waters of the sun-drenched streams. It was a place of elemental currents very similar to the ancient feypaths where promises were often broken.

Before golden light touched the wintered land, the final wave of noble warriors moved silently through the ancient feypaths leaving the old females and children behind in the protection of the faery woodlands.

Many hours had passed since Lord Tynan and the first and second waves of warriors traveled the fey-paths to attack the fortress.

Bryna could wait no longer.

She found Edwin making ready with the third wave that would back up the attack.

"Edwin?" she said, planting herself in front of him.

He looked up. "My Lady?" He returned his dagger to its sheath at his waist and picked up his round shield. "You should not be here. We leave for the feypath. "

"Aye, and I go with you."

"Nay, I think not, my Lady." Though his words were resolute, his face had colored a wee bit.

"I go with you Edwin, or I go without you," she stated. "Either way, I go to Kindred."

Above the hills, storm clouds had gathered in

menacing shapes of dark gray, reflecting her mood.

Edwin looked up at the swiftly darkening sky and swallowed hard. "Aye, my Lady. I can see that."

The feypath Tynan had chosen smelled of mold and decay.

Bryna coughed from it, walking behind Edwin at the end of the line of warriors. Tynan's tribesmen had refused to let her lead, so she contented herself with following even if she was the last person to arrive.

"The stink worsens," someone muttered up ahead.

She agreed, but thought the smell nothing unusual. Derina often remarked on the unearthly stink, saying it bore the faeries' taint of spitefulness. "Spitefulness for what?" Bryna had asked. "It is spitefulness born out of envy," her teacher had replied, but never explained.

Now she covered her nose and mouth, shaking her head at the foul air and focused on the path ahead.

Thin rock formations hung from the stone ceiling, dripping tears of milk. Beneath their feet, black pebbles crunched in the soil.

"By the light of the faeries, it stinks in here," Edwin complained hoarsely in front of her. "How much worse can it get?"

"Far worse," Bryna answered, knowing it for truth. "Doona think of it."

Like the rest of the men, Edwin wore a gold neck ring and matching arm bands. Blue dye marked their naked chests in the runes of Kindred. All wore daggers sheathed at their waists and gripped swords and shields in their hands.

Up ahead, the feypath narrowed, causing several of the larger men to crouch and grumble.

Bryna tried to look over Edwin's shoulders. "Have we reached the change in the fey light?"

"Aye, it appears up ahead. It is as you said, the strange light guides us."

Lavender light permeated the feypaths. Mysterious and flowing, it thrived in the shadows, a symbiotic life not of this world. Yet, the closer to Kindred one came, the lavender deepened, shades of violet and plum, an opulence not seen before.

Bryna felt the light on her face, felt all things in this path that were of intolerance and faery. In preparation for her journey with the warriors, Rose had woven sprigs of rowan into her hair to ward off the evil. It was the only concession she agreed to. For, unlike the rest of the warrior women that preceded them, she avoided the girdles of chain and other personal adornment, choosing instead to wear her old gray gown in case of capture. She reasoned, if the Roman's believed her taken against her will, she might be able to help Tynan and his tribe.

"Verra close," one of the men called up ahead, his voice lost in the cry of the winds that lived in the tunnels near the sea. The unearthly lament echoed in their ears, hauntingly beautiful, sending chills down Bryna's spine.

"I doona like this." Edwin planted a hand against the wall. "The tunnel narrows up ahead."

"The feypaths were not intended for the big men of the faery tribe, but for the willowy shape of the faeries. It worsens the nearer we are to the fortress," she reassured as best she could.

He looked at her, strands of red hair blowing across his youthful face. "How do you know, my Lady?"

She pushed aside her hair and tapped an ear. "Listen, Edwin. You can hear the echo of the sea crashing into the cliffs below the fortress."

He looked back down the tunnel. "With this wind, I can barely hear it."

"We are close, trust me."

They continued to follow the path marked by the three stone markers of those who went before. Steps quickened, a feeling of anxiousness filtered down the ranks.

Bryna felt it too, except . . .

The sound of the winds had changed.

She listened, warm air lifting her hair off her nape and shoulders.

Red fire and crystals flashed in her mind.

Jewels.

Red Jewels.

A faery prison.

A golden territorial goddess, enraged.

She stopped and held her head, lost in the black anger that had engulfed her mind, a mountain of red jewels and blue flames that did not burn.

"My Lady?"

Bryna struggled against the fury consuming her senses — and then it was gone, lost in the wind, lost in her mind.

She gave him a reassuring smile. "I am fine, a momentary weakness. Please Edwin, we fall behind the others."

His face showed his indecision, then he nodded. "Stay close to me."

"I will. Please, let us go."

Up ahead, the warriors had disappeared around a corner.

Edwin and Bryna hurried their steps. They came to a sharp corner and stopped. On the opposite wall, a blue shimmering half-moon rock had slid aside allowing the warriors to slip through in small groups.

"We are beneath the fortress," Bryna said excitedly.

"Aye, it will not be long now."

Waiting their turn, they stepped into the opening of the half-moon rock.

Purple darkness invaded their sight.

For a moment, Bryna felt disoriented, lost in a swirling black emptiness of envy, jealousy and resentment.

"Doona stop." Edwin tugged on her hand, pulling her with him.

They plunged out of the icy coldness into the dank dungeons of the Roman fortress.

Each breathed a sigh of relief as they regrouped with the others.

"What is that? Never have I felt such malice," one of the women warriors rasped.

"A lingering of fey and spite," Bryna explained. " 'Tis a faery realm of in-between, a rebuff that has no bearing on us."

The woman nodded, already turning toward the battle at hand. The warriors began to disperse, according to their lord's battle plan.

Edwin moved closer to her. "I will see you safely to Lord Tynan, my Lady."

Bryna knew the youth would not leave her side. She looked around. Far larger, this dungeon looked older than the one she had rescued Tynan from.

Torches burned on the walls, sucking up the cool shadows with orange and blue flames. She stepped out into an empty corridor. The temperature this far below ground felt cool and damp against her skin, a constant no matter the weather above. Beads of moisture glistened on the gray stone of the walls. At their feet, rats scurried around corners, upset by this latest invasion into their domain.

She looked down the corridor. Metal gates hung open on their hinges, gaping jaws of death.

"I told you to wait in the woodlands."

Bryna pivoted and looked up. At the top of a flight

of stone steps, a painted savage glared down at them. Leather straps criss-crossed a glistening chest, anchoring the leather scabbard that held his sword on his back. A jeweled dagger glittered in his right hand.

"I had to come, Tynan."

His breath frosted the cold air in rapid bursts at the top of the steps. "Why did you disobey me?" he demanded.

"The faeries call to me."

"The faeries," he echoed irritably, securing the dagger at his waist. He descended, taking two steps at a time, landing beside her on silent feet.

"Is Kindred ours?" Edwin asked eagerly, coming up beside her.

"Aye, lad, except for a few pockets of resistance, Kindred belongs to us once again."

"You are hurt, Tynan?" Bryna touched his arm.

"Nay, the blood is not mine, faery." He turned his attention back to his younger kinsman. A dark brow rose, an obvious demand for an explanation.

Hastily, Edwin bowed. "Sire, I brought your faerymate to you for safe-keeping."

"In the middle of a bloody battle?"

"Sire, if I dinna bring her here, I feared she would come alone. Your faerymate is persuasive."

"You mean mule-headed, lad."

"I asked him to bring me," Bryna came to Edwin's defense.

"Asked him? I doubt that."

"If you must be angry, then be angry with me."

"I am not angry." Dark amethyst eyes slid to her. "I would have sent for you, impatient one, if you but waited."

"I could not wait. The faeries call to me." She would not deny them her help this time.

"The faeries always call; you must choose when to answer or your life is not your own." Turning back to Edwin, he gestured to the steps. "Lad, see Ian in the main hall." He squeezed the youth's shoulder. "Thank you for bringing my faerymate safely through the fey-paths. I know that could not have been easy."

Edwin bowed, then climbed up the steep steps, leaving them alone.

Bryna found herself under scrutiny. He scowled at her small smile.

"So, faery, you are here now. Tell me why you could not wait until I sent for you?"

She was about to answer when the cool air in the dungeon suddenly changed to a foul, bone-chilling cold. Torchlight flickered on the walls.

"An evil cold searches and now comes to us," Tynan muttered, looking over his shoulder.

Bryna followed where he looked and saw an entrance to a dark and ominous looking tunnel.

"Do you smell that?" She wrapped her arms around herself, shivering.

"The stench smells of death. Doona move from here." He stepped away from her to stand in front of the tunnel.

It was as if time shifted, removing all presence of life. Even the creatures that had called the dungeons their home seemed to have left rather than face this unknown sorcery.

"We are in the deepest part of the ruins near the ancient tombs." Tynan ran his right hand along the stones framing the tunnel. "It is a place long forgotten."

"Do you sense the Sorcerer, Tynan?"

He looked over his shoulder. "Do you, faery?" he asked, his voice intent.

A sick feeling of awareness stirred in Bryna's stomach. "I sense darkness and power, red jewels in blue flames that do not burn." Something horrible waited in that tunnel. "The faeries are down there, methinks."

"I do not doubt it." He turned back to the tunnel.

The unnatural cold abruptly dissipated.

Gone.

As if it had never been.

Bryna stared at Tynan's stiff back. "Have you found Derina?" she asked.

He did not answer.

"Tynan?"

He looked over his shoulder. "The old druidess?" He shook his head, coming back to her. "Not yet. My men know not to harm the sightless one."

He inspected the tunnel once again.

"What do you sense?" she asked.

"I think I hear faery calls. Their pleas for freedom are

distorted somehow." He shook his head. "I canna tell."

"We must help them."

"Aye, I will. But first, I must secure the fortress."

A fight broke out at the top of the staircase between tribesmen and a few remaining Roman soldiers. Voices challenged, bellowing out in rage and battle.

He pushed her back against the wall, instantly protective. "Stay here, Bryna. Obey me in this."

She nodded.

He raced up the flight of stone steps to aid his fighting tribesmen and then disappeared from her sight.

Bryna pushed away from the hard wall. Wiping cold sweaty palms on her gown, she stared at the tunnel with a mounting sense of urgency.

"I am here," she whispered.

Streams of white light slowly crept from the strange tunnel's entrance like the stems of flowers, budding into brilliance then fading into smooth blackness. Warmth surged into her body, so very different from the strange cold that had come before.

Her pulse quickened.

A flute's haunting melody rode the shimmering air currents, the sound unpleasant, forced and distorted to her ears.

"COME, FAERY," a faint male voice called to her in echo. "COME, BRYNA OF LOCH GUR."

She looked into the tunnel. Sloping walls glistened with moisture.

"HELP US!"

She took another step. A heavy purple mist greeted her just inside the tunnel's entrance.

"Show me the way to you."

The mist retreated into the perilous tunnel, spent waves receding from the shore.

Bryna followed.

✳✳✳

Tynan raised his sword and dispatched the last of the Roman soldiers from this earthly place. The small pockets of resistance were more of a bother to him than a burden. The fortress belonged to him now.

He forced himself to take a step back. His men swirled in over the fallen enemy and dragged the dead away. He did not like killing, but did what he must to reclaim Kindred.

The air shimmered suddenly.

His blood ran cold.

Blackness came out of nowhere and wrapped his mind in coiling malignancy. His heart pounded wildly, but not from the battle.

Wrongness.

It permeated his being.

His hand tightened on the sword's hilt.

Then he heard it, faery whispers, distorted and dark, calling her to them. *Bryna*.

Fear for her sucked at him.

"Nay," he bellowed. Pivoting, he ran back down

the flight of steps.

"Bryna!"

Too late.

He knew it even as he raced down the steps, charged toward the tunnel and crashed into an invisible wall of spellbound darkness.

Pain exploded in his limbs.

Darkness clouded his vision.

Decay filled his nostrils.

Invisible, clawed hands tore at his shoulder, sinking into his flesh and drawing blood.

Tynan raised the reassuring weight of his double-edged sword and brought it down, fighting to free himself of the Evil One's spell.

CHAPTER 13

A FEELING OF OTHERWORLDLINESS GRIPPED her, of dampness and in-between, a pulsing that predated history.

The faeries were near.

Bryna moved deeper into the shadowed tunnel, following the receding purple mist. The isolated sound of the sea warned her to go no further. On the high ceiling, roosts of insect eating bats waited for the passage of daylight, dropping feces on the tunnel's floor. Blindworms and slugs slithered around her feet in the pungent layers of bat dung, retreating from the mist and the sense of death.

"COME TO US." the faeries called urgently. "COME AND FREE US FROM THIS PLACE OF RED NIGHT."

A heavy purple mist swirled around her ankles, masking the dung and squishy sounds her shoes made. It beckoned her to quicken her pace, crawling up her legs, warming her skin; the way freezing does before death.

"I come," Bryna called. She pushed aside huge centipedes that crawled along the edges of a narrow opening and slipped through.

"HURRY."

"Have patience," she said in reproach, their calls shrill and hurtful in her ears.

The tunnel swept downhill and suddenly all forms of life disappeared. She squeezed around a stone obstruction shaped like a hunched man, the purple mist disappearing quickly ahead.

"Wait for me," she ordered.

The mist slowed its pace.

Up ahead, light appeared.

"Where does he imprison you?" she asked the mist. "Show me so I can find you."

"IN THE CENTER. WE CANNA SEE BEYOND THE BLUE FLAMES. HURRY."

Bryna hurried, tripping over fallen stones that littered the dirt path.

"IN HERE."

At the mouth of a wide cavern, the mist disappeared. She stopped, taking a moment for her eyes to adjust to the bluish light.

"Where are you?" She looked around. A feeling of openness and displacement skittered down her spine.

She stood at the mouth of a massive cavern with four white stone pillars marking the entrance. Hundreds of jagged cracks ran down the length of the floor, skirting fallen stalactites and opening into a large crater in the center of the cavern.

"IN THE CENTER!"

Bryna moved into the cavern. Enormous burn marks licked at the ragged edge of the crater.

The bluish glow providing the cavern's half-light came from the huge crater.

Bryna blinked at the wonder of it. Within the crater rose a mountain of red crystals, an astounding sight of crimson and power.

"WE BE IN HERE."

She moved to the edge of the crater of jewels and looked down. Shafts of heated air flushed her cheeks. Tiny blue flames danced and glowed in the individual jewels, gatekeepers locking the magical within. She took a deep breath to steady her heart.

"I am here." She hovered at the crater's edge. "Tell me how to free you."

"HE COMES," they warned in shrill voices. "BEWARE."

"Who comes? The Sorcerer?"

"THE BETRAYER."

She looked up.

A white robbed creature stood on the opposite side of the crater. Unmoving, like a white pillar of salt against a backdrop of blue shadows, he stared at her in predatory silence. He stood taller than most men, a gaunt frame just beginning to bend with age. Deformed feet peeked out from beneath the hem of his robe.

He bowed from the waist, a gesture of respect that surprised her.

"SHOW HIM NO WEAKNESS," the faeries warned in her mind.

Stepping back, Bryna's skirt caught on one of the

thousands of cracks that scarred the stone floor. She tugged on it, tripping momentarily on a fallen stalactite.

The Betrayer remained watchful.

Struggling to maintain her eroding calm, Bryna notched her chin up. As a slave, passiveness and insecurities had ruled her, but no longer.

She had found the imprisoned faeries. Tynan's goddess was amongst them. She must find a way to free them, and her.

The Betrayer walked around the crater. The taint of him was unmistakable, foul and unclean.

He stopped a few feet from her, this being of malicious intent, his face in blue shadow. Bryna presented a strong front. Gnarled hands adjusted the white hood and then he leaned forward slightly, sniffing at her in a strangely familiar way.

"It would seem," he said quietly, "I have found the missing faery."

"*DOONA LET HIM TOUCH YOU.*"

Bryna forced herself to look up within the hood. Black brows slashed across a skeletal face, singed gray and heavily lined. She met deep-set, violet eyes that watched her with undisguised concentration.

"You are the Sorcerer?" She forced the question through her lips. She had never seen the man's face. The question lay there in the silence, waiting for his response.

"You speak to me?" he said in swift amazement,

and then regained his self-possession. He gestured to the crater. "They doona speak to me, ever. No matter how I plead, they doona forgive."

Bryna glanced at the crater. "Why do you want the faeries forgiveness if you imprison them?"

"I forswore the promise."

"What promise?" Bryna stared at the violet color of his eyes, and the familiar slant of his mouth. Anguish tightened his features.

"A past never forgotten, never forgiven." He shook his head and sighed heavily, eyes dulled to lifelessness. "I am noble tribe. I am *Tuatha Dé Danann.*"

The Sorcerer was one of Tynan's people? She could not believe it.

"Is he here?" he asked, a trace of excitement in his tone.

"Who?" she prompted.

"The one that is mine. The one whose scent clings to your fine skin."

Tynan? "Nay," she lied softly. This fiend wanted the Dark Chieftain for some horrible purpose. "He is not here. I come alone."

"Foolish faery. Lies transform your face. You canna lie to me. No one can lie to me." His features contorted into a mask of raw hatred and Bryna took an involuntary step back.

"I want him. I want my blood back!" He waved at the jewels. "I hold the faeries forever, if need be. For the Dark Chieftain, I wait. With his death, they will have no choice but to speak to me, for only I then will have the ancient blood. The prophecy returns to what should have been, and then I shall plant my seed in the territorial goddess' womb and all shall be forgiven."

Bryna took a shaky step backwards. He was maddened.

His gaze speared her with a lurid passion. A slow smile curved his lips, a deeper understanding dawning.

"Goddess," he murmured. "You canna run now that I know your mortal form, goddess of the silver eyes." He laughed, a vile, menacing sound. " 'Tis your womb I seek. You were meant for me."

She shook her head, frightened by his directness. *What did he mean by mortal form?*

He pointed again to the red crystals. "Your brethren made me this way. Spite and willfulness, they doona forgive. Well, neither shall I."

"Doona let him touch you, Bryna."

He cocked his head. "Bryna." He said her name slowly and then offered his hand. "I will not harm you, Bryna. Come to me, my silver-eyed beauty. You are my territorial goddess, destined from birth. You shall mate with me." When she did not respond, he scowled and dropped his hand. "You deny me?"

"I am not the goddess."

A smile of tolerance curled his lips. "The Dark Chieftain believes you are."

"He is mistaken," Bryna stated firmly.

"Is he?" The Betrayer's gaze slid back to the red jewels. "You have come for the faeries, have you not? You wish to speak to them? Come, talk to them. I allow this."

With a peculiar rolling gait, he walked to the far side of the crater, creating an illusion of safety in distance. His white robe swept around him, hiding his deformed feet.

Bryna touched her temple with trembling fingers. Insistent voices called to her from within the jewels, whispers of silk and petals in a warm wind laced with urgency. She stepped nearer the edge of the crater, drawn by the blue flames. At first, she did not see them, but then her eyes caught upon movement and her senses heightened and their ethereal images materialized. They were beautiful and magically intertwined within the flames, slim as birch trunks with catlike eyes and translucent skin.

"Pretty creatures?" the Sorcerer inquired, knowingly. "I have always thought them beautiful and treacherous. You are different from them."

Bryna raised angry eyes to the Sorcerer. "Free them."

He shook his head. "I have felt their vile breath and prejudice. In a moment's whim, they condemned me." He spread his hands wide in supplication. "They lack tolerances you see."

A rock fell somewhere behind the Sorcerer and he smirked.

"Come, my Centurion friend. Come join us."

Bryna let out a startled gasp. "You."

"Witcheyes, you have caused me much inconvenience. Are you surprised that your master is not dead? I am harder to kill than these barbarians."

She struggled to remain calm. Deeply hollowed eyes focused on her with such hatred that she took a reflexive step back, only to collide with an immovable wall.

"Easy, Bryna," Tynan reassured. "I am here." Above his faerymate's bright head, his gaze locked with the Evil One. In his mind, the faeries continued to call out to him, their demands insistent and sharp.

"Demanding sprites," Tynan muttered in disgust, used to their ploys. "They have no patience."

"Nay, they do not," the Sorcerer agreed, which did not surprise Tynan in the least. He had always suspected the Evil One was bound to the faeries in some way.

"Tynan." His faerymate whispered urgently, gripping his bloody forearm.

"I am all right." He pushed her gently behind him for safety.

"She must stay," the Evil One said firmly.

"Out of harm's way," Tynan snarled.

"Agreed. The goddess appears to care for you, great chieftain. I find it odd, but then you carry the ancient blood and it does call to them." The Evil One gestured to his left. "Have you met the invader of our land?"

Tynan looked right, taking in the cowardly Roman

who had run when his soldiers had fallen.

"At last I know who I had held in my chains." The coward shook his sword at him.

Tynan acknowledged the gesture with scorn.

"At last," the Evil One said, and Tynan turned back to his true enemy, detecting a tone of elation in the fiend's voice, a warning of the wickedness yet to come.

"I am here, Evil One. Release the faeries. Imprisoning them serves no purpose."

"It serves my purpose. Let them wait and learn patience as I have. They have grown too demanding. Did my spell hurt you, chieftain?"

"Little," Tynan said.

"A minor dalliance spell laced with darkness. I would have thought you would be injured more. 'Tis the fey blood that gives you the strength."

"No spell of darkness holds me. I see yonder rat still scurries to do your bidding."

The Centurion's swarthy face turned bright red with the insult. "Bastard."

"We must all have our servants." The Sorcerer waved for the man to stay. "My aim has always been to find you and then weaken you." He paused. "Be you mine, Tynan?"

Tynan stiffened at the familiar phrase.

"Ah, you remember my sacrificial altar."

"I remember your stink."

"Do you remember how weak you felt?" The

Sorcerer raised his arms, white sleeves billowing outward. "Remember, chieftain."

His withered voice rose in a dark incantation. Black darkness shot from his outstretched hands, wrapping around Tynan, binding him with weakness.

Tynan felt his soul withering. His sword tilted down, the tip grazing the ground. He stumbled forward, lost in the darkness . . .

With his last thought, he reached out for Bryna.

Suddenly a chant of pure beauty filled his mind. Bryna's faery voice joined his brethren in song, an instant knowing of it. Her small hand reached for his wrist.

The darkness wavered and he saw the Centurion and Sorcerer cowering. The song hurt them somehow, even as his soul returned from the encroaching oblivion. He squeezed his faerymate's hand, was whole again, and pushed her behind him. He looked up and locked glances with the repulsive fiend. A violet lunacy glared at him from across the red crystals.

His faerymate had broken the spell. He did not know how, but thought only of what he must do to save Kindred.

"Evil One," he snarled. "Is that the best you can do? A Roman rat and a weak spell?"

The fiend straightened, spittle running down his chin. "Goddess Witch, curse you."

"Your fight is with me, not her," Tynan growled. "Come and test the Dark Chieftain's sword. If afraid, end the cowardly rat who waits for your direction."

"I am the true Dark Chieftain," the Sorcerer bellowed, "I am the ancient blood liege of KINDRED, not you."

"You speak idiocy."

"Do I?" He pulled his hood back, a jerking movement of wretchedness. "Look at me, Tynan. Look at me! Doona you know me?"

Tynan gripped the sword hilt tighter. "It matters not to me by what name you call yourself."

"It matters, Tynan. I am Cormack, Lord Knight of the *Tuatha Dé Danann*." His mouth turned upward in an ugly way, both grimace and triumphant smile. "I am your father."

Behind him, his faerymate choked back a gasp.

My father? He cringed deep down inside, where all the childhood needs and weakness had hidden on his journey to adulthood. Hurt, loss, rage, and finally disbelief fought for control of his heart. He studied the cruel skeletal face and gleam of violet eyes . . . and knew the Sorcerer's words for truth. This repugnant creature was his father.

"Father," he said.

"So, you believe me?"

"I heard whispers that the Evil One belonged to the *Tuatha Dé Danann*."

"The whispers are true."

"The truth changes nothing."

"Does it not?" Cormack stepped forward, sure o his power. "Have you no questions for me, my son. Are you not curious about your mother? About wha happened to her?"

"She died," Tynan replied without any emotion. He would not let it sway him to anger and foolishness.

"Aye, by my own hand."

"Murderer." Tynan snarled an oath of fury.

"This is your fault, goddess." His father pointed at Bryna. "Your fault I fell under a mortal woman's power and broke the promise."

"Nay, 'tis your own fault," Tynan shot back. "You are a weak chieftain, Cormack, and do not deserve the promise."

"Weak, am I?"

"Aye, weak in honor and heart. Weak in strength and power that you blame a woman for your own sins and weakness."

"That creature standing behind you is not a woman. Have you seen her true form, my son? Have you gazed onto her real likeness and felt passion in your blood? Nay, you have not, or you would not defend her so."

"Weak chieftain, you see only the outside wrapping and take no responsibility for your own actions."

"I am not weak," his father hissed. "For what has been done to me, you must pay, Tynan, you who came of a mistake and should never have been born. You will not steal my right of claim. I am the true Dark Chieftain. Your blood and the blood of the territorial goddess must mingle and spill into the land as one. Then my seed shall spill into her womb."

"Come then, Father." Tynan flexed his sword. "Come meet your fate." He gave his faerymate a quick glance and turned away.

Bryna could not move.

She met the Sorcerer's enraged gaze and through his eyes saw a reflection of another form, another self, willowy and cat-eyed. It terrified her.

"Roman, bloody my goddess for the mating."

"Bryna, move!" Tynan roared, bolting toward her, but he was too late. Somehow, the Centurion had moved between them. With his sword, he swiped at her head. Bryna ducked, but he cut her back into a stream of blazing fire.

Stumbling in pain and shock, she ran around the crater.

"Fool! Doona kill her," the Sorcerer shrieked from somewhere behind.

Suddenly Tynan was there, his powerful sword protecting her from the Centurion's downward thrust.

She crawled to the edge of the crater, her body cold and trembling. Reaching behind, she felt for the wound, her hand coming away smeared with warm blood. It trickled down her rump and thigh to the soil. Everything tilted into narrowing grayness.

"COME TO US, BRYNA. COME TO US. WE CAN HELP YOU."

She blinked back hot tears.

"Goddess."

Bryna looked up into the Sorcerer's white face.

"Your mortal form is pleasing to me." A dark

lustful smile lit his face.

"Stay away from me." She scrambled back to the crater's ledge.

He followed her, bent and vengeful in his pursuit. "Why did you not come for me those years ago?"

"I doona know what you are talking about."

He came down on one knee beside her. "Did you wish to punish me for claiming another woman? If you would have but shown yourself, I would have set her aside. But you did not come! This is your fault. Now I must kill what should have come from your womb."

Bryna shook her head, leaning away from him.

"With his death, only I remain with the ancient blood, then the faeries of Kindred have no choice but to speak to me, the true Dark Chieftain. You were destined for me, Bryna, not him. When I mate with you in Tynan's blood, I shall fulfill the prophecy and be redeemed." He pulled out a small black spider from within his robes.

"Know you this, goddess?" he asked.

"Nay!"

Tynan heard Bryna's cry. He charged back to her with the Centurion shrieking in pursuit. Grabbing his father around the neck, he pivoted, pulling away from his faerymate just in time to meet the Centurion's blade.

His father kicked out in response, catching Bryna hard in the cheek. She lost her precarious position on the crater's edge, and with a startled cry fell down into the pile of red crystals, out of his sight.

The blue light of the false flames winked out.

Crystals exploded into a thousand shards.

Red light filled the cave with vindictive faeries.

"*FREE!*"

They focused on the true Dark Chieftain.

Warmth infused Tynan's battle weary body.

His wounded shoulder healed instantly.

A river of fey strength surged into him.

With a swift sword thrust, he ended the Roman leader's worthless life. The cowardly invader gurgled in shock, crumpling to the ground, dead.

Swinging around, Tynan dragged his thrashing father back to the edge of the crater.

"Bryna!" he called out.

His father panted in his arms. "She is dead! She is dead! Now both of us are doomed."

"Nay, I'll not believe it." He stared into the thick swirls of pink smoke rising from the crater.

Suddenly, the air shimmered all around them.

Faeries took form.

Unblinking eyes stared with raw malevolence in bright shades of silver, gold, and copper.

"Nay," his father spat at them. "I am the true Dark Chieftain."

The faeries hissed in unforgiving rage. Sheer wings buffeted the air in flight.

"Nay!" Tynan called out, but retribution would no

be denied. He staggered back, pulling his father with him. A deep painful droning filled his ears. Whiteness exploded in front of his eyes.

And then . . .

. . .the Evil One, his father, dissolved into gray dust and nothingness.

Tynan stepped back, his arms empty. "You had no right," he said tightly, unable to condone his father's death.

The buzzing eased.

"WE HAVE EVERY RIGHT, DARK CHIEFTAIN."

He took a deep breath. "Clear the air so that I can see," he commanded.

A warm faery wind rose in the cavern, clearing the pink smoke.

In the crater, among the shattered red crystals, Bryna lay face down, unmoving.

He took a step forward and felt an icy tingling.

Wisps of gold took form and Tynan found himself facing a creature of twilight. She stood between him and the crater where Bryna lay.

Beneath lashes tipped with silver, eyes of pure gold stared back at him, hard, fathomless, and covetous. White-gold hair waved about delicate, elfin features. A thin web-work of gold threads covered a white, wraithlike body. Wings of gold and white lace stilled on her back.

"I AM YOUR GODDESS."

Tynan stepped around her.

"Bryna!" Sheathing his sword in the leather scabbard strapped to his back, he climbed down into the crater and knelt beside his faerymate. Blood glistened from the wound on her back.

"Bryna," he whispered, terror clutching at his heart.

Her face turned slightly to him. "Tynan?"

"I am here." He kissed her cold cheek. Gently, he lifted her from the shattered jewels.

"The Sorcerer?"

"He is dead."

He felt the cool press of her face into his shoulder. "I am sorry, Tynan."

His lips brushed her forehead in response. "You are safe now, faery. Let me carry you out of here."

He fitted her in his arms, careful of her back wound, and stood.

At the crater's edge, the faeries gathered. They were slight and luminous creatures watching him with unblinking eyes.

"Are the faeries free?" his brave faerymate asked against his neck.

Tynan watched the golden goddess step forward, balancing on the edge of the crater.

She stared at him with cruel possessiveness. Wings of lace beat silently in the air, sending a chill down his spine.

"Aye," he replied softly. He held Bryna close. "They are free."

CHAPTER 14

TYNAN LEFT BRYNA IN ROSE'S safe care at Kindred. He had a promise to keep and could no longer delay.

In the fey woodlands, nocturnal creatures stirred from their sleep and stilled at the glittering faeries gathering in the clearing. It had not been this way since the first black-haired chieftain bowed and rejected the Faery Queen and she, in outrage, cast the magical *geas* upon him.

Tynan entered the clearing. He paused near an ancient oak and disrobed as was the custom. His guarded gaze swept the ancient stone well. Shards of light shimmered in silver, copper and gold from the faeries. The brightness hurt his eyes. He could just make out the tiny white roses growing between the vines and silver thorns at the well's base.

He had been born the son of a weak chieftain and understood his obligation to his tribe and to the land. Over the years he accepted it, satisfied with what he had to do. Now, he found his heart aching for a flame-haired faery with gray eyes.

With his right hand, he picked up his sword. Leaning down, he gripped the shield with his left. Naked, except for his torc and arm bands, he walked toward the primordial well and stopped several feet in front of it. Dropping to his knees, he bowed his head in supplication and waited. The ground felt hard and warm against his skin. His hair fell unadorned in a black waterfall down the tense muscles of his broad back.

Outside the woodlands, snow blew in wintry gusts, carpeting the land in a tapestry of white. Here, in this faery place amongst the great oaks, holly, and yews, spring bloomed eternal, cradled in a warm mist.

"I am here," he murmured.

A long silence came to the clearing.

"So AM I."

Tynan stiffened at the sound of the lilting voice.

He felt her move behind him, a golden and vain creature of twilight.

Her cool scent was one of *Anemone*, named Windflowers because the flowers never opened unless the wind blew. Her fragrance floated in the air, a beguiling scent of yearning and arrogance.

"You COME TO HONOR ME?" she asked.

Tynan felt the possessive brush of long tapered fingers at his temple.

"Are you the territorial goddess?" he asked. Even with his eyes closed, the otherworldly light hurt.

"How DARE YOU NOT RECOGNIZE ME, CHIEFTAIN."

His jaw tightened. "My eyes are closed, goddess."

"You NEED NOT SEE ME WITH YOUR EYES TO KNOW ME. I AM THE GEAS IN YOUR BLOOD BY ANCIENT PROMISE. You BELONG TO ME."

"BELONGED," a male voice stated from somewhere above him.

Tynan kept his eyes closed against the cutting light.

"NAY, THIS CANNA BE. HE BE MINE BY ANCIENT PROMISE, THIS DARK CHIEFTAIN. THIS ONE I CLAIM AS IS MY RIGHT," she protested.

Tynan shifted uneasily, feeling a tug at his scalp.

"THIS ONE," she murmured longingly. "I WANT THIS ONE."

A brush of gold gently smoothed through his hair. A terrible tension built in him at her continued caress. He felt golden threads weaving through his soul, trying to bind him to her.

"HIS BLOOD BOILS FOR ME. SEE THE TENSION IN HIM."

Tynan breathed in his fury. He knew she spoke to someone else, someone of power.

"ANSWER ME, CHIEFTAIN. DOES YOUR BLOOD NOT HEAT FOR ME?"

"I answer only to my goddess. I do not know if you are she."

She jerked his head back. "I AM YOUR GODDESS."

"BLODENWEDD," a voice warned. "RELEASE HIM."

Her hands slipped through his hair. Golden threads evaporated.

"STAND ASIDE," the male voice commanded.

Tynan knew the faeries gathered here to see the fulfillment of an ancient promise as they, too, suffered from his father's betrayal. From the tiny, prankish piskies who were no taller than a mouse, to the nasty spriggans with large heads, the knockers who worked underground, the gentle small people who lived in faery gardens with perfume, and finally to the good people who helped his ancestors build Kindred. They all suffered with the land.

"DARK CHIEFTAIN," the male voice commanded, "LAY DOWN THINE OFFERING."

Tynan heard the velvet compulsion in his mind and suspected the voice belonged to the dangerous Faery King.

He placed his sword and shield on the ground beside him. They were tokens of his honor and strength. He had come to fulfill his *geas* and mate with the territorial goddess. A heavy disgust settled in his body at the thought of lying with a creature of twilight and cold mist.

Bryna.

His heart and body warmed with thoughts of her. His *geas* calmed in fulfillment of her.

It felt right to be in her arms, to be sheathed in her softness. He wanted Bryna as his faerymate, not the vain, golden creature that played with his hair.

The golden creature hissed at him, sensing his thoughts. The harsh brush of her hand against his cheek warned of her displeasure with him.

Tynan turned away instinctively, his countenance hard.

"YOU SEE BLODENWEDD, HE DOES NOT LIKE YOUR TOUCH. HIS GEAS RECOGNIZES ANOTHER GODDESS."

His *geas* recognized Bryna as the territorial goddess. He had left her safe in the fortress with the rest of his tribesmen. Work had already begun on rebuilding Kindred.

"HE BELONGS TO ME BY ANCIENT PROMISE."

"BLODENWEDD, MY WHITE FLOWER, YOU BE SO YOUNG IN THE WAY OF THINGS. NO CREATURE BELONGS TO ANOTHER. EVEN THE ANCIENT PROMISE ABIDES THE HEART'S CALL."

Silence paused in the clearing.

Tynan held his breath, sensing a change in the air.

"OPEN THINE EYES, DARK CHIEFTAIN, SO WE MAY KNOW THY HEART."

Tynan forced his eyes open and stared at them. Silver, gold, and copper light shimmered and softened, no longer hurtful. The delicate petals of the purple orchids bloomed beside red yewberries, silver ferns, and fallen acorns. Black wolves walked beside boars, pigs, and badgers. Faeries sat on snails or on the backs of blue hares. Some stood in their red velvet coats. Some hovered, their sparkling diamond wings beating silently. The woodland's good people were the only ones near human size. The only ones able to mate with a mere mortal. Once upon a time, the good people were of the *Tuatha Dé Danann*, but their bonds with enchantment changed them, made them *draiochtach agus sidhe*, magical and faery.

"LOOK YOU HERE, CHIEFTAIN."

Tynan did as commanded.

Like an immortal king, a male faery with long white hair sat atop a granite boulder flanking the ancient well.

He wore a long coat of silver, black breeches, white stockings, and gleaming, silver shoes buckled with diamond drops. Silver eyes stared unblinkingly at him. Full lips curved with mocking amusement.

Tynan met the male faery's gaze. This one decided his fate.

"DO YOU KNOW WHO I AM, DARK CHIEFTAIN?"

Tynan nodded.

"I AM NUADA, FAERY KING, HOLDER OF ALL SOVEREIGNTY."

As a boy, he had heard of the great Faery King who led and won the battle against the Fir Bolg. Losing an arm, he had been replaced by Bress mac Eladan, only then to grow another arm and reclaim his sovereignty.

"I am here," Tynan said simply.

"AYE, YOU BE HERE. BUT NOT THINE HEART." Diamond eyes watched him intently. "WILL YOU LAY WITH BLODENWEDD AND GIVE HER A CHILD OF THINE LOINS TO RESTORE LOYALTY AND BOUNTY TO THE LAND?"

This is it, Tynan thought. "Aye," he replied. He would rather die nobly in battle than lay with this golden creature of twilight.

"WILL YOU LAY ONLY WITH HER?" the Faery King

asked, his tone that of taunting enjoyment. "GIVE UP THINE MORTAL LIFE AND IN SO DOING PAY FOR YOUR FATHER'S DISGRACE AND BETRAYAL?"

Tynan reeled back. He never truly understood the sacrifice of his faery *geas* until now, this moment, when his response lodged in his throat. He loved another, as his father once did. However, Tynan knew he was a stronger chieftain; his choice would not doom the land to more years of grief. His sense of honor forbade it, and he set the desire of his heart aside.

"Aye," his voice quivered only slightly when he answered. "Aye," he repeated more firmly, a willing sacrifice. "I will fulfill the promise."

Dark amusement glittered in Nuada's eyes and Tynan tensed.

"EVEN THOUGH THINE SEED TAKES ROOT IN ANOTHER GODDESS'S WOMB?"

Tynan felt his stomach drop. "Bryna."

"AYE, THAT ONE." Nuada murmured, reading the chieftain's thoughts. He wondered if the prideful mortal would follow where he led.

Blodenwedd hissed in protest. "IT MATTERS NOT."

Tynan and Nuada both ignored her. Tynan regarded the Faery King. A tiny smile curved the white-haired creature's lips, and suddenly he understood what his body had known all along.

"Bryna is my territorial goddess," he stated boldly.

"DESTINED SO." Nuada nodded in agreement. "BUT,

ALAS, STOLEN FROM US."

"I have met your faery obligation, then," Tynan said firmly.

Nuada arched a white-winged brow. *"DO YOU BE-LIEVE IT TO BE SO?"* he asked.

Tynan did not hesitate. "It is so."

"A WISE CHIEFTAIN YOU BE, THEN." Satisfied with the chieftain's answer, Nuada sat back on the boulder and straightened his long silver coat with seemingly casual indifference. He had greatly disliked the other chieftain named Cormack, a young man of insult and arrogance. In punishment, he had secretly ordered the newborn territorial goddess stolen and placed among humanfolk. It had been a foolish impulse that resounded throughout the land in hurtful ways, terrible ways that bestowed unforeseen consequences. Now, he must wait for the unfolding of time, a mingling of burdens past and obscure futures. For what had been lost long ago, had now returned.

Bryna stood on the parapets in the purple twilight of the ending day seeking solitude in her grief. They were near the end of *Feabhra*, February, the *mi na ngaoth*, month of winds, and Tynan had gone to her, had gone to his goddess.

Her heart welled in misery. She had not known it

would hurt so, this deep plundering ache inside her body. Since Tynan had left, her thoughts strayed often to the battle in the tombs and what the Sorcerer Cormack had said.

"That creature standing behind you is not a woman. Have you seen her true form, my son? Have you gazed onto her real likeness and felt passion in your blood? Nay, you have not, or you would not defend her so."

Bryna trembled inside her soul. A cloak of lavender blew about her chilled body, a chill of fear, not of cold. She inspected her hands, turning them this way and that before touching her face. "What am I?" she bitterly whispered to the winds.

In the sky above, an unearthly cry answered and she looked up. A flock of black and gray hooded crows flew, holding her attention. It was said if an unmarried girl threw stones at scald crows, she would know the direction from which her new mate would come. Bryna looked away. It was also said that scald crows were the emblem of Macha, one of the three sisters of Mor-rioghanna, goddess of battle and carnage. She hoped the battle and bloodshed were finally over and the land would grow fertile once more. She looked to the black sea, a light mist settling over the rocky cliffs, questioning her own nature.

"Child?"

Bryna turned and felt a surge of warmth. "Teacher," she replied, bowing her head respectfully. "Have the villagers moved all your things back to the cottage?"

"Aye, they did. I still say that I doona like hiding."

"They only meant to keep you safe during the battle."

"I know this and am grateful." Her teacher moved closer to the edge of the parapets and looked out with sightless eyes. "How is the wound on your back today, child?"

"It gives me little pain. Rose's herbs ease my discomfort greatly."

"At least that simpler is good for some things," the druidess said, far too sweetly.

"Teacher," Bryna said firmly.

Derina waved her hand in dismissal. "I dinna seek you out to talk of that one."

Bryna waited, her eyes becoming shadowed.

"Child, there is talk of another territorial goddess among the chieftain's people."

"I know."

"You are the territorial goddess, I say, handfasted and bedded. They all are fools."

Bryna dusted off her gray skirt without saying a word, her shoulders locked in tension.

"Is that why you stay with me in my cottage, child?"

"I like your home. It is at the edge of the village and I can see farmlands in the distance. Each morning I walk in the garden toward the western walls of the fortress where horses and cattle graze in quietness."

"Aye, bounty returns to the land joining, with the mild winter; a good spring comes this year. It is because the chieftain joined with you that this bounty comes to us once again."

"Mayhap, but it is a trial-marriage, not permanent."

"Doona take the handfasting so lightly. The land responds to you."

Bryna sighed heavily, not wishing to argue. "Let us go inside. Evening comes on fast wings and I am getting cold." She took Derina's thin arm.

The druidess pulled free in mild protest. "I can find my own way, child of the faeries. I am not blind. Not like some others in this noble tribe."

"Aye, not blind," Bryna managed a slight smile, "just willful sometimes."

"Most times."

Bryna laughed softly at that. "True."

They made their way carefully back down the wooden steps into the dusk-covered courtyard.

"My stomach rumbles in hunger," the druidess murmured in annoyance.

"Aye, I hear it." Bryna walked at the druidess' slow pace.

"The ground feels hard and cold beneath my feet."

"Mayhap you would do well to accept Rose's offering of new shoes," she suggested.

"That one only knows how to torture plants. What does she know of good shoes?"

Bryna sighed. "You must learn to get along with the simpler, Teacher. This is not like you." She returned Edwin's wave from the newly built stables. He called that he would join them in the feast hall soon.

"Who is that?" the druidess asked.

"Edwin, and doona change the subject."

Horses nickered contentedly out in the paddocks.

"Ah. He is a good one, that youth."

"Edwin is good. Teacher, did you hear what I said?" she prompted wearily. "You must learn to get along with the simpler."

"Are the mews finished, child?"

Bryna gave up and glanced left at the unfinished mews, housing for the tribe's hunting birds. The simpler and the druidess would work it out themselves.

"Nay, not yet. Mayhap another month."

"Have they prepared the gardens?"

"They appear to be worked on." Beyond the stable and mews, the inner gardens of the fortress showed signs of work for the spring planting of vegetables and herbs.

"Are we at the keep yet, child? My feet grow sore."

Bryna looked at the druidess. "I doona understand why you will not accept the shoes from Rose. Here, the steps are in front of us." She assisted the druidess up the steps. In the day's ending light, the gray stones of the keep appeared laced with slivers of silver. Well-fed wolfhounds, set loose to act as watchdogs, barked in greeting at their heels.

"Leave the dogs alone." The druidess gestured, more with impatience than any malice.

"I have seen you feed these dogs with table scraps.

I doona think a simple pat will do any harm. Why are you so bad-tempered this eve?"

"I am, always grouchy when I am hungry."

Bryna climbed the remaining steps and pushed at the tall doors. They swung open easily on newly oiled hinges.

She followed her teacher in. "Smells like sweet cakes."

"Tell me what you see, child. Have they finished the clean up?"

"Wall torches flicker on clean white walls. Tapestries are hung on either side of the great hall. I have seen the repair of the two natural spring enclosures within the tombs. Cisterns and large tanks are to be constructed. In the storage area, rooms fill with honey and acorns. Large quantities of firewood, hemp, dry wool, and rags are being stocked for the poulticing of wounds."

"A wise chieftain."

"Aye," Bryna agreed. "In front of us the servants carry platters of steaming food to the feast hall. Do you wish to go in?"

"My stomach wishes it, even if I do not."

Bryna looked toward the hall in thoughtfulness. "Teacher, I am not really hungry this eve. I will see you at the cottage later."

"Nonsense, child. We go through this every night. You are handfasted to the chieftain. Your rightful place is here in this hall."

"It is a trial-marriage, a temporary madness," she re-joined, but there was something else too. She had not felt right of late and wished only to lie down and rest.

Her teacher snorted in displeasure. "Madness. Bah. If you did not show up, that Hawkboy would come and find you anyway. Now, let us go in before I faint of hunger."

Bryna bit her lip and nodded. "As you wish." They walked the length of the entrance hall to the feast hall. Many of Tynan's warrior tribesmen had come for the evening meal. Others, with families, chose to stay at home and end the day among themselves.

"Is the fire lit, child? My bones rattle."

Bryna glanced at the hearth. The druidess seemed to complain a lot these days; Bryna could only attri-bute it to her age. "Aye, a roaring fire sends heat and light from the hearth. Trestle tables and benches have been set in rows."

"The same as last eve?"

"More tables, methinks."

"Here, Bryna!" Hawk waved from the long table on the dais.

"I doona smell him. Is he clean?"

Bryna laughed softly. "Aye, my teacher. The boy is clean."

"A first, I must say. Usually I can smell him from across the meadows."

Bryna guided the druidess past the other long tables to the dais.

Hawk sat at the head in his father's large wooden chair in a clean green tunic and breeches. He stood in welcome upon their approach.

"How do I look, Bryna?"

"Most fine, Hawk." She turned in greeting to the simpler.

Rose sat on the boy's left in a gown of dark blue wool. Sprigs of dried rosemary and holly adorned her gray streaked braids.

"Good eve, Rose," Bryna said.

"Good eve, Bryna," the simpler replied warmly, her blue eyes dipping right. "And to you, ancient one."

Derina grumbled something about interfering simplers and Bryna pinched her teacher's arm, warning her to behave.

"Bryna, sit here next to me." Hawk pulled out the empty chair to his right.

"I think not, Hawk. That chair is meant for your father's new faerymate."

The boy frowned looking down at the chair and then back to her, a child's confusion mirrored in his brown eyes.

"Bryna, Hawk has waited to take his meal with you." Rose gestured to the chair. "Please, sit and join us."

"Oh, do sit, child, and stop making a fuss," her teacher said tightly, taking her seat beside the simpler.

Bryna could see there was no hope for it. She made her way around to Hawk and took the seat.

"The tribe elders are in meeting, so I am the lord in charge."

Bryna smiled. "What of Ian? I thought your father left him in charge."

"I have his permission."

"Oh, well, then I must obey."

The boy beamed and returned to his seat.

A servant carrying a trencher of meat moved between her and Hawk. They were serving roasted boar this eve with pudding and pancakes. Her stomach rolled into revulsion. She looked away while the servant filled the platter she would share with Hawk. Over the past few weeks, food smells made her unwell.

She must have noticeably paled, for immediately a goblet of warm milk and honey was thrust into her hand with an order to drink.

Too queasy to argue, Bryna took a sip. Sweetness flowed down her throat, easing the nausea.

Opening her eyes, she set the goblet down on the table and found everyone looking behind her.

"Better, faery?"

The Dark Chieftain had returned.

She dropped her hands in her lap. "Aye, Tynan. My thanks." She bent her head, unwilling to turn around and meet his new faerymate. She felt fragile suddenly and wished only to retire.

"Welcome home, Father." Hawk rose from the chair and slid in beside the simpler in his customary seat, that is, when he did not take supper with the other tribe children. "Please, sit and tell us of the faeries."

Bryna held still, every nerve in her body strung taught with tension. The Dark Chieftain of Prophecy, of fate and of future, moved to her left and took his seat like any mortal would. She could not take her eyes from him.

"The faeries remain the same as always, Hawk," he answered in that deep velvet voice that she had missed.

"Did you meet the Faery King?" the boy prompted.

"Aye. I met Nuada."

"What is he like and what . . .?"

With Tynan conversing with his son, Bryna glanced over her shoulder and saw only empty space. Behind her, a tapestry of four white horses hung, their flowing manes braided with silver ribbons.

She turned back slowly, confused by the absence of his new faerymate.

"Are you well, faery?"

His violet eyes were watchful and intent and all she could think of was how she missed him. "I am well."

"Does the wound on your back still give you pain?"

"Rose's herbs speed the healing."

"I am glad to hear it." He turned the platter around so that the choicest portions faced her. "Are you hungry, Bryna? The food looks verra good this eve."

She stared at the offering in his hand and swallowed hard. No way could she even think about eating that.

"She retches," Hawk replied, plopping a piece of

meat in his mouth.

Bryna looked up and saw Rose correct the boy with a swat on the arm.

"Well, she does!" he said indignantly, rubbing the spot.

"Retches?" Tynan murmured, and Bryna found herself once more under scrutiny.

She reached for her goblet and sipped the honeyed milk. "I eat well enough. I am not used to the richness of the food."

"It is the same as any other day, Bryna."

"I am not hungry."

"Tell us about the faeries, father," Hawk interjected, and Tynan turned back to his son, giving her a small respite. Bowing her head, she took a shaky breath, battling a new onslaught of queasiness.

All around her people seemed to move in slow motion.

She saw Tynan nod to Rose's question.

" 'Tis done," he answered and Bryna wondered what had been done.

In her graying vision Hawk stood up, his youthful face pinched in worry.

"I doona want a faery for a mother," he decreed loudly. "I want Bryna!"

Bryna closed her eyes and fainted into her pudding.

CHAPTER 15

THE SOUND OF THE RAIN woke her.

She lay in a large bed under a pile of white furs. The ceiling above showed runic symbols etched in fading black ink at its center.

Bryna closed her eyes and listened to the soothing sound of the rain outside. She liked the way Derina's herbs scented the air with a soothing fragrance. Turning on her side, she snuggled deeper in the warm pelts.

"Do you intend to sleep another day away?"

Her eyes flashed open. She bolted upright in bed; white furs tumbled to her lap.

"Tynan?" She blinked, trying to focus. He relaxed in a black chair beside a hearth.

"I frightened you, faery?"

"I dinna expect you to be here."

"Where else would I be this early in the morning?" he rejoined softly.

"In your bedchamber at Kindred."

"This is my bedchamber, Bryna. Look around you."

Upon the walls opposite the hearth, two large tapestries graced the walls. At the foot of the bed, batches of dried fragrant herbs lay upon a massive chest of blond wood.

She rubbed her temple. "What happened?"

"You fainted in your pudding the day before yesterday."

"I have been here since then?" She could not believe it.

"Aye."

"I doona remember how I got here." A trace of panic tinged her voice.

"Easy, faery, I carried you."

"Oh."

From beneath lowered lashes, she looked around once more, only to confirm her fears. "This is your bedchamber?" What must his golden goddess faery-mate think?

"Our bedchamber," he corrected.

She did not understand that comment and looked back at him.

The hair, drawn away from his face, added a sensual tone to his features in the morning's light. He wore a black tunic and breeches. His long legs were crossed at bare ankles in repose. On the table beside him, he caressed a copper goblet.

"Are you chilled?" he asked, taking a sip of ale, his gaze never leaving her. "I will add more wood to the fire."

Bryna glanced down at her nakedness and gasped. She jerked the furs up to cover herself. "Where are my clothes?"

"You doona need clothes to sleep, faery."

He set the goblet back down on the table. At his elbow, a clay bowl topped with a black wick waited to be lit.

Behind him, she could see the window. Outside, the gray rain gave way to heavy, white snowflakes.

" 'Tis snowing," Bryna remarked.

He glanced over his shoulder. "Do we talk of the weather now?" His dark brow rose in mild annoyance.

Bryna understood his displeasure, but not his actions. Why did he bring her to his bedchamber if he wanted to be with his golden faerymate? His *geas* meant an obligation to her, a compulsory obligation that was no longer necessary. She was no longer necessary.

Clutching the white pelts to her breast, she shifted to the edge of the bed, farthest from him, not realizing that she offered him an enticing view of a white back and dimpled buttocks.

"The wound on your back is almost healed, faery."

"Aye." Her toes touched the cold wood floor and she shivered.

"Bryna, what are you doing?"

"I-I must leave."

"I doona think so."

"OH!" Strong arms wrapped around her. Muscles flexed and she abruptly found herself in the center of the large bed, positioned under him.

Bryna swallowed and looked up. "I must leave

here, Tynan."

"Why?"

"I doona want to cause you dishonor with your faerymate. I should not be here."

His head tilted, a wolfish smile came to his lips. "You would never cause me dishonor, Bryna." He nuzzled her cheek. "I have missed you. It has been too long between us."

Bryna sucked in her breath and pulled back. He sat up and with a quick jerk, the black tunic flew over his head.

"Nay, 'tis wrong," she argued, but not as strongly as she should. Next, he stood, removed his breeches and came back to the bed. Leaning over her, his powerful arms braced on either side of her head.

"We are handfasted, Bryna," he breathed against her lips. " 'Tis never wrong between us." His tongue skimmed her lips and slid inside, sending sparks of fire into her bloodstream. He tasted of sweet cakes.

She kissed him back, clutching at his shoulders, unable to help herself. He groaned in her mouth, tasting of male need and once more positioned his body over her.

Bryna forgot about his golden goddess faerymate.

Forgot about honor and ancient promises.

All the discomfort and nausea she suffered those days since he had left melted away, replaced by pleasure and a warm ache.

His weight settled over her, hips rocked against

the furs protecting her woman's softness.

"Faerymate," he breathed, kissing her cheek, her temple. "Take me."

Faerymate. The word stuck in her head. Need and pleasure ebbed and Bryna turned away.

He lifted his head, blinking through a thick haze of male desire.

"Please, let me go." She placed a firm hand against his chest. "I will not betray your faerymate."

"My faerymate?" he echoed and grinned. "Nay, I canna let you go."

She looked back at him in disbelief. "You would force me?"

"Nay, faerymate, I but give you what you need."

"Tynan," she said in exasperation, "I am not your faerymate."

"We are handfasted, do you deny this?"

"I do not."

His head lowered in response, warm satiny lips brushed at her ear.

Bryna shoved at his chest. "Stop. I canna think when you do that."

He acquiesced with a silent nod, and traced his lips down the slim column of her throat.

Grabbing a handful of hair, she jerked his head back.

"Ouch," he murmured.

She stared into his crinkling eyes, finding no humor in the situation. "The golden one is your territorial goddess and your faerymate, is this not so?" She would have her answer.

"Nay, faerymate."

Bryna released his hair, searching his face. "I doona understand you."

"Forgive me, I should have told you. Mischief on my part. Bryna, you are my territorial goddess, stolen from your true destiny and raised in the mortal way. My *geas* and body recognized you before my mind did."

Bryna could not move.

"See the growing darkness in my eyes, faery? It is our bond, a showing of my desire for you. From your womb, I will build a kingdom of dawn."

"How can this be?"

"Look at me, faery." His voice was soft and compelling in the morning silence.

Bryna turned back to him.

"Search your heart, you know I speak the truth of it."

"But, I dreamed of another . . ."

"Aye, there is another," he agreed acidly, "young, golden-eyed, and self-indulgent. She took the place of the one stolen."

"She is the territorial goddess?"

"Aye, but not mine." He kissed her cheek. "Tell me what you feel, faerymate."

"Uncertainty."

"Then let me remove your doubt. Fulfill the ancient promise with me." He urged against her lips. Shifting, he pulled the furs out from between them. "Welcome me into your body, goddess."

He kissed her then, a kiss of forever and pledges long ago made. She spread her legs, welcoming him into her feminine cradle. The moisture of her arousal bathed the tip of his manhood and his body tightened in response. Bracing above her, he entered her body in a slow slide of seduction. His hips moved leisurely, building a cauldron of fire in her. Deeply, repeatedly, he thrust into her until she arched in a hot, liquid frenzy.

Bryna tossed on the pillow, whimpers escaping her throat. Her legs wrapped around his hips, urging him on.

Sweat glistened on their straining bodies.

Deep strokes.

Deeper still into her gliding heat.

Fiery contractions rippled in her womb.

Gasping, she cried out his name. Her body convulsed against him in a shower of blinding rapture and soul-piercing passion.

Tynan grasped her hips, deepening his thrusts to prolong her pleasure until she sobbed uncontrollably.

Then he surged into her one last time, lost in the throes of a splintering male possession.

Bryna awoke slowly to an empty bed.

The snow had stopped outside and bright afternoon sunlight filtered to the planked floor. Memories of Tynan's touch sent a warm ache through her.

She was his territorial goddess, his faerymate, destined and handfasted as prophesied. As prophesied, she mused, but her heart was in it now. Somehow, this yearning would not settle for anything less than his heart.

"FINALLY, YOU WAKE."

Bryna sat up, clutching the white furs to her bare breast. In the window's light, a golden goddess stood in stillness.

"DO YOU KNOW ME?" the goddess asked, a small hand pulling back a hood of golden webs.

Bryna saw a face of elfin loveliness and skin the color of white flowers. She saw a bit of herself reflected in curve and color. "I have seen you in my dreams," she answered.

"AYE. I VISITED YOU THERE. I AM BLODENWEDD. I HAVE COME TO MEET THE GODDESS WHO STOLE THE HANDSOME CHIEFTAIN FROM ME."

"I dinna steal him," she replied stiffly. "He chose me."

"HIS GEAS CHOSE YOU," the goddess corrected, and then frowned as if recognizing something distasteful. "I DID NOT KNOW YOU BE SO BEAUTIFUL IN MORTAL FORM. HAIR THE COLOR OF FLAMES AND SUNLIGHT, WINGED BROWS OF BLACKEST PITCH, SKIN OF PUREST VIRGIN SNOW, A MOUTH OF MOIST ROSE PETALS, YOU BE MADE FROM MANY HUES."

"So are you," Bryna replied.

"I BE ONLY MADE FROM THE SHADES OF GOLD AN

SPRINKLES OF SILVER. YOU BE OF ALL THINGS. DO YOU CARRY HIS SEED?"

Bryna pulled back at the unexpected question.

"WELL, DO YOU?"

The way Blodenwedd stared at her stomach made her feel uneasy.

"YOU DO," the golden goddess stated with a frown.

Bryna touched her stomach. "I have not been sure until this moment. Aye, I carry his seed."

"I AM RESENTFUL. HE BELONGED TO ME."

Bryna watched the other's agitation with a growing sense of calm.

"HOW CAN YOU BE HIS TERRITORIAL GODDESS WHEN RAISED IN THE MORTAL WAY?"

"How do you know that I was raised in the mortal way?"

"OUR FAERY KING SAID AND SO IT MUST BE SO. YOU WERE NEVER AMONG US. NEVER SHARED IN WHAT BE OUR RIGHT. I BE SADDENED FOR YOU."

Bryna did not think so. "I doona miss what I doona know."

"DOES THE LAND EVER SPEAK TO YOU?"

What Bryna felt, she could not describe.

Blodenwedd took a step forward. "FALSE GODDESS. HIS GEAS CHOSE YOU. A MISTAKE, I CLAIM, BUT THE FAERY KING DOES NOT LISTEN. UNFAIR. UNFAIR." Her eyes flashed in anger, fists clenched.

The Dark Chieftains of the ancient line were

destined to mate with a territorial goddess from long ago. Yet, they were allowed one choice and Bloden-wedd knew this.

One choice only.

The heart selected.

To break the obligation and kill the chosen territorial goddess was to act contrary to nature and to court death. Yet, she could not fathom how this one had been stolen and then suddenly reappeared without the workings of the powerful Faery King. Killing a chosen goddess would only result in the chieftain's insanity and the land returning to ruin. She was not foolish. The silver-eyed goddess watched her serenely, a controlling of emotions that made her uneasy.

"A CHIEFTAIN CAN NEVER ACCEPT ANOTHER FAERY MATE, ONCE CHOSEN. UNLESS DEATH COMES."

"Unless death," Bryna echoed. "But I am not so easily killed, golden one."

"I HAVE NOT COME TO KILL YOU."

"Have you not?"

"FALSE GODDESS. I BE NOT STUPID. THE CHIEFTAIN WOULD KILL ME." She tugged the hood of golden web back over her head. "I MUST ABIDE BY OUR LAWS, THOUGH IT ANGERS ME TO DO SO." She looked up, eyes glittering with envy. "MINE I SAY. MINE."

Bryna stared back defiantly. "Were you behind my stolen destiny?"

The goddess pulled back in insult. "NOT I. NEVER I. NEVER, I SAY."

"Do you know who, then?"

"NAY. DOONA KNOW. DOONA CARE. I TELL YOU ONLY THIS. A PROMISE BETWEEN US, GODDESS TO GODDESS. SHOULD THE HANDSOME CHIEFTAIN TIRE OF YOU, I WILL TAKE HIM FOR MY OWN. FOR NOW, THE DESTINY OF FAERY LIES IN YOUR HANDS AND I MUST ABIDE BY THIS." She stepped back into the shafts of afternoon light filtering in from the window, her golden cat eyes cold and hard. "BE WARNED, FALSE GODDESS, INVADERS ARE COME."

The air in the room shimmered with gold light, then the goddess was gone.

Bryna took a deep, quaking breath. "False goddess, you are such a fool," she muttered, and dropped her head in her hands. A painful drawing centered in her womb. It was a sign of wrongness with her pregnancy that she understood all too well and had no control over. At moments like these, she could feel her true self, concealed, waiting for acknowledgement that she did not know how to give. She did not know how to be faery and until that time, a precarious future waited.

She climbed off the bed and stood on shaky feet. Her mind turned to Blodenwedd's last words of warning.

Invaders are come.

She needed to speak with Tynan.

Bryna attended to her personal needs quickly, dabbing at the spots of dried blood on her thighs. Preparing rags for any further blood spotting, she donned a woolen gown of dark lavender with a matching fringed cloak. Feeling a little weak, she left her hair unbound and left the bedchamber. Slowly, she made her way down the center staircase and outside to the windy courtyard. Stormy gray skies promised more snow. Her gaze searched the wind-swept parapets above, where she found him standing alone.

Tynan stared out at the black sea. He felt the weight of responsibility heavily this day. Much work needed to be done to fortify Kindred against the return of the Roman invaders. If not the Romans, then another invader would come to claim the rich, green, fertile land. He must protect his tribe and his faery brethren from what was to come. Establish one kingship, he mused, form alliances with the other chieftains of Munster, Leinster, Connacht, and Ulster. It would not be easy. The *Tuatha Dé Danann* were different, no longer purely mortal. Mayhap their future lay with the faeries, mayhap not. Only destiny would tell.

He felt her presence. "Do you come to warn me of the snowstorm?" he asked, continuing to look out to the sea.

"Methinks no warning is needed."

"Aye, the air is cold and the sea restless. Skies darken to night when they should be bright with day. Does the sea speak to you, faery?" Tynan continued to look outward, enjoying the scent of her carried to him by the air.

"Aye, the waves speak to me."

"What do they say?"

"Good afternoon, Dark Chieftain of Kindred. Go inside before you get wet."

Tynan threw back his head and laughed. Turning to her, his smile quickly faded.

Wrapped in a hooded cloak, his faerymate appeared a frail waif. "Bryna, are you ill?" he asked in concern. Dark circles mirrored gray eyes, glassy with fatigue.

"Tired only."

"Come." He took her arm and led her back down the newly built stairwell where they could be out of the wind and assured of privacy. "You should not have come out here."

"I had to speak with you."

"Then send one of the servants to fetch me."

"I could not, I had to come. Tynan, invaders come," she said distinctly, holding her hood in place.

Tynan released her and stepped back. "From where?" he demanded, focusing intently on her. "The sea?"

Bryna shook her head. Burnished gold curls slipped out of the hood. "I doona know," she whispered urgently.

"Doona know." Tynan scowled. "Do you sense this, or do these gloom words belong to the golden goddess?"

She stiffened in surprise. "You knew Blodenwedd visited me."

"Aye, I sensed her presence. She made sure of it. Now,

answer me. Does the land or sea warn you of invaders?"

"Nay, I sense only contentment, but she is the true goddess, Tynan. Her senses . . ."

"Hush." The tightness in his chest evaporated. "You are my territorial goddess. I listen only to your words and wisdom, not the gloom and doom of a spoiled child."

"Tynan, you should not take Blodenwedd's warning lightly."

"I do not, but her senses are not confined by time and place. Does she warn us for today or for twenty summers come pass?"

"She dinna say and I doona know."

"I know. You are linked to me, by blood and ancient promise. Your senses guard for our time, a sentinel for here, now, and our future. That is all that concerns me."

"Tynan, I am sorry. This faery awareness does not come easily for me."

"It will." He touched her arm and found her shivering. "Is this why you seek me out in the cold?"

She nodded.

He opened his cloak and pulled her chilled body into his arms. "You feel like ice."

She stepped between his braced legs, slim arms wrapped around his waist. "You feel like fire."

He closed the cloak around her trembling shoulders and rested his chin on the top of her head, concern furrowing his brow. He would speak to Derina and Rose later. Could his babe be weakening her, or some illness draining her? Dread settled in the pit of his stomach.

"Warmer?" he asked.

"Hmmmm."

Tynan bent and swung her up into his arms. "You would do better out from this cold."

She buried her face against his neck, unexpectedly and without protest. Tynan took the remaining stairs down and strode across the frosty courtyard with her light weight in his arms.

"Where do you take me?"

"Back to bed."

She lifted her head, a glimmer in the otherwise dull gray of her eyes.

"No more of that," he scowled, "until I know you are well." He headed for his keep.

"I am pregnant."

"I know. Bryna." With a powerful shove of his shoulder, the keep's doors flung open. He strode into the brightly lit hall with the cold wind following him in.

Ian appeared immediately by his side. "Sire?"

"Fetch Derina and Rose," Tynan ordered softly, "my faerymate is ill."

Ian nodded and disappeared back out the door.

"You knew I was pregnant?" she inquired with a trace of anger in her tone.

Tynan climbed the center staircase. Stopping on

the third step, he turned and barked out orders to the servants waiting at the bottom of the steps. Their faces were all grim with worry for they served him out of choice, not slavery. Tynan wanted food and a hot bath brought to the lord's bedchamber for his faerymate.

The servants immediately set to the tasks.

He felt a tug on his hair. "How do you know?" she demanded when he turned back to her.

"The Faery King told me." He took the rest of the stairs two at a time and went down the hall to their bedchamber.

"Oh, him," she murmured weakly, and rested her head back against his shoulder. "I wonder how he knew."

Bryna closed her eyes, strength draining to cramping and pain.

CHAPTER 16

TYNAN'S HEART HURT, A DEEP drawing wound not meant to ever heal. *Damn the faeries.*

Midnight had come to the land of the *Tuatha Dé Danann* in shades of crimson pitch, a moonless sky, and stars of dirty white. The air tasted foul in the fields and in the halls of Kindred.

He stood by the roaring hearth in an empty feast hall. For just a moment, he could not believe Rose's softly spoken words.

"Tell me again." He sat down in a wooden chair and dropped his head in his hands.

"Lordling," Rose whispered.

He looked up. "Tell me!"

Fire sparks of blue and red spiked in the hot air beside his thigh. He did not feel the intense heat of the flames, only the icy fear coiling around his heart.

"Her womb bleeds. Derina and I both feel she will lose the babe this night."

Tynan looked into the flames. "By the goddess, I am Kindred's ancient heir, the Dark Chieftain of the *Tuatha Dé Danann*. With my sword and wits, I can best most men. I doona know how to fight this battle of life and win."

"You canna win when death has chosen."

Within his inner fey sight, Tynan saw shapes move. He glanced at the closed doors of the empty feast hall. Outside those wooden doors, he knew Ian and Edwin guarded his privacy. The rest of his tribe receded into the night to await the dreaded news.

He looked up and collided with his son's frightened eyes.

"Hawk, I thought I told you to go to bed."

"I canna sleep with death near."

Tynan pulled the boy into his arms. "Death comes not for you."

"Will Bryna die?"

Tynan looked up at the simpler, looked at her bloodstained apron.

Rose smiled sadly. "I doona think so, Hawk. Bryna is of *Daoine Sidhe*. She is young and strong. She will have other children that will bring loyalty to the land."

Tynan released his son and stood. "If she is my true territorial goddess, why does she lose the babe?"

The simpler paled.

"Answer me. Has my *geas* chosen wrong?"

"Derina thinks it is because Bryna has not accepted her true faery self. Until she does, your seed will not take. You must love her with your full heart and being."

Tynan guided his son into the chair and thought about what the simpler had said.

He had fought long and hard for his tribe to re-claim their heritage. He already admitted to himself that he cared greatly for her. How much more did the Gods and Goddesses want? How much more would they demand of him? He cared for her in his way.

Damn them.

Tynan raked a hand through his hair. He strode to the windows at the end of the feast hall.

His chest felt tight. Breath constricted in his throat. At his order, tapestries covered the windows at night to keep the cold outside. He grabbed the edge of the woven cloth. For a moment, he stared into the jet black eyes of a pair of hunting kestrels.

With a growl of rage, he tore the tapestry down and flung it to the floor behind him.

He stared out at the starless night locked in a red haze of fury . . . at himself. Red clouds hid the moon. Torches lit the courtyard and parapets and he could see his men standing guard, tension in their postures. They waited as all of his tribe waited, for this endless night to pass.

This was his fault. Once he suspected her with babe, he should never have touched her. Damn his lust. Damn his *geas*.

"When can I see her?" He looked over his shoulder.

Rose had not moved from beside Hawk.

"Soon, in a few hours." Her voice pitched high to carry across the hall.

"She has not yet lost the babe," he stated rather

than asked.

"Nay, not yet. But soon."

Tynan's stomach clenched. "How can you be so sure?"

"I am, Lordling. Ask not how."

Thoughts of Bryna writhing in pain upstairs nearly undid him.

This was his fault.

His fault. *What more can I give?*

The simpler came up beside him. "Lordling." She touched his arm. "This thing is not your fault."

"Aye, it is mine, Rose," he replied icily. He looked back to the unforgiving night. "I need to be with my faerymate."

"Most men want nothing to do with the birthing, let alone something like this."

"I am not most men."

"I need to be with Bryna too," his son stated, coming up behind them.

"Nay, Hawk." Tynan shook his head. He would not subject a child to witnessing death in this tragic manner.

"I wish to be there with Bryna."

"Hawk." Tynan knelt in front of his son. "You shall guard the door and keep the faeries away. Can you do this for me?"

"Aye."

"I will not let death take her, Hawk." He pulled his son into his arms and held him tightly, drawing comfort from his small body and the simple scents of hay and horses in the boy's hair.

Blood stained the linens.

Bryna tossed in agony, in sweat and in pain, panting for breath. She wanted to run away but her body did not have the strength to obey her.

Tynan's warm chest pressed up against her naked back, giving her strength. "Breathe, faery."

She bit her tongue from crying out. The contractions worsened. It hurt so very much, but she would not cry out. Never would she cry out. Not even when the villagers tried to burn the heart shaped birthmark off her hand did she allow a whimper to escape.

Her chieftain mate held her tenderly, his arms strong. "Bryna listen to me."

She shook her head.

"You must let our child go."

"Nay," she cried, her fingers digging into his forearms.

He kissed her temple, sweet comfort and sorrow. "Let him go, Bryna. He was meant for better things than here."

Grayness closed in upon her and Bryna lost consciousness at the first light of dawn. A final, great flushing of dark blood stained her pale thighs and the white bed linens.

Death had claimed the chieftain's heir.

It was done.

Tynan stood near the window, numb with shock. He watched Derina and Rose clean the blood from Bryna's limp body. His fists clenched and unclenched at his sides in helpless rage.

Outside, the morning sky darkened to a stormy, lead gray. Howling winds turned into a wintry gale of sleet and rain. The tops of trees bent low to the ground in mourning and grief. Temperatures dropped, stealing the warmth of life from the air.

"We wait now," Rose murmured, helping the ancient druidess tuck the pelts around Bryna's still form.

"How long?" Tynan asked, his voice sounding hoarse to his own ears.

"Until she awakens, Lordling. Darkness and grief stain your features. Go rest. Nothing more can be done here."

Tynan shook his head. "I will not leave her, Rose. Take the druidess and go. I wish to be alone with my faerymate."

The simpler nodded. With bloody linens in one arm, she guided the ancient out of the bedchamber.

The door closed behind them, leaving him with his faerymate and his grief.

✳✳✳

Tynan stared at the small still form in his bed. In a desperate voice he pleaded, "Bryna, doona leave me."

The gale's howling wind outside was his only answer. He turned and punched the wall. "You canna have her." Pain sliced through his hand and up his arm. "Do you hear me? You canna have her." Icy rain pelted the windows in answer.

Long hours passed.

And when still she did not awaken, Tynan slipped into bed with her. He held her gently, comforted by the sound of her slow, steady breathing.

In her unconsciousness, Bryna floated in a strange purple mist to the woodland dells, faery gardens, and moorland caves filled with perfume and music. Graceful elfin folk with pale, delicate complexions and luminous jewel eyes, welcomed her. She went with them, became one with their number, losing all sense of time and place.

In dreams, she danced with the virtuous souls of the pagans and ate ripe, purple plums from the perfect orchards. At the edge of dusk, the enchanting creatures brought her to a field of wild flowers that lay between a rocky road and cliffs spotted with thickets of silver thorns.

"A choice," the elfin folk said, pointing down the path. They kissed her gently on the cheek, one by one, and then stepped back, disappearing into the purple mist.

Alone, Bryna stood at the beginning of a winding path of white stones. She listened to the sound of the flute music in this fey place and to a man's breathing.

A choice.
To leave or to stay?

✳✳✳

Bryna opened her eyes and saw the gray ceiling above her. Her first feeling was of soreness.

Turning her head on the pillow, her sleepy gaze settled on Tynan. He slept soundlessly beside her, fully dressed in a black tunic and breeches, his braided hair badly mussed. Dark circles lived under his eyes and a gaunt paleness showed beneath the dark growth of a beard.

She shifted and winced.

Tynan's eyes flew open. He rose on an elbow, instantly alert.

Bryna's eyes widened at the stark intensity in his face.

"You came back," he murmured with relief.

"Where did I go?"

"To a fey place, I imagine."

Fey? Bryna remembered a field of wild flowers and blades of tall, blue-green grass.

The image blurred to a white stone path, and then a sea of blood.

She blinked in memory of it, and a physical pain washed over her.

Blood.

Loss.

Grief.

An emptiness settled inside her womb where her child had been. "I have lost our babe," she murmured.

He pulled her into his arms, his body warm and strong and full of life. "He was not meant for us, Bryna."

She clung to him, tears of misery streaming down her cheeks. "I am so sorry, Tynan." Words of remorse locked in her throat. "My fault . . ."

"Nay, faery. It is the way of things, sometimes. Doona blame yourself."

After a time, when sorrow had spent, they lay in each other's arms. In the courtyard outside, a child's delighted shriek mingled with the bark of the wolf-hounds. Tribesmen called to one another. Horses neighed in greeting and life moved on.

Bryna listened and took comfort in the sounds. The purity of her fey self took hold, a natural inclination for the positive and encouraging. "We will have other children," she whispered.

Above her head, Tynan's eyes closed. "Do not think on that now." Never would he risk her life in childbirth again.

*** *** ***

A fortnight had past since suffering the loss of her unborn babe. Bryna lay motionless and alone in the big bed. Her emotions still felt raw inside her, but her fey self tempered it with hopes for the future.

She spent most days in the bedchamber sleeping or staring out the window to the courtyard below, physically healing and sipping Rose's demon bane tea.

Healing.

For some reason, her body needed more time.

The feelings of loss and melancholy would soon ease into a sense of sadness and regret. She knew this.

If only Tynan did not stay away.

Derina and Rose would visit often, their presence a great comfort to her. The warmth of *Marta*, March, the busy month, filtered through the windows. Days lengthened pleasantly, birds were gone a mating, hibernating badgers awakened, and hardy farmers began to plough fields with their oxen. Each day the courtyard filled with Tynan's tribesmen and local traders. Each day the loss inside her eased.

Each day he stayed away.

From just outside the bedchamber, she heard soft footfalls and looked to the entrance.

"Afternoon, child," Derina said from the doorway.

"Afternoon, my teacher."

"I bring a gift from the chieftain. Do you feel up to walking?" Her teacher held up a gray gown of fine thread.

"Please, come in." Pushing the pelts aside, Bryna climbed out of bed and went to the druidess. She touched the soft fabric of the bodice. " 'Tis beautiful."

"Put the gown on and come walk with me outside.

The sun is high in the sky, child. I have a need to stretch my legs."

Bryna looked at the gown and then back to her teacher. She smiled. "I would like that."

She shrugged out of the white bedrail and donned the gray gown. The bodice hugged her breasts and nipped at her waist.

"Does it fit, child?"

"Verra well, Teacher." Long sleeves, crossed with thin silver ribbons, hugged her arms

"Hold out your hand, I have my own gift for you."

Bryna held out her hand.

"Here." The druidess dropped two golden combs into her palm. "For your hair, child. Pull it away from your face. Let us go. You have been too much inside of late."

"Teacher, these combs belonged to your mother."

"They are yours now, child." The druidess closed Bryna's fingers over the combs. She shuffled back to the window. "No tears. The time for grieving must pass. Let us go and enjoy what is left of the day."

With a few quick brush strokes, Bryna managed to tame her hair into some semblance of order. She placed the combs on either side of her temples and pulled the curls away from her face. Sitting down on the bed, she slid her feet into her brown boots.

"Have you seen Lord Tynan?" she inquired.

"He gave me the gown to bring to you."

"Do I need a cloak?"

The ancient shook her head. "Nay, the sun is warm."

Bryna straightened and smoothed down the folds of the gown. "I am ready."

Her teacher nodded and gestured to the door. "We will walk slowly."

Bryna smiled. "As always, my teacher."

They walked through the sunlit courtyard out to the village at the ancient's pace. Children played with the wolfhounds, tossing sticks in the warm air for the dogs to catch.

When they came to the end of the courtyard, Bryna turned and asked, "Where is he?"

"This way, child, in the meadow between the village and fortress."

They came upon a group of twenty men battling with practice swords in the field. Loud voices rose in taunt, others in advice.

"Thrust under," one man called.

"You thrust under," another answered in annoyance.

Bryna stepped closer to see. Tynan stood with his back to her, parrying with another tribesman, whom he quickly overwhelmed.

"Go to him, child." Her teacher pointed to the waiting servant girls with water buckets on the side. "Bring him water to quench his thirst."

Bryna walked over to the water buckets.

"I think that is enough for today," Ian offered, striding into the circle, having noticed his chieftain's faerymate.

Tynan said nothing. He still wished to fight. His gaze snagged on the bright head making its way through his men.

Bryna.

His fingers eased on the sword. He quickly sheathed the practice weapon at his waist and nodded to Ian, acknowledging the man's attempt to warn him.

"My thanks, Ian." He nodded. "Time for rest. Go clean up. There are plenty of sweet cakes this eve for everyone."

Ian stepped away. "Practice is ended," he called out to the men. "Go and clean up."

Carrying a water bucket, Bryna pushed through the multitude of sweaty men. Placing the water bucket at Tynan's booted feet, she knelt before him in the dirt. With two unsteady hands, she filled the wooden ladle.

"Water to quench your thirst?" Would he refuse her offering and embarrass her in front of his men, or would he drink from her hands?

Tynan knelt and cradled her hands. Leaning forward, he drank from the ladle. Bryna felt soft lips brush her thumb, his breath tickling the index finger of her other hand.

She sensed the men dispersing quietly all around them, but that was all. Her world centered on her mate. His black hair had been plaited with two braids at each temple. The rest of the raw silk fell in a single plait down his back.

"My thanks," he murmured.

Bryna held still under his slow appraisal.

"More water, Tynan?"

He nodded.

She dipped the ladle into the bucket and held it out to him.

"Are you well?" he asked.

"Aye, I feel much improved." She was so glad to be near him. "My thanks for the gift, Tynan. The gown is lovely."

"The color suits you." He took the ladle and drank, lashes lowering, locking her out.

Bryna did not know that images of dark blood flashed in his mind and that he could still feel her cold, limp body in his arms. Had she been more aware, she would have realized that her chieftain mate blamed himself for the death of their unborn son.

"My thanks for the water." Dropping the ladle in the bucket, he rose and walked away.

Bryna stared after him, unable to match his actions with the burning need in his eyes. He did not want her, she understood with a sudden clarity. Her gaze fell to the ground, a familiar comfort when in turmoil. Tynan's *geas* stirred his body, changing the amethyst in his eyes to black amber. The man himself did not want her.

Swiping the tears from her cheek, she remembered Blodenwedd's warning, " . . .should the chieftain tire of you, I will take him."

"Fool of a chieftain," her teacher grumbled from behind her. "He does not see the truth."

"He is no fool." Bryna answered, climbing to her feet. "Forgive me, Teacher. I feel suddenly fatigued and need to return to the keep." She walked quietly away, her heart returning to numbness, as it had been when she had served in slavery to the Romans. In the days that followed, she did not approach the Dark Chieftain again, but found value in simple things and in helping his tribesmen.

Yet, when the nights approached, she would cringe inside, for they were the most difficult to get through. In the evening, she would take her meal in the bedchamber alone. Afterward, she would curl up in the bed, staring into the shadows on the wall that were born by the fires in the hearth. When the moon rose high in the night sky, he would come to their bed. Lying atop the pelts, his back to her, he slept without a sound.

She lay awake, feeling his physical exhaustion and listening to his breathing. With a heavy heart, she would wonder when he would send her away and call for Blodenwedd. When her eyelids grew heavy, she would sleep and dream of terrible things.

At dawn's first light, he would leave again.

Inspect the new chariots, mews, and stables . . .

Supervise the restoration of the tomb and farms . . .

Practice with his warriors . . .

Search the countryside with his patrols for Eamon . . .

And another night would come and pass.

Many days and nights went like this until last night . . .

Last night had been different.

Bathed in the white light of the full moon, he had held her with surprising reverence, thinking her asleep. His bare chest pressed into her back. She remembered the warmth of him and the whisper of his words. *I doona know what to say to you, faery. How you must hate me.*

When morning came, he had left her alone again.

Bryna stared at shafts of morning light streaming in from the window. She dinna hate him. Why would he say that? Did he think she blamed him for the loss of their babe?

Guilt washed over her at her own selfish need. Why did she not see that he had suffered as greatly as she did?

She climbed out of bed with a new sense of purpose, determined to talk with him. Standing in front of the hearth, she sought warmth from the cool morning air, composing herself. It was time for both of them to heal and move on with life.

"Creature of twilight, what do you see in the burning embers?"

Startled, Bryna turned around and faced a druid in a hooded brown robe. He had closed the door securely behind him.

"Eamon?" She recognized that voice.

"Aye, 'tis Eamon."

He came into the room and moved beside her, unthreatening.

"What do you see in the embers?" he asked again.

Bryna glanced at the ashes and smoldering remains of last night's fire. "Why are you here?" She felt uncomfortable in his presence. "Your chieftain sends men out searching for you."

"Aye, but they will not find me." He continued to stare at the dying fire.

"What do you see in the embers? Do you see your fate?"

Bryna glanced at the hearth. "They are but embers, Eamon, nothing more," she answered, slightly perplexed by his fascination.

"Nay, they are signs of a life ending." He dropped the hood back and turned to face her.

Bryna flinched at the feral look that came into his eyes.

"I have come to claim what should have been mine," he snarled.

She bolted for the door, but a large hand grabbed a handful of her hair and yanked.

Bryna went flying backwards and landed hard on her hip in front of the hearth. She swallowed back her cry of pain, unwilling to show him weakness. Instead, she glared defiantly back at him through tear-filled eyes.

He knelt before her. "You are lovely, I have always thought so." His arms braced on his knees. "Faery whore," he said with vehemence, "you should have been mine."

"I belong to Tynan." She kicked out, catching him in the upper chest and sending him backwards, but like most warriors, he recovered his feet in one fluid motion.

Bryna scrambled back on all fours.

His lips curved in a sneer. "Faery whore, you belong to the man that wears the mantle of the Dark Chieftain. And soon I will be that one." He towered over her. His gaze raked her body. "I smell the stench of him on you."

Bryna scrambled to her feet and backed away.

"But his seed does not root in your faery womb," he gloated, pressing her back. " 'Tis a sign of weakness in him."

"The weakness is mine, not his."

He grabbed her by the shoulders and pulled her into his arms. He smelled of bitter ale. Bryna shoved against him. "You have no right. Let go of me."

His face darkened in fury. "No right?" he choked. With a massive fist, he clipped her jaw.

Pain exploded up her cheek. Blood pooled in her mouth and dimness strayed into her vision. Her head rolled listlessly on her shoulders.

"That is better," he breathed. "I like the silence of a woman's breath."

Her eyes glazed. She could no longer think clearly.

He dragged her back to the bed and tossed her down on the furs, but she slid to the floor in a limp heap.

He chuckled softly and opened the heavy lid to her trunk, pulling out her lavender cloak.

"Stand up." Grabbing a handful of silken hair, he pulled her to her feet.

Bryna wavered on weak legs.

"Hold still," he commanded irritably, draping the cloak around her shoulders. He pulled the hood up to hide her bright tresses and fastened the brooch at her shoulder to hold the cloak in place.

"Know how long I have waited to touch you?" he said. "I have wanted you since first I saw you."

Bryna tried to focus on the voice and fuzzy image in front of her. Grayness invaded her sight and she collapsed, unconscious.

Eamon frowned as he caught her. "Mayhap I hit you too hard." He pulled his brown hood over his head to hide his features and swung her up in his arms. "Come, goddess." He peered out the doorway to an empty hall. "We go to the woodlands."

CHAPTER 17

THE BIRDS REMAINED ODDLY QUIET, a distinct warning that Tynan could not ignore.

Heat shimmered in the late morning air, adding to the feeling of growing unease inside him. He could not shake the feeling of wrongness coiling in his stomach.

He crossed the muddy courtyard to the stables and stopped. Turning back, he scanned the area. A warm breeze blew his hair away from his face. His hand rested easily on the hilt of the sword at his waist. He searched his surroundings. Wolfhounds nestled by the front of the keep. Workers repaired the parapets. Tribesmen bartered in morning trades. Horses neighed in contentment in the outside corrals.

"What is it?" Ian called from the stables. Tynan shook his head. He could give no reason for his unease.

Edwin joined Ian. They both stood just outside the stable, watching him.

"What do you sense?" Edwin asked with concern.

Tynan did not answer right away. "I sense a change in the wind, something dank comes."

Ian stepped forward. "From Ulster?" He knew the

messenger from the Ulster King had arrived yesterday.

Tynan shook his head. "Nay, he thinks us faery cursed and will have nothing to do with us."

"So, it is as you said."

"Aye. They fear us. We have no ally there." Tynan did not believe they would fare better with the Connacht, Leinster, or the Munster kings. The *Tuatha Dé Danann* were the faery tribe, separate from mortal men and part of the *Daoine Sidhe*. He envisioned Kindred becoming like the faery woodlands, a haven of magic and heavy mist seen only by those of faery blood.

"Good then," Ian stated. "I canna condone their superstitious ways."

"Aye," Tynan agreed. The other tribe's blood practices were barbaric. "I doona believe in the sacrifice of innocents for fair weather and fertility."

Ian nodded. "I've increased our presence in the village and posted more guards. Our search parties have found no sign of Eamon. Does your faerymate sense this danger?"

Tynan shook his head again. He dinna know what Bryna sensed. He had stayed away from her hoping his *geas*, his magical obligation to mate, would calm. But it did not. Each night he came to her bed, wanting the closeness of her. Each morning he left in the same state, plunging into the day's work, hoping to exhaust his body and drive the burning lust out of his system.

Tynan faced Ian. He had come to see the first foal

of the season and put Bryna from his mind.

"Show me Cloud's foal."

He followed Ian and Edwin back into the first stable. This building housed twenty horses at a time. The scents of fresh hay and leather combined with the smell of a new birth.

Standing outside a wooden stall, they looked in upon Ian's dappled gray mare, Cloud. The mare's large blue eyes watched warily from beneath long white lashes. She stood seventeen hands of sleek muscle, the fleetest horse in their stable.

Beside her, a pitch-black foal with one white fetlock tottered on long, spindly legs.

" 'Tis a good sign for a birth this early in the year."

Tynan joined Edwin in resting his arms on the top of the wooden stall. Their gold arm bands shone brightly. Unlike many of the other tribes that preferred bright colors, the men of *Tuatha Dé Danann* adapted the colors of the night and fey woodlands, dark blues and purples and shades of black. Swords and daggers were always sheathed at their waists, a readiness that he insisted upon.

Cloud nickered encouragement to the swaying youngster, testing his legs in the clean, yellow straw.

"His long legs hint of swiftness to come," Tynan said in observation.

"Aye, he favors my Cloud. The foal is yours, Tynan."

Tynan squeezed Ian's shoulder. "I am honored, Ian. If the foal is as fast as his dam, my chariot will fly among the gods."

Edwin chuckled. "That gray mare can outrun a hawk in full flight."

"Nay, not a hawk in full flight," Ian mocked.

"We shall see, Ian, we shall see." Tynan leaned over the stall.

"What will you name him?" Edwin asked.

Tynan looked at the black foal. "I will call him Black Spear."

" 'Tis a fine name," Ian murmured.

"May he be as swift as a spear," Edwin concurred.

Tynan watched the foal's progress. "Within a few short hours he will have his balance under him and we will know."

The foal looked up at them with curious black eyes as if only now realizing that he had an audience. Tynan wished to have shared this moment with Bryna.

He did not realize how long he stood in silence before Ian spoke.

" 'Tis not good to stay away from your mate," Ian said softly.

Images of blood-stained sheets filled Tynan's mind.

Ian turned to Edwin. "Lad, give us a moment."

Turning, Edwin walked outside and closed the stables doors behind him.

Ian rested his arms on the stall in a thoughtful stance. "My wife and I have wished to keep this secret, but methinks you should know of it and mayhap it will help you. Aya and I lost our first child in much the same way as you and Bryna."

Tynan looked over at the older man. "I did not know, Ian."

"No one knew, except Rose, and she agreed not to speak of it to anyone. I tell you this more out of understanding than sympathy. There is no reason for losses such as this, and I blamed myself for touching Aya even after I knew she was with child."

"I touched Bryna," Tynan said tightly.

"I suspected. It does not matter."

"It matters." Tynan's hands gripped the top of the stall, causing Cloud to shy away.

"Easy, girl," Ian said. Reaching out, he stroked the mare's muscular shoulder. The horse soon quieted and the black foal found his way to his first warm meal.

"We tried again for a babe. When Aya carried our second, I stayed away from her. Yet, she lost that babe too. Only she and I knew, another secret kept out of shame." Ian pulled his hand back and rested it on the stall. "The third time the goddess blessed us. Aya bloomed like wild flowers in sunlight. She grew strong as the child did in her womb, and her appetites increased."

"Appetites?"

"I have five sons and two daughters, sire. They doona grow on trees."

Tynan chuckled and patted his man on the back. "They are fine children, Ian."

"Aye, they are. Do you understand what I am

trying to say? It does not matter if you touched her or not. When death calls, there is nothing any of us can do. Go to her, sire. The worst thing would be for you to stay away. Bryna grieves, too, though she hides her tears well. Only together can you heal."

Tynan looked back to the black foal and raked a hand through his hair. "I doona know how to approach her."

"Do as you always have done."

Suddenly, the mare's gray head shot up sharply, pink nostrils flared in agitation.

"What, Cloud?" Ian straightened and glanced over his shoulder.

"She senses something," Tynan said, his hand resting on the hilt of the dagger at his waist.

Cloud neighed loudly and pawed the floor. Horses in the paddocks answered her with upset whinnies. Outside, the wolfhounds began barking.

Tynan glanced at Ian.

"Trouble," Ian murmured.

Tynan agreed. "Take Edwin and a few of our men and begin a search," he ordered, and bolted out the stable doors. Already, his tribesmen were at alert, groups fanning out. Out of the corner of his eye, he caught sight of the lead wolfhound, Shadow, sniffing at a servants' entrance to the keep.

Drawing his sword, Tynan ran across the courtyard to the dog.

"Show me, Shadow." He pushed the side door

open, noting the broken lock.

The scarred dog took off at a run down the narrow corridor with Tynan chasing after him. Servants made way as they raced through the keep, the animal heading for the center staircase, his nose to the floor. A sick dread settled in his stomach when the dog ran up the stairs and headed straight to his bedchambers.

Tynan followed more cautiously, his grip tightening on the hilt of the double-edged sword.

A hint of rosemary scented the air.

"She is gone," the ancient druidess whispered shakily, standing in the center of his bedchamber.

The vile scent of acid sweat overpowered his faerymate's soft lavender fragrance.

"Eamon," he said icily.

"Aye, that one."

Shadow whimpered, pacing back and forth in the corner near the window.

Tynan went to the dog and knelt. Three drops of blood glistened on the floor.

With a swift downward thrust, he buried the tip of his sword in the floor. The dog jumped back on all fours, teeth bared, hair bristling at his shoulders.

Reaching out, he patted the dog on the head to reassure him. "Not you, dog." He stood slowly and turned back to the blind druidess with the white hair.

"Teacher." He called her by the name Bryn used, showing his respect. "Where does he take my faerymate?"

"The feypaths," she said, almost trancelike in her pose. She turned, empty eye-sockets piercing him with a sudden chill. "Dark Chieftain, my faery sight canna see beyond the purple light of the feypaths. You must start your search there."

Tynan's gaze settled on his sword, the tip buried deep in the wood floor. It still wobbled from the force of his anger. "Eamon knows but one feypath, to and from the faery woodlands."

***

Eamon grinned in triumph. It proved incredibly easy to slip past the servants and take what belonged to him. A druid's unobtrusive dark robes had served him well in his enemy's place. He could barely contain his delight.

He cast his eyes to the territorial goddess walking in front of him. The floor length lavender cloak hid her slender form. Flame colored hair fell down her back in unruly lengths.

She belonged to him now. He could hardly wait to take her womb and become the Dark Chieftain.

"Is it always this dark in here? It strains my eyes."

Bryna looked up. The unreal light shifted, tarnishing the rocks and walls of the feypaths with its sepulchral smear. "It is not this dark, usually. Shades of purple light have muted and blurred into gloominess," Bryna answered softly. "We trespass here."

"I doona like it."

"Most mortals would not." For Bryna, the color soothed her faery soul. A cool breeze blew in the tunnels, carrying the murmurs of thousands of vindictive sprites. If Eamon heard the sound, he did not acknowledge it.

"After I have you, I will be powerful and immortal."

"Think me immortal, Eamon?"

"You are a goddess."

"Immortality is a gift, Eamon, a gift that I dinna receive. As a goddess bound by prophecy to a chieftain, I live a mortal's life."

"I know you are immortal. Doona lie to me."

Bryna stepped gingerly around a sharp ledge of shiny black rocks. "I doona lie, Eamon." Her bare feet were cut and bleeding from walking on the rocky dirt path.

"I doona want to talk of it now."

"As you wish."

"Stop talking."

Bryna bowed her head in acknowledgement. Dampness clung to the air, weighing down her limbs. The sound of Eire's wild sea, lashing against the cliffs, echoed in the tunnels. Tenderly, she felt for the swelling at her jaw. It still hurt to the touch, a minor ache, compared to her throbbing feet. Ahead, gray walls of stone flowed into the feypath's purple light, yawning outward into a black void.

"It stinks in here," Eamon complained.

She glanced over her shoulder.

Distaste showed clearly on her captor's face and she felt a sense of pleasure upon seeing him so discomforted.

"Fey spitefulness," she replied.

"Speak up."

"You breathe faery spitefulness."

He scowled at her. "Nay, 'tis the rot of some dead animal."

"You think so?" She continued walking.

"So serene, so cool, my icy goddess," he taunted. "You lost his heir, Bryna. Think he will come for you after that?"

Memories of that horrible night flooded her mind in a blur of feelings and colors. She had lain in strong arms, bleeding and exhausted with scents of Rose's stonecrop and garlic remedies scenting the air, and the flicker of yellow candlelight on wall tapestries.

"Do you remember?" he goaded behind her, confident in his superiority.

"I remember," she responded serenely to her captor, this vanquisher who knew nothing but his own envy and resentment and sought to rip her heart asunder.

"Already Tynan warms another's bed. Do you remember when he rejected your water offering in the meadow? Proof that he no longer cares for you. He has abandoned you, where I would take you willingly in my arms."

"I am pledged to the Dark Chieftain," she replied

simply, unwilling to be drawn in by him.

"You will be mine, Bryna. I would never hurt you like he has."

The scent of lies fouled the air. She covered her mouth and coughed, turning away.

"Aye, it stinks of rot in here." He shoved her forward. "I would sooner leave this place. Move faster."

Bryna walked on, leaving a blood trail for Tynan to follow. She did not pause, her bleeding feet carrying her forward.

"Must you touch everything?"

"I am the territorial goddess, Eamon. The land calls for my touch."

"Your touch," he growled, "slows us down." He grabbed her arm and dragged her forward.

Bryna allowed him to pull her along without a fight.

The purple light in the tunnels dimmed and the sound of the dark sea had grown distant. She prayed to the mother goddess for strength, fighting the urge to ask Eamon to slow the pace or even to stop and rest for a moment. Wet pain licked at her feet.

She stumbled and could not help a painful grimace.

"What?" He stopped and faced her. "Tell me," he demanded.

She stared at the long scar wrinkling his chin.

"My patience grows thin with your silence, Bryna."

Bryna found herself pushed roughly against the wall. The folds of the lavender cloak opened, revealing the bloodstained hem of her white bedrail.

He looked down and cursed. "You think to leave a blood trail for him?"

"Tynan does not need a blood trail to find me."

Her captor's face turned red in fury. "I will just carry you, then."

✱✱✱

Tynan crouched low in the cool purple light of the feypaths. A thin gold torc rested on his collarbone and gold arm bands wrapped around biceps.

It was always twilight in the feypaths, always foul with faery spitefulness. His long black hair fell unadorned down his bare back. Kneeling, he caressed the single strand of auburn hair between his fingers.

He wore the runes of Kindred upon his chest, a vow of protection and promise cast in blue dye. Black breeches glistened with sweat from his long chase. He curled the single strand of hair around his fingers and reverently tucked it into his waistband beside his jeweled dagger.

Looking up, he regarded the two tunnels before him.

He had a choice to make.

Tynan reached for his battle sword. He had placed it carefully on the ground when he found a strand of Bryna's hair. With one fluid motion, he swung the sword back into the leather scabbard tied at his back.

Slowly he stood, his features hard and feral.

Breathing in the damp air, the coppery scent of her blood rode the currents of the feypaths and he knew that she had intentionally left a blood trail for him to follow.

He emitted a primitive snarl of vengeance and bolted for the right tunnel.

CHAPTER 18

"EAMON, PLEASE PUT ME DOWN," Bryna made her request in a small, breathless voice. He had flung her over his shoulder like a sack of grain hours ago, and she gritted her teeth from the soreness in her stomach.

"Shut up," he growled. "This is your own fault, stop complaining."

Biting her lip, Bryna's head drooped low. In her misery, she thought of Tynan and felt a deep regret. Silence roared in her ears, a kind of melancholy set in, for she could not fathom a life without him.

"Damn faeries." Eamon stumbled and then muttered an oath. "I have had enough carrying you." With a grunt, he leaned forward.

Bryna slid off his shoulders and landed on shaky legs, feeling slightly faint. She took a moment to regain her composure, grateful for the small respite that her captor seemed to give her.

"Better?" he asked.

She nodded. Hard fingers cupped her chin, tilting her face up for closer inspection.

"Never have I realized the beauty of our fey brethren. The sight of you fills my body with need."

Bryna pulled out of his hand, sickened by his

touch. She pointed behind her. "Look there, Eamon. The half-moon rock is just to the right."

He peered around her, a sly grin appearing on his face. "Aye, I remember it." He walked over. His hands slid up and down the purple crystallike stone, searching for the indentation.

"Where is the lever? Ah, I found it."

The fey rock slid open in silence.

"Come." Grabbing her wrist, he dragged her through the opening. Tainted darkness bled into their senses, a lingering of in-between from a fey to a mortal place. With the next step, they passed through and entered a small clearing.

They paused in moonlight and Bryna took the fragrant air deep into her lungs. She looked out upon the land of her heritage. A heart shaped boulder stood to the right. At its base, a spray of wild flowers, in shades of white and purple, fluttered from the increasing south winds. In the distance stood a tribe of wild goats, their white coats ghostlike against the night's rocky landscape.

She sensed a rainstorm coming and tasted the fierce sweetness of the tempest on the tip of her tongue.

Eamon shoved her forward impatiently. "Let us go. I wish to be in the woodlands before sunrise."

Bryna walked out into the open fields, the feather caress of grass at her ankles. All around primeval moonbeams swept the land, lighting the way. Soil, centuries old and rich with enchantment, cushioned her, reaching out to heal the raw pads of her feet. Bowing her head, Bryna murmured heartfelt thanks to the land goddess for her soothing gift.

As a slave, she had been impressionable, passive to those who demanded control. Stolen and molded by isolation, she had become something she should never have been. No longer would she drift through life insecure and controlled by others.

She BELONGED now.

In the midst of this ordeal, she was just beginning to understand her rightful place. She recognized the envy and resentment that drove Eamon, the fury that tainted his mind for things he had no right to. This trespass against her would never be redeemed in the minds of her brethren. For Eamon, it would be a journey into forever darkness.

"I doona remember it taking so long to get there."

Bryna glanced at her captor's scowling face. "It is the same distance as it always has been."

"The faeries play a game with me."

"The faeries doona play games with you, Eamon."

He pointed to their left. "I doona remember those rocks."

Bryna looked at the ancient ring bank of fissured and split stones. " 'Tis a sacred rebirth stone formation and has always been there. Mayhap my brethren allow you to see it this time in preparation for your arrival."

He gazed uneasily at her and Bryna perceived a

crack in his confidence. He did not like that the faeries knew of his coming. He wanted to control them because he feared them.

"My brethren's enchantment stirs in the air. Can you not feel it, Eamon?"

"I feel nothing. Keep moving."

Bryna walked on, her head held high. "You canna control my brethren."

"When I am Dark Chieftain I will control all things."

"The Dark Chieftain is the protector of all things, not the master."

"There is no difference. Look over that rise. The woodlands peek out of the white mist."

Bryna looked ahead.

Her step became strong and true.

Her captor no longer pulled her forward.

She walked on of her own accord.

Her faery spirit poised for the upcoming battle.

Rain fell in torrents.

With ghostly speed, Tynan raced into the heavy faery mist. Lightning flashed across the sky, illuminating his way. Thunder boomed in disruptive violence above him, angry at his delay.

He ducked under an ancient canopy of oak trees, drenched to the core of his being. With his back pressed against a massive tree trunk, he dragged air into his lungs. Steam rose from the heat of his flesh and exertion. He felt oddly refreshed and renewed from the rainstorm's enchantment, despite his long run. His lungs no longer burned. His heart no longer pounded in his chest.

Pushing away from the ancient tree, he threw his head back and breathed deeply.

He felt strong and refreshed, his body invigorated and swift.

He scanned the woodlands, focusing with his senses. Branches of the massive oaks swayed in the rain cast winds. The smaller yews and hollies bowed in worship to the moving spirit of the storm. Nostrils flaring, he took in the familiar scents of this fey place.

"Tell me where she is," he called out softly to the woodlands.

He caught sight of several pairs of yellow eyes. The pack of black wolves watched him in the darkness. Wild pigs, searching for acorns, grunted in wet pleasure, unconcerned by the close proximity of the predators. Enchantment streamed in their blood as it did in his.

A rustling sound came from his right and a badger crossed his path, foraging for food.

In the treetops, the kee-kee cry of kestrels echoed hauntingly above the wind and then he felt it — a presence of white and air.

Perched on the lower branch of a massive oak, a large snowy owl watched him with unblinking yellow eyes.

"Messenger from the faeries, where is my faery-mate?"

The bird hooted at him as if to say, listen . . .

Tynan tilted his head and paid attention with every one of his senses.

Then he heard them . . .

Faery voices.

Calling.

He took off at a run for the primordial well in the clearing.

CHAPTER 19

IN THE NIGHT SKY, THUNDER roared in protest of the rainstorm's sudden abatement. It had come and gone in formidable power, leaving behind a fearsome silence.

"Kneel!"

Bryna hit the ground hard on her knees.

"I am here," her captor called out to the faeries, one hand wrapped hurtfully in her hair. "Show yourselves. I have brought my goddess."

Silence answered them.

Tears welling in her eyes from his hold, Bryna stared at the thicket of silver thorns surrounding the base of the sacred well. Granite boulders stood behind in threadbare coats of green and brown moss.

"Answer me," he called out, muttering an impatient oath and releasing her. Stepping back, he removed the wet druid robe, flinging it aside. Underneath the guise, his green tunic and breeches were dampened. At his belt rested a dagger and sword. He looked around and came back to face her. "Why do they not show themselves?"

"They will, Eamon," she said calmly despite her inner quaking.

His gaze narrowed at her and Bryna sensed a

terrible intent.

"Mayhap a little demonstration is in order," he said, and then gestured. "Remove those clothes."

Bryna shook her head. "Nay, Eamon. I will not." Her fists clenched tightly in her lap.

"Do as I say."

"I will not."

"Doona test my temper. I said remove those clothes."

She shook her head defiantly. In the shadows of the ancient trees, a wind stirred the leaves. A clear whistling sound penetrated her ears.

"WE BE HERE," her brethren whispered.

Bryna touched her ear in acknowledgement.

Her captor scanned the clearing. "What is that murmuring sound?" he demanded.

"The faeries."

He grabbed a handful of hair and jerked her head back. "Why do they not show themselves to me?"

Bryna stared up into hateful eyes. "In their time they come, Eamon. Release me."

He did, then back handed her across the face. Bryna fell back, her cheek stinging from the blow.

"Doona play your fey games with me," he growled in rising temper. He ripped the heavy cloak from her shoulders and tossed it into the mud.

"Stand up."

She shook her head.

He grabbed her by the hair once again and pulled her roughly to her feet.

Dressed in only a sodden bedrail, Bryna glared back at him.

"I see why Tynan has lain with you." He released her hair and cupped her face. "I will not hurt you, Bryna, if you but obey me. My touch can be gentle too."

She pulled back in revulsion.

"Doona turn from me when I speak to you." His hands gripped her shoulders. There was a terrible entreaty in his voice. She flattened her hands against his chest and pushed against him, seeking her freedom. "I would rather die than endure your touch."

His body stiffened in front of her, large fingers digging into her flesh. Bryna bit back a cry of pain and looked up into his hardened face. He was watching her, eyes bright with hatred. "I will make you die little deaths each time I come between your thighs." He shook her. "Shall we begin now in this fey place?"

Suddenly, a blinding light burst upon them, a brilliance gone in the next breath, a faery intervention.

Silver, gold, and bronze luminosity shimmered upon the dark branches of the trees. The clearing buzzed loudly with the drone of bees.

"I see them!" He shoved her roughly aside and Bryna slid, landing in the mud on her side.

"They come. I knew they would come at my call," Eamon said excitedly. "They recognize me as the Dark Chieftain."

All around, the woodlands were alight with agitated faeries.

"WE BE HERE." They called to her, reassurances that rode the air currents of the night.

"Come." Eamon beckoned, his steps taking him to the clearing's perimeter and away from her. Unwinking eyes stared out from the darkness. "I have come to mate with the territorial goddess," he declared loudly.

"I doona think so," Tynan answered, his voice low and dangerous.

Bryna pushed sodden hair from her face with a trembling hand and stared with wide eyes.

Tynan stood between her and her tormentor, gripping the hilt of a glittering, double-edged sword.

"You came after me," she said softly, her heart full of joy.

His gaze flickered to her. In that briefest of moments, where light balanced over shade, she glimpsed a smoldering fury deep within his amethyst eyes. The intensity of it stole her breath away, for she did not know if it was meant for her or Eamon.

Tynan turned away from his faerymate and faced his cousin.

"You," Eamon gritted out, striding forward and unsheathing his sword.

"I am here, Eamon," Tynan said evenly, keeping his anger in check. He stood poised for battle, watching the flush of hatred stain his cousin's cheeks.

"You have no right!"

"Again, cousin, you seek that which does not

belong to you."

"I have earned the right of challenge. I am the stronger one."

"You challenged and lost," Tynan replied coolly. "Have you forgotten the morning of the bonfire? Has your mind grown weak and feeble as your body? I give you one last chance. You trespass here, for she belongs to me and only to me. Drop down your sword now, for I am the Dark Chieftain of Prophesy. Not you."

Eamon bellowed and attacked, but Tynan anticipated it and sidestepped. With a sharp downward thrust, he slashed a deep groove in his cousin's strong right arm. Blood spewed from the gash. His cousin only grunted, raising his sword despite the severity of the wound. Tynan knew it would take more than a single blow to slow him down. The battle was just beginning.

The two deadly blades met in a loud crash, filling the clearing with the piercing sound of scraping and ringing iron. They fought savagely, their blows hard, rapid, and deadly.

Bryna rose clumsily to her feet. Her back pressed against the boulder beside the well. She shivered in fear and cold, unable to look away. When Tynan staggered back from a slash in his thigh, she jammed her fist in her mouth. The land responded to her silent screams with gusts of cold wind and darkening thunderclouds. In a loud burst of crackling lightning, rain fell upon the ground once again, drenching the battling warriors in the territorial goddess's enchantment.

Tynan felt it.

Felt the surge of strength flow into his weary limbs.

The rain, he realized, the rain was enchanted. *My faerymate*. With fluid ease, he shifted on his injured leg, able to carry his weight once again, and lifted his sword.

His cousin grinned triumphantly, rain distorting his features into something vile and evil. "You are not so strong now, Tynan."

"Neither are you," Tynan countered, waiting. Blood soaked his cousin's right side from the arm wound. They were both badly hurt. It would come to a test of wills.

"Did you enjoy your visit with the Sorcerer?" his cousin sneered. "I see he dinna teach you to bow to your betters."

"The Evil One," Tynan said in sudden understanding. "You betrayed me?"

"Aye, I did. Too trusting you are, cousin. 'Tis a simple task to slip a potion in your drink. I had followed you to the stream that night and watched you collapse. I should have let you drown in the black waters, but that feeble Sorcerer wanted you for some sacred ritual."

"You know nothing of what you speak, Eamon," Tynan replied tightly.

"I know this," Eamon spat in fury. "I must finish

what the Sorcerer could not and claim my rightful place as the Dark Chieftain. You may have bested me once, but never again."

"Come then, cousin. Come and taste your death." Tynan saw the imminent strike and wielded his sword upward, meeting his cousin's downward thrust.

"You canna win, Eamon." Tynan gripped the hilt of his sword with both hands, power radiating through him into the deadly blade, making him strong. "Drop the sword and live."

Uncertainty flashed in his cousin's eyes for just a moment. "Nay!" he roared, overwhelmed by his hatred and jealousy.

Swords clanged above the sound of the driving rain. Lightning flashed in the sky directly overhead, followed by an explosion of thunder.

Tynan forced Eamon back. "Yield, Eamon. Doona force me to kill you."

"Never!"

He parried his cousin's stroke and then drove his sword deep into the other man's belly.

It was done.

Eamon stared down at himself in bewilderment, at the sword embedded in him.

Blood splattered the rain-soaked earth.

An unearthly stillness came to the clearing.

Tightening his grip on the hilt of his weapon, Tynan jerked the blade out as Eamon's sword tumbled from his hand and landed in the mud at their feet.

Death was approaching.

Clutching his bleeding stomach, his cousin lifted his head, eyes glazing and searching. Tynan knew he looked for Bryna.

"I could have loved you, g-godddess." A gurgling sound rose up from his cousin's throat.

Leaning forward, Tynan removed the dagger from Eamon's belt and tossed it aside. His cousin dropped to his knees in a rain pool of blood and mud, his eyes glazed with the ending of his life.

"May you find peace, Eamon," Tynan said softly, feeling Bryna come up beside him. "May the envy darkening your soul finally release you."

His cousin slipped silently to the ground, locked in death's cold embrace. Eamon's envy, Tynan thought, would betray him no longer.

✳✳✳

The rain had stopped, leaving glittering raindrops like tiny diamonds everywhere.

Bryna felt her heart pounding. She had helped Tynan. A whisper and understanding and then power surged into her and she knew instinctively how to aid her chieftain mate. Rain had fallen, seething with energy from her and all of it directed into Tynan, replacing the strength he had used before coming to the clearing.

She stood trembling now, a sodden butterfly,

empty, relieved and frightened because he had come.

His *geas* was what drove him.

But he had come.

Fought for her.

And won.

" 'Tis finally done," her chieftain mate said, pointing his sword to the ground and leaning heavily upon it.

"Tynan," she said achingly, wanting to say so much more.

Reaching out, he touched her bruised jaw, an undisguised emotion clouding his features. "I regret not getting here sooner, faery."

"You are here now." She curled her hands around his thick wrist and pressed her face into his warm, calloused palm.

"I am here now," he readily agreed. His thumb caressed her cheek. "Dinna you think I would?"

Her brows drew together. "I dinna know."

He tilted her chin up and she looked up at him, her heart in her throat.

"Foolish faery," he murmured roughly. "You are mine."

He staggered then and she pulled back, gripping his wrist.

"Your fey strength leaves me, faery. It seems Eamon's blade has cut far deeper than I thought." Black lashes splayed down upon pale cheeks. The sword fell from his hand.

He tilted forward.

"Tynan!" Bryna tried to cushion his fall but he was so much larger than she was. They landed hard in the mud. She managed to break most of it with her own body and protect his head from hitting the ground.

Unconscious and sprawled heavily on top of her, she could not breathe from the weight of him. His bristled cheek pressed into the white hollow between her thinly covered breasts. Hot breath scorched her skin.

"Tynan?" She cupped the back of his head with her left hand.

Silence answered her.

She tried to turn him over on his back, but lacked the strength. The hilt of the dagger at his waist dug into her thigh. Changing tactics, she slipped out from under him, rocking back and forth, using the slippery mud to ease her way.

Bryna pushed wet hair out of her eyes and moved near his hip. Kneeling, she leaned forward, trying to inspect his wounded leg, but the wound was in the front of the thigh.

Pushing at his waist, she tried turning him over on his back, a hopeless task until he groaned and then rolled over on his own, flinging arms wide.

Bryna paled. Even covered in mud, his leg wound caught her attention immediately. The deep gash ran the length of the front of his right thigh.

Carefully, she began to rip open the pant leg.

"Help me," she called out to her brethren, not looking up. A clear whistling sound came to her ears.

"Hurry," she commanded, a territorial goddess asserting her authority. "Blodenwedd, I need water from the well."

The woodlands filled with golden fey light.

CHAPTER 20

THE SUN PEEKED THROUGH THE canopy of the pristine woodlands, welcoming a new morning and Tynan awoke to a feeling of warmth and dryness. He became aware of his surroundings, slowly waking from dreams of peace and contentment. He stared up at a ceiling of wooden rods interwoven with dried branches and curving twigs. The sky shone brightly through a gap in the top thatching. Outside, a blackbird's song greeted the new dawn.

He caught the smell of musty animal skins and rose to his elbow. He lay in a bed of white sheepskins. Beyond the bed, in the center of the round house, flames crackled in the fire circle.

Tynan's eyes closed in memory. *Clearing. Swords. Rain.*

He opened his eyes. *My sword? I need my sword.* "Bryna?" Pushing himself up, he located his sword and scabbard lying on an old goatskin at the base of the bed. He tried reaching for it but pain cut through his leg, stealing his breath and strength.

"Tynan, stop." His faery strode in, carrying a pile of twigs, and dropped them in the corner. "What are you doing?"

"Give me my sword." He gritted his demand through clenched teeth.

"Nay, lay down."

"Bryna, give it to me."

She shook her head. "There is no need for it here. We are safe, Tynan."

His gaze flickered to a red hem of faery webs by his hip. The fey fabric swirled around dainty bare feet. He looked up slowly.

A creature of silver and flames, of in-between and mystery, watched him.

"What are you wearing?" he blurted out. "Faery webs?"

"A fey gift." She leaned forward, touching his forehead with the back of her hand. Sheer and strapless, except for five silver threads scooping one shoulder, the red faery gown hugged her curves indecently.

"No fever." She straightened, pushing her hair back over her shoulder. "How do you feel?"

Tynan scowled. "How long have we been here?"

"You have slept for two days."

He could not recall anything beyond the battle. "Where is this place?"

"In the woodlands."

He studied the dilapidated roundhouse. Wild vines grew over the entranceway, crawling up the structure's walls. "This is a faery place?"

"It is."

He looked back at her, a feeling of uncertainty

washing over him. "You are different, Bryna."

" 'Tis the fey gown."

Nay, not that, he thought. There was a complete-ness to her now; the insecure waif was gone.

"Hungry?" she asked.

Tynan glanced down at himself. He felt stiff. Shifting, he tested the ache in his lower body. Sharp pain erupted down his right thigh, causing him to feel queasy.

"Tynan, doona move around so much."

With a muttered curse, he jerked the skins off and stared down his nakedness at a heavily bandaged thigh. The pungent scent of garlic, stonecrop, and healing flesh hit him like a fist.

"What is that smell?"

"Poultice, stitching, healing herbs and faery whis-pers," his faerymate explained softly.

"I stink."

A faint blush tainted her cheeks. "Aye, a wee bit for now. I'll bathe you later."

"Where are my clothes?"

"I cut your breeches off to get at the wound." She shrugged. "Your boots are over there in the corner."

He did not want his boots. He wanted his clothes. Tynan scrutinized the bodice of the red dress, his eyes narrowing. One more shrug and she would spill out of it.

Her small hands caressed the fabric self-conscious-ly. " 'Tis a gift from the faeries. Doona you like it?"

"Nay, 'tis indecent," he said irritably.

"Indecent?" She glanced down at herself. "Everything is covered except my shoulders and back. The faeries have clothes for you too."

"Not bloody likely."

It was obvious she wanted to smile, for her lips quivered a moment and then stilled. "Blodenwedd says your body was meant for the faery webs."

Tynan scowled. She knew perfectly well what he thought of the spoiled Blodenwedd.

"Are you hungry, Tynan? I prepared a stew."

"Thirsty," he said, more in annoyance. He hated being confined this way and he stank worse than the pigs. He yanked the pelts back over himself to block out the pungent smell and looked up. The dress opened down the back, an inviting path to the top of her curved bottom.

"Bryna?"

She glanced over her shoulder, her hands gripping the handle of the water bucket.

"Where is the back of the gown?"

"There is none because the webs interfere with my wings."

"Wings?" he choked.

She set the bucket down beside him and knelt. Scooping up the water with a chipped clay bowl, his faery held it out in offering. "The water is verra cold from the well, so drink slowly."

"You have wings, Bryna? I doona see them."

"So they tell me," she replied with a slight nervousness to her voice. "They are folded and unseen for now."

"Unseen," he echoed, feeling an odd regret. It made him wonder at her faery form. He took the bowl from her outstretched hands and drank deeply, despite her warning to go slow. It seemed his stomach agreed with her wise advice, for he had to fight back a grimace of discomfort.

"Would you like the stew now?"

"Aye." He nodded, feeling scolded by her gaze.

Leaning around him, she rolled some of the older animal skins and propped them behind his back so he could sit more comfortably. "I will be a moment."

She rose and went back to the cooking pot near the fire circle.

"Do you feel the wings?" he asked.

She tilted her head, a peculiar frown to her profile. "I am not sure what I feel, Tynan."

Retrieving a large clay bowl she scooped the contents of the stew with a ladle. "I have kept this warm since yester eve, hoping you would awaken." She returned, kneeling beside him once more. The faery gown spread out around her shapely legs.

"What is in it?" Tynan took the warm bowl from her hands.

"Lamb and vegetables." She handed him a wooden spoon with scalloped edges and a vine handle.

" 'Tis just a spoon, Tynan. No need to scowl at it,"

she said sweetly.

For a moment, he thought she would take it out of his hand and start feeding him like a babe. "I am not scowling at it," he replied glumly. "I have never seen anything like it before."

" 'Tis for eating."

He gave her a slanted smile and then looked down at the stew. His mouth began to water. He dug in with the spoon, tasting succulent meat and vegetables, and found himself ravenous. He ate quickly, lost to his body's needs.

"Slowly, Tynan. You have not eaten in two days and your stomach may object."

"Do you have more?"

"Aye, but first drink this." She handed him a cup of honeyed milk. "It will coat your stomach. 'Tis the faery healing that causes the immense hunger in you."

"Faery healing as in faery whispers?" Tynan asked, drinking the sweetened liquid. It only made him hungrier.

"Aye, faery whispers to make you strong." She brought another steaming bowl of stew to him and knelt near his hip.

He consumed that one, too, and handed her the empty bowl.

"More?" she prompted, her gaze steady and patient. She looked amused with him.

"Nay, faery." The heat of the food warmed his body, pulling him down. His eyelids drooped in heaviness.

"Sleep now, Tynan. 'Tis the healing that calls to you. Doona fight it."

"Is there something in the stew, Bryna?"

"Nay, just fey wishes for a fast recovery." She removed the rolled up pelts from behind his back and helped him slide down. "Rest now, close your eyes."

"A fine faery healing, I canna keep my eyes open."

She caressed his cheek, her fingertips brushing his eyelids. "Bed rest is what you need."

"I need . . . to return to Kindred," he said stubbornly, his body unwilling and weighty.

"In time. The faeries have saved your leg, now give yourself time to heal."

"They will always remind me of it too," he complained sullenly and then gave a mighty sigh. Sleep claimed him.

"Willful." Bryna smiled gently, sitting back. "Heal my heart."

"HE WILL HEAL."

She stiffened at the sound of the Faery King' smooth voice from behind her.

"HAVE YOU SHOWN HIM YOUR TRUE SELF, HONOR?"

"NAY." Bryna said softly, not turning around.

"SOON THEN, HONOR."

Clutching the empty bowl in her lap, she gave curt nod.

✳✳✳

The morning sun rose on another day.

Tynan dreamed of wings made of filmy white lace and silver threads attached to a beautiful woman's shoulders.

Slowly the dream world released him and he became aware of a gnawing heat in his leg and a cool wetness gliding down over his body. Opening his eyes, he stared at a pair of incredibly healthy breasts pushing against a lace-work of delicate, silver webs. They brushed against his cheek as she reached across him, a settling of pelts and movement of air. He closed his eyes, caught between primitive desire and a dull, weakening ache.

"Tynan?"

He peered at her from beneath his lids, a look of moldering disquiet.

She hesitated. "How are you feeling today?"

"I still smell like rancid garlic."

Her eyes crinkled in laughter. "That is not you." She pointed to the large clay bowl near her hip. "I am replacing the old poultice with this one. The garlic is not as pungent as before."

He considered arguing with her, then thought the better of it. "How does my leg look today?"

"Verra well. You heal quickly, Tynan. I see no sign of infection."

He grunted.

She sat still, gazing at him with those deep gray eyes.

He thought of pulling her down in the bed beside him. "What are you wearing now, silver threads?"

"Doona you like this one?" She looked down at herself.

" 'Tis the same as the other." He struggled to sit up and realized she had the pelts off him again.

"This one has sleeves, Tynan." She pushed him back down, her strength overpowering him in his weakened condition.

"I would not call those threads sleeves."

Her eyes flashed at him "You are bad-tempered in the mornings. If you promise to lie still and let me replace the poultice, I will change back to my bedrail. It is clean, though ripped."

"Doona change," he grumbled, feeling out of sorts lying there naked and helpless like a newborn babe.

"May I finish, then?"

He waved at her to continue, his gaze shifting away

A cool cloth glided down his healing thigh, causing him to flinch.

"What are you doing to me now?"

She smiled, a little curve to her lips. "As I told you I must put the new poultice on your leg." Reaching in the clay bowl, she cupped handfuls of a greenish mixture and put it over the wound. "It speeds the healing, Tynan."

"It feels warm," he said, slightly surprised.

"Aye, did you think it would not be?" She wrapped a white cloth around his thigh.

He frowned a little. "It still stinks."

"A wee bit, nothing like before." She sat back and surveyed her work, her hands green from the poultice. "How does the wound feel?"

Tynan shifted, testing the bandage. The ache in his leg had diminished, giving way to another bodily need. He became aware of a building pressure to relieve himself and glanced hopefully at the entranceway.

She turned to where he looked and smiled. "The pale afternoon light filters in, turning the vines to silver this day."

He had not noticed. He caught sight of a brown wren foraging and wished only to join the bird beyond the holly bush.

"Tynan?"

He gave her a wan smile.

"Does the wound pain you?"

"Not like before." He sat up.

"Where are you going?"

She had that authoritative tone of the simpler. Rose's influence, no doubt. He motioned to the open entranceway. "I need to go outside."

"Why?" she asked, her lovely brows arched in confusion.

He had no intention of explaining what should be obvious.

"*He has needs, Honor.*"

Tynan looked up. A halo of silvery light and glitter took form in the entranceway, then strode in.

"Nuada," Tynan said in relief. The silver garbed Faery King came to stand before him, hands on his hips and a curious quiver to his lips.

Tynan found no amusement in this situation.

"*I SHALL TEND THE CHIEFTAIN, GODDESS. GO. IT BE TIME.*"

Tynan looked to his faerymate, but she had already stood and left without explanation.

Night fell in shades of deep, black velvet.

A myriad of candles glimmered through trees thousands of years old. White roses bloomed in fey wildness amongst a thicket of thorns surrounding the enchanted well.

Bryna knelt in the moonlit clearing. A flowing gown of white webs hugged her form, leaving her back bare. Clusters of faery diamonds decorated the bodice, sleeves, and entire length of the train.

She bowed her head. Blodenwedd attended her, a kind of penance, no doubt ordered by the Faery King.

Bryna inhaled and took on her fey form as the faeries had taught her.

Her eyes changed.

Black pupils became catlike slits surrounded by a sea of gray.

Gossamer wings materialized.

Formed of silver lace, they unfolded from slender shoulder blades and stretched out behind her.

Her skin whitened, transforming to silk and the color of virgin snow.

And her hair.

Gold and red hues wove into every strand, glittering with heat.

"Are you sure?" Blodenwedd asked.

"Aye." Bryna shivered with a guarded awareness. "Show me the ways of the *Daoine Sidhe*, so I may learn and protect the *Tuatha Dé Danann*."

Blodenwedd nodded. Her body faded into the night. Fey winds blew through woodlands fragranced with blooms and fatal, mortal enchantment.

Bryna closed her eyes.

The soft wind kissed her cheeks.

Her hair turned into the color of immortal flames.

Behind her lids, a purple light came into being.

She saw the ancient faery fort of Kindred.

She felt her body link with the magical life force of the land. From the waterlogged bogs to the salty wind; from the mysterious shamrocks to the ancient oaks; from the wild goats to the sea gray seals — all linked.

Everything shimmered around her.

All endless.

She breathed in the revelation of BELONGING.

To Bryna it meant peace in her soul, a completeness where none existed before. To Tynan and his tribe, it would mean a strong future and fulfillment of the Dark Chieftain Prophecy for bounty and loyalty.

Bryna ceased being lost and became by right of

birth . . . a territorial goddess in full bloom.

It felt very good, indeed.

She had been raised in the mortal way. Her first instincts would always be mortal.

However, the rest would be pure goddess. Her lips curved into a smile.

The fey wind dwindled to faery whispers and silver threads that transformed into butterflies.

All became what should have been.

She was goddess.

Only one thing remained to complete her transformation.

Only one thing remained to gain faery approval of her handfasting, her trial-marriage.

Only one thing remained to permanently bond her with the Dark Chieftain.

She must show him her true self, and in so doing complete the prophecy with his acceptance. She dare not allow herself to think of his rejection.

Bryna folded her wings against her back and returned to her mortal self.

✳✳✳

Another morning came.

Tynan's wound healed, the mark of it disappeared, as is the fey way. His full strength returned.

In the cool air, he stood staring down at the black webs covering his body. Like the course of a stream, the enchanted fabric flowed over skin and muscle, outlining his form. He felt more naked than clothed. The Faery King brought the clothes himself and asked that he put them on.

Tynan could not refuse. He chuckled at himself now, a sudden creature of twilight and depth and wondered what Bryna would say when she saw him.

Turning, he grabbed the leather wrapped scabbard resting on the table. Shrugging into the straps, he anchored it across his shoulders and down his back.

"Blodenwedd is right," his faerymate murmured from the entranceway. "You were born to wear the faery webs."

"They are comfortable," he reluctantly admitted.

She smiled at his tone and walked around him. "You feel better, Tynan?"

"Aye."

Picking up the sword where it lay on the goatskins, she held it out to him, palms opened, balancing the deadly, double-edged blade and leaving him access to the hilt.

"Thy sword, Dark Chieftain," she whispered.

Tynan looked at her and saw the serene manifestation of the faeries in her features, enhancing her beauty. A muscle twitched at his jawline. "You are different, Bryna." He did not reach for his battle weapon.

She nodded. "Different, and yet the same."

Tynan inhaled the new, subtle difference in her scent. It coursed through his veins, heating his blood

— a mysterious blending of moonlight perfume and lavender, of turbulent storms and summer rain. He lost himself in her silver eyes. Something flickered in their depths, sorrow or desire. He could not be sure, for it disappeared as it had come, suddenly.

"The faeries have treated you well?" he asked.

"They are my brethren."

Tynan's hand slid over the sword's wooden hilt with what he hoped was an easy grace. He had never felt more awkward.

"You are as they now?" He inspected the blood groove down the center of the weapon with the tip of a finger.

"I am more, and less of what they are, part of twilight, between two worlds, belonging to neither and both."

He nodded, stepping away from her, not understanding. His palm glided over the smoothness of the blade before sliding it into the scabbard at his back. The sword felt familiar, the only thing familiar here in this fey place.

"You doona need the sword."

"I always need my sword, Nuada." He looked over his shoulder at the Faery King. "My thanks for your healing."

Nuada dipped his head and looked to Bryna.

"We await you by the falls, Honor."

Tynan's gaze narrowed in suspicion. "What is this about?"

"WORTHINESS. ACCEPTANCE."

He glanced at Bryna, but she refused to meet his gaze.

"COME TO THE FALLS NOW, HONOR. IT BE TIME AND THE DARK CHIEFTAIN BE HEALED."

Tynan recognized the direct command. With that, the Faery King vanished, leaving them alone with only shafts of silver light.

"Why does he call you Honor?"

"It is my true fey name."

"Do you wish me to call you by this name?"

She shook her head. "I am Bryna, not Honor."

Tynan looked toward the entrance. "They await us," he whispered. "I feel them."

"Come, Tynan."

Tynan's hand shot out and grabbed her forearm, holding her in place.

"What do I sense, Bryna? Whose worthiness? Whose acceptance? What does the Faery King ask of you?"

"He asks of my worthiness and your acceptance."

Tynan understood immediately. "He does not give his approval to our handfasting?"

"Nay, not yet. He is angered that we handfasted without faery permission."

"Handfasting is a trial-marriage. It was the only way I could protect you."

"He knows this and it tempers his annoyance. But for our marriage to become permanent, you must accept me."

"Accept you? I chose you. You are mine by ancient promise, my territorial goddess. Look at me, Bryna." He pulled her gently closer. "What is his other demand?"

Tears glistened in her eyes. "He questions my ability to give you children."

Tynan glared at the entrance in fury. "He has no right."

"Tynan, he has every right."

"Nay, he does not." Tynan guided her out of the roundhouse. "Let us be done with this foolishness. You are mine by ancient promise, by honor-mark, by claim, by handfasting. I will accept no other, damn them. How many approvals do I need to claim my mate? Show me this place we need to go."

He followed his faerymate to an isolated path between the trees.

"I have not been here before."

" 'Tis the sacred place of revealing. Blodenwedd showed me yester eve. It is a place of waterfall called the Falls of the Orchids."

Before them two massive oaks stood guard at the entrance of a boundary of boulders.

"Come," she gestured. "The falls lie beyond."

He followed her, entering a clearing of lush jade carpet sprinkled with blades of golden grass. Beyond the carpet, a waterfall fell from a tower of rock to a small black pool. Spray and mist coated the land, giving it an otherworldly appearance. Lichens and mosses clung to fissures in flat rocks and along either side of the waterfall.

"This is a fey place of revealing. My brethren have chosen not to share it with mortals."

"Selfish sprites," Tynan remarked under his breath.

"Some things must be kept separate, Tynan."

He grunted, unwilling to give agreement. The temperature dipped as they came forward, marking the serene world of in-between. Around them thousands of fragrant orchids grew with white to creamy green blooms borne on many stems surrounded by fleshy leaves. Amidst the flowers her brethren waited, shimmering and silent in their unblinking regard.

The Faery King sat atop a boulder to the left of the waterfall.

Tynan left his faerymate's side and walked over to the boulder to face the king. He stared up at cool jeweled eyes in open challenge.

"She is mine by ancient promise," he stated strongly, passing over formal greetings. He had had enough of faery interference in his life.

"PROMISES CAN BE BROKEN."

"Not this one," he answered.

Nuada's smile did not reach his eyes. "YOU HONOR-MARKED, HANDFASTED, AND MADE THE CLAIM WITHOUT GAINING OUR APPROVAL FIRST."

"Do you question my *geas*?"

The Faery King blinked, a single shifting within. "WE QUESTION NOT THE PROMISE, BUT HER ABILITY TO

GIVE YOU CHILDREN. THE PROPHECY MUST CONTINUE."

"She will bear my children."

"CAN YOU GUARANTEE THIS, DARK CHIEFTAIN? SHE HAS LOST YOUR FIRST SEED."

"I will accept no other." Tynan held the fey king's gaze. They could not force him to choose another.

Nuada's lips tightened, showing his displeasure. He had the power to wipe the chieftain's memory clean of Honor, if he so chose. "PRIDEFUL AND STUBBORN."

"Aye," Tynan agreed. "She is mine."

"THEN TURN TO THE WATERFALL'S POOL AND VIEW THE TRUE FORM OF YOUR GODDESS. TELL ME IF YOU STILL ACCEPT HER. TELL ME IF YOU WILL LAY WITH A CREATURE OF TWILIGHT. I WILL KNOW IF YOU LIE."

Tynan looked over his shoulder.

In the misty waters of the waterfall pool, Bryna knelt, head bowed, body trembling. Water lapped gently at her thighs.

Silvery lacewings stretched out behind her in the glorious display of her kind.

"Bryna?" he said in wonderment. Never had he seen so beautiful a faery. He moved to the edge of the black pool.

She looked up at him, a creature of twilight and legend. Uncertainty shone in transformed eyes. Silvery tears streamed down pale cheeks, catching in the crease of quivering lips the color of yewberries.

He went to her and knelt in the warm waters.

Cupping her face, he stared into her catlike eyes. "Bryna, you are beautiful to me in any form."

She grabbed his wrists with cold hands, holding on in this place of judgment. "Be sure, Tynan," she said achingly.

"I am." He kissed her lips, a sweet claiming and promise for the future.

Behind them, the Faery King's lips thinned even more. He gave a curt nod of approval. He would give Honor a sennight to conceive before removing the chieftain's memory of her. He had run out of patience. Long ago, he had ordered a territorial goddess stolen and misplaced in punishment for a weak chieftain's insult. He could have done far worse. For now, he would wait.

CHAPTER 21

AFTER BIDDING THE FAERIES FAREWELL, Bryna and Tynan entered the feypaths. It was early afternoon.

Before them, the cavernous tunnel opened into the colors of soft purple upon gray shades, at odds with the deeper discordant shadows beyond.

"This feypath is different than the other one, faery." He touched the cool stone outlining the walls.

"I have chosen another feypath for our journey." Bryna could sense Tynan's revulsion. He stood poised, assessing the danger.

"It smells different," he said, his gaze searching.

Behind them, the purple half-moon rock slid silently back into place.

"It is less foul, Tynan."

He made no move and Bryna stepped around him to lead.

His hand shot out, holding her gently in place.

"Tynan, the faeries' spitefulness stains the feypaths to keep mortals from using them. I can do nothing to remove the taint, but there is no reason for you to suffer. So, I have chosen this path because it is less foul."

"Less foul." His tone marked his disbelief.

"Come." She urged him forward. " 'Tis as safe as the other feypaths we've traveled."

"You know this way, Bryna?"

"Aye. With my fey awakening has come the knowledge of many things, including the ancient feypaths. There are many paths to Kindred. This one," she gestured forward, "is more direct and, as I have said, less foul."

"Safer, faery?"

She shook her head. "None of the faery feypaths are truly safe."

"Why is that?"

She looked down the tunnel. "Envy."

"Envy?" he echoed, not understanding.

"Have you not guessed, Tynan? The faeries envy mortals. They envy how mortals feel and respond to the natural world."

"Why? They have so much." He released her arm.

" 'Tis hard to explain. If you and I stand beside a flower in a meadow, I will hear the breath of a butterfly before he lands on a flower. A mortal would simply be pleasantly surprised. They envy that feeling of unexpectedness, of the unforeseen."

"Are you envious?" he asked, his eyes watchful.

"Nay, I feel with the heart of a faery goddess and a mortal woman."

" 'Tis hard to be caught in between."

Bryna regarded him thoughtfully. Did he really understand what she was?

"Come." He took her hand. "Let us see this fey-path that you have chosen for our journey." He led her forward.

They walked for hours through the strange, desolate tunnel. A faint chill and an odor of mild decay clung to the humid air. Black pebbles littered the dirt floor. Intermittent stone tunnels appeared on either side of their path, opening into vast graves of nothingness.

Bryna's steps began to slow.

"Tired, faery?"

She shook her head. Though the faery awakening in the clearing and the revealing at the falls had weakened her physically, she did not want Tynan to suffer the feypaths any longer than necessary. "We must go on. I doona want you to spend a night in the feypaths."

"It is not as bad as first I thought. Let us rest here." He pointed to an outcropping of rocks shaped in a cross. "Enough hours have passed that it feels like night to me."

Bryna did not argue. Wearily, she sank to her knees near the crosslike outcropping of rock and minerals.

Tynan could feel the faery magic of the tunnel against his tingling skin. He tried to peer into the purple darkness. "Do you sense the fey magic?" he asked.

When no answer came, he turned around. In the eerie darkness, his faerymate curled upon herself on the ground, fast asleep. The silvery webs of the enchanted gown had darkened, obscuring the outline of her body. Flame colored tresses spilled about her shoulders to the hard ground. Her lips were parted in a deep slumber.

A faint smile curved Tynan's mouth. *Stubborn faery. Sleep comes to you despite the strangeness here. Mayhap it is no longer strange to you.*

He lay down behind her, wincing slightly at the remaining tightness in his healed thigh. Gently, his arm slid around her small waist and pulled her back into his chest.

"Tynan?" she murmured sleepily, snuggling back into him.

"I am here, faery. Let us sleep for a while."

"Aye," she whispered.

He buried his face in the silken waves of her hair and closed his eyes. She smelled of lavender and sanctuary even here, within the feypath. He felt slumber rising up to claim him, but it would be a light resting, for already his senses were tuned to threat and hazard. He respected his fey brethren, but never would he trust them.

They slept for eight hours, although Tynan could not be sure. He felt rested and turned onto his back.

"Morning."

He looked over and stared into a pair of lovely silver eyes.

" 'Tis morning, you think?" he inquired softly.

"Aye, on the outside land. We best be going."

He nodded and stood.

Reaching up, Bryna placed her hand in his, a touch

that warmed her soul. Effortlessly, he pulled her to her feet.

"I have a longing to return to Kindred."

"So do I," Bryna agreed and led the way.

After they had walked for a time, vines began to thicken along the ivory cast ceiling and walls.

"Faery, I am to assume we cannot eat these berries." He looked to her for confirmation.

Bryna glanced at the blue-black fruit ripening on the vines. She knew he was hungry, but then so was she. "That could be dangerous."

"They are poisonous?"

"Nay, not poisonous but I doona know how a mortal's stomach would react with fruit tainted with faeries' spitefulness."

He grinned. "Not verra well."

"Nay, I think not."

He touched a berry then glanced back at her.

"Can you eat them?"

"Methinks my stomach might strongly object."

He nodded and looked back down the tunnel. "We need to eat."

"It is not far."

"The immensity of these brown vines could easily trap a man."

Bryna regarded the vines. Large heart-shaped leaves grew vigorously across ceiling rock and down cracks in the walls. The purple flowers were pipe shaped, prickly, and foul smelling.

"The vines grow thicker further in." He fingered the sturdiness of one of the leaves. "You said we are not far from Kindred."

"Aye, the vines lead us to Kindred's back garden. Methinks an hour or less for the rest of our journey."

"At least there are no thorns."

She laughed softly. "There is that."

Reaching back, he pulled his sword out of the scabbard and prepared to cut a path for them.

"Nay, Tynan," Bryna cried out in alarm, grabbing his sword arm. "Doona cut them. The vines are living and will let us pass. We need only ask them. Please lay down your sword."

He looked at the vines suspiciously. With a fluid upward motion, he flipped the sword, sheathing it perfectly in the scabbard at his back. "Never have I spoken to vines."

"I know." She stepped forward; a whispered request, and the vines opened a path for them.

He stood there, staring.

"Shall we continue?" Bryna asked.

"By all means, faery." He gestured forward. "Let us continue."

An hour later, they came upon a half-moon rock.

Tynan searched for the lever underneath and the rock slid open.

"After you, faery. Sunlight awaits."

Smiling, Bryna stepped through the fey opening into a place of in-between, a momentary coldness, a feeling of displacement and obscurity, and then...

They were outside.

Blue sky.

Green earth.

Sweet air.

She took a deep breath, her face upturned to the fragrant warmth of the afternoon sun. "It feels good to be outside once again."

"Aye, it does," Tynan murmured.

From somewhere near, a child's voice rose in laughter. Behind them the hedgerow and vines returned to their growth pattern, hiding the entrance to the ancient feypath.

Bryna's gaze glided over the back garden. A small grove of sacred oaks stood far off to the right, acting like a wall to the garden and shadowing the evergreen hollies that guarded the waning year when winter came.

"It feels like *Meitheamh*, the month of weddings," she said.

"*Aibrean* and *Beltane* are gone?" Tynan found it hard to believe that April and May had passed and they were into the month of June.

"Aye, Tynan. The cottage and falls were belonging to the faery world. Time moves differently there. Here in the mortal world, it feels like *Meitheamh*."

"The cottage and falls were of faery?"

"Aye, they are a place no mortal has ever seen. Here, under this magnificent blue sky the land

whispers of midsummer to me and so it must be."
The passage of time could sometimes be contradic-
tory between the faery and mortal worlds, and that
recognition did not come easily to her. For now, she
simply breathed deeply of the fragrant air, an enjoyment of life in her lungs.

Her chieftain mate stepped forward, hands on his
hips, overlooking his land. "It feels good to be back."

Bryna watched him. He stood apart from her, a
stance of power and alertness in the sunlight. His left
hand rose, shading eyes that scanned the area.

"The land is serene, Tynan."

"Aye, so I feel it."

The black faery webs enhanced his flawless form.
It was as if the Gods and Goddesses gathered to craft
him in nature's excellence.

"You are very quiet, faery."

Warmth crept into her cheeks. "I simply observe
the black webs."

"Do they meet with your approval?"

"They are fey."

"That they are." He glanced back at her. "But I see
another kind of appreciation in your eyes."

Bryna smiled and looked away. She stepped forward into an abundance of angular reddish-brown
stems and yellowish buttonlike flowers.

"Mugwort," he said in observation. "The druidess
insists the plant keeps elves and evil away."

"Elves hate the scent of this herb."

"I will not argue with a goddess about that." He held out his hand. "Come, walk with me, I wish to view my land before we are noticed, and the chieftain's responsibility is set upon my shoulders once again."

Bryna placed her hand in his and walked beside him. Along a low wall of stones, a dirt path opened. Patches of wild strawberries grew in and out of the shade, spreading outward toward the fields. The low growing, creeping plants covered almost half an acre.

"Your tribesmen doona see us," Bryna remarked, shielding her eyes.

"When they raise their heads from the strawberry patches they will."

"Lordling!" The simpler had come to her feet in the middle of a particularly succulent strawberry patch. Ian turned, looking to where she pointed.

"They see us."

"So it would seem, faery," he chuckled. "Ian wonders how we got into the back garden without alerting his posted sentries."

"Will you tell him of the garden's feypath entrance?"

"I will tell him because he must guard us well. Do you object?"

She shook her head. "As long as those you tell are respectful."

"Then you must teach us, goddess, how to be respectful."

She looked up at him. "The way you respect the faery?"

"The way I respect you."

Somewhere to their right, Hawk let out a bellow.

Tynan turned at the sound. "So much for a quiet homecoming."

The boy came at them at a dead run, trampling through strawberries. Bryna stepped back allowing Tynan to catch his son and swing him up in his arms.

The boy wore only blue breeches; his bare chest and feet were stained with pink juice. "Hawk, you smell of strawberries." Tynan laughed quietly and turned to Ian.

"Welcome home, sire."

"My thanks, Ian. It is good to stand on Kindred's soil once more." He looked around at his gathering tribesmen. "Word travels quickly. How are our people?"

"Quiet and well guarded," Ian answered. "Eamon?"

"We will talk later."

"Bryna!" Hawk cried.

Laughing softly, Bryna stepped forward.

There was a collective silence and Tynan scanned the faces of his tribesmen. He saw respect and joy and found his heart well pleased.

He glanced over his shoulder at his smiling faery-mate. No longer the shy, remote girl he had once brought to his woodland fort, Bryna had become a territorial goddess in full bloom, a goddess who would protect the *Tuatha Dé Danann* with her life.

"Are there any strawberries left, Hawk?" she teased his son.

"Aye, Bryna. I've picked them all day until my fingers hurt. Rose said my mouth is red from too much picking."

"Why is that?" Tynan set his son down.

"I ate only a few," the boy protested, straightening his pants' waist and leaving a new trail of red stickiness.

"A few?" the simpler echoed, coming up to them and wiping her hands on a stained rag tied to her belt. "More like a garden's worth."

"I dinna eat a garden's worth, Rose," Hawk said indignantly.

"With all that fruit, you are sweet now."

"Rose, I am not sweet." He shoved away at his black hair. "I am a boy."

Tynan looked over at Bryna. When their eyes met, she laughed, a sound of musical bells like none other the tribe had ever heard. Grinning himself, he wiped the strawberry juice from his son's chin.

"She sounds like music," Hawk said in surprise and wonder.

"That she does. You have a belly full of sweetness. Let us hope it stays there."

"What do you mean?"

"It means," his faerymate knelt beside his son, "if you eat too much of a thing it may bring pain to your belly for a short time."

Hawk paled. "Pain?"

She pressed her palm against the boy's full stomach

and smiled gently. "But not this time, methinks."

"I will not eat anymore today."

"Good." Tynan pulled Bryna to her feet and squeezed her hand.

"Good," the simpler repeated, and turned to embrace Bryna. "Welcome home."

Tynan turned to Ian.

"My faerymate and I must rest. Have the tribe elders gather in the main hall on the morrow. We will talk then."

Ian nodded. "Done, sire."

Tynan guided his faerymate forward through the crowd of his people. "Come, faery."

He wanted a hot bath, food, sleep, and Bryna in his bed, but first, he needed to walk around Kindred and feel the rich soil beneath his feet.

"Rose, take Bryna to our chambers," he ordered. "Have a warm bath and hot food prepared."

"Aye, Lordling."

"Tynan?" His faerymate started to protest. "Are you not coming?"

"I would like to walk the land first, faery."

She looked beyond him, her eyes clear and bright and said, "I understand."

"Go with Rose and Hawk. I will not be long."

"As you wish."

He watched Hawk escort Rose and Bryna where two guards stood at alert by the kitchen's double doors. When they disappeared into the keep, he turned back to Ian and lowered his voice.

"What month is this, Ian? It doona feel like *Aibrean*."

Ian did not hide his surprise. " It is *Meitheamh*."

"Two months lost." His faerymate had been right. He turned back to face the eager countenances of his tribesmen.

"It feels good to be home. When twilight wanes on the last Sunday of the month, we shall celebrate Midsummer's End and the return of my faerymate." Tynan held his hands up for quiet. "Aye, I know you all like celebrating. So do I, and it is long overdue at Kindred. Now, go before you overrun the gardens," he commanded. "Otherwise, we must face the simpler's wrath and I fear I am not up to it this day. We all know of Rose's protectiveness toward her plants."

Several women laughed. "I would rather face her temper than that of the old druidess," a young man muttered, walking away.

Tynan's tribesmen followed, going their own way, some back to chores, some back home, news of their chieftain's return spreading quickly.

"Ian," Tynan said, "walk with me."

The two men headed for the stables, one dressed in a fine brown tunic and breeches and the other in glittering black faery webs.

Tynan wanted to take a quick stroll around Kindred before returning to his chambers. He scanned the finished corrals with approval. Cloud and several other mares grazed quietly at the high end of their paddock while their foals played in mock battle. He saw Spear nip at the hindquarters of a young gray that came too close.

"Sire?" Ian frowned. "Two months lost?"

Tynan rubbed his chin. "To my way of thinking, I left only a few days ago."

"I have had search parties in the hills and feypaths for two months now looking for you."

"I doona doubt it, Ian. Faery time is different from our time. I canna explain it. Send word to bring our men home. There is no more searching."

"Done."

They stopped under the parapets.

Above the horizon, the setting sunlight changed the colors of the land to pink and lavender.

Tynan studied the inner courtyard filled with his tribesmen. Pigs and goats stood off in their pens. Horses and wagons stood by the stables. People bartered among themselves. There were so very many. A deep calm flooded his being. "It feels good to be home," he murmured, adjusting a sleeve.

Ian cleared his throat. "These black clothes are made by our brethren? I have never seen anything like it before."

"They are faery webs," Tynan answered while shielding his eyes and checking the unfinished parapets. The walkway along the inner width of the parapets, when finished, would connect the different towers of Kindred to one another.

"Faery webs?" Ian echoed.

"Aye," Tynan chuckled. " 'Tis a long story, Ian."

"They are the webs of a condensed night that only a Dark Chieftain may wear," the ancient druidess explained loudly, coming up behind them.

Both men spun around.

"Teacher," Tynan warned. "Be careful your silent step does not startle a warrior." He did not want to see her hurt for Bryna's sake. In her brown robes, the ancient blended with the shadows under the parapets.

"A warrior should be more alert," she said testily.

"Do you need something, Teacher?" Tynan asked.

"Aye, I do."

With a raised brow, he watched in disbelief as the druidess pressed her open palm upon his stomach. Bent fingers sent a pulsing heat through him.

"The webs accept you," the ancient murmured. "Spirits and night. Good. Verra good."

"Old crone," Ian said beside him, "remove your hand. We will have none of your eerie ways here."

"Do you fear the touch of an old woman, Dark Chieftain?"

"I doona fear anyone's touch."

The ancient looked pointedly at Ian.

"Ian," Tynan turned to his friend, knowing the druidess wished to speak with him alone.

Ian understood too. Bowing, he walked stiffly away with a muttered oath.

Tynan turned back to the ancient. "We are alone.

Say your words."

"Verra well. Kindred needs heirs."

"I know my duty."

"You honor-marked, claimed, and handfasted with the territorial goddess."

"You tell me of things I already know, Teacher. Tell me of things I do not."

"The faeries remain uncertain of Bryna's ability to give you children."

"They gave their approval."

"Approvals can be withdrawn," she replied.

"Damn you, say it."

"Abundance now, famine tomorrow."

"Speak clearly," Tynan commanded, his tone laced with irritation.

"The faeries came to me last night in a dream. If Bryna does not conceive within a sennight, another goddess they choose for you. Your memory will be wiped clean of her."

"They would not dare," he growled in fury.

"Oh, they dare. You will have no memory of her and no choice but to accept a new goddess mate."

"Can they do this?"

"Aye. Who shall stop them? The ancient prophecy must be fulfilled. The Faery King grows ever more impatient with each passing hour. My Bryna deserves happiness. This is an uncertain time for her, an uncertain time for us all. The longer you wait, the weaker your tribe, and the more intolerant the faeries become."

"Damn them."

"Now hold still and let me touch you."

Her cold palm pressed hard into his stomach, sending icy shivers up his spine. He felt as if the breath were being drawn out of him. He put his hands on his hips. "By the goddess," he muttered.

"Defiant," she said under her breath. "The faeries will have trouble with you." She dropped her hand away. "Willful too."

"Aye, I am. They will not steal my memory of her. Now that you touched me, what do you see?"

The ancient's lips thinned. "You have learned to control the faery *geas*. You shall not control it," she spat in anger. "This eve of the crescent moon thine seed must flow in fertile ground, or you risk all."

"I will not take her tonight. I will not be told what to do."

"If you doona take her, you damn your tribe to poverty and wretchedness."

Tynan's eyes narrowed to slits of twilight.

"And you damn her." Empty eye-sockets crinkled. "No longer your chosen goddess, what do you think they will do to her? Banish her, they will. Do you hear me, Dark Chieftain?"

"I heard you," Tynan answered low and strode angrily away.

✳✳✳

"Bryna, child?"

"Teacher!" Bryna bounded from the wooden chair nestled beside the hearth. She hugged the druidess in a tearful embrace. "I have missed you," she whispered.

"Ah, child, me too. Let me look at you with my fey sight." Derina pulled back, her head tilting.

Bryna stood still under her teacher's appraisal. She wore an empire line gown made of faery webs and moonbeams.

Her teacher smiled. "You are the goddess now."

"As if you dinna know. Come in and warm yourself. The coming night brings a chill to the air and I now how your bones ache." She guided her teacher round the large wooden tub warming in front of the hearth.

"Water for the chieftain's bath - a good faerymate ou are." Turning toward the table, the ancient sniffed the air. "Food and flowers I smell."

"Aye, curious one. On the table, white candles ght a food tray bearing boar meat, goat cheese, and bread. Two silver goblets stand beside a flask of ale." he walked over to the bed. "On the bed there lie many fragrant rose petals."

"Ah, a thoughtful gesture from the chieftain's eople." The ancient nodded and smiled. "Child, I inna stay long. I came only to see that you are well."

"I am well." Bryna walked back to the druidess. "Methinks you have other words to say."

"The chieftain is restless."

Bryna ran a finger along the tub's edge. "Restless is an odd word to use. What do you truly mean?"

"Uncertainty and fear."

She looked up. "You speak like a bard now?"

Her teacher sighed in exasperation. "It is all clear to me."

"But not to me."

"Your uncertainty breeds his reluctance. He will not touch you this night, or any night thereafter."

Bryna walked over to the hearth and stared into the flames. "What do you see?"

"Child, he fears his seed will take your life."

"It will not," she said softly.

"It almost did."

"That unsure time is gone now."

"Child, if you are the territorial goddess, confident and true, the chieftain's seed will root in fertile ground and the land shall prosper. The faeries will be satisfied. If not . . ." she shrugged.

Bryna glanced over her shoulder at her teacher. The face that regarded her seemed more heavily lined with age and worry. "The faeries are satisfied and have given their approval. We have time."

"Do you?" the ancient prompted. "The faeries are intolerant, child. They can withdraw their approval at any time. Fulfill the prophecy and take his seed. Ensure the future."

Bryna turned back to the flames. Her heart agreed

She had sensed the Faery King's edginess at the falls, a need to quicken her joining with the chieftain.

"Child, the *Tuatha Dé Danann* face many futures. They may become as faery and live with the land, or dwindle to mist and disappear for all eternity."

"They will not disappear," Bryna said, her faith strong, an echo of the knowing inside her.

"You know this for certain?"

Nothing is for certain, she thought.

"My goddess knows many things," Tynan said from the doorway, his tone showing his irritation.

Bryna turned to her mate. He stood tall and regal in the faery webs, a darkening scowl on his face.

"Tynan, please." She wished these two would learn to have more tolerance for each other.

Her teacher turned toward the doorway. "The chieftain is right, child. We shall talk another time. I ask that you consider what I have said."

"I will consider it," Bryna replied.

"I bid you good eve, then."

"Good eve, my teacher." Bryna bowed her head. "Do you need assistance?"

"Nay, I can find my way." Her teacher paused before Tynan. "Be careful, Dark Chieftain, that your silent step does not startle a druidess and cause havoc upon the land."

"Leave," he said, pointing to the outside corridor.

"I am. You doona have to be so ill-tempered."

Tynan snarled an oath and shut the door behind

the druidess. He leaned back against it. "By faith, that woman can tax a man's patience."

"Derina has her ways, but she means well."

"I will have to take your word on that, faery."

"Come, Tynan." Bryna gestured to the wooden tub by the fire and walked over to it. "I have kept the water warm for your bath." She looked back at him. "Or, would you prefer food to sate your hunger?"

He straightened away from the door, a slight hesitancy in his stance. "You are wearing more fey webs? I doona recognize this gown."

She touched the ivory bodice lovingly. "I found three web gowns in the bedchamber. They are gifts from the faeries. I bathed and put this one on. Do you not like it?"

"It is lovely," he grumbled, his gaze sliding away. Moving into the room, he shrugged out of the strap that anchored the sword and scabbard to his back.

Bryna went to assist him. "Here, let me." She took the leather scabbard from his hands and positioned it beside the bed within easy reach.

When she straightened, he had placed his dagger on the table and was gazing thoughtfully at the petal covered bed.

"Bryna, where did all these rose petals come from?" He picked up a petal and fingered it.

"Derina says they are from your people, a welcoming home gift."

"And, what do you say?" he inquired.

Bryna looked to the bed and smiled. "They are a faery gift. Fragrant flowers such as these, white brimming with pink, do not grow this time of year."

"Ah, another fey gift. I wonder what the faeries want this time." He tossed the petal back on the bed and glanced at the tub. Bryna could see that something other than the druidess had upset him.

"I wish to wash the stink of the feypaths from my skin. Is the water warm?"

"Aye, Tynan." She walked around the tub to the other end where she had kept five buckets warming close to the fire. She lifted one of them to empty into the tub.

"Wait, faery." He came up behind her, his hand sliding over hers where she held the bucket's handle. "Let me lift them."

She stepped aside while he emptied four of the five buckets into the tub, bringing the water level near half-full.

Straightening, his gaze slid back to her and Bryna felt the fey connection that bound him to her. She also felt his discipline, the inner battle that waged between his dread of the past and his need for her.

"Do you need assistance?" she asked.

"For what?"

"Removing the fey webs?" she replied innocently. The time for hesitancy between them was over. Standing here in the privacy of their bedchamber with the warmth of the fire at their backs, Bryna's heart grew bold.

She was ready to embrace the prophecy, to embrace the destiny that had once been stolen from her. She was ready to embrace her chieftain mate and all that would come thereafter.

"Come, Tynan, you canna wash with the fey webs clinging to your noble skin." Stepping closer, she reached out, her hand catching at his lean hip, webs and magic clinging to her flesh. A small flash of blue light and the black webs came away in her hand, leaving him gloriously naked.

He looked down upon himself, a slight tightness around his lips. When he glanced at her sideways, his eyes had darkened to slits of fire, setting a preordained heat to her fey blood.

"Let me wash the stench of the feypaths from you," she said.

The air seemed to heat all around them, setting the room to shadows and waverings of gold. His gaze slid away, releasing her, and he stepped into the tub. Bryna released a pent-up breath. He was going to be willful. Kneeling beside the tub, she removed his arm bands and torc and placed them on the floor behind her.

"It is a large tub," she murmured.

"Aye, I asked the carpenters to build one for me. I dislike folding my body to fit."

"You are bigger than most men."

He grunted noncommittally and Bryna could no

help but smile.

Hot water lapped over his stomach and thighs, turning his skin red. He leaned his head back on the rim of the tub and closed his eyes.

"The water is warm?" Bryna asked.

"Aye."

His face and shoulders shone in the candlelight with a fine sheen of sweat, a very strong temptation for a goddess bent on seduction and fulfillment of a prophecy. Muscular arms rested on the rim of the tub. His eyes were closed, black lace splayed against flushed cheeks.

"I would assist you in your bath."

"So it would seem."

She took one of his hands and opened his fist. "Let me ease your strain."

Without waiting for his reply, she dipped her hands in the hot water and soaped his arm. With slow strokes, she worked her way across his broad shoulders, collarbone, neck, and upper chest, then down his other arm.

"Lean forward."

He did as she requested.

Gathering up his hair, she soaped his back, feeling the tense muscles beneath her hand. He was fashioned of firm flesh and powerful muscle, an enticing combination of mortal and fey bloodlines.

With the clay bowl, she scooped up the water and rinsed the soap away, her fingers gliding up and down in a slow caress.

"Wet your hair, Tynan."

Leaning back, he slid under the water to wet his hair. When he came back up, she was waiting.

"Keep your eyes closed." She lathered up his mass of hair. Raw black silk streamed through her fingers. She would have liked to feel it upon her bare breasts.

"Rinse." She pushed his shoulders down.

He complied, sliding back under the water again, immersing his head. Water lapped over the tub's edge, wetting the front of her and making the fey gown nearly transparent.

When he came up again, Bryna scooped water from the one remaining pail and rinsed all remaining soap from his hair. She quickly plaited the length into a single braid and rested it over the rim of the tub so the heat of the fire would dry it quickly.

Candlelight caressed his features in a tantalizing display of shadow. She slid forward a little on her knees, drawn by her own desires for him. His eyes remained closed in a false repose, his jaw firmly clenched.

With soapy fingers, she traced his face, stroking the tension and roughness of his bristled cheek.

Cupping handfuls of water, she gently cleansed his skin, the tips of her fingers brushing his lashes. A faery god could not have made her a more handsome mate.

"Tynan, please sit and lock your hands behind your head."

He complied with her request, but slowly, as if his

desires were pulsing near out of control. Soon, she thought, soon he would leave his doubts behind. Soon, they would be one again and all that should have been would come to pass.

Washing the silky hair under his arms, she retrieved the clay bowl and with repeated dips in the water, flushed the soap away. Her movements were purposeful, the bowl brushing against his lower stomach once, twice . . .

He opened his eyes.

Black amber stared at her from a beneath wet, shiny lashes.

"Finish it," he said roughly. He lowered his arms and gripped the rim of the tub.

Obediently, she leaned forward and soaped his thighs.

He held himself rigid under her touch and Bryna knew his restraint neared breaking.

"My brethren have healed you well," she whispered. "No scar mars the thigh."

"Bryna," he said tightly.

With a single finger, she traced the rippling stomach muscles and down. His arousal pierced the veil of soapy water.

"You play with fire, faery," he said with a savage intensity that set her heart alight.

Her hand slid beneath the gentle ripple of water to measure the silken length of him.

"Goddess's Blood." He manacled her wrist and shot out of the water. It splashed over the rim, splaying her and the fire in the hearth.

He dragged her to him. Wet heated skin met cool damp faery webs.

"Bryna, what do you want of me?"

She looked up at him and spoke with her heart. "I want you, Tynan. Put your hands on me. I want your fire and seed in my womb."

"All you had to do was ask me, faery."

"Did I not just ask?"

"You shall have me then, my water goddess." Scooping her up in his arms, he stepped out of the tub and carried her to the bed.

He followed her down upon the soft pelts, his mouth fastening on hers with a hunger born of desire.

Bryna eagerly matched his need with her own.

Her hands locked in his wet hair, holding him to her.

Her chieftain mate.

Her heart.

Her soul.

Her love.

Raw, elemental strength and beauty burned in her arms.

His lips left a trail of moisture down her throat. His hands were everywhere, freeing her from the white webs. Cupping the creamy fullness of her breasts, Tynan's mouth latched on to her right nipple. He suckled first one breast and then the other, sending a liquid fire to her woman's core.

She tossed restlessly under him, struggling to get closer.

He released her glistening nipple, working his way down her satiny stomach to the auburn fleece guarding her womanly center. Gently, he parted her thighs and eased her open with his tongue, tasting the hot, sweet nectar of her response. She pushed down into his mouth.

"Tynan, please," she begged. "I canna wait."

"Soon, faery." He flicked his tongue over her, wanting her ready for him.

He eased up her trembling body, kissing every delicious curve of her.

Balancing his weight on his arms on either side of her head, Tynan stared into the passion-glazed eyes of his faerymate. She humbled him, this waif goddess of strength and purity. He would suffer any anguish if this joining left him an heir that would not hurt her in the birthing.

Bryna lifted her hips to the blunt tip nudging her aching cave.

"Take me then," he rasped and slid into her dewy sheath.

Faery to Mortal.

Goddess to Chieftain.

Soul to Soul.

Bryna cried out in the ecstasy of the joining. He stretched her passage with exquisite pressure, stealing away her ability to breathe.

"By the faith," he rasped, a sheen of sweat glistening on his brow, holding still inside her.

Bryna rolled her hips, wrapping her legs around his hips to pull him deeper.

"I dinna want to hurt you," he warned, battling his own wants, for it was no longer his *geas* that drove him. That fey compulsion was slowly receding, being replaced by something far more intricate to the heart.

"Never would you hurt me." Bryna pulled him down. "Be with me, Tynan."

His head dropped to her shoulder. Slowly, he began to move his hips, sliding within her tight passage.

Throbbing.

Pulsing.

Building to an ancient rhythm.

Stirring her blood with yearnings, as only he could.

Taking her deeper and deeper into the ancient magic that flowed in his veins from the first Faery Queen.

Bryna strained against his pulsating penetration. Pleasure deepened within her womb.

"Come with me." Tynan kissed her shoulders, grinding his hips to meet her needs. His lips sought her jaw, where he had marked her long ago with his honor-mark.

She arched under him, her fingers digging into his flesh.

Air exploded out of her lungs.

A searing rain of molten, silver flames consumed and carried her to the edge of her being.

Bryna cried out, her body straining against his.

Tynan flung back his head in an agony of passion. With a guttural roar, he spilled his seed deep in her fertile womb, fulfilling the prophecy.

Fulfilling the ancient promise.

Conceiving his heir.

He collapsed on top of her, heat and sweat clinging to their skin. His face buried in the hair at her nape.

His heart steadied against her breast, a slowing down of time and energy, until an exhausted sleep pressed in and claimed him.

Bryna pressed her cheek to his, his body sliding to the side of her in slumber.

"I love you, my heart," she whispered. For a long while, she listened to his breathing and the crackle of the fire before closing her eyes to seek her own rest.

CHAPTER 22

BONFIRES AND TAR BARRELS BLAZED in the warm night air, bringing a sense of anticipation to all those present. Masses of ropes, dipped in tar, were hung from an iron chain along the perimeter of the inner courtyard, but at a safe distance from the stables, mews, and animal pens.

Tynan watched all with a critical eye from his wooden chair on the newly erected dais in front of Kindred. When satisfied with the precautions taken, he nodded to his people.

"Begin," he called out. He could wait no longer for Bryna to join him.

With a single torch, the ropes lighted in a fire celebration of Midsummer's End and of the safe return of the chieftain's territorial goddess. A gentle roar rose among the onlookers as the fire, signifying both light and rejoicing, raced across the ropes with the speed of lightning.

Leaders of the fire festival, men and women dressed in fine red garments, walked among the cheering revelers with small torches and twigs with streaming red ribbons.

In the shadows, Bryna stood alone. She could not

look away from the dais and her chieftain mate. The black faery webs enhanced Tynan's dark, mystical allure. He wore no personal decoration, unlike the rest of his people who showed off their brightly colored tunics and girdles of chains.

She pulled her gaze away and looked out among the people. The *Tuatha Dé Danann* were on a precipice. Some, like the line of Dark Chieftains, had faery blood in their veins, binding them to an ancient calling. Others, like Ian and Edwin, were still completely mortal. Only time would tell if the tribe went the way of the faeries or returned to their mortal ways. Even Bryna did not know this.

She glanced back at Tynan. He sat motionless, his gaze searching restlessly over the crowd for her. Hawk climbed up on his father's lap, his face alight with the rare fire spectacle.

Bryna knew she belonged on the dais with them, yet she could not move from the shadow of the tar barrel where she stood, hiding. There lived a strange emptiness in her heart these days, for although Tynan treated her like a cherished mate, he had yet to speak of love.

"Child, you should be up there with the chieftain." Her teacher came to stand before her, and Bryna sensed a dispute coming.

"I should," she agreed, but did not move to comply. Maidens danced in the courtyard, faces eager and bright with promise. A whirlwind of magic and moisture blew in from the surging sea, bringing clouds and the threat of rain.

"Why do you stand here in the shadows?" Derina demanded, jerking the brown hood down to her shoulders.

"Sometimes, I need the shadows," Bryna replied calmly, yet beneath her surface the pounding of the *bodhran*, the ancient war drum, throbbed in her blood.

"Foolishness, you doona need the shadows. You need him. His heart picked you, child, not his *geas*."

Bryna looked back at her teacher. "What did you say?"

"I am surrounded by willfulness."

"Teacher," she warned.

"Child, the chieftain loves you, though he does not speak it. His child already roots in your womb."

Bryna started to argue, but stopped. She looked down her body, her right hand sliding over her stomach in wonder. "I am with child?"

"Aye, you carry the next heir."

She did not ask how the druidess knew. "I doona feel weak or ill," she murmured, her senses turned inward.

"Why should you?"

"Last time I felt a draining inside me."

The druidess huffed with impatience. "Last time you dinna accept your faery self and your faery self could not accept the child. You are different now. When was your last moon time?"

"I have not had it since coming from the faeries."

"Good."

Bryna felt heat rise in her cheeks. "Must you know everything?" She blinked back tears of joy.

The druidess's empty eye sockets crinkled. "For a goddess, you know very little. His *geas* awakens only after his heart chooses one born of faery. Dinna I tell you this?"

"Nay, you did not."

"Being the territorial goddess, you should know it. Once love comes, the chieftain's *geas* is reborn in the next heir, carried through his blood, and passed on until the next awakening."

"I dinna learn the ways of the faery until a short while ago. You should have told me about his heart's choice. This does not come natural to me, this fey awareness."

"It should."

"The only thing that comes natural is the sensing of men's lies and the coming of storms, like the one approaching now."

"A storm comes?" The druidess looked around.

"Ah, so you doona know everything," Bryna said triumphantly.

"You are in a temper tonight," her teacher complained, pulling her hood back up. "Must be the babe growing in you."

"I am not in a temper," Bryna argued.

"You are prideful and stubborn and that one over there," she pointed a bent finger at Tynan, "is scowling at me like the black evil himself. I doona like it."

Tynan watched the exchange between his faery-mate and the ancient druidess with growing irritation. Bryna belonged beside him in the celebration, not skulking in the shadows.

Last night she had joined her body to him in a mating of such pure pleasure that he grew hard thinking of it, yet he sensed a strange distance in her that he could not breach.

Blazing masses of rope hung between them, silhouetting his faerymate in the shadows of the fire. The sound of the drum beat loudly in his ears.

When the druidess walked away and Bryna raised incredulous eyes to him, he shot out of the chair.

"What?" Hawk gasped in surprise, almost toppling over.

Tynan handed his son to Ian and jumped off the dais into the crowd. He came to her side in just moments.

"Bryna, what did the druidess say to upset you?"

She looked up into his eyes, a faint blush staining her cheeks.

" 'Tis nothing, Tynan. You know how Derina can be."

"I know. Why did you not join me on the dais?"

"I needed to stand apart for a time."

"Apart from me?"

"Aye, for a little while. I had a need to listen to the land."

His gaze skimmed the horizon. "Do you sense invaders coming?"

"Nay," she hurried to reassure him. "The land is calm . . ."

"Calm?" He looked back at her, his eyes narrowed in observation. "You tremble before me. Your hands press to your stomach protectively, causing me to wonder if you are ill."

"Nay, not ill."

Tynan's nostrils flared when she looked away from him.

Above them, lightning arced, illuminating the overcast sky in black and gold. Thunder exploded in ageless magic, releasing a waterfall of silvery rain. Turbulence reigned beneath his faery's serene exterior.

He turned his face towards the dark purple sky, his eyes blinking against the raindrops. "Another one of your rainstorms comes, faery."

"They are not my storms."

"They most assuredly are your storms." He glanced back at her, the passion of the tempest streaming through his blood, his link to his goddess mounting with each breath. "You will talk to me this eve of what bothers you."

She did not answer.

Done being patient, he scooped her up in his arms.

"Tynan, put me down!"

"Not until I know what is wrong and put an end to this silence between us."

Unmindful of the pouring rain, he carried his faerymate towards the steps of the Keep. People had run for cover everywhere, leaving only the flames hissing at the rain, an ongoing battle of primordial forces between water and fire.

Tynan entered Kindred and climbed the center staircase two steps at a time.

"Put me down," his faerymate commanded with all the authority of a goddess.

"Aye, I will." Tynan strode across the landing into their chambers. He kicked the door shut behind him and entered their bedchamber.

"Tynan!"

He dropped her unceremoniously in the center of their bed, where she quickly scrambled back to the edge.

Tynan stepped back, mindful of the shapely limbs that could lay a man low.

"*Daoine Sidhe*," he warned. "You are drenching the fire celebration."

Standing, she flung wet curls out of her eyes and glared at him, her eyes bright with anger and some other emotion he could not fathom.

"Strong emotions in you seem to trigger rainstorms."

"I dinna mean to bring the storm, Tynan. It happens sometimes." She moved away from him. Unclasping the gold brooch under her chin, she pulled the drenched cloak from her shoulders.

"The elemental force of the storm surges in you, faery. I feel it in my blood."

Bryna felt every raindrop as it kissed the land in

joyous completion of its journey. She had not realized that Tynan sensed it as well.

She turned to face him and found him studying her damp, gray gown. It had been his first gift to her.

"No faery webs to tempt me tonight?"

She looked away.

"I wish to end this distance between us, here and now."

"There is no distance, Tynan."

"You hold yourself from me, even when I am deep inside your body." He backed her up against the wall. "Talk to me." His head lowered, warm lips brushed hers. "Talk to me."

Bryna thought to push him away. Instead, her fingers curled in the wet silk at his temples, holding him close, returning his kiss. He tasted of rain and cherries.

There was a wildness in him tonight that reverberated with the thunderstorm. She should have known he would be sensitive to her nature, to the pulse and link of the hills, the lochs and the sea.

Warm hands slid up her thighs, lifting the hem of her gown.

He broke the kiss and Bryna felt a wrenching inside her, an echo of the disturbance inside him.

"Bryna," he said in an agonized whisper, his lips caressing her cheek. "I love you, please love me." Large hands cupped her buttocks and lifted her. "Love me, faery."

"Oh, Tynan." She wrapped her arms around his neck, her heart brimming with joy. "I love you so." The black faery webs responded to her happiness, to her willingness to join, truly and fully this first time in the ways of the fey. They slit open over his manhood. He shifted and embedded himself in her honeyed sheath.

Bryna threw back her head, lost in his love, lost in the rainstorm, lost in his fire and forcefulness of her chieftain mate. Her nails scored the black webs covering his sinewy arms.

"Take me, faery."

He belonged to her now, only to her.

Bryna took him.

Took him.

Cherished him.

Loved him.

The powerful, ancient rhythm of his thrusts set the pace, but she enhanced their coupling as only a territorial goddess could.

The air shimmered around their straining bodies in a veil of gold and silver. Love for him poured out of her, weaving a spell of faery passion around them.

Fire roared through his blood with a deep intensity. Tynan became one with his faerymate and the thunderstorm, lost in the sensation of a primal force beyond anything he had ever experienced.

They blazed.

Hotly.

Passionately.

His faerymate soared in his arms, climaxing in a white-hot explosion of brilliance.

Tynan closed his eyes and threw back his head. Light burst behind his lids. With a violence bordering on pain, he spewed his seed into her womb in a luminous eruption that robbed him of his strength.

His legs weakened under him.

With Bryna in his arms, he slid to the floor still deeply embedded in her, her legs wrapped around his hips, the folds of the damp gray gown hiding where they remained joined.

He struggled to breathe, never having felt anything like this mating before. His faerymate cupped his face. "I love you, Tynan. You are the air that I breathe."

Tynan stared into pools of glittering mist. His chest tightened with strong emotions. "I love you, faery. I always have."

Tears welled in her eyes. "I dinna know."

"I dared not admit it even to myself."

"Why?" The single word burst out of her.

"I thought if the faeries knew my true feelings they would use them against me. I could not survive if they took you away."

"I would never allow that, my heart." She smiled through her tears, her hands cupping his face. She thought of the child she carried. "Tynan, would you allow a territorial goddess to give you another gift?"

"Another gift such as this?"

"Nay, my love." She took his right hand and pressed it firmly to her stomach. "I carry your heir."

He stared at her in amazement, his eyes searching and then dropping to her stomach.

"You are not ill this time?"

"Nay, we are strong and healthy." She wiggled on his lap to prove her point, piercing the dread that had found its way between them.

"Shall I show you?" Her hands locked on his broad shoulders to hold on. Her legs tightened around his hips.

He chuckled low and shook his head. "Bryna, I need a few . . . BY THE GODDESS!"

Tynan's head flung back. He bucked, coming off the floor and for a second time that night, he experienced a climax like none before.

And for a third . . .

And for a fourth . . .

EPILOGUE

Summer slipped away on shortening days, making way for the newborn cold. Snow fell on the land and from the sea came a blustery *Feabhra,* February, wind.

Tynan paced the hall all day, his leather boots soundless. Time went by in a blur of apprehension.

He wore a gold torc about his neck, and a black woolen tunic and breeches. His hair fell unadorned to his waist except for a braid at each temple. Dagger and sword had been set aside long ago. He prayed silently to the mother goddess for the birthing to go easy on both his faerymate and son.

He stopped at the foot of the staircase, staring again at the landing that led to his chambers. Servants scurried up and down the stairs, their hands full of items gathered at Derina's and Rose's bidding.

Herbs.

Cloths.

Buckets of hot water.

"How long does it take for one wee babe?" Hawk asked nervously, standing in his best green tunic between Ian and Edwin. He had even washed his hair for the occasion.

Ian crossed his arms and leaned against the wall.

"Babes have their own way of doing things, even if they are born of magic."

Tynan glared at Ian.

The older man simply shrugged. "The snow-storm ends and twilight approaches. The babe will be born then."

Tynan peered at the windows. The snowstorm had indeed ended, leaving the land awash in purple light.

An otherworldly scream tore from his chambers above. Blood drained from his face. Turning, he looked up the staircase.

Upstairs, Bryna panted as the last of the labor pains left her body.

"Please, Rose," she whispered shakily, "let me see him."

"Easy, child." Derina helped Bryna sit up in bed just as Rose came to the edge. The simpler had cleaned the babe and swaddled him in white cloth. Bryna held out her arms, then found them filled with tiny warmth. She looked down. Her son's eyes were not the lavender of twilight, but the silver gray of rain. He stared up at her from beneath black lashes and gurgled loudly.

"We know who the father is by that thatch of black hair." The simpler smiled, stepping back.

"Aye, that one," Derina grumbled, gathering the soiled cloths. "Hair black as pitch. Eyes pierced of twilight."

"Eyes of silvery mist," Bryna corrected. Her son

had a small, heart-shaped mole on the big toe of his right foot.

"Eyes of silvery mist," her teacher mumbled. "That will change."

"Mayhap," Bryna replied, but knew it would not. The faery *geas* of her chieftain mate would pass from son to grandson and awaken in that time, but that was many years away.

Suddenly, the sounds of heavy footsteps were heard coming up the stairs. Her chieftain mate barged through the door and stopped, his face pale with dread.

Bryna smiled gently. "Come, Tynan." She held a hand out to him. "Come and meet your son."

He appeared to be in a daze, walking slowly forward, unaware of the departure of the simpler and druidess. He eased himself onto the edge of the large bed, careful not to disturb her.

"Are you well?" he asked hoarsely, touching her face.

Bryna held his calloused hand to her cheek and kissed his thumb. "Both of us are well, my love."

"Both." He peered down at the fretting babe in her arms, his face illuminated with wonder. "He is so small, Bryna," he murmured in awe.

"He is small for now, though our son has your big hands and feet."

"Our son," he murmured in a voice shaky with emotion.   Touching his son's wrist, a tiny hand instantly gripped his little finger. Her chieftain mate laughed loudly, his face alight with love and mirth. Leaning forward, he kissed her cheek tenderly. "I love you, faery."

"And I you, my heart." She turned to him, her lips brushing his, her heart warmed with joy and contentment.

She had found home.

She had found love.

She finally BELONGED.

. . . and the land glimmered with faery blessings for promises well-kept, and true love found.

- THE END -

- NOTES ON TEXT -

Aile Niurin -	Hell Fire
Áine -	Another name for universal mother goddess.
Bodhran -	A Celtic war drum.
Dana -	Universal mother goddess.
Daoine Sidhe -	Faery folk.
Duil -	Desire.
Draiochtach agus sidhe -	Of magical and faery.
Eire -	Ancient Ireland.
Fey -	Faeries.
Feypaths -	Underground secret passages created by faeries.
Fortnight -	Fourteen days or two weeks.
Fir Bog -	Belgians, mystical settlers of Connacht, known as the bag men.
Gá -	Need.
Geas -	A magical obligation.
Idir -	Between.
Laigin -	Ancient name of Leinster.
Meahd -	Balance.
Milkwater -	Goat milk and water drink.
Mi na ngaoth -	Month of winds, February.
Months -	Months - Eanair (January), Feabhra (February), Marta (March), Aibrean (April),

Beltane (May), Meitheamh (June), Nollaig (December).

Sennight - Seven days or one week.

Sidhe - Gaelic name for the *faeries* in both Ireland and the Highlands of Scotland.

Teastaigh - Madness and want.

Torc - A neck ring, commonly made of gold or bronze.

Tuaicthe - Anguished hearts.

Tuatha Dé Danann - Collective term coined in the Middle Ages for the people of the goddess Dana.

Tir Na n'Óg - Land of the youth.

Yn Drogh Spyrryd - Evil one, dark druid or sorcerer.

Woad - European plant of the cabbage family, formerly cultivated for a blue dye extracted from its leaves.

AUTHOR'S NOTES

While researching on the Internet a few years ago, I came across an article in British Archaeology, no.14, May 1996 regarding the Roman occupation of Ancient Ireland. It immediately caught my interest since at the time; Rome was reputed as never having invaded Ancient Ireland.

Here is an excerpt:

"In May 1996, British Archaeology reported on disputed findings of a Roman fortress in the coastal site of Drumanagh, Ireland. Richard Warner, Keeper of Archaeology and Ethnography at the Ulster Museum writes, "... In short, early medieval Ireland has all the appearance of being, culturally, an heir to the Roman world of which we are supposedly to believe, it was never a part."

I had found the article at British Archaeology site at: wwww.britarch.ac.uk/ba/ba14/ba14feat.html.

August 2004
I have recently found a wonderful site on mythic Ireland: www.mythicalireland.com

FOR MORE INFORMATION
ABOUT OTHER GREAT
TITLES FROM
MEDALLION PRESS, VISIT

www.medallionpress.com